# JODI PICOULT

## THE

# BOOK

## OF

# TWO

# WAYS

HODDER &
STOUGHTON

First published in the United States by Ballantine Books
An imprint of Random House, a division of Penguin Random House LLC, New York.

First published in Great Britain in 2020 by Hodder & Stoughton
An Hachette UK company

1

Grateful acknowledgment is made to John and Colleen Darnell for providing Egyptian text
translations throughout the novel as well the images on pp. 31 and 171. Used by permission.
Photo on page 26: *Inner coffin of Governor Djehutynakht* Egyptian, Middle Kingdom,
late Dynasty 11 - early Dynasty, 2010-1961 B.C., Object Place for Label: Notes: Egypt
(Deir el-Bersha, Tomb 10, shaft A) Findspot: Egypt, Deir el-Bersha, Tomb 10, shaft
A (Djehutynakht), Notes: Egypt (Deir el-Bersha, tomb 10 shaft A) Cedar, Length × width ×
height: 224.1 × 75 × 80 cm (88¼ × 29½ × 31½ in.) Museum of Fine Arts, Boston,
Harvard University-Boston Museum of Fine Arts Expedition 21.962a.

Quotes from "The Nine Contemplations of Atisha" by Rev. Joan Jiko Halifax
(Upaya Institute and Zen Center, www.upaya.org). Used by permission of the author.

A CIP catalogue record for this title
is available from the British Library

Hardback ISBN 978 1 473 69240 4
Waterstones and WHSmith exclusive Hardback ISBN 978 1 529 33790 7
Trade Paperback ISBN 978 1 473 69241 1
Ireland and Airside Trade Paperback ISBN 978 1 529 33806 5
eBook ISBN 978 1 529 33807 2

Printed and bound in Great Britain by
Clays Ltd, Elcograf S.p.A.

Hodder & Stoughton policy is to use papers that are natural, renewable
and recyclable products and made from wood grown in sustainable forests.
The logging and manufacturing processes are expected to conform
to the environmental regulations of the country of origin.

Hodder & Stoughton Ltd
Carmelite House
50 Victoria Embankment
London EC4Y 0DZ

www.hodder.co.uk

# THE
# BOOK
## OF
# TWO
# WAYS

*Also by Jodi Picoult*

Songs of the Humpback Whale
Harvesting the Heart
Picture Perfect
Mercy
The Pact
Keeping Faith
Plain Truth
Salem Falls
Perfect Match
Second Glance
My Sister's Keeper
Vanishing Acts
The Tenth Circle
Nineteen Minutes
Change of Heart
Handle with Care
House Rules
Sing You Home
Lone Wolf
The Storyteller
Leaving Time
Small Great Things
A Spark of Light

*Jodi Picoult and Samantha Van Leer*

Between the Lines
Off the Page

*For the Stage*

Over the Moon: An Original Musical for Teens

To die will be an awfully big adventure.

—J. M. BARRIE, *Peter Pan*

# PROLOGUE

. . .

My CALENDAR IS full of dead people.

When my phone alarm chimes, I fish it out from the pocket of my cargo pants. I've forgotten, with the time change, to turn off the reminder. I'm still groggy with sleep, but I open the date and read the names: *Iris Vale. Eun Ae Kim. Alan Rosenfeldt. Marlon Jensen.*

I close my eyes, and do what I do every day at this moment: I remember them.

Iris, who had died tiny and birdlike, had once driven a getaway car for a man she loved who'd robbed a bank. Eun Ae, who had been a doctor in Korea, but couldn't practice in the United States. Alan had proudly showed me the urn he bought for his cremated remains and then joked, *I haven't tried it on yet.* Marlon had changed out all the toilets in his house and put in new flooring and cleaned the gutters; he bought graduation gifts for his two children and hid them away. He took his twelve-year-old daughter to a hotel ballroom and waltzed with her while I filmed it on his phone, so that the day she got married there would be video of her dancing with her father.

At one point, they were my clients. Now, they're my stories to keep.

Everyone in my row is asleep. I slip my phone back into my pocket and carefully crawl over the woman to my right without disturbing her—air traveler's yoga—to make my way to the bathroom in the rear of the plane. There I blow my nose and look in the mirror. I'm at the age where that's a surprise, where I still think I'm going to see a younger woman rather than the one who blinks back at me. Lines fan from the corners of my eyes, like the creases of a familiar map. If I untangle the braid that lies over my left shoulder, these terrible fluorescent lights would pick up those first gray strands in my hair. I'm wearing baggy pants with an elastic waist, like every other sensible nearly-forty woman who knows she's going to be on a plane for a long-haul flight. I grab a handful of tissues and open the door, intent on heading back to my seat, but the little galley area is packed with flight attendants. They are knotted together like a frown.

They stop talking when I appear. "Ma'am," one of them says, "could you please take your seat?"

It strikes me that their job isn't really very different from mine. If you're on a plane, you're not where you started, and you're not where you're going. You're caught in between. A flight attendant is the guide who helps you navigate that passage smoothly. As a death doula, I do the same thing, but the journey is from life to death, and at the end, you don't disembark with two hundred other travelers. You go alone.

I climb back over the sleeping woman in the aisle seat and buckle my seatbelt just as the overhead lights blaze and the cabin comes alive.

"Ladies and gentlemen," a voice announces, "we have just been informed by the captain that we're going to have a planned emergency. Please listen to the flight attendants and follow their directions."

I am frozen. *Planned emergency*. The oxymoron sticks in my mind.

There is a quick rush of sound—shock rolls through the cabin—but no screams, no loud cries. Even the baby behind me, who shrieked for the first two hours of the flight, is silent. "We're crashing," the woman on the aisle whispers. "Oh my God, we're crashing."

She must be wrong; there hasn't even been turbulence. Everything has been normal. But then the flight attendants station themselves in the aisles, performing a strange, staccato ballet of safety movements as instructions are read over the speakers. *Fasten your* seatbelts. *When you hear the word* brace, *assume the brace position. After the plane comes to a complete stop you'll hear* Release your seatbelts. *Get out. Leave everything behind.*

Leave everything behind.

For someone who makes a living through death, I haven't given a lot of thought to my own.

I have heard that when you are about to die, your life flashes before your eyes.

But I do not picture my husband, Brian, his sweater streaked with inevitable chalk dust from the old-school blackboards in his physics lab. Or Meret, as a little girl, asking me to check for monsters under the bed. I do not envision my mother, not like she was at the end or before that, when Kieran and I were young.

Instead, I see *him.*

As clearly as if it were yesterday, I imagine Wyatt in the middle of the Egyptian desert, the sun beating down on his hat, his neck ringed with dirt from the constant wind, his teeth a flash of lightning. A man who hasn't been part of my life for fifteen years. A place I left behind.

A dissertation I never finished.

Ancient Egyptians believed that to get to the afterlife, they had to be deemed innocent in the Judgment Hall. Their hearts were weighed against the feather of Ma'at, of truth.

I am not so sure my heart will pass.

The woman to my right is softly praying in Spanish. I fumble for my phone, thinking to turn it on, to send a message, even though I know there is no signal, but I can't seem to open the button on my pants pocket. A hand catches mine and squeezes.

I look down at our fists, squeezed so tight a secret couldn't slip between our palms.

*Brace,* the flight attendants yell. *Brace!*

As we fall out of the sky, I wonder who will remember me.

MUCH LATER I would learn that when a plane crashes and the emergency personnel show up, the flight attendants tell them how many souls were on board. Souls, not people. As if they know our bodies are only passing through for a little while.

I would learn that one of the fuel filters became clogged mid-flight. That the second filter-clogging light came on in the cockpit forty-five minutes out, and in spite of what the pilots tried, they could not clear it, and they realized they'd have to do a land evacuation. I would learn that the plane came in short of Raleigh-Durham, sticking down in the football field of a private school. As it hit the bleachers with a wing, the plane tipped, rolled, broke into pieces.

Much later I would learn of the family with the baby behind me, whose row of three seats separated from the floor and was thrown free from the aircraft, killing them instantaneously. I would hear about the six others who had been crushed as the metal buckled; the flight attendant who never came out of her coma. I would read the names of the passengers in the last ten rows who hadn't gotten out of the broken fuselage before it erupted in flame.

I would learn that I was one of thirty-six people who walked away from the crash.

When I step out of the examination room of the hospital we've been taken to, I'm dazed. A woman in a uniform is in the hallway, talking to a man with a bandaged arm. She is part of an emergency response team from the airline that has overseen medical checks by physicians, given us clean clothes and food, and flown in frantic family members.

"Ms. Edelstein?" she says, and I blink, until I realize she is talking to me.

A million years ago, I had been Dawn McDowell. I'd published under that name. But my passport and license read Edelstein. Like Brian's.

In her hand she has a checklist of crash survivors.

She puts a tick next to my name. "Have you been seen by a doctor?"

"Not yet." I glance back at the examination room.

"Okay. I'm sure you have some questions . . . ?"

That's an understatement.

*Why am I alive, when others aren't?*

*Why did I book this particular flight?*

*What if I'd been detained checking in, and had missed it?*

*What if I'd made any of a thousand other choices that would have led me far away from this crash?*

At that, I think of Brian, and his theory of the multiverse. Somewhere, in a parallel timeline, there is another me at my own funeral.

At the same time, I think—again, always—of Wyatt.

*I have to get out of here.*

I don't realize I have said this out loud until the airline representative responds.

"Once we get the doctor's paperwork, you're clear to leave. Is someone coming for you, or do you need us to make travel arrangements?"

We, the lucky ones, have been told we can have a plane ticket anywhere we need to go—to our destination, back to where the flight originated, even somewhere else, if necessary. I have already called my husband. Brian offered to come get me, but I told him not to. I didn't say why.

I clear my throat. "I have to book a flight," I say.

"Absolutely." The woman nods. "Where do you need to go?"

*Boston,* I think. *Home.* But there's something about the way she phrases the question: *need,* instead of *want;* and another destination rises like steam in my mind.

I open my mouth, and I answer.

# LAND / EGYPT

· · ·

*I have heard these songs that are in ancient tombs,*
*What they say about aggrandizing the one on earth,*
*And diminishing the necropolis.*
*But why is such done against the land of eternity,*
*A just and righteous place without fear?*
*Mayhem is its very abomination!*
*No one there dreads another.*
*This land, without an opponent,*
*Is where all of our families rest*
*Since the beginning of time.*
*Those who will be born after millions and millions,*
*All shall go to it!*

—From the Tomb of Neferhotep, as translated
by Professors Colleen and John Darnell

MY MOTHER, WHO lived and died by superstitions, used to make us say together before we went on a trip: *We're not going anywhere.* It was meant to trick the Devil. I can't say I believe in that kind of thing, but then again, I didn't say it before I left home, and look at where that got me.

Walking outside of the airport in Cairo in August feels like stepping onto the surface of the sun. Even late at night, the heat is a knife on your skin and comes in pressing waves. I can already feel a line of sweat running down my spine; I didn't come prepared for this. I find myself in the middle of other people's transitions: a rumpled, dazed group of tourists being herded into their minivan; a teen dragging duct-taped luggage from the back of an open cart to the curb; a woman securing her head scarf as it blows in the breeze.

Suddenly I am surrounded by men. "Taxi?" they bark. "You need taxi?"

There's no hiding the fact that I'm a Westerner; it's clear from my red hair to my cargo pants and sneakers. I nod, making eye contact with one of them, a driver with a thick mustache and a long-sleeved striped shirt. The other taxi drivers fall back, seagulls in search of another crumb.

"You have suitcase?"

I shake my head. Everything I have is in the small bag I carry over my shoulder.

"American?" the man replies, and I nod. A wide, white grin splits his face. "Welcome to Alaska!"

It is startling to think that fifteen years have passed, but that lame joke is still the go-to gag for visitors. I get into the backseat of his car. "Take me to Ramses train station," I say. "How long?"

"Fifteen minutes, *inshallah*."

"*Shokran*," I reply. *Thank you.* I am stunned at how quickly the Arabic comes to my lips. There must be a space in the brain that stores the information you assumed you'd never need again, like the lyrics to "MacArthur Park," or how to multiply matrices, or—in my case—anything Egyptian. When Meret was little, she used to say *lasterday*, which might mean five minutes ago or five years ago—and that is where I am right now. Like I stepped back into the moment that was left behind when I abandoned this country. Like it has been waiting all this time for me to return.

With the window down, I can already feel dust settling on me. In Egypt, everything is covered in sand—your shoes, your skin, the air you breathe. It even gets in your food. The teeth of mummies are worn down by it.

Although it is nighttime, Cairo is alive in all its contradictions. On the highway, cars share the space with donkey carts. Butcher shops with meat hanging outside cozy up beside souvenir stands. A souped-up muscle car zooms past, leaving a throb of rap music in its wake that tangles with the loudspeaker reverb of the *salat isha,* the nightly Muslim call to prayer. We drive along the Nile, trash stewing on its banks. Finally, Ramses Station comes into view. "Fifty pounds," the driver says.

There are no set taxi fares in Egypt; the driver tells you how much he thinks the ride is worth. I pass him forty pounds as a counteroffer and get out of the car. He gets out, too, and starts yelling at me in Arabic. *"Shokran,"* I tell him. *"Shokran."* Even though this scene is common and nobody bats an eye, I feel my pulse racing as I walk up to the train station.

It is not easy to get to Middle Egypt as a Westerner. Tourists are not supposed to use the trains, so I don't buy a ticket and instead wait for the conductor to find me and play dumb. At that point, the train is already moving and it's too late, so he shrugs and lets me pay. Hours later, when I get off at my stop, in Minya, I am the only white person in the station. I'm nearly the *only* person in the station.

I was supposed to arrive at 2:45 A.M., but the train has been delayed, so it's just after 4:00 A.M. It feels like I have been traveling for twenty-four hours straight. The only taxi driver at the Minya train station is playing a game on his mobile phone when I knock on his window. He takes one look at me, rumpled and dragging. *"Sabah el-khier,"* I say. Good morning.

*"Sabah el-noor,"* he replies.

I give him my destination, a little over an hour away. He takes the eastern desert road out of Minya. I stare out the window, counting the *gebels* and *wadis*—hills and valleys—that rise in the darkness at the horizon. At the security checkpoints, where boys too young to grow a beard hold battered old machine guns from the sixties, I wrap my scarf around my head and pretend to sleep.

The driver keeps stealing glances in the rearview mirror. He is probably wondering what an American is doing in a taxi in the heart of Egypt, the one section that isn't on tourist itineraries. I imagine what I might say to him, if I had the courage or the language to do so.

One of the questions I ask my clients is *What's left unfinished?*

What is it that you haven't done yet, that you need to do before you leave this life? I've heard nearly every response: from fixing the front door where it sticks to bathing in the Red Sea; from publishing a memoir to playing a hand of poker with a friend you haven't seen in years. For me, it's *this*. This dust, this tooth-jarring ride, this bone-bleached ribbon of landscape.

In a previous life, I had been planning to be an Egyptologist. I fell in love with the culture first, when we studied Ancient Egypt in fourth grade. I remember standing at the top of the jungle gym and feeling the wind and pretending that I was in a *felluca*, crossing the Nile. My prized possession was a guidebook from the Tut: Treasures of the Golden Pharaoh exhibit that my mother had found at a secondhand bookshop. In high school, I took French and German, because I knew that I would need those languages to translate research. I applied to colleges that offered Egyptology programs, and studied on full scholarship at U Chicago.

Most of what I learned about Ancient Egypt can be boiled down to two subjects. The first is historical—Egypt was ruled by thirty-two dynasties of pharaohs, split across three main time periods: the Old Kingdom, the Middle Kingdom, and the New Kingdom. The First Dynasty began with King Narmer, the pharaoh who unified Upper and Lower Egypt around 3100 B.C.E. The Old Kingdom is best known for being the time the pyramids were built as tombs for the kings. But around 2150 B.C.E., civil war broke out in Egypt. There were forty-two separate territories—or nomes—each headed by a nomarch. During this period, each nomarch was fighting for his own nome. There were alliances, but the pharaoh in the north didn't rule over a unified Egypt; instead, it was like the Egyptian Game of Thrones. The Middle Kingdom began when a king named Mentuhotep II reunified Upper and Lower Egypt around 2010 B.C.E. That lasted until the Hyksos invaded from the north and a period followed where rulers were from foreign lands. It wasn't until King Ahmose crushed the Hyksos that Egypt was reunited again during the New Kingdom, in 1550 B.C.E.

The second key subject involves Ancient Egyptian religion. Much of it was related to the sun god, Re—who, as the sun, was pulled across the sky daily in a long boat called the solar bark—and Osiris, the god of the Netherworld. Osiris was also the corpse of the sun god, and so they were flip sides of the same coin. This was not a logic bomb for the Ancient Egyptians because Osiris and Re were simply two faces of the same entity, like the Christian trinity of the Father, Son, and Holy Ghost. Every night, Re visited Osiris and reunited with his corpse, which powered him up to make the sun rise the next day. The Egyptian model of the afterlife imitated this cycle: the deceased's soul was reborn daily like Re, and reunited nightly with its corpse.

A lot of what we know about Ancient Egypt comes from tombs, so we have proof that great pains were taken to prepare for dying, and what came afterward. Even people who don't know much about Egyptology have heard of the Book of the Dead—or, as Ancient Egyptians called it, the Book of Going Forth by Day. It's a New Kingdom collection of spells to help the deceased make his or her way to the afterlife—but it evolved from earlier, lesser known funerary texts. First came the Old Kingdom's Pyramid Texts: spells to ward off evil creatures, words to be spoken at funerary rituals by the dead king's son, and instructions for the deceased to reach the next world. By the Middle Kingdom, funerary texts were found painted on the coffins of nobles and other citizens, including spells to restore family relationships, because death can separate us from people we love; spells to help the deceased travel with Re in his solar bark to defeat Apep—the serpent of chaos—who tried to suck the water out from underneath; and spells to help the deceased become one again with Osiris every night.

Also part of these Coffin Texts was the Book of Two Ways, the first known map of the afterlife. It was found only in certain coffins in Middle Egypt during the Middle Kingdom, usually painted on the bottom. It showed two roads snaking through Osiris's realm of the dead: a land route, black, and a water route, blue, which are separated by a lake of fire. If you follow the map, it's like choosing between taking the ferry or driving around—both ways wind up in the same place: the Field of Offerings, where the deceased can feast with Osiris for eternity. There is a catch, though—some of the paths lead nowhere. Others push you toward demons or circles of fire. Embedded in the text is the magic you need to get past the guardians of the gates.

The first passage I ever translated from the Book of Two Ways was Spell 1130: *As for any man who knows this spell, he will be like Re in the sky, like Osiris in the Netherworld, and into the circle of fire he will descend, but no flame will be against him forever and ever.*

Forever and ever. *Neheh djet.* Time, for Ancient Egyptians, moved differently. It could be linear and eternal, like Osiris. Or it could be cyclical, with daily reincarnations, like Re. These were not mutually exclusive. In fact, to have a good death, you couldn't have one without the other. The tomb was the connective tissue, the magical battery that provided the juice for eternal life. Most Egyptologists studied the images and hieroglyphs in a vacuum, but as a young academic, I started to think about their placement in the coffin, and the Book of Two Ways on the floor. What if the mummy inside was meant to activate the magic, like a key?

The versions of the Book of Two Ways that have been published have come almost exclusively from coffins of nomarchs from the necropolis at Deir el-Bersha, a sprawling collection of rock-cut tombs of nobles, a city of the dead. Fifteen years ago, I was a graduate student working in those tombs, trying to prove my thesis.

*What's left unfinished?*

As the driver turns south, bringing me back to Deir el-Bersha, I glance out the window again, struck by the beauty of the sky yawning over the desert. It's blue and pink and orange, the stripes of a day that's only beginning. A star winks at me for a moment before it's swallowed by the sun.

*Sirius.* I've arrived in Egypt the day of the Sothic rising.

Because Egypt is a valley, you can see stars there like nowhere else, and the Ancient Egyptians tracked the rise of groups of stars in their solar calendar. Every ten days, a new group of stars would appear in the east at dawn, after being absent for seventy days. The most important of these was the star Sirius—which they called Sothis, or *Sopdet.* The Sothic rising signaled rebirth, because it occurred in the season when the Nile would flood and leave silt to fertilize their crops. To celebrate, Ancient Egyptians would travel to festivals, often leaving graffiti where they went. But mostly, they would get drunk and have sex—it was like Coachella, every time the Nile overflowed.

Wyatt once told me that at these festivals, the Ancient Egyptians would purposely drink to the point of vomiting, so that they imitated the Nile flood. *Those Egyptians,* he said, *knew how to live.*

I look up at the sky again, searching for Sothis. Just like the Ancient Egyptians, I see it as a sign.


DEIR EL-BERSHA IS located smack in the middle of Egypt, opposite the town of Mallawi on the east bank of the Nile. Only people authorized by the government are allowed entry because of damage from ancient earthquakes and recent lootings.

I stare at the scenery until I see the familiar rock-cut tombs. Dozens of tiny metal doors are lined up in a striated row of limestone, like a hotel carved into the walls of the *wadi,* the valley. A death hotel. I can pick out exactly where I spent three seasons in the tomb of Djehutyhotep II, the overlord of the Hare nome. Below it, covered with staging, is the newest tomb. I squint, but I can't see any activity there.

That's not the only thing that's new in Bersha. There are sprawling modern cemeteries that didn't exist in 2003, just a little south of the tombs. Beside a mosque, there is now a brightly painted church for Coptic Christians. Along the banks of the Nile, Egyptian farmers walk on narrow raised paths between their fields, or heap the flat fans of date palms into a donkey cart. And then suddenly, we are at the Dig House. I pay the driver and step out of the taxi, sand flying up around me.

The house has changed, too.

It was built out of mud brick in 1908 by a British architect, Gerald Hay-Smythe, to match medieval Coptic monasteries. The porch had collapsed before I arrived as a grad student, and no one ever got around to fixing it. But now, I see, the porch has been rebuilt.

There are no vehicles parked outside, and there's a stillness to the house that speaks of emptiness. I walk past a patch of wild onions and a rusting bicycle into the outer courtyard. Sheets and shirts and *galabeyas,* the long caftan garments worn by locals, hang on crossed clotheslines. Fifteen years ago, the Egyptian family who looked after the Dig House and the Egyptologists inside it would string our laundry up like this. All our bedding smelled like sunlight.

"Hello?" I call out. There isn't a door to knock on, just an open archway. Hesitantly, I step forward, and startle a cat. It yowls and leaps onto a crumbling sill, where it judges me with narrow eyes before disappearing inside the open window.

I walk down the long corridor that separates the quarters of the local caretakers from those of the archaeological team. A fine layer of grit covers the floor, the walls, everything. "Is anyone home?" I say, but the only sound is swing music crackling from a speaker in the throat of the house. I peek my head into a room without a door, which has a stack of old twin mattresses printed with the Disneyfied faces of Cinderella, Snow White, and Sleeping Beauty. Further down the hall is the entrance to the magazine—the storage facility where we would put any finds that we might want to look at during a future season. I can't help myself from stepping through the doorframe, where in the dim light I scan neatly labeled cardboard boxes, stacked on shelves. Suddenly I whip around, certain I'm being watched. On a folding table is a mummy that was in this room long before I ever was, and will likely be here long after I leave. "George," I murmur, calling him by the name everyone else had, fifteen years ago. "Good to see you again."

Further down the hallway is the bathroom, an individual shower and a toilet. I use the facilities, fingering the frayed sign still taped to the back of the stall door: THINGS YOU SHOULDN'T FLUSH: ANYTHING YELLOW, TOILET PAPER, YOUR HOPES & DREAMS.

*"Min hunak,"* I hear, a voice getting closer. *Who's there?*

I have literally been caught with my pants down. I spring up, wash my hands, and hurry out of the bathroom to try to explain myself, only to come face-to-face with a memory.

As if it were yesterday, I see this man with his weathered brown skin and gentle hands setting a platter of fresh salad in front of me at a table. He's ageless, frozen in time, the same caretaker who looked after the house when I was a graduate student. "Hasib?" I ask.

His eyes widen, and hearing my accent, he switches to English. "Hasib was my father."

I blink. "You're . . . *Harbi*?"

Harbi had been a boy back then, though one of our best workers. He'd done whatever Professor Dumphries asked—from rigging staging so that we could scrutinize hieroglyphs at the top of the chamber wall to standing for hours in the hot sun with a mirror canted to capture the light so that we could accurately copy rock art.

His gaze narrows. "Dawn?"

"You remember me?" I say. If Harbi does, maybe he will not be the only one.

"Of course I do. You brought me Superman."

Every time I flew through Heathrow, I'd pick up a comic book for Harbi and a Cadbury bar for Hasib. "I came empty-handed this time," I confess. "Is your father still here?"

He shakes his head. "He died."

Muslim clients of mine have always been better with death language than my Christian clients, who tend to be terrified of that transition. "I am so sorry to hear that," I tell him. "I have many great memories of him."

Harbi smiles. "As do I," he says. "My son and I now see to the Dig House." He frowns. "*Mudir* did not tell me you were coming."

When I hear him say *Mudir*, the director, I immediately think of Dumphries, who had held that title as the head of the Yale Egyptology program. But of course, there is a new director now. Wyatt.

"It was sort of a last-minute decision," I hedge. "Where is everyone?"

"It's Friday," Harbi says, shrugging. Fridays had been our days off, when we would often take trips to other dig sites. "They were visiting Sohag overnight."

Sohag is another Yale archaeological mission, about three and a half hours south. "When will they be back?"

"Lunchtime, *inshallah*."

"Would it be all right if I wait?" I ask.

"Yes, yes," Harbi answers. "But you must be hungry, *doctora*."

I feel my face color. "Oh," I correct, "actually, I'm not. A *doctora*." It makes sense for Harbi to assume that a visitor would be another Ph.D., like the ones from Yale, and that the girl who worked here for three seasons as a grad student would have completed her dissertation.

Harbi looks at me for a long moment expectantly. When I don't say more, he starts walking down the hallway. "But you are still hungry," he says.

I notice his limp and wonder what happened: if he fell on-site, if his injury pains him. But I can't ask personal questions, not when I am unwilling to answer any myself.

"I'm not very hungry," I say. "Don't go to any trouble . . ."

Harbi ignores my comment and leads me to the largest room of the Dig House, which functions as a work space as well as a dining hall. "Please make yourself at home." Leaving me behind, he shuffles toward the tiny kitchen, his rubber sandals scratching along the tile floor. Under the dome of mud brick is the same table where we ate all our meals, the wood still scarred and spotted. But it's what's different that takes my breath away. Gone are the rolled sheaves of Mylar and ragged stacks of manila folders and papers. Instead, a jigsaw puzzle of desks on the other side of the room is covered with computers—cables snaking like sea monsters and twined around each other, rigged into surge protectors that balance precariously, straining to reach a wall outlet. There are tablets charging and two impressive digital cameras. On the far wall is a giant printed rendering of the complete epigraphic copy of the colossus-hauling scene from Djehutyhotep's tomb—the one that I had worked on with Wyatt that entire last season. I recognize the careful drawings I made with my own hand on Mylar, reproduced now in ink, with Wyatt's translation in the margin. If I needed proof that I was once here, that I had done something worthy—it is literally right in front of me.

I step through the French doors onto the patio just as Harbi returns, balancing a stack of plates. "Please, sit," he urges, and I slip into my old spot at the table.

He has brought a bowl of salad—chopped tomatoes, cilantro, and cucumbers—soft cheese, and *aish shamsi,* bread that is leavened in the sun before baking. I don't realize I am starving until I start to eat and cannot stop. Harbi watches me, smiling. "Not hungry," he says.

"A little," I admit. Then I grin. "A lot."

For dessert, he brings *bas bousa*—a mixture of coconut and honey and partially milled semolina. Finally, I sit back in my chair. "I think I may not eat for the next three days."

"So then you are staying," Harbi replies.

I can't. I have a life halfway across the world, a family that is worried about me. But there is something so unreal about being back here, as if I've been able to simply rewind the clock, that makes this feel like I am just pretending. It is like when you are having a wonderful dream, and you know you are dreaming, but you tell yourself not to wake up.

It is a few moments after Harbi returns to the kitchen that I realize he didn't ask a question, but stated an assumption. That he'd already made this choice for me.

And that I didn't correct him.


My mother used to say that blue eyes were bad luck, because you could see everything that a blue-eyed person was thinking, but I didn't heed the warning the first time I met Wyatt Armstrong. I was a newly arrived transfer to Yale in 2001, a grad student with fifty dollars in my savings account and a shared apartment. I had been in town for three days, and as far as I could tell, the only weather in New Haven was a cold, driving rain. The night before the semester began, I was on my way home from Sterling Library when it started to pour. Desperate to protect the haul of books in my arms—including several hefty volumes of Adriaan de Buck's Coffin Text transcriptions—I ducked into the first open doorway I could find.

Toad's Place was—well—hopping, even for a Wednesday night. The bar was a mix of Yalies and Quinnipiac girls, who got bused in and tottered up and down York Street in heels and miniskirts that barely covered their asses. Inside, undergrads jockeyed at the bar, brandishing fake IDs like FBI badges. A metal band thrashed somewhere in the back, drowning out the fizz of a group of girls cheering on two guys engaged in a drinking contest.

The floor was sticky beneath my sneakers and the room smelled like Budweiser and weed. I glanced outside at the sheet of rain, weighing the lesser of two evils, and made my way to the end of the bar. I climbed onto a seat and set my stack of books on the bar, trying for invisibility.

Of course, I noticed him. His shirtsleeves were rolled up to the elbows and his hair, gold, spilled over his eyes as he reached for the shot, tossed it back, and then slammed the empty glass upside down on the scarred bar. The entourage around him erupted, cheering: *Mark! Mark! Mark!* But he didn't smile or raise his arms in victory or console the loser. He just shrugged as if he knew that this would be the outcome, and accepted it as his due.

Asshole.

There were legacies at U Chicago, but at Yale, they seemed to be the norm instead of the exception. I hadn't been here very long, but the few students I'd met seemed to be ripped from the pages of *Town & Country*. My roommate, whom I'd found through a flyer on a bulletin board, came from the Hudson Valley and was obsessed with dressage. I assumed that had something to do with fashion, until I saw her in her horseback riding gear.

Suddenly the guy looked up, his blue eyes catching mine. They made me think of the heart of a glacier, of how, when you touch dry ice with your bare skin, you cannot let go even if you try.

He opened his mouth, and let out a long, low burp.

Disgusted, I turned away as the bartender put a napkin down in front of me. "What can I get you?" she asked.

On my budget, I couldn't afford a drink, but I also couldn't wait out the rain without ordering something. "Soda water?"

"She'll have Hendrick's, straight up. Twist of lime." The guy had moved to take the seat beside me, so seamlessly and silently I hadn't noticed.

The first thing that surprised me was his accent—British. The second was his utter arrogance. "No thanks."

"It's on me," he said. "And I'm usually quite good at guessing someone's signature drink." He nodded at a girl in a sequined bustier who was dancing by herself. "Skinny margarita or, God forbid, a rosé spritzer." Then he gestured to two men in matching motorcycle leather making out. "Fireball whisky." He pointed to me. "Martini. Did I get it wrong?"

I did prefer gin, but I would have rather died than admit that to him.

"My mistake: three blue cheese olives," he called to the bartender, and then he turned to me again. "You're a savory sort of woman, aren't you." A grin ghosted over his lips. "Or perhaps you're *unsavory*."

That was enough. Even if the rain and wind had reached hurricane force, it had to be less painful than sitting next to this conceited moron. I reached for my stack of books, but he plucked one from the top and opened it, skimming the hieroglyphs.

"Egyptology. I didn't see that coming." He handed me back the book. "Are you an ancient artifact of cultural significance?" he murmured, leaning a fraction closer. "Because I dig you."

I blinked. "Does that line actually *ever* work?"

"Fifty-fifty," he said. "I have a backup. How about I'll be the cultural relativist and you assume the missionary position?"

"I'm glad you're into history, because that's what you're about to be." I took a long sip of the martini and hopped off the barstool. "Thanks for the drink."

"Wait." He touched my arm. "Let me start over without the BS. I'm Wyatt."

"Liar."

"I beg your pardon?"

"Your friends called you Mark."

"Ah, that's a nickname, short for the Marquess of Atherton."

"*You're* a marquess?"

"Well, no." He hesitated. "The marquess is my father. I'm merely an earl." He lifted his glass to mine, clinking the rim. "English through and through, all the way back to William the Conqueror, I'm afraid, and inbred ever since." He flashed a smile then, a real one, as if letting me in on a joke. Suddenly I understood how he had gotten to be such an entitled dick. It had nothing to do with being an earl. It was that when he smiled—wide and almost apologetic—people probably fell all over themselves.

"So," he said. "You are . . . ?"

I set my glass down on the bar. "Leaving," I replied.

THE NEXT MORNING, I was the first one in the small seminar room where Ian Dumphries, the head of Egyptology at Yale, had invited all of this year's graduate students to kick off the academic year. I'd already met him during interviews when I was applying to the doctorate program. Unlike many other Egyptologists, he didn't focus only on one narrow facet of the discipline, such as mud brick architecture or the battle of Kadesh or Egyptian grammar. He published widely about all sorts of topics: the Book of Two Ways, Middle Kingdom archaeology, the history of Egyptian religion, and even an occasional demotic ostracon. Given what I hoped to write for my dissertation, I wanted a mentor who was open-minded. I found Dumphries utterly brilliant and equally terrifying, so I was surprised when he greeted me by name. "McDowell," he said. "Welcome to Yale."

The biggest reason I had come to this university was because I knew that here I would get to work at Deir el-Bersha. Back in the 1890s, the necropolis had been the domain of a British Egyptologist, Percy E. Newberry, who worked with Howard Carter (of later Tutankhamun fame). The oversight of it had changed hands many times before 1998, when Yale acquired the concession, which was supervised by Professor Dumphries.

Five more graduate students entered, tangled in a messy knot of conversation. There were only seven of us in the entire department at Yale, which had been another selling point for me. They sat down at the seminar table, chatting with an easy familiarity. I was the only new doctoral candidate this year.

"Good to see you've all survived another summer," Dumphries said. "I'd like to introduce our newest sacrifice, Dawn McDowell.

We've poached her from Chicago. Why don't you all give her a thumbnail introduction of who you are and how you got here?"

The roots of my curiosity absorbed the schools they'd studied at, their dissertation topics. Just as the last student was wrapping up, the door burst open. Wyatt Armstrong strode in, balancing a box of Dunkin' Donuts coffee and another of Munchkins. "Sorry I'm late. It's a long and sordid story involving a cement mixer, a crying infant, and a Komodo dragon, but instead of boring you with all that I come bearing conciliatory pastries and mediocre coffee."

I stared, my heart pounding, calculating the odds. In a school with 7500 graduate students, how could I possibly wind up in a tiny department with the one person I'd hoped to never see again?

I wondered how Dumphries, starched and buttoned up as he was, would react, but he just shook his head and smiled slightly. "Sit down, Wyatt," he said, in the tone an exasperated parent saves for the child who drives him crazy, but whom he secretly loves beyond reason. "You're just in time to tell Ms. McDowell who you are and why I keep you around."

Wyatt slid into the empty chair next to mine. If he was surprised when he saw my face, he didn't show it. "Well, hello, Olive," he drawled.

"It's Dawn."

He raised a brow. "*Is* it," he murmured. "I studied Egyptology at Cambridge and came here three years ago. I'm a linguistics wonk so I TA in all the undergrad classes on hieroglyphs, hieratic, and demotic. My thesis title is 'Ritual Speech and Interlocutory Verbal Patterns in the Coffin Texts.' I spent six months coming up with something that sexy, so don't go stealing it."

"The Coffin Texts?" I repeated.

"Dawn plans to study the Book of Two Ways," Dumphries interjected.

Wyatt pinned his gaze on me. "Guess you and I are going to be all up in each other's business."

"I'm not a philologist," I qualified. "I'm just trying to fill in a gap in the research." I turned to the other grad students, offering context. "Pierre Lacau published the text from the Book of Two

Ways coffins in Cairo in 1904 and 1906, but most of the coffins have never been published as *coffins*." Now that I was warming up to my favorite subject, my words came faster. "I want to write about the iconography. You can't just look at the map of the Book of Two Ways without thinking of the coffin as a microcosm of the universe. Imagine the front side of the coffin is the eastern horizon. The back side is the western horizon. The floor is the Netherworld, with its map. The lid is Nut, the sky goddess, and going into the coffin is like going back into her womb—getting reborn from the coffin to the afterlife. The mummy fills all the space between heaven and earth."

Dumphries nods. "So Wyatt's thesis will be a new translation of the Book of Two Ways. And Dawn's thesis will collect all the illustrated representations of the Book of Two Ways for the first time."

One of the other students smirked. "You guys should publish as a matched set."

"Funny you should mention that," Dumphries said. "Dawn's too humble to tell you herself, but she already published a chapter of her dissertation in the *Journal of the American Research Center in Egypt*."

I blushed. It was nearly unheard of for an undergrad's work to be accepted by a journal of Egyptology; I knew that was in part why Yale had wanted me. I was fiercely proud of it. "It was called 'The Corpse Makes the Coffin Whole,'" I added.

Feeling the heat of Wyatt's gaze, I turned. "That was *yours*?" he said.

"You *read* it?"

He jerked his head, a tight nod. He glanced at Dumphries—so effusive in his praise for me—his lock on teacher's pet suddenly less solid. Something shuttered in Wyatt Armstrong at that moment, armor sliding into place.

FOR THE NEXT month, Wyatt and I did an excellent job of avoiding each other unless we were forced to interact, which happened Mondays and Wednesdays at 9:15 when we both TA'd sixteen undergrads in Dumphries's course Gods of Ancient Egypt. Even then, we sat on opposite sides of the seminar table. Then, in October, we were told that we would be accompanying Dumphries and the class on a field trip to the Boston Museum of Fine Arts to see the new exhibit on the Book of Two Ways.

I had only seen the map of the Netherworld in books. Nothing was going to spoil the excitement I felt at being so close to an image of the Book of Two Ways. Not even Wyatt.

The day of the trip, Dumphries stood in the front of a classroom in the museum, clicking through a series of excavation slides from Deir el-Bersha. "Imagine it's 1915," he began, "and you're an Egyptologist who's found a thirty-foot burial shaft under a pile of boulders in a necropolis from the Middle Kingdom. You've cleared the debris, and you've just crawled into Tomb 10A for the first time. You let your eyes adjust to the darkness and what do you see? A coffin, with the decapitated head of a mummy sitting on top of it."

A student in front of me shook his head. "Fucking Indiana Jones shit, man."

Beside me, Wyatt snorted.

"Tomb 10A belonged to a nomarch named Djehutynakht, and his wife, also named Djehutynakht."

Wyatt leaned toward me. "Imagine how confusing sorting the post must have been," he murmured.

"They lived around 2000 B.C.E., in the Middle Kingdom, and ruled one of the provinces of Upper Egypt. Sometime in the four thousand years between their death and the early twentieth century, grave robbers broke into the tomb, stole the gold and the jewels and all the valuables, and threw the headless mummy into the corner. Then they set fire to the chamber, so they didn't leave any evidence behind. But some of the material in the tomb survived and was brought to the MFA by Harvard Egyptologists in 1921. This is the first time it's been exhibited."

I stared at the slide on the screen: the mummy head, wrapped in its frayed linen, brown with ancient resin. It had hand-painted eyebrows and slightly bulging eye sockets. Its mouth turned down, as if it were mildly disappointed.

An undergrad raised her hand. "Where's the rest of him?"

"Egypt," Dumphries replied. "But is it the rest of *him?* Or *her?* Amazing to think that we've had four thousand years to figure this out, and we still don't have all the answers." He flipped to the next slide. "The evolution of the Coffin Texts and the Book of Two Ways was more about changing tastes in funerary decoration than it was about more people having access to the blessed afterlife. As coffins became more common in the Middle Kingdom, those spells that used to be on precious papyri could now be painted on the wood of the coffin."

He clicked again, and the slide became the familiar image of the Book of Two Ways, its snaking blue and black lines and the red lake of fire that kept them from crossing.

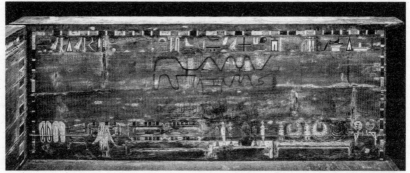

PHOTOGRAPH © 2020 MUSEUM OF FINE ARTS, BOSTON

"The Book of Two Ways is yet another confirmation of the unity between Re and Osiris," Dumphries explained. "The main purpose of Re's journey through the Netherworld is to unite with the corpse of Osiris. The roads through the Netherworld are for Re to travel to reach Osiris. The goal of the deceased is to become both Re and Osiris, in order to attain eternal life."

He traced a finger over the wavy lines on the projected image. "Mind you, the Book of Two Ways doesn't actually mention *two* ways. Just . . . *ways*. The black and blue roads are not labeled directly, but we can imagine them as a land and a water route to the Netherworld that lead to the same outcome."

Dumphries glanced around the room, and I realized he was looking for me. "McDowell," he said. "Tell us what the key to resurrection was, according to the Book of Two Ways."

"Knowledge," I said, straightening. "That's why the texts were placed *in* the coffin. They're spells the deceased has to have in order to pass all the obstacles en route to the shrine of Osiris."

"Exactly. And frankly, who *doesn't* need knowledge to survive tests in this world . . . or the next?" He faced the students. "Questions?"

A student raised his hand. "Will this be on the midterm?"

Dumphries flicked his eyes away, dismissive. "Next?"

"Did you have to be super rich to have the Book of Two Ways painted in your coffin?" another student asked.

"The ones we've found at Bersha have come from nobles of the Hare nome, but a good death wasn't linked to economic status. Every Egyptian could become an *akh*—a transfigured soul."

A third student raised her hand. "What about gender? Did women get the map, too?"

"Yes," Dumphries said. "It's been found in the tombs of noble-women."

Wyatt crossed his arms. "There are some Egyptologists who claim that women had to take on male characteristics to become an Osiris, much like a female pharaoh would wear the ritual false beard of the king."

"I doubt it," I said. "The word *corpse* in Ancient Egyptian is already feminine. And there's a woman's Middle Kingdom coffin where the spells have pronouns that were all changed from male to female, tailored to the deceased."

Wyatt and I stared at each other, facing off, as Dumphries shut the projector. "If Mommy and Daddy are done arguing," he said drily, "we're going to turn you loose in the museum. Armstrong, McDowell, I pass you the torch."

While Dumphries left with the museum curator to look at objects from Bersha that weren't on display, Wyatt and I herded the under-grads through the MFA. He was the primary TA; even if I'd wanted that position I wasn't as adept at teaching hieroglyphs. I had to admit, he was good at it.

Wyatt gathered the undergrads in a semicircle at the doorway of the new exhibit. The undergrads held packets with hieroglyphs that had been copied from the coffins they were about to see firsthand. The girls, and some of the guys, were gazing at Wyatt as if he had just created the cosmos. I knew that there were undergrads who signed up for Dumphries's courses because of the British TA who, if you believed the gossip, was apparently Harrison Ford and the Second Coming all rolled into one.

"We tend to think of literacy in Ancient Egypt as black and white—either you could read or you couldn't. In antiquity, it was actually a continuum. If you were a priest or a bureaucrat, you'd learn hieroglyphs. If you were training to be a scribe, you learned hieratic—the cursive form of hieroglyphics—for everyday use in contracts and wills and village documents. But even if you were in the public, you could still recognize basic symbols, the way we'd know a stop sign by its shape even if we couldn't read the letters on it. All of you are going to hopefully achieve the reading level of a bureaucrat. Let's get to it, then."

The Ancient Egyptians can be credited with developing our alphabet. When early Semitic speakers traveled from what's now Israel to Egypt, they didn't have a writing system. They saw the Egyptians writing their names on rock and wanted to do it, too. So they picked hieroglyphs that represented common objects—water, an eye, a bull's head—and used them to form the first letters of those words in their own language.

Wyatt walked into the exhibit, stopping in front of a case that had the exterior panel of Djehutynakht's coffin. I scanned the columns of hieroglyphs painted on the ancient cedar, looking for the owner's name.

The ibis stood for *Djehuty*—the ancient Egyptian name of the god Thoth. The squiggle was a line of water, the letter *n*. The stick beneath was *khet*. The circle with the horizontal lines were *kh*—repeating the sounds of the stick—and the loaf was *t*. When you translate hieroglyphs, you do it in two steps, the first of which renders the sounds of the hieroglyphs into a script that uses alphabetic signs. So the transliteration was *ḏḥwty-nḫt*—

"Djehutynakht's coffin," Wyatt announced. "What's the first thing we need to figure out?"

"Which way the faces point in the signs," a girl answered. "Because you read toward the faces."

"Right. So in this case, the bird faces left, which means . . . ?" He glanced at the girl.

"We're reading the columns of text from left to right."

"Exactly. Now, one of the reasons it took so long to decipher hieroglyphs is because they're not purely phonetic or purely ideographic. It's a mixture, with an additional sign type thrown in just to confuse you further—a determinative. Determinatives are like clues to give you information about the meanings of the words near them."

The students crowded closer, squinting at the images on the exterior of Djehutynakht's coffin. They were greenish blue, some standing out in stark relief against the strip of eggshell paint, others so faint they could barely be distinguished from the grain of the wood. "Who can find an ideogram?" Wyatt asked.

A kid beside him pointed to the thin canine figure perched on a pedestal. "The jackal."

"Very good. The jackal is the god Anubis, or as an Ancient Egyptian would say, *Inpu*. The hieroglyph writes his name. But what comes before it?"

He underlined a series of signs with his fingertip on the glass.

It was one of the very first combinations of hieroglyphs I had ever learned, because it was so commonly seen.

"*Hotep di nisu*," Wyatt read. "An offering the king gives on behalf of . . . ?"

"Anubis," said the boy who'd pointed to the jackal. "The god of embalming."

"Right. He's quite important for mummies," Wyatt said, and then he grinned. "And daddies. What's next? What are these four pots tied together?"

"The offerings are in them?" a student suggested.

"No, because it's not an ideogram," said another girl. "It's a phonetic hieroglyph. The picture of the pots tied together writes the word *khenet*. It has nothing to do with pots. It's just a cheat for writing three letters of the alphabet: *khn-n-t*."

Wyatt's eyebrows raised. "Well done."

The girl's cheeks flushed crimson. "That means so much coming from you!"

"Oh, dear God," I said under my breath.

As he launched into another transliteration tutorial, I became transfixed by a model that had been found in Tomb 10A along with the coffins of the Djehutynakhts. Two weavers, carved of wood, were kneeling by a loom. The women in the front were spinning flax. Amazingly, after four thousand years, the threads of the flax and the loom were intact, the way they would have been the day they were set in the burial chamber, with the rest of the models and pottery and *shabti* statues.

"Time for a scavenger hunt," Wyatt said, handing out a list of objects. "Pick a partner, you'll be working in teams. The answers are somewhere in this exhibit. First pair to come back to me with pictures on their phone gets ten points on their next homework assignment. And . . . go!" He turned to me as the undergrads dispersed. "Was I that stupid once?"

"Do you really want me to answer that?" I said.

Wyatt wandered toward the coffins of the Djehutynakhts. "No," he said. "But look at this."

We both stood, hypnotized by the Book of Two Ways on the inner coffin of Governor Djehutynakht. There was the red rectangular door to the horizon. The blue water and black land routes through the Netherworld. The crimson line between them, a lake of fire. After so many years of studying this through pictures and drawings, I felt like I had reached the Holy Grail, only to find it locked inside a glass exhibit case.

"I wonder who first looked at that and thought it was a map," Wyatt murmured.

"Well, the coffin wasn't empty. It's pretty clear that the deceased was meant to stand up and walk one of the two paths to reach the Field of Offerings."

"Not to poke holes in your theory," Wyatt said, "but this Book of Two Ways was on the *wall* of Djehutynakht's coffin. So . . . that sort of disproves your point."

I stepped away from him, staring at the richly painted cedar panel of the front inside of the exterior coffin. There was a false door through which the *ba*—part of the soul—could pass between the afterlife and this world. Djehutynakht was painted in front of the false door. The text nearby requested offerings from the king and Osiris: incense, wine, oils, fruits, meats, bread, geese.

In the interior coffin, Djenutynakht's mummy would have been placed lying on his left side, eyes looking east. Spells from the Coffin Texts wrapped around the inside walls, protecting him like another layer of linen.

"The Coffin Text spells surrounded the mummy for a reason," I said quietly.

"Yes," Wyatt agreed. "Papyri disintegrate, and cedar doesn't. Look, I don't mean to be a jerk—"

"But it comes easily to you?"

He shrugged. "They're texts, Olive. It's a stretch to try to squeeze them into your theories about iconography."

I folded my arms. "My name is *Dawn*. I hate when you call me Olive."

Wyatt leaned close to the glass, his breath fogging it. "I know," he said. "That's why I do it."


As the Dig House bakes in the late-afternoon sun, so does everything living. The fans can't keep the air circulating fast enough, and heat shimmers from the mud brick walls. A fly that has been circling

my lunch collapses on the scarred table. The alfalfa and corn growing along the Nile drape their lank arms over each other, a line of
drunken soldiers staggering home.

This is the time of day when, as a grad student, I trudged back
from the dig site with the sun forging a crown on my head. Sometimes we would work in the magazine, but more often, we made up
for our early-morning departures by drifting to each of our rooms
and taking a nap.

I think back to my old room, with the fan I had to jerry-rig with
duct tape in order to work. I would strip down to my underwear on
the narrow twin bed and pretend to sleep until I heard the knock on
the wall between us. I'd knock back. While the rest of the house was
hibernating, he would slip into my room, curl his body around
mine, and we would burn each other alive.

Harbi offers to make up a cot for me, but that feels presumptuous.
After he goes back to his living quarters, I am left to wait alone.

It is nearly 10:00 A.M. at home. Brian will be at work. Meret will
be at school.

I should tell them where I am.

But there are some feelings that the English language just doesn't
fully capture. An emotion like grief spills over the confines of those
five letters. The word *joy* feels too compact, stunted, for what it
evokes. How can you even put into words the confession that you
made a mistake, that you want to turn back time and try again? How
do you say it without hurting the people who have been sitting across
from you at the breakfast table for fifteen years, who know your
Starbucks order and which side of the bed to leave you at a hotel?

So instead, I poke around the Dig House, trying not to snoop.
Avoiding the laptops and iPads that litter the main room, I slip into
a small alcove behind it. There are narrow cedar shelves inside,
stacked with books. When I was a grad student, we used them for
research. Plucking a few newer-looking journals off the shelves, I
sit down on the floor cross-legged, and begin to reconstruct the history of Wyatt's success.

In 2013, he found the tomb of Djehutynakht, son of Teti, who
lived during the Eleventh Dynasty just before Montuhotep II reuni-

fied Egypt. This Djehutynakht—as common a name during the Middle Kingdom as John—was known to scholars from some hieratic ink graffiti he left in the tombs of his ancestors, touting the work he had done restoring the damage there. And yet, the location of Djehutynakht's own final resting place had never been located.

Then came the 2003 discovery of a dipinto—ink written on stone—which offered a clue. The message described a visit by a later nomarch—Djehutyhotep—to Deir el-Bersha to see the Sothic rising, during which he stayed overnight in the forecourt of Djehutynakht's final resting place.

I bite my lip, running my fingers over the familiar image of the hieratic, followed by Wyatt's hieroglyphic translation, to clarify how he read each sign.

How *we* read each sign.

*hsb.t 7 3bd 4 pr.t 14 hr hm n nswt bity h3-k3.w-rꜥ ꜥnh d.t r nhh*
*hrw pn iwt pw ir.n iry-pꜥ.t h3ty-ꜥ hry-tp ꜥ3 n wnw dhwty-htp r dw pn*
*r m33 pr.t špd.t*

*ii.n=i ḥnꜥ ḥry-ḥb.w ḥm.w-kꜣ m-ḫt šzp.n=i sš m ḫnw r-nty ḫpr pr.t špd.t*
  *ꜣbd 4 pr.t 15*
*iw sḏr.n=n m wsḫ.t n is n ḏḥwty-nḫt ms n tti nty mḥ [. . .] r [. . .]*
*pr.n=n m ḏw pn m wšꜣw [. . .]*

*Regnal year 7, fourth month of Peret, day 14 under the majesty of the
king of Upper and Lower Egypt Kha-kau-re, living forever and ever.*

*On this day, the count, hereditary noble, and nomarch of the Hare
Nome, Djehutyhotep, came to this mountain to see the rising of Sothis.*

*After having received the letter from the Residence foretelling the rising
on fourth month of Peret, day 15, I came together with the lector priests
and mortuary priests.*

*We spent the night in the forecourt of the tomb of Djehutynakht, born of
Teti, which is [. . .] cubits from [. . .]*

*In the deep of the night we went forth from this mountain [. . .]*

It's breathtaking, seeing this in its final, published form, and I
find myself riveted by each line and symbol. Yet when I close my
eyes, I can feel the rock under my hand, still warm from the sun.

More proof that once, I was here. That what I did mattered.

I scan the journals, but there's nothing in them yet about Wyatt's
discovery of the tomb. Then I spot a slim bound volume on the bottom shelf. The title is printed on the spine: *Ritual Speech and Interlocutory Verbal Patterns in the Coffin Texts.*

I look at the date on the title page: 2008. Wyatt's thesis, finished
and published after I left.

I am halfway through the first paragraph when he notes an
article—"The Corpse Makes the Coffin Whole"—published by
McDowell in 2002.

My breath catches in my throat. I touch my fingertip to my own
last name.

*Conversations with the author of this article in front of a coffin at the
Museum of Fine Arts in Boston challenged my original thesis,* Wyatt
wrote. *During the course of my grammatical analysis, I mapped out
where different speech patterns (first person, dialogue, third-person nar-*

*ration) occurred on the coffin, and in the process realized that the texts were distributed according to a geographical pattern corresponding both to parts of the body and parts of the Netherworld.*

"You've got to be kidding me," I say softly.

*It is impossible,* Wyatt concluded, *to separate the grammar from the context.*

It may have taken years, but I got him to admit I was right.

I realize that the words are swimming on the page, and I wipe my eyes. I am about to shut the book when I notice the first footnote in Wyatt's thesis. In academia, the first footnote is often how the author of an article will dedicate the piece to someone. At the bottom of the page Wyatt has written his inscription, a poem translated from P. Chester Beatty, presented without comment.

> *One unique is the sister, without her equal, more beautiful than all*
> *    women.*
> *Behold her like the star,*
> *Having appeared in glory at the beginning of a good year.*
>
> *Shining of excellence, luminous of hue;*
> *Beautiful of eyes when glancing, sweet her lips when speaking—*
> *For her no word is excessive.*
>
> *Long of neck, luminous of chest;*
> *True lapis is her hair,*
> *Her arms putting on gold,*
> *Her fingers like lotuses.*

To anyone who might read Wyatt's thesis, this would be taken at face value: a beautiful example of Ancient Egyptian love poetry.

That is . . . to anyone but me.

THE FIRST EUROPEAN to visit Deir el-Bersha was a Dominican friar, Johann Michael Vansleb, who wrote about his visit to the "hieroglyphick cave." What people who aren't Egyptologists don't realize is that the art is not just fine lines and chicken scratch. It fills the walls and the ceilings of tombs with vivid cobalt, russet, turquoise, yellow, ocher, pitch black. The figures show movement, sound, emotion. These aren't just monuments to the men and women who were buried inside. They are stories.

Unlike the later New Kingdom tombs of royals, where texts about how to get to the afterlife were written on the walls and images of the gods were the norm, the tombs of nomarchs in the Middle Kingdom were filled with scenes of ordinary life. You'd see cooking, grinding grain, dancing, games, music, wrestling, basenji dogs, hunting, sex, trapping game, winemaking, harvesting, building, plowing. The tomb of Baqet has an entire wall of wrestling holds. There's one tomb where the owner is pictured with a pet griffin on a leash, to suggest that the man was an explorer—someone who had traveled so far and so wide he met a magical creature at the edge of the known world. There were cryptographic hieroglyphs meant to be puns and puzzles for visitors. All in all, you couldn't walk into a Middle Kingdom tomb without thinking that these people had fun, even four thousand years ago. Their tombs were celebrations of here and now—what you did during your life and what you would take with you after you died.

In July 2003, I was back at the Dig House for my third season in Deir el-Bersha with Yale Egyptology. It was not our normal season—that was in January—but Professor Dumphries had scheduled an extra trip before the start of the fall semester because of an upcoming publication deadline, and there was no way I was missing it, even if it was brutally hot. Wyatt and I were working in the tomb of Djehutyhotep II, who ruled in the mid-Twelfth Dynasty.

We had a routine. Every morning, my alarm would go off at 4:30, and I would stumble in the dark to pull on my long-sleeved cotton shirt and khakis, and to lace up my boots. Whoever got to the table earliest got the first omelets that Hasib would make and didn't have to wait. I was usually the fastest, along with an osteologist from England, who was working with us that season. There was also a first-year grad student, a conservator who was cleaning some of the art in the tomb, and Dumphries.

Wyatt was always the last to get to the table, his hair wet and shaggy, his eyes bright. He was the type of cheerful morning person that the rest of us wanted to kill. "Well," he announced, as forks clattered against plates. "I'm a four, if anyone's wondering."

"Out of a possible ten?" asked Yvonne, the osteologist.

"More like a possible hundred," I murmured.

"It's not a ratio," Wyatt said. "It's the Bristol stool scale. Type four: like a smooth, soft sausage—"

"Shut up," I said. "Please. For the love of God. We're eating."

Dumphries laughed. "It's good to monitor, in the desert. I'd put myself at a Type three, actually."

"Clearly *someone's* a Type two." Wyatt grinned at me. "Mild constipation."

"If I'm having any digestive issues, it's because you're a pain in my ass," I replied, and the others laughed.

I usually managed to time my breakfast so that as Wyatt sat down, I could get up and begin to pack my bag for the day. I had to spend eight hours with him inside a rock-cut tomb, but outside of that, I tried to stay out of his presence. Every other grad student on digs worked so hard during the day that by eight o'clock at night we were fast asleep, but Wyatt wasn't like every other grad student. He didn't fear Dumphries's censure—in fact, he courted it, brandishing a bottle of whiskey one night that he'd carried down from Yale and challenging the rest of us to a game of Never Have I Ever; playing poker with Dumphries until midnight; teaching the local workmen how to curse fluently in English.

As Wyatt regaled the table with a story that began with the Bristol Royal Infirmary, which developed the scale, and ended with an overweight bulldog and Prince Charles, I rose from the table and moved into our work space, to pack up.

I rolled up a fresh sheet of Mylar and set it next to my bag. Then I checked the contents: a small mirror, a dozen Sharpies, brushes, a notebook, a camera, a centimeter scale for measurement, a bottle of water, and printouts of the reference photos of the scene we were working on. Packing the bag had become a science, because I had to carry it all the way to the dig site. Dumphries and the larger equipment went in the Rover; underlings walked.

"T minus five," Dumphries announced, and he stood up from the table, heading to collect his own materials and to talk to Hasib.

I glanced down at my bag again, sensing something missing. My scarf. I wore it to keep out the blowing sand and dust, but I must have left it in my room.

I hurried down the hallway toward the sleeping quarters and was on my hands and knees, crawling under my iron bed frame to get the scarf where it had dropped, when Wyatt stuck his head through the door. "That's an improvement, Olive."

"Why are you in my room?" I shimmied backward and sat on my heels, the scarf caught in my hand.

"I've lost my notebook."

"Why would *your* notebook be in *my* room?"

"I don't know," he said. "That's why I'm looking for it."

I got to my feet. "Ask the last person in your family that died." He blinked. "What?"

"That's what my mother says. It's a superstition. She's Irish."

"Of course she is. No wonder we get on like oil and water."

I shrugged. "I'm not the one without a notebook."

Wyatt ran a hand through his hair. "I don't know the last person in my family who died."

I turned off the light beside the bed, and the fan. "Sounds like a *you* problem."

"For fuck's sake. Fine, then. Uncle Edmond, from Surrey."

I folded my arms, and raised my brows.

"Uncle Edmond," Wyatt ground out, "where's my notebook?"

Suddenly Dumphries appeared in the doorway. "There you are," he said to Wyatt, holding out a small brown notebook. "Is this yours?"

I breezed past them both. *"Erin go bragh,"* I murmured to Wyatt.


THE TOMB OF Djehutyhotep II had an entry that always reminded me of *Planet of the Apes*—an impressive rock-cut stone façade, listing to the left after years of earthquakes and quarrying and robbery. The architrave and doorway were carved and decorated with Djehutyhotep's titles and the names of the kings under whom he served. The porch was supported by two fluted columns, and the outer chamber had a large desert hunting scene and fishing scene. A narrow doorway led to the inner chamber—the spot where I worked that July—which was 25 feet deep by 20 feet wide by 16.5 feet high. Inside was the most famous scene in the tomb: a massive statue of Djehutyhotep II being transported. It was accompanied to the left by a large image of Djehutyhotep joined by his family and guards and important officials. The gate of the building where the statue was being hauled was on the right, and in front of that gate were people bearing offerings. In Egyptian art, you'd see hierarchic scale—the most important people were the biggest—but you also would see composite perspective. The faces of the individuals were in profile, but the eyes were straight on. The artists back then would take the most salient feature—eyes, or for the torso, a nipple—and emphasize it.

The best-known publication of the tomb was from 1894, by Percy Newberry. Working under him to create the drawings were Marcus Blackden, and seventeen-year-old Howard Carter—long before his own discovery of Tutankhamun's tomb. But there were errors in the Newberry publication—bits that were incomplete and inaccuracies that only became evident if you were standing in front of the actual wall, like Wyatt and I were. It was our job, that season, to find and record those mistakes, so that Dumphries could publish a corrected version.

It was early morning in the tomb, and the air was already stagnant and blistering. Mohammed and Ahmed, two of the Egyptians we had working with us that season, were using the total station to mark elevation points. The first-year grad student was sitting outside the tomb, sorting broken potsherds into types: bowls and cups, bread molds, jars, and anything unusual—like a piece with a stamp on it. I had brushed off the surface of the statue-hauling scene I was working on and had finished the daily struggle to affix the Mylar to the rock wall surface with masking tape. Mylar was an entire level of hell, as far as I was concerned. In the heat, it got gooey and limp; in the winter, it grew hard and stiff. The thinner it was, the worse it held up in this kind of heat—but the thicker it was, the harder it was to see through in order to trace the hieroglyphs. It wasn't particularly efficient, but it was all we had at the time—a way of taking a three-dimensional inscription on the wall and putting it onto two-dimensional paper.

I glanced over at Wyatt talking to Mostafa, the antiquities inspector. Mostafa had expressed an interest in learning hieroglyphs, and Wyatt was endlessly accommodating, drawing in the dust of the tomb floor or finding a sign on the wall. "This one, that looks like a touchdown?" Wyatt tested.

I glanced over, surprised he knew the word from an American sport.

He had drawn the biliteral sign for *ka*, the part of the soul that has to do with what's handed down from generation to generation. While Mostafa tried to remember that, I turned my attention back to the wall.

Harbi was holding a large mirror to shine the light from the entrance of the tomb to fall from left to right over the area of text I was studying. When tracing, you had to pretend that light was coming from the upper left at a forty-five-degree angle, and if the hieroglyph happened to be in sunken relief, you'd draw a shadow line, slightly thicker.

I lifted my Sharpie from the Mylar, squinting at a detail I couldn't quite see.

"Harbi," I said, "can you get me a little more light here?"

He was young and wiry and strong, wrestling with the large mirror to try to direct the light where I needed it. But given the placement of that particular sign, he couldn't shine it close enough.

"I've got an idea," I said. I hopped off the ladder I was standing on and rummaged in my bag for my small mirror. "Aim up here," I told Harbi, pointing to a spot above my head on the wall. I held up the hand mirror, catching the stream of light he directed that way, and bounced it down to the sign I wanted to scrutinize.

"This one's my favorite," Wyatt was saying.

He pointed to the sign he had sketched into the dirt:

Mostafa frowned. "A pistol?"

"In a matter of speaking," Wyatt said. "Think more . . . below the belt."

"It is a phallus?"

"Yes. As a preposition, it means *in front of*."

*Of* course *it did*, I mused.

"There's a bit in the Coffin Texts where the deceased talk about each part of themselves, from their fingers to their toes to their ears to their phallus, and each part is a different god." Wyatt pointed to the symbol in the dirt. "I'd call mine Re. Because it, too, would be resurrected nightly."

I tweaked the little hand mirror so that a beam of light struck Wyatt directly in his eye. He winced, holding up his palm to block it.

"Hey, Wyatt?" I said sweetly. "You planning on working today?"

He stood, wiping the dust off his hands. "Lesson time is over, my friend," he said to Mostafa. "I've got to earn my keep." He scuffed out the picture he'd drawn with one boot, and then walked underneath the ladder I was perched on.

"I can't believe you did that!" I said.

"Taught Mostafa a hieroglyph?" he said innocently.

"No . . . you just walked under the ladder."

"Let me guess. Another superstition from your Irish mother." He rummaged for a Sharpie in his own bag. "What should I do to keep the whole tomb from falling down around me, then?"

"My mom would say you should walk through the ladder again, backward. Or cross your fingers and keep them crossed till you see a dog."

"A dog . . . ?" He shook his head. "I'll just take my chances and live on the edge." He spread one hand over a section of Mylar and began to trace hieroglyphs he could reach from his spot on the ground. "The only superstition my family ever adhered to was to not leave a finger of brandy in the decanter. You have to finish it. But I don't know if that was superstition or alcoholism."

"My mother has so many of them."

"What's the oddest one?"

I thought for a moment. "Don't put your feet on the table, because it's where God's face is."

"On the table?"

"Allegedly. And if you give someone a handkerchief as a gift, it means the recipient's life will be full of sadness," I added. "Oh. And breaking dishes is lucky."

He turned to me. "Did you break a lot of dishes?"

I noticed that the light Harbi had been trying so hard to catch for me touched Wyatt's hair effortlessly, like a benediction. "Yeah."

"Then maybe she was just trying to make you feel better. I'm told mothers are supposed to do that."

I glanced at him, but there was enough bitterness in his tone to suggest that his own mother might not have been very kind. The Wyatt I knew was a titled white guy with all the privilege in the world; maybe his mother had forgotten to pick him up from cricket practice once.

And yet as soon as I thought that, I felt embarrassed.

Before I could question whether Wyatt might deserve more than my usual scorn, we were interrupted by Dumphries. "Hello, my chickens," he said. "How's our colossus?"

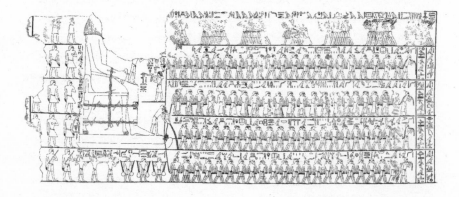

I came down from the ladder and stood beside him. Wyatt joined us, and we all looked at the image of the tremendous statue of Djehutyhotep II being hauled. It had been much more impressive, once. In 1890, the inscription was damaged—all the hieroglyphs to the left had been hacked out. There was also graffiti scrawled over other parts of the text—Coptic, from people who had lived in the tombs, and Greek, from ancient tourists. Our job was basically to replicate this image, with all its scarring from age and erosion and mankind, and to hypothesize about missing pieces. In the Middle Kingdom, autobiographical inscriptions were pretty straightforward, but there was always a weird turn of phrase or grammar that was time-consuming and hard to translate, that required reference books and publications. In those cases, two heads were better than one.

That's why Dumphries had assigned us both to the task.

He clapped us both on our shoulders. "So let it be written, so let it be done," he joked, quoting Ramesses II from the movie version of *The Ten Commandments*. "Which as you know is complete bullshit."

He wandered off to check on the others as Wyatt and I climbed back into position. "So," Wyatt said drily, "did you know the Cecil B. DeMille movie used this scene of the colossus as a reference?"

Dumphries had told us that fact at least twenty times in the two weeks we'd been here. "Why no," I said, deadpan. "That's totally news to me."

Dumphries loved to talk about everything that the movie got wrong. The film made it seem like when a pharaoh said something was law, no questions were asked. But Egyptians were big on tribunals. Even when a pharaoh was presumed assassinated, like Ramesses III, an independent panel of judges was set up and everyone had to be interviewed before a sentence could be meted out to his murderer.

I was working on sketching the overseer, who stood on the actual statue, directing those who were hauling it.

"Did you ever see *The Ten Commandments*?" I asked Wyatt.

"Every Easter," he replied.

"They got this part wrong. The overseer wasn't holding a whip. He's clapping. Look."

All of a sudden Wyatt was scaling the opposite side of the ladder.

He traced a finger over the hieroglyphs beside the overseer. "Words spoken: keeping time for the soldiers by . . . can't read that bit . . . Djehutyhotep, beloved of the king." He met my eyes. "He's the DJ."

"Dropping that sick beat." I laughed.

"DJ Hutyhotep," Wyatt said. "Whassup, Deir el-Bersha! Lemme see some hands in the air!" He leaped off the ladder, pointing to the men who were hauling the colossus. "That's not all Cecil DeMille cocked up. The guys dragging this thing aren't enslaved. There's a missing part, an inscription, that says it was hauled by three troupes of recruits, along with the sculptors and quarrymen who carved it."

"Yeah, but Charlton Heston had to be in the shot," I said, and just then I lost my balance.

I would have crashed onto the stone floor, but somehow Wyatt was there, and we collapsed together in a heap. He rolled, taking the brunt of the fall, his arms tight around me.

In this tomb where time had stopped, it might have well been just the two of us, suspended. His hands flexed on my shoulders and I could see actual fear in his eyes—not for himself, but for me. "Are you all right?" he murmured, and pressed against the length of him, I could feel his voice better than I could hear it.

*Was I?*

Then he grunted beneath my weight, and I rolled off him. "Thanks for breaking my fall," I said.

"Thanks for breaking my knee." He flexed the joint and stood. "And here I thought *I* was supposed to have the shit luck."

Somehow, we had managed to tear off the Mylar as we tumbled to the ground. I groaned, thinking of what a pain it would be to hang it again in just the right position. But with the Mylar removed, I couldn't help but be impressed by the beauty of the art: the rich red skin of those hauling the statue, the faded yellows of the stone figure, the turquoise faience necklace of the domineering nomarch walking behind, the delicate pleated white of his robe. "My name is Ozymandias, King of Kings. Look on my works, ye Mighty, and despair!" I murmured, quoting Shelley.

Wyatt settled beside me, staring up at it. "Wrong colossus," he said.

I knew that. Shelley had written his poem about the massive model of Ramesses II. "Yeah," I conceded, "but same basic idea."

Wyatt was quiet for a moment. "I think that Djehutyhotep would be delighted to know that four thousand years later, we're talking about him. Just by our saying his name, he lives on. I mean, look." He waved his arm around the tomb. "The names, the deeds, the autobiographical texts all over the place—that's because tombs were meant to be visited. That's how memories get preserved." Wyatt looked at me. "It's why we want to publish, isn't it?"

I shook my head. "You think we'll be immortalized? Two insignificant grad students who are a footnote in one of Dumphries's papers?"

Wyatt laughed. "I won't forget you, Olive. No matter how hard I may try."

I punched his shoulder. "That's not the same as being remembered."

He smiled at me. "*Isn't* it?"

I DO NOT know how many hours pass while I'm sitting cross-legged on the floor, reading Wyatt's dissertation. The sun has sunk so low that my eyes burn, trying to find enough light to read. There are lamps, but I don't want to get up to turn one on. I'm too afraid that all this will disappear; that I will wake up in Boston and this will be only the filmy soap left from the bubble of a dream.

*Although the Coffin Texts do not say that the coffin is the microcosm of the Underworld, the arrangement of texts shouts this (McDowell, 2001)*, I read.

*Spell 1029, the first spell of the Book of Two Ways, describes the rising sun:* Trembling befalls the eastern horizon of the sky at the voice of Nut. For Re does she clear the ways before the Great One, Osiris, when Re perambulates the Netherworld. Raise yourself, O Re!

I close my eyes, seeing in quick succession a series of memories:

Harbi peeling an orange in the front yard; my own hands and nails, brown with dust; the unlikely relief of hot tea on a blistering day. The ache in my arches after a day on my feet. The tail of a white scarf floating behind me on a bicycle. I am riding the handlebars, Wyatt is pedaling.

*Nut is the sky goddess, the mother of Osiris. The Underworld is also in her body; the coffin can be Nut, and thus the mummy in her womb becomes Osiris.*

I remember the way the moon sat on the sill of my window, watching me sleep. The scrape of sand underneath my bare thighs. The purr of my bedroom fan, wheezing to life after a power outage. The sound of his breathing.

*The term* raise yourself *signifies specifically what a mummy does—as in awaken—so here Re* is *a mummy; here Re* is *the deceased in the coffin.*

When we were here during the season, there was always so much dust and sand that every night, I would rinse my eyes out with a saline wash, and blink to find the world new again. That's what it feels like now, to read the explanation of the theories I never got to prove.

"My God."

I look up, straining in the near dark to see. Wyatt looks just like I remember. Older, but only in breadth of his shoulders, the lines that fan from the edges of his eyes. All the remaining light in the room is drawn to his hair, still gilded, a crown for a prince.

"I didn't believe it when Harbi told me," he says.

I get to my feet, still holding his dissertation. Between us, I feel a shifting wall, as if we are magnets with like poles that keep us at a fixed distance. And I also feel what it could be like if one of those poles flipped.

Wyatt isn't smiling, and neither am I. I lift my chin. "You once told me you'd do anything for me," I say.

"Dawn—"

"I want to work here," I interrupt. "I want to finish what I started."

# WATER / BOSTON

. . .

*Life asked death, "Why do people love me but hate you?"*
*Death responded, "Because you are a beautiful lie and I am*
*a painful truth."*

—*Unknown*

WHEN I GET home, Brian is waiting. He stares at me as if I am a hallucination, and then he approaches me cautiously—the way you would move toward a feral animal or someone whose world has gone to pieces around her. He folds me tightly into his arms. "Jesus Christ, Dawn," he says, his voice shaking. "I thought you were gone for good."

Slowly, my arms come up to embrace him. My eyes drift closed. I actively shove away the memories that rise, and force myself to only see forward.

What if it's that easy to start fresh? I remember how, when Meret was little, she had a toy that was an enclosed tablet of tiny metal filings that could be moved with a magnetic pencil. After drawing whatever it was she wanted to draw, she could pull a lever and all the filings fell to the bottom of the tablet, making a blank slate. But after a few months of use, there were hazy black shadows of former pictures she'd drawn caught in the very fibers of the toy. Even as she created pictures over them, I could see the ghosts of her imagination.

"Dawn," Brian says. An apology, a beginning.

"I don't want to talk about it." It's too raw. Maybe one day, but this is not that day.

He nods, slipping his hands into his pockets. It's something he does when he is nervous. "Are you . . . all right?"

"I'm here, aren't I?" I try to say this lightly, but the reply sinks like fog, making it harder to see.

"This is my fault."

I don't correct him. If it wasn't for what he did, or didn't do, I would never have left in the first place.

"Is Meret—"

"She's in her room." I head to the staircase, but Brian's voice tugs at me. "She doesn't know. I didn't want to scare her."

I pivot. This, I suppose, was either meant to protect Meret, or meant to protect Brian. No matter what, it's an unexpected gift right now.

Meret's bedroom always surprises me. Although it has been years since we decorated it for a baby girl, I still expect to see it in pinks and yellows, with a wallpaper border of dancing hippos. Sometimes when I am sorting through the laundry now and see her brightly colored bras, I am startled by them, because just yesterday I was folding onesies printed with ladybugs, cotton dresses with tutus built in.

Although she's a teenager now, her walls aren't covered with Sia or 21 Savage. She has a vintage Adolphe Millot insect graphic and overblown photos of microscopic onion epidermal cells and elodea root. Meret has wanted to be a scientist like her father since he helped her make her first baking soda volcano in the kitchen sink at age four.

The lights are on in her room, and she is asleep on top of the covers. A book—*Lab Girl*—is on the floor, where it's tumbled out of her hands. I set it on the nightstand and go to turn off the lamp, but she stirs, blinking up at me. "You're back," she whispers. I wonder what Brian *did* tell her. If she heard us arguing, before I left.

I pull back the covers so she can crawl into bed. Her pajama top rides up, exposing a plump roll at the waistband of the bottoms. I bite my lip—she hates how she looks, which is a function not just of being fourteen but also of being the daughter of two parents who are thin. I spy something purple balled up in the trash can—it's the shirt that I bought her for her birthday. When she unwrapped it, Meret had plastered a smile on her face, but I saw her finger the label, Junior XXL. *Mom,* she had said, *I'm not that huge.* I felt terrible. But wouldn't it have been worse if I'd gotten her a size down, and it was too small?

*At least I remembered her birthday,* I think.

"Stay with me till I fall asleep?" Meret asks.

In another universe, I wouldn't be able to say yes.

I stroke her hair and take this as a boon—the mood swing that puts me in her favor again; the fact that I've been forgiven for my birthday gift; the mixture of grief and relief in Brian's eyes for something that nearly happened but didn't.

I think about the fact that even though I walked out of this house, I've somehow wound up right back where I started.


WHEN I WAS little, I used to read the obituaries, and one day I asked my mother why people die in alphabetical order. My mother didn't answer. She spit on the floor, because to talk about death was to invite it into the household. She was Irish and superstitious—a double dose of stubbornness—she put safety pins in my clothing to ward off the evil eye, she taught us never to whistle indoors and if we left the house and had to come back in, we were to look in a mirror or our luck would turn. I never heard my mother talk about death, in fact, which is why it's so ironic that she is the reason I am a death doula.

I was a graduate student on my third dig season in Egypt when I found out she was dying. She had Stage 4 ovarian cancer that she had chosen to hide from me and my brother. Kieran had only been thirteen, and she hadn't wanted to worry him. I was pursuing my passion, and she hadn't wanted to interrupt that. My father, a U.S. Army captain, had died in a helicopter crash when my mother was pregnant with Kieran, which meant that I suddenly had to take charge. I was furious that my mother hadn't told me she was sick. I sat by her side in the residential hospice, leaving only to be home in time for Kieran when he returned from school. I watched her fade into the sheets, more a memory than a mother. Then one day near the end, my mother squeezed my hand. "Your father died alone," she said. "I always wondered if he was scared. If there was something he wanted to say." *Are* you *scared?* I wanted to ask. *Is there something* you *want to say?* But before I could, my mother smiled. "At least I have you," she had said.

I thought about my father, halfway around the world by himself when he took his last breath. I thought of my mother, hiding an illness that had eaten away at her until she was only a shell of the woman I remembered. Death is scary and confusing and painful, and facing it alone shouldn't be the norm.

I realized I could do something about that.

With my mother's death, my life as I knew it was over. I couldn't go back to Yale, since I was now Kieran's guardian. I needed a job, and I found it working at the same hospice where my mother had been. At first, the director hired me out of pity, just so that I could pay bills. As an academic I had no practical skills, so I ran the reception desk and acted as girl Friday and visited with the patients. It was that, the visiting, that I was particularly good at. I liked collecting their stories, mining their histories, putting together the pictures of who they used to be. It was, after all, what archaeologists do. One day the hospice director suggested that I might have a future in this field. I took online classes to get my MSW and became a hospice social worker. I was responsible for getting DNRs signed, for asking about funeral home arrangements, for ascertaining if families were strapped financially. I supported both the patient and the caregiver, who were each carrying such heavy loads. I used to think of my job as taking those massive backpacks off their shoulders for an hour and giving them that time to get squared away before they had to pick them up again. But one hour was never enough, and there were elements of the job that chafed—like having too many patients and endless paperwork; or having to smile through a hospice doctor's terrible jokes ("Rectum? I hardly knew him!"). Or the way patients had to be recertified at ninety days to make sure they still met hospice criteria . . . while those who didn't make the cut were still ill enough to need care or help to process what was happening to them.

After almost a decade of hospice work, I heard about a course called Intro to Death Midwifery. It made sense to me—just as we have birth midwives for the transition from the state of being a single person to becoming a mother, why not have death midwives for the transition from the state of life to that of death? I called up, but the course was full. I told the instructor I would bring my own snacks, my own chair, if she would just let me be a fly on the wall. From the very first words of the instructor—that death doulas hearken back to a time when people didn't die alone—I was enthralled. *Doula* is Greek for "woman who serves"—and just as birth doulas know that there's discomfort and pain that can be managed during labor, death doulas do the same at the other end of the life spectrum.

I started my own business as a death doula five years ago, and it's still something that most people have never heard of. There's a National End-of-Life Doula Alliance, NEDA, which creates core competencies and has a proficiency assessment for doulas to pass, but it's still pretty much the wild west of caregiving. Medicare doesn't cover my services, and what I do means different things to different people. God knows there's a need—the "silver tsunami" of baby boomers are aging and have busy kids who can't be caregivers or children who don't live nearby. Society is culturally shifting, and there's a need for support. Plus, there's a rise in the consciousness movement that reinforces we are only on Earth for a short time.

Doulas don't perform medical tasks—I'm not covered by liability malpractice insurance. I work in homes, nursing homes, inpatient hospices, assisted living facilities. Whereas the hospice model is a team, the doula works solo, doing all but the medical care. I can be with a client round the clock, but I don't have to be. It's really up to the individual, and it may change as the illness progresses. I listen. I keep caregivers calm. I make sure someone isn't alone if they don't want to be. I gather information and share it—about funerals, or what to expect during the dying process. I anticipate what is going to be needed and create a plan for it—such as a vigil, or a church memorial service. I provide referrals to chaplains or doctors. I'll give physical and emotional comfort through foot massage, chakra cleansing, visualization, meditation, guided breathing. I may help a caregiver with a basic daily task—brushing teeth, showering—but that's an individual preference, too. I'll get dry cleaning, groceries, or take a client to a doctor's appointment.

Although I work in tandem with hospice professionals, I also know that some care isn't medical—it's holistic, and spiritual—and I provide it. Maybe that's creating a home funeral, or assisting the families in washing and laying out the body. Maybe it's arranging for acupuncture for pain relief, or giving business advice on selling a car that's sitting in the garage and hasn't been driven since 1970. Sometimes I help families wrap up the affairs of the deceased, taking social security cards and bank information and encrypting and destroying them when I'm finished. A death doula is one-stop shopping; I am a general contractor of death. The way I describe it is like this: if you want butter pecan ice cream at 3:00 A.M. and you're on hospice, you might be able to ask a volunteer to get you some when he or she next visits. If you hire a death doula, and you want that ice cream at 3:00 A.M., she'll get it for you. And if you hire *me*, I will already have it waiting in the freezer.

After nearly thirteen years of end-of-life work, I know that we do a shitty job of intellectually and emotionally preparing for death. How can you enjoy life if you spend every minute fearing the end of it? I know that most people—like my mother was—are afraid to talk about death, as if it's contagious. I know that you are the same person when you die that you were when you were alive—if you are feisty in life, you'll be feisty at the end of life. If you are nervous when you're healthy, you'll be nervous on your deathbed. I know that people who are going to die need me to be a mirror—to look in my eyes and know I see who they used to be, not who they are right now.

After thirteen years of this work, I thought I knew a lot about death.

I was wrong.

. . .

I FALL ASLEEP in Meret's room and stay there all night. In the morning, Brian and I move in a careful ballet. We speak only when necessary, and even then it's in details rather than emotions. He is leaving today to give a keynote at the Perimeter Institute in Waterloo, Ontario, on his work in quantum mechanics, and it is a Big Deal. Fifteen years ago, a theoretical physicist who believed in parallel universes was considered fringe, and now less than half of the scientists in his field cling to those older beliefs.

I'm grateful that he's taking a business trip, because it prolongs the inevitable. I do not go into the shower until Brian is downstairs making coffee; in the kitchen, we try not to look each other in the eye, saying all the right things so that Meret will not think that there is anything strained between us. He doesn't want to push me, because he is afraid of the outcome; I don't want to be pushed for the very same reason. So I pour Brian a to-go cup; he kisses Meret on the top of the head and grabs his overnight bag; he leaves for the airport just before Meret does to catch the bus that will take her to STEM camp.

For the first time since I've come back home, I am alone in the house. With a deep breath, I let go of all the studied pretense, bury my face in my hands, and wonder how to go back to normal.

Suddenly, the front door opens again. I call out, "What did you forget?"

But it isn't Meret, like I expect. Brian is standing at the threshold of the kitchen, holding his keys like an afterthought. "You," he says. "I forgot *you*." He walks in and sits down across from me at the table. "I can't do this, Dawn. We have to talk."

We already did, and look at where that got me.

"I don't know what you expect me to say," I tell him.

Brian looks down at the table. "You don't have to say anything. You just have to listen to me."

I know her name: Gita. I know that she went to Cambridge before coming to Harvard as a postdoc. I even remember when Brian took her out to dinner with other colleagues to try to convince her to come to their physics program. *Is she a good fit?* I had asked. *Do you think you can work with her?*

The next time I heard of her was when Brian told me he had taken her out to lunch, because she didn't seem to blend in with the other postdoc students. I thought it sounded exactly like Brian: kind to a fault, trying to circumvent a problem before it really started. Often, he was so wrapped up in his work he forgot to study interpersonal cues, and I thought that it was a positive step to care about a new recruit's happiness. Then, a week later, Gita asked him to help her with car shopping. She had heard that it was easier for dealers to fleece a woman if she didn't have a man there with her to kick the tires or ask about fuel efficiency. Brian had complained about it to me—*I'm not here to babysit*—but he had gone with her, and she rolled off the lot in a Toyota RAV4. A few weeks later he brought home a basket of Cadbury Flakes and Crunchies and Twirls and Rolos, a gift that made Meret burst into tears because she thought there was a subtext to receiving a bucket of candy. *Gita brought it from England,* he had said, truly bewildered. *It was supposed to be a present.*

But then he had agreed to go to Gita's apartment after work to help her set up an air-conditioning unit. He did not remember that it was his daughter's birthday, and that we were supposed to be having a celebratory dinner. Instead he followed Gita like a puppy to her place. He had stripped down to his undershirt and hauled the unit upstairs and settled it in the bedroom window as directed and, with characteristic thoroughness, had sealed it into place with plastic and duct tape so no bugs could come in through the cracks.

I sent him two texts: *Where are you?* and: *Meret's birthday???* He read them but responded to neither.

He came back into the living room to find Gita wrapped in his discarded dress shirt, sitting on the couch with a bottle of chilled champagne and two glasses. As a *thank-you,* she said.

Brian said he left immediately.

I believed him as he choked through this confession. I believed him, because had he actually taken Gita up on her offer, the guilt would have rolled off him in waves instead of just roses.

"Why didn't you answer my texts?" I demanded.

"I was in the middle of putting in an air conditioner," Brian said.

"Then why didn't you answer them when you finished?"

He spread his hands, because he knew whatever he said was not going to come out right. "I'm sorry, Dawn. I'm so sorry. This is all my fault."

"I have to go," I muttered.

"Go? Where?"

I rounded on him. "I don't think you get to ask me that right now." Even as I ran out the door, I could feel him tethering me, solid and immobile, like the weights that secure balloons at party stores, when all they want to do is rise.

THAT WAS THEN; this is now. We cannot go on coexisting in this house without negotiating a treaty of some kind. "I'm listening," I say.

He threads his fingers through his thick hair. "I don't know how to erase what happened."

That passive construction. As if he was a bystander; as if he had no complicit role.

"I didn't do anything with her," Brian says. "I swear it."

"If you didn't *do anything*," I repeat, "then why didn't you tell me you were going to her apartment that day? Why ignore my texts?" I swallow. "Why act like you had something to hide?"

"Because I felt like an idiot when I realized I had forgotten Meret's birthday."

I stare at him. "Do you really think that's why I left?"

He winces. "I thought . . . I thought I could be helpful. I didn't know she wanted more than that. And I . . . I realize now that I should have."

I believe this, too. Sometimes Brian is so literal that you have to hit him over the head to get him to understand a subtlety. But I also believe that he has a secret, one maybe that he hasn't admitted to himself—that, faced with a beautiful girl and champagne and possibility, for one second, he had wished he was in a different timeline.

He may not have acted on it, but that doesn't mean it wasn't a betrayal.

Brian's shoulders are hunched; he bends closer to the table. It takes me a moment to understand that he is doing something I have never seen him do during the long tenure of our marriage.

He's crying.

Brian has always been so steady and thoughtful and capable, the spool to my kite, the grounding to my electricity. When I literally had nowhere else to go in the world, he offered me his home. After I watch a patient die in front of me, I embrace him and remember how it feels to be alive. He's consistently been able to save me. Until now.

To see him shaken and unsteady feels like the world is a little off-kilter, familiar but somehow wrong, like parting your hair on the opposite side. Something vibrates deep inside me, a note I recognize as pain. This is marriage, I realize. A tuning fork of emotion.

The muscle memory of our relationship has me moving out of my seat before my mind catches up. I stand in front of Brian and stroke his hair, because I can't stand to see him hurting, even if the reason is because he hurt *me*.

He is out of his seat like a shot, grabbing on to the lifeline I am offering. And honestly, it *is* one. Life, as we know it for the past fifteen years, has been irrevocably altered by a young physicist's attentions, and this is a hint of how to turn back time. It's a trail of breadcrumbs, made from a thousand embraces just like this one. This is familiar ground.

There is a sense of completion in coming into the arms of the person who has held you for fifteen years, like rolling into the softest spot of the mattress or answering the last clue of the Sunday crossword. It's heat from the fireplace filling the room. It's the homing pigeon, spying its roost.

But there is also selective amnesia, a whitewashing, and even as my skin soothes to Brian's touch, my mind is grasping at the smoke of the old argument that drove us apart.

I cannot help myself—I bury my face in the collar of his shirt and breathe in deeply. Soap. Starch. No roses. My eyes drift shut.

Then suddenly I snap upright. "Your speech."

"Fuck the speech," Brian says. "There'll be another opportunity."

I smile a little. "In another universe, you already gave it, and received thunderous applause."

"In another universe, I got booed off the stage."

I look at Brian's eyes, spruce green darkening to black as he stares at me. As a scientist, he has never been good with words; but even in his silence I can map the trajectory of his thoughts. Brian's mind works in kets, the little boxes that physicists use to talk about the quantum state of whatever is inside the brackets. Or in lay terms: the way a thing truly is—in this case, our marriage. "In another universe, we're already naked," I say.

Weeks later I will take this moment in time and I will turn it over in my mind like a snow globe. I will wonder why I said that, when guilt was still thick between us. Maybe I wanted to see if we could get close enough for there to be no room for blame. Or maybe, after all that has happened, instead of arguing over the past it was just easier to be flagrantly, viscerally in the *now*.

He stares at me, waiting—*hoping*—for absolution. For the knowledge that even though the last time we were together I couldn't get away from him fast enough, I am back now.

I pull my shirt over my head.

Brian kisses me and takes over, tugging down my shorts. He catalogs every inch of me that he uncovers. Then he lifts me onto the kitchen counter and stands between my legs. I fumble with his belt, shove down his pants. His hands are parentheses on my hips, holding together a tumble of utterances: *this, please, now*. In one swift move he drags me forward, wrapping my legs around his waist as he pushes into me. His teeth scrape my neck; my nails brand him. He begins to move, but I won't let him put any space between us, and we rise together like a chimera. He lets go at the same moment that I tighten around him, and when I remember where I am a moment later, it is because I can still feel the jump of his heartbeat inside me.

I find Brian staring down at me with a smug grin. "Well," he says.

I laugh.

We have what I assume is an ordinary married sex life—a couple of times a week, motions we have mastered for an economy of time, a guarantee of pleasure, and a solid night's sleep. Whoever comes first makes sure that the other gets there, too. It is always good, and it is occasionally great. Like just now. When *sex* isn't the right word, anymore. It's more like spilling over the boundaries of your own body to fill someone else's, and having them do the same to you.

In many ways, this is a microcosm of marriage. There is a lot of *Did you use up all the creamer?* and *Are you going by the post office today?* but every now and then, there are moments of transcendence: when you rise in tandem the moment your daughter crosses the stage at fifth-grade graduation; when you glance across the table at a dinner party and have an entire conversation in silence; when you catch yourself looking around at your home and your family and think: *This. We did all this.*

Brian had fallen for me fast. He once told me that when he was with me, he didn't fade into the background. Food tasted better. The air was crisper. He said I hadn't just changed his world. I'd changed *the* world.

Brian reaches for a dish towel and hands it to me, the messy business of love that no one ever has to deal with in Hollywood. *What do they do?* he has whispered to me at movies. *Sleep in the wet spot?* He kisses me lightly and pats the marble counter. "Promise me you'll scrub this before you cook on it," he says, and starts to withdraw.

I hook my ankles together and trap him, looking into his eyes. It's something you don't do a lot, when you've been with the same person as long as I have. You glance, you skim, you catch his gaze, but you don't really drink in his features as if they are an oasis in the desert. But now, I stare and stare until Brian fidgets, and gives me a sheepish smile. "What?" he asks. "Is there something on my face?"

"No," I say. But I see it, finally—the wonder. The belief that he might wake up and all of this will be a dream. *Oh,* there *you are,* I think. *The man I fell in love with.*

. . .

I MET BRIAN at the communal kitchen in the hospice where my mother was dying. We crossed paths at the coffee machine. I knew, after a few days, that he liked flavored coffee—hazelnut or French vanilla—and that he was a lefty. There was always a residue of graphite on the comma of his hand, as if he'd spent the day writing in pencil.

I brought a lunch snack most of the days I was sitting with my mother, and sometimes I would eat it at the scarred little table in that communal kitchen. Brian was there, too, making mathematical notations that were so tiny I had to squint to see the numbers. They were figures I didn't understand; factorials and exponents and equations way beyond my AP Calculus memories.

"Good day or bad day?" I asked him. This was the hospice equivalent of *How are you doing?* which, in hospice, was always: *dying*.

"Bad day," Brian said. "My grandmother has Alzheimer's."

I nodded. I was grateful, at that point, for my mother's lucidity.

"She thinks I'm a Nazi, so I figured it would be better if I left the room." He scrubbed a hand through his hair. "It kind of sucks, you know. To have your body survive the Holocaust and your brain be the part of you that quits."

"You're a really good grandson, to be here all this time."

He shrugged. "She raised me. My parents died in a car crash when I was eight."

"I'm so sorry."

"It was a long time ago." Brian watched me open a bag of Goldfish. "Is that all you're eating?"

"I didn't have time to go food shopping—"

He pushed half of his turkey sandwich toward me. "It's your mom, right?"

It wouldn't be hard to figure that out, and it still hurt, knowing that someone else had asked questions, had made judgments, had pitied me. "It's not rocket science."

"No. Quantum mechanics."

I glanced up, confused, and found him hunched over his papers again, scribbling.

"You don't look like a physicist." I glanced at the sea glass of his eyes, and the hair that kept falling into his face because it was too long.

"How am I supposed to look?"

I felt my face heat up. "I don't know. A little more . . ."

"Greasy? Frayed?" He raised an eyebrow. "How about you? What do you do, when someone isn't dying?"

The way he said it, so frankly and honestly, was the first thing I liked about Brian. No euphemisms, no subtlety. At the time, I found that directness refreshing. But I also couldn't say the words out loud—that I was an Egyptologist who'd been ripped out of Egypt and who couldn't see a path back to completing my Ph.D. That, unlike with numerical equations on paper, there wasn't an easy way to solve my problem.

"I've never understood quantum mechanics," I said, steering the conversation away from me. "Teach me something."

He turned to a fresh page and drew a tiny circle. "You ever hear of an electron?"

I nodded. "It's a particle, right? Like, an atom?"

"Subatomic, actually. But for our purposes, you only have to know it behaves like a sphere. And one thing we know about spheres is that they can spin, right? Either clockwise or counterclockwise." He drew a second circle on the page. "The thing is, electrons are supercool because they can spin clockwise *and* counterclockwise at the same time."

"I call BS."

"I don't blame you. But, actually, there have been tons of experiments that can only be explained with this phenomenon. For example—imagine taking an opaque screen that blocks out all light. Now cut two little holes in that screen—let's call them slit 1 and slit 2. If you shine a laser beam onto the slits, and you block slit 1, you'd expect to see a little blotch of light on the wall in the distance aligned with slit 2. If you block slit 2, you'd expect to see a little blotch of light on the wall in the distance aligned with slit 1. What happens when we open both slits at the same time?"

"You see two blotches?"

His eyes lit up. "You'd think so, right? But no. You get a whole row of blotches of light uniformly spaced out in various intensities. It's called an interference pattern. The only way physicists can explain it is that the light that comes out of slit 1 must be interacting with the light that comes out of slit 2, because we know that when only one slit is open you get a single blotch on the wall . . . when the other slit is open you get a single blotch on the wall . . . and when they're both open, you get something you've never seen before. Then Einstein came along and told us light isn't a jet stream, it's all individual particles, so maybe the pattern comes from individual particles from different slits hitting each other. Scientists slowed the laser to a point where only one photon was going through a slit at a time, figuring that the weird pattern would disappear. But it didn't. And physicists were left with the explanation that the one photon actually does go through both slits simultaneously, interfering with itself. Even though every evolutionary instinct bred into us revolts against the idea." He glanced at me. "That interference phenomenon is what makes your laptop work, in case you still think I'm bullshitting."

"What does this have to do with the electrons?" I asked.

"We know they spin both clockwise and counterclockwise," Brian said. "So let's say you put an electron in a box. There's a little trigger next to the electron that will activate if the electron spins clockwise, but it won't activate if the electron spins counterclockwise. If the trigger activates, it will send a signal to a gun, which will fire, and kill a cat."

"That's a big box."

"Work with me," Brian said. "So if the electron goes clockwise . . ."

"The trigger activates, the gun goes off, the cat dies."

"And if the electron goes counterclockwise?"

"Nothing happens."

"Exactly." He looked up at me. "But what happens if that electron spins both clockwise and counterclockwise at the same time—as we *know* it can?"

"Either the cat is dead or it isn't?"

"Actually," Brian corrected, "the cat is both alive and dead."

"How postapocalyptic," I murmured. "Nice story, but I've never seen a zombie cat."

"That's pretty much what Niels Bohr said, too. He knew that the math said this was happening, but he had never seen a live-dead cat either. So he figured that there had to be something special about the act of observation that made the cat stop being both alive *and* dead, and instead become just alive *or* dead."

"Like human consciousness?"

"That's what John von Neumann suggested. But what makes humans so special that they can determine the outcome of a quantum system to collapse into a single defined state? What if it's not a human . . . what if a ferret is watching? Or what about the cat in the box? You *know* it has a vested interest in the outcome. So does it have the power to collapse the state of the electron, or trigger, or gun?" Brian said. "The collapse theory was the one the cool kids believed until the 1950s, when Hugh Everett III came up with another reason why we don't see zombie cats walking the earth. He said that just like the electron and the trigger and the gun and the cat are quantum objects, so is whoever or whatever is observing what's in that box." He drew a little stick figure wearing a skirt, waving. "At first, she is standing outside the box, and doesn't know what she's going to see when she looks inside. But the minute she lifts the lid . . . she is split into two distinct copies of herself. In one version she sees a cat with its brains exploded all over the box. In another, she hears a meow. If you asked her what she saw, one version is going to say the cat is dead, and the other will say the cat is alive. The observer only ever sees one outcome, but never both, even though the laws of quantum mechanics tell us that both versions of that poor damn cat exist. And the reason she sees only one outcome is because she's trapped in one of the timelines and is unable to see the other one." He grinned at me. "That's Everett's whole deal. The reason we don't see zombie cats or electrons spinning both ways at the same time is because the minute we look at them, we become part of that mathematical equation and we ourselves get split into multiple timelines, where different versions of us see different, concrete outcomes."

"Like a parallel universe," I said.

"Exactly. I've been using the word *timeline* but you could easily say *universe*. And the reason this matters isn't because there are cats in boxes, but because we're all made up of molecules, like those electrons. If you zoom in and zoom in and zoom in, everything we do is explained by quantum mechanics."

"What happens to those two different timelines?"

"They get farther and farther apart. For example, the observer who sees the dead cat might be so bummed out she drops out of grad school and becomes a meth addict and never invents the technology that would help us develop a cure for cancer. Meanwhile, the observer who sees the live cat thinks she is onto something and becomes the dean of physics at Oxford." He ran a thumb over the stack of papers he had been working on. "That's what I'm doing. Slowly destroying my career by insisting that the multiverse is constantly branching off, creating a new timeline whenever we make a decision or have an interaction."

"Why would that ruin your career?"

"Let's just say the physicists who believe it are outliers. But one day—"

"One day they'll be calling you a genius." I hesitated. "Or maybe that's already happening in some other timeline."

"Exactly. Everything that *can* happen *does* happen—in another life."

I tilted my head, staring at him. "So in another universe, my mother isn't dying."

There was a pause. "No," he said. "She's not."

"And in another universe, we never met."

Brian shook his head, and a blush rushed over his skin like the tide. "But in *this* universe," he said, "I'd really like to take you out to dinner."


WHEN I COME out of the shower, Brian's overnight bag is sitting on the bed. I hear the water start again in the bathroom and stare at it.

With a groan I turn away and pull on underwear, a pair of shorts, a tank top.

I run a comb through my hair and twist it into a braid and there's no reason anymore for me to be in the bedroom, except that I can't leave.

The shower is still running.

I move toward the duffel and tug the zipper open. Brian's Dopp kit and shoes are on top. I set them aside and pull out a cotton sweater and sniff it. There's something floral there—is it roses, again? Or am I imagining it?

"Dawn?"

He stands behind me, a towel wrapped around his waist. My hands go numb, body freezes. Caught in the act. I am a thief, a spy. I am Daisy, wallowing in Gatsby's clothing.

"I thought . . . we were okay," Brian says.

"Because we had sex?" I reply. "I'm pretty sure you were the one who told me that doesn't mean anything."

"I didn't have sex with her." Brian sits on the bed and pulls the sweater out of my arms.

"No. You just *thought* about it."

I am being spiteful and nasty and unforgiving. I am licking my wounds with poison. Brian has apologized; I should forgive him. Shouldn't I?

But he was with *her* the day of Meret's birthday. He missed dinner. He came home wrapped in the scent of roses—on his clothes, in his hair, strewn across our marriage.

"Do you like her?" I force myself to ask. The words feel like knives in my throat.

"Well . . . I mean," Brian stumbles. "I hired her."

"Wrong answer," I snap, and I get off the bed. I am halfway out the door when he grabs my wrist and spins me around.

"I have never loved anyone but you."

Once, there was an earthquake in Boston. I was driving Meret home from preschool and along the route, a few trees had fallen. It was a tiny earthquake compared to the ones on the San Andreas

Fault, but for people who are not used to having the ground shudder beneath their feet, it was shocking.

I went about the day, making mac and cheese for Meret for lunch, taking her to the park to push her on the swings, turning her over to the babysitter so that I could check in on a hospice patient. The woman was wide-eyed, chattering about how the bed had shimmied across the floor with her in it; how her pill bottles had tumbled from the shelf like they had been pushed by the hand of a ghost. *Did you feel it?* she asked me, but I shook my head. Because I had been in the car, the tires rumbling just as the earth did, I didn't even know something had happened until she told me. A catastrophe had subtly changed the world, and I hadn't even noticed.

Brian will not let go of my hand. He traces my knuckles with his thumb. "Please, Dawn. I know I can't undo it. But it will never happen again."

I believe him. I just don't trust him.

"I fucking hate roses," I say, and I walk out of the bedroom.

HERE'S THE INSANE thing about resuming your old life when it's nearly ended: it is business as usual. Your heart may be broken, your nerves may be shattered, but the trash needs to be taken out. Groceries must be bought. You have to fill your car with gas. People still depend on you.

On the way to the home of a new potential client, I call my brother. As a neurosurgery resident, he rarely picks up, so it's startling when I get him instead of voicemail.

"Kieran?"

"Dawn?"

"I didn't expect you to be there."

I can hear the amusement in his voice. "Sorry to disappoint you. I just got out of surgery. What's up? Wait, let me guess. You have a weird rash."

Granted, I tend to call him when I have a medical question, like if the flu has hit Boston yet, or what to do for plantar fasciitis, or any of a dozen other things that he tells me he can't answer because they're not his specialty. "I'm not sick. I just really wanted to hear your voice. I . . . missed you."

"Shit, forget the rash, you're sicker than I thought. Maybe you should come straight to the ER."

"Shut up," I reply, but I'm smiling.

"So what's really going on?" my brother asks.

I hesitate. "I was trying to remember if Mom and Dad ever fought."

"Can't help you. On account of I was only a zygote when Dad was still alive."

"I know," I say.

"Is this about you and Brian?" Kieran asks. "You never fight."

"There's a first time for everything, I guess."

He waits, expecting me to expound, but I am reluctant to say more.

"Look, Dawn, you have nothing to worry about. You and Brian, you're like the *rule*. The standard. You're the marital equivalent of the sun coming up every morning and the sky being blue when you open your eyes. You'll be together until the end of time. That's what you want, right?"

"Yes," I say. "Of course."


AT THE HOSPICE, we used to have a cat that predicted death. It was a tabby that never had a name other than Cat, as far as I know, but she lived in the building and there was a line item in the budget for her food. We had two therapy dogs that came in to see patients, but the cat was quintessentially standoffish and wouldn't suffer being petted. Her only use, as far as I could see, was to let us know when someone had less than twenty-four hours to live.

Without fail, if I went into a room and found the cat curled up at the bottom of someone's bed, they died shortly after. I don't know if it was a sixth sense, or some kind of olfactory cue—I know dogs have been trained to sniff out some cancers—but that damn cat had a hundred percent success rate.

After I became a hospice social worker, it was nearly a full year before someone died in front of me. (Even now, many of my clients die when everyone leaves the room, as if they have been hanging on by sheer force of will to the people who will miss them.) One morning, I walked into Judith's room at the hospice facility and Cat was staring at me, flicking her tail.

Without alarming her daughter, Alanna, who was the primary caregiver, I did a quick survey of Judith. She was unresponsive, her breathing thick. I looked at the cat, nodded, and she jumped off the bed and slunk from the room.

"Alanna," I said, "if there's anything else you need to say to your mother, I'd say it soon."

Immediately tears sprang to the woman's eyes. "It's already her time?"

If there is one thing I've learned while doing the business of death, it's that it comes as a surprise, even in hospice.

I pulled up a chair beside her. Alanna leaned forward, unconsciously holding her breath every time her mother inhaled. Cheyne-Stokes breathing—which sometimes happens when a person is dying—is a cycle, slowed inhalations followed by faster pants, and then no respiration at all, before it starts up all over again. The pattern repeats every few minutes. Even though it is a normal occurrence as the respiratory system shuts down, it sounds agonizing, and it is hard to listen to, especially for family members who know that this is the beginning of the end.

My job is to support not just my patients but also their caregivers. So I tried to distract Alanna, asking how the night had been, and when her mother had last opened her eyes. Finally, when I realized that Alanna was coiling tighter and tighter, I asked her how her parents got engaged.

I once read that every story is a love story. Love of a person, a country, a way of life. Which means, of course, that all tragedies are about losing what you love.

When someone with a terminal disease can't stop fearing the future, it's comforting to look to the past. We tend to forget that we were all young, once. And that there was a time when we had beginnings, instead of endings.

Alanna looked up at me. "My mom and dad came from really different backgrounds. Dad had family money, but my mom had next to nothing. They decided to take a trip to the national parks, and my mom showed up with a cooler full of sandwiches, because every time she'd gone somewhere as a girl her mom packed all their meals. It was like she never even considered restaurants as a possibility."

I imagined Judith, wherever she was at that moment, listening to her own history and smiling on the inside. We know that of all the senses, hearing is the last to go.

"They went to Old Faithful," Alanna said. "My dad had been planning to propose. But there was some random guy who kept asking questions, and my mom—who had read everything she could about the geyser before the trip—kept answering him. How often does it erupt? About twenty-two times a day. How high does it reach? Around 130 feet. How hot is the water? Over 200 degrees Fahrenheit." She smiled faintly. "My dad was losing it. So finally he tapped my mom on the arm and said, 'I have a question.' He got down on one knee, and asked, 'Where does all the water go?'"

I laughed. "What's the answer?"

"I have no idea. She never gave it to him. She just said yes."

We looked down at Judith, who let out a puddled sigh, and stopped breathing altogether.

Alanna went still. "Is that . . . is she . . . ?"

I didn't respond, because I needed to make sure it was a cessation of breathing, not just a moment of apnea. But after five minutes had passed without another breath sound, I told Alanna that Judith was gone.

She pressed her forehead to her mother's hand, still clutched in her own. She was sobbing hard, and I did what I always did—rubbed her back, soothed, gave her a moment for her grief. I slipped out of the room to the front desk. "We need a nurse to come in and declare a death," I said, and then went back to comfort Alanna.

After a little while, she sat up, wiping her eyes. "I have to call Peter." Her husband. And probably a dozen other relatives. Her eyes were swollen and slightly wild.

"It can wait a minute," I said. I wanted to give Alanna something to take away with her. "Judith told me many times how much it meant to her to have you here."

Alanna touched her mother's wrist. "Where do you think she is now?"

There are all kinds of answers to that question, and no one is more right or wrong than another. So I told her what I knew for certain. "I don't know," I said, and I gestured toward the body. "But she's not in there."

Just then, Judith's jaw moved, and she drew in a deep, viscous breath.

Alanna's gaze flew to mine. "I thought she was . . ."

"So did I."

The nurse appeared, looked at the breathing patient, and raised a brow. "False alarm?"

I tell this story a lot at conferences and workshops: that the first person who died in front of me did it twice. It always gets a laugh, but it's not funny, not at all. Imagine Alanna having to grieve her mother a second time. Imagine if the worst thing in the world happened to you, and then you had to experience it all over again.

MY POTENTIAL NEW client has the same birthday as me. Not just the month and date, but the year, too. I have been the death doula to clients who are younger than I am, and in a few terribly sad cases, to children. In the past I have been philosophical about it: it's not my time, it is theirs. But today, I look down at my intake form and it feels like a metaphor.

Winifred Morse lives in Newtonville, in a small duplex that backs up to the green run of the Boston College Law School campus. She is dying of Stage 4 ovarian cancer, and unlike most of my clients, she called me herself. Usually I get inquiries from concerned family members, who want me to come in to support a loved one without telling the client what I do, as if naming a death doula is what will trigger mortality itself. I don't take those jobs, because it feels dishonest to me, which means that I often have to tell a caregiver to wait until the client herself is facing down the barrel of death and accepts that she needs support.

I drive to her home and stand outside for a moment, closing my eyes and taking a few deep breaths to release the tension in my shoulders and spine, pushing Brian to the far corners of my mind. Right now, the only problems I will let myself have are Winifred Morse's problems. I can worry about myself on my own time.

Her husband, Felix, answers the door. He is at least six foot five, all hooks and angles, like a praying mantis. When I introduce myself, he smiles, but the joy stops short of the fill line. "Come in, come in," he says, and I find myself in a foyer whose walls are covered with modern art. There are canvases where soft pink blots look like the curves of a woman, from a certain angle. There are some with angry black slash marks, like the claws of a beast trying to rip its way free from the frame behind. There is one that has the most painstaking gradients of blue from top to bottom, like all the moods of the sea. It makes me think of my mother.

I do not know much about modern art, except that it is supposed to evoke feeling, and I can't drag my eyes away from that painted ocean. "I like that one, too," Felix says, coming to stand beside me, his hands in his pockets and his elbows sharp. "Win painted it when she was pregnant with Arlo."

I file that information away, wondering where her son is, and how he is processing her illness. "She's an artist, then," I say.

Felix's mouth twists. "She was. She hasn't painted, really, since she got sick."

I touch his arm. "And how about you?"

"I'm no artist. I can't even draw a stick figure. I teach driver's ed." He looks at me, sheepish. "I wanted to be a doctor, but my grades weren't good enough. So I figured out another way I could save lives."

I try to imagine Felix cramming his frame into the passenger seat of a car, patiently instructing someone to turn on their signal before pulling away from the curb. "I wasn't talking about work," I say. "I meant . . . how are you feeling? Are you eating? Sleeping?"

He looks at me curiously. "Shouldn't you be asking Win that?"

I always pull the caregiver aside for a private conversation when I see a client. Sometimes, they notice things about a loved one that I would not—like a shaking hand when reaching for water, or restlessness at night. They'll tell me if a client isn't sleeping, if she's moody, if she's seeing people who aren't there. Sometimes a client will put on a brave face and not admit to pain or fear when they're with me, but a caregiver always tells the truth, because they think it will help me give them the answer to the question they can't ask their loved one: *when and how will it happen?*

Anticipatory grief is real and devastating. It can run the gamut from *How will I survive alone in the world?* to *What do I do when the Internet cuts out, because she's always been in charge of calling the cable company?*

"I *will* ask her those questions," I tell Felix, "but part of my job is making sure you're okay, too." I glance around the entryway, where—scattered among the artwork—are the trappings of illness: a walker, a pair of compression socks, a prescription packet on a side table. "Your whole life has been taken over by cancer, too."

He is quiet for a beat. "My whole life," Felix murmurs, "is her whole life." He glances up at me. "You'll see. I've never met anyone like her. When I think about her not being . . . here anymore, I can't picture it. I can't imagine anyone taking her place. There's going to be this Win-shaped space when she's gone, and I'm scared it's going to be bottomless." When he stops speaking, his eyes are damp, and he seems startled to find me there. "I'll show you," he says.

He leads me into the rabbit warren of the house, which has more twists and turns than I would have expected for a tiny duplex. Win is in the study, where floor-to-ceiling bookshelves spread behind her like the wings of a great eagle. She is moving slowly postsurgery, but still moving, shuffling her feet as she puts a book back in its place. She turns to me, and I instantly mark the effects of chemo and radiation and drug therapies: the paper-thin skin, the slightly jaundiced whites of her eyes. Her collarbones jut out from above the neckline of her shirt. Her hair is soft and downy new growth, like the fuzz of a duckling. Her abdomen is distended with fluids.

"You must be Dawn," she says, reaching out a hand.

Even in her diminished state, there is a crackling, an energy that pulls focus, so that you cannot help but have your attention drawn right to her. Her eyes are an unholy gold, set against her dark skin. I imagine how magnetic she was before she got sick. Felix never stood a chance.

"It's really nice to meet you, Winifred," I say, and I mean it. One of the reasons I love my job is because of the people I meet. True, I lose every single one of them, but in a way that's why it's even more important that I am able to get to know them before they're gone.

"Call me Win," she says, and she grins. "It's quite the misnomer, since I apparently won the Death Lottery."

"*Dying* is a misnomer. You're alive, until you're not." I slide a glance toward Felix. "Besides, if we're talking about unlikely labels, his name takes the prize. Felix Morse basically means *Happy Death* in Latin."

Win laughs. "I think I like you."

That is basically the point of this initial meeting—not only to see if my potential client feels comfortable with me, but to see if *I* feel comfortable with *her*. In Win's case, her age is a factor, too. I can't project myself onto my work, consciously or unconsciously. I can't serve as a death doula if I'm thinking, *What would I want in this situation?* Or *This could be me.*

When I was in Chicago as an undergrad, I volunteered at a domestic abuse shelter. There was a woman there about my age, who had lost her father when she was young, and who had a two-year-old she had to take care of, and she just got under my skin—to the point where I couldn't sleep unless I knew she had eaten that night, that her son had eaten, and that she was not at home with her violent husband. The volunteer coordinator called me in and told me I wasn't going to last long if that was how I approached every case. *She's not you*, the coordinator said. Since then, I've learned to maintain my distance, but sometimes, it's too hard to do that, and those are exactly the jobs I shouldn't take. There are boundaries I cannot cross, even in a field that routinely collapses the space between people.

"Why don't we sit down?" I suggest.

Win and Felix settle on a leather couch, I pull up a side chair. "So," I start, "what would you like me to know?"

"Well, to begin with, the doctors told me I have less than a month," Win replies.

I watch Felix's fingers tangle with her own. "That's why they call it 'practicing' medicine," I say. "They may give you a certain amount of time to live, but they really don't know. It might be longer, and it might be shorter. My job would be to make sure you're prepared no matter what happens."

"We probably should talk about cost," Felix says.

"We will," I reply. "But not at this visit. This is really just a first date. Let's see if we're compatible—and then we can start planning our future." I won't decide whether to take on a client (or let a client hire me) until the second visit. That first encounter needs to settle.

I turn to Win. "How are you feeling today?" I always start with the physical, and then move on to emotional well-being.

"I'm up," Win states. "I showered."

I understand what she is telling me: today is a good day. There are some where a client isn't up to leaving bed, or putting on clothes.

"Is there any swelling around the surgical site?" Win shakes her head. "How about your hands and feet?"

The questions follow a pattern: *Do you have any pain? Are you warm enough? Have you eaten today? How have you been sleeping?* I ask Felix if hospice has provided them with a morphine kit—a comfort measure that stays in the refrigerator, along with other meds, in case they are needed immediately, before a hospice nurse can arrive.

"Do you feel like you have the support you need?" I ask.

Win looks at Felix, a whole conversation caught between them. "I do. But I wish he didn't have to. It's not fair to him."

"It's not fair, period," Felix mutters.

"Let me tell you what my role is, as a death doula," I say, leaning forward. "I'm here to assist you and make sure your needs are met right now. I can help you with anything that's left undone—I can work with you to plan a funeral; I can help you organize your will or your finances; I can clean your garage if the clutter is driving you crazy. I can comb through a storage facility if there's a picture in there of your grandmother you really want to see. I can take you to see an opera one more time, or read *Fifty Shades of Grey* out loud to you. I can organize your social media accounts so that your friends know you've died, when the time comes. I can help move you outside, so you can watch the birds."

I deliver this the way I always do: matter of fact, no sugarcoating or pretending that death is not inevitable. "Is there anything you *don't* do?" Felix asks, joking.

"Windows," I reply, and grin. "For real, though—medication. I can't prescribe it and I won't administer it. That's up to you. So are diaper changes, if and when necessary. I will help with a bedding change or a wheelchair transfer, but that's really the job of a caregiver and it's a liability for me if I'm alone with Win." I turn to her. "All you have to do is tell me what will create greater peace for you, at any given moment, and I will do my best to make it happen."

She stares at me, unblinking. "Will you be here when I die?"

"If that's what you want," I say, "then yes."

The room settles around us, a cocoon, and inside it we have already begun to change. "How will you know when that will be?" Win asks softly.

"I'll be in contact with your medical team. And there are signs and symptoms that the body is shutting down."

Win continues looking at me, her eyes narrow, as if she is weighing her next words. "I like you," she says finally. "You don't bullshit me."

"I'll take that as a compliment."

"You should," Win says. "How did you get into this business, anyway?"

"My mother died in hospice, and it turned out I was good at helping people prepare for death."

"You must see some crazy sad stuff."

"Some of it's crazy sad," I admit. "Some of it is just crazy."

"I can't imagine some of the things you must have been asked to do," Win muses.

"During my internship as a social worker, I was paged to the ER for a man who was brought in dead on arrival—along with his kids' sixteen-year-old babysitter. He was having an affair with her, and they decided to do meth, and since he'd already taken Viagra he had a stroke and died. The girl was hysterical, and the nurses were trying to get in touch with his family. The wife and kids showed up, but the dead guy still had an erection, so I had to ask the doctor to figure out a way to hide it so the kids wouldn't see it. We wound up taping it to his leg and covering him with six blankets. *Six.* Then I slipped out of the room to put the babysitter into a taxi. She asked me if I thought she should go to the funeral. I told her I thought she should reconsider her life choices in general."

Win bursts out laughing. "I promise you that you categorically will not have to tape down my erection when I die."

"Well, if I do, I'm charging extra." Win is someone I could see myself being friends with, had we met under different circumstances. That alone is probably enough reason for me to realize I need more distance; yet I somehow know she will become my client. "Is there anything I can get you right now?" I ask.

"Time," Win says immediately.

"I was thinking more along the lines of a pillow, or a chocolate chip milkshake," I answer. But if she is worried about time, it is likely because of the fear of leaving people she loves behind. Felix. Or her son. "We could Skype Arlo."

"If you can do *that*," Win says, "I will leave you everything in my will."

"Arlo's gone," Felix explains. "He died three years ago."

"I'm so sorry. I'd like to hear more about him." But for the first time in our visit, a wall has come up between us, and Win shifts subtly away from me. Eager to change the subject, I try a simpler question. "What have you been doing today?"

She looks up, allowing me to draw her back out. "I've been reading up on Willard Wigan, the microsculptor."

"Microsculptor?"

"He's an artist, but his art fits inside the eye of a needle or on the head of a pin," Win explains. "You need a microscope to see it."

"Felix tells me you're an artist, too."

"Wigan's quite famous. I . . . only dabbled," Win demurs.

"Past tense."

She ignores what I've said, choosing instead to talk about the artist. "I'm fascinated by the idea of walking past a piece of art because you can't see it with the naked eye. Imagine all the times you've told yourself, *Oh, it's nothing*. Well, nothing can be pretty goddamned big."

I look at Win and know she is seeing the trajectory of her disease: that first twinge, that dull ache, the way she dismissed it at first. I look inside myself, and I think of Brian.

Lifting my chin, I smile at Win and Felix. "Tell me how you fell in love," I say.

FELIX TELLS ME that Win was wearing a yellow sundress that looked like electricity wrapped around her body, and he couldn't turn away. Win says that's not accurate. He couldn't turn away because he was paid to make sure she didn't drive off the road or into a tree.

They swap off, telling their story. They finish each other's sentences, as if the words are a sweet they're trading bite by bite.

Win says she had never met someone who was so steady. Ten and two, he had told her. That's how you keep your hands on the wheel so nothing surprises you. Somehow, she had gotten to her late twenties without anyone imparting that life lesson.

Felix says that he knew he was in love when she told him she knew all the words to "A Whiter Shade of Pale."

Win says he had kind eyes.

Felix proposed after he took her bowling. Win had grown up with candlepins in New England, and had never used a big, heavy ball. When she drew her arm backward, the ball popped off her fingers and smacked Felix in the mouth, knocking out his two front teeth.

He asked her to marry him at the emergency dental surgeon's office.

It was a sure thing, he tells me. If she didn't love him, he figured she could still be guilted into saying yes.

. . .

ON MY WAY home from Win's, I pull into a lot near Boston Harbor. It is by no means on my way, but it's the place I go when I want the world to stop spinning.

On any given day in the summer, you can see the whale watching boats, as large and steady as the prey they search for, tourists streaming on board like krill through baleen. There are ice cream vendors and couples with selfie sticks and men dressed up like Colonial patriots promoting historical tours. In the distance you can see the USS *Constitution,* and in the other direction, the angled roof of the New England Aquarium, where my mother would teach kids who weren't us about mollusks and sea stars and tide pools.

My mother was the first person to bring me here. She had Kieran in a baby sling across her chest and she held my hand so tight it hurt. "When I first came to Boston," she told me, with her lilting accent— which always reminded me of summer, and the way bees would bounce from blossom to bright blossom—"it was the last place I wanted to be. I'd come to this spot every day because I thought maybe, if I looked hard enough, I could still see home."

There was no way that Ireland was visible, even on the clearest of days, but it didn't stop her from hoping.

"One day I couldn't wait anymore, and I jumped into the harbor from this very place and started swimming."

None of this had surprised me. My mother was meant for the ocean. In Ireland, she used to swim off the coast of Kerry each morning, no matter how cold the water. She told me that dolphins followed her and that sometimes she would swim for hours and wind up so many miles down the coast that her father would have to come and pick her up in his old truck. When she was pregnant with me, she swam for hours at a YMCA. I was a breech baby, the midwives said, because I had no idea what gravity was, which way was up, which way was down.

My mother said that for a while, no one noticed her in the water. Her stroke would have been clean and sure, slicing between buoys and boats until the waves turned darker and choppier, the invisible line where the harbor turned into ocean. She told me that a cormorant guided her, its elegant white belly an arrow forward as it flew overhead. She told me that night had already fallen when she was picked up by the captain of a tugboat who only spoke Portuguese and who kept pointing to her legs and shaking his head, as if he were otherwise convinced she was a mermaid.

"Here's the thing, Maidan," she told me, using her nickname for me, the Irish word for *morning*. "I almost made it. The ocean's different in Ireland, you know. Sweeter, less salt. And I could see the shoreline. I was *that* close."

I believed her, when I was little. Now, of course, I know it is impossible that one small woman might have swum across the Atlantic in a matter of hours. But that doesn't really matter, does it? We all have stories we tell ourselves, until we believe them to be true.

My mother spent most of her life wondering who else she might have been, if she hadn't left Ireland. An Olympic swimmer, maybe. Or just someone who worked in her father's pub. A different man's wife, a different girl's mother.

I've thought about that, too. If you had asked me fifteen years ago, I would have said that by now, I'd be published and well established in the field of Egyptology. Maybe I would be a curator for the Met, living in Chelsea, with subway maps memorized and a little dog I took running in Central Park. Maybe I'd be a professor with my own concession in Egypt, taking students twice a year and pulling secrets out of the dusty earth. Maybe I'd teach at Queen's College at Oxford, wandering the stacks of the Ashmolean or presenting at the annual conferences for Current Research in Egyptology in Madrid or Prague or Krakow.

Maybe I would be at the Grand Café on High Street, scrambling through my purse to find a few pound coins for my latte, when the man behind me in line offered to pay instead.

Maybe that man would be Brian, in town to give a guest lecture on multiverses at Oxford's physics department.

This is what I tell myself: that we were inevitable.

That it was meant to be.

. . .

WHEN MERET WAS seven, Brian bought her a microscope for Christmas. I argued that it was an expensive gift for a child who really shouldn't be playing with glass slides, but I was wrong. Meret spent hours hunched over it, switching among the five magnification settings, looking at prepared slides of dragonfly wings, cucumber ovaries, horsehair, and tulip pollen. She would meticulously use tweezers and swabs to make her own specimens, highlighting them with eosin or methylene blue. Her bedroom walls were filled with magnified drawings of what she saw: the lace of an overblown lilac leaf, the tangled spaghetti of bacteria, geometric evil eyes of onion cells. That was the beginning of her love affair with science, and to date, it hasn't stopped.

Teachers love her, and why shouldn't they? She is smart and curious and wise beyond her years. They look at her and they see what she has the potential to become. Other students, though, can't seem to get past how she looks.

When most kids in elementary school began to outgrow their round bellies and chubby cheeks, Meret didn't. It is not that she isn't active or that she doesn't eat healthily. It's just how she is made, and if that isn't everyone's standard of perfect, then maybe they just have to revise their damn standard.

But.

I remember what it felt like to be fourteen. I remember looking in the mirror and not recognizing myself. I know that's what Meret sees, when she forces herself to see her reflection—although I also notice the way she avoids that at all costs. What's different is that my body was changing, and that's what made me uncomfortable. For Meret, it's the opposite. Her body stays the same—curved, softer, larger—and that's what she is desperate to hide.

Last year, when she started wearing clothes that were bigger than mine, I told her that sizing wasn't standard; that I could wear a four in some brands and an eight in others. She stared at me for a long moment. *That's exactly the kind of thing a skinny person would say,* she told me, and she locked herself in her room for the rest of the day.

As her mother I am damned if I do and damned if I don't. If I cook only vegetables for dinner, she thinks I'm judging her. I try to completely avoid the topics of food, of exercise, of therapy, of weight. I know every time someone tells her she is the spitting image of me, she is thinking: *yeah, buried under the extra pounds*. I wish I knew how to get her to see that her name describes her: a homonym for a word that means *worth*.

Brian is equally at a loss. He was never overweight as a kid; he isn't now. His relationship with Meret has one advantage over mine, though—she does not look at him and compare herself. Maybe for that reason, the bond they have has always been a little fiercer, a little *more*. Say what you will about Brian, but he loves being a father more than anything in the world. He would have had ten more kids, but that wasn't in the cards for us, and eventually we stopped trying. *Clearly,* he would say to me each month, when I told him—again— that I wasn't pregnant, *we can't improve on the original model*.

This summer, Meret is at a STEM camp for teenage girls. We had to nearly force her to go, but since she will be moving into a new school next year as a ninth grader, this gives her the chance to make some connections with new kids before the academic year begins. It seems to be working. She keeps talking about a girl named Sarah, who like her, is a budding biologist. Today she texted me, asking if she could go to Sarah's for dinner.

Which is why I'm surprised when she walks through the front door while I'm cooking for myself and Brian. "Hi," I say. "What are you doing home?"

"Don't I live here?" she asks, and flops down on the couch. She immediately takes a throw pillow and covers her midsection. I don't even know if she realizes that she does that, every time she takes a seat. "What's for dinner?"

"I thought you ate at Sarah's," I say, and wince, because I don't want her to read between the lines and think that I'm criticizing her for being hungry.

"I did and I didn't." Meret picks at the tasseled edge of the throw pillow. "I mostly picked."

I glance up, sympathetic. "Did they make pork?"

Meret hates pork. She has boycotted it ever since she learned that pigs are smarter than any other domestic animal. "No, fried chicken and Caesar salad." Color rises in her cheeks. "It's hard, you know. If I only eat salad, they're thinking, *Poor thing, she's trying so hard*. If I eat the chicken, they're thinking, *Oh*, that's *why she's huge*."

I wipe my hands on a dish towel and walk into the family room to sit beside her on the couch. "Baby," I tell her, "no one is thinking that."

"She asked me to come over Saturday to hang out."

"That's great!" There is too much cheer in those words.

Meret sinks lower into the couch.

"What did you work on today?"

Her face lights up. "We isolated the DNA of spinach."

"Wow." I blink. "Why?"

"Because we *can*. It looked like cobwebs." She drops the pillow, talking with her hands. "Did you know we share eighty-five percent of our genes with zebra fish? And that less than two percent of our DNA actually has the instructions to make proteins? The rest is called 'junk DNA,' because it's just a bunch of random sequences that doesn't seem to be code for anything important."

"That's a lot of wasted space in a chromosome," I point out.

"Yeah. Unless it *is* important and no one's figured out the DNA Rosetta stone yet."

I tug on one of her curls. "Maybe that's going to be your big contribution to science."

She shrugs. "You know what they say. If you need the right man for the job . . . get a woman." Then, suddenly, she launches forward and hugs me. Adolescence is like summer weather in Boston— storms chased by sunshine, in the span of a minute. Occasional hail. And every now and then, a cloudless sky.

I wrap my arms around her, as if I could cocoon her again, and keep anything bad from happening. I remember what it felt like to have her settled under the umbrella of my rib cage, to have a double beat of a heart. I still do. It's just harder to hear, sometimes.

Just then Brian comes in. After calling the Perimeter Institute and canceling his speech at the last minute, he went to his lab. He tosses his briefcase onto the kitchen counter and eats a slice of mozzarella off a platter of caprese salad I've made. "Ugh," I say, "not before you wash your hands."

"She's right," Meret says. "A single gram of human poop can contain a trillion germs."

"So much for being hungry . . ." Brian leans down and hugs Meret, and then, after only a tiny hesitation does the same to me.

I breathe in. Neutrogena shampoo. Old Spice.

I exhale.

"Meret isolated DNA today," I tell him.

He whistles. "How much is this camp costing?"

"It was vegetable DNA. But still." Suddenly she leaps up. "Oh! But thank you for my birthday present! It's perfect."

He must have bought her something and left it in her room when I was visiting with Win. His gaze slides to mine as Meret hugs him. "I'm sorry it was late," he says.

"That's okay," Meret tells him.

I feel, for just a moment, a pang of jealousy. Why does he get a free pass, every time; why am I always judged?

I know parents with more than one kid say they love the kids equally, but I don't believe it. I think it is the same in the other direction. A kid will say they love both their parents the same amount, but when there's a rough edge, sometimes that ragged border fits flush against one parent, and prickles against the other.

I just wish, sometimes, I could be the one she loves more.

But I never say this. I paste a smile on my face, and I ask Meret, "What did Dad get you?"

Before she can answer, Brian interrupts. "I almost forgot. I bought tickets for a thing Saturday at MIT. Guest lecturer in zoology who's going to talk about the time she was bitten by a vampire bat and chased by a gorilla. Rumor has it she's bringing a live octopus."

"Sounds cool," Meret says.

"But you were invited to Sarah's." I try to catch Brian's eye, to silently urge him to not push; to realize that spending time with another teenage girl is a lot more important than meeting a cephalopod.

"I never said I was *going*." Meret glares at me. "She wants to hang out at her pool."

It is ninety degrees out, and humid. "That sounds perfect." I look meaningfully at Brian. "Doesn't it?"

"Yeah," he says. "I mean, I'm sure we can watch the lecture online."

"I'm. Not. Going."

"But, Meret—"

She swings around, her fists balled at her sides. "If I go to her pool, I have to take off my shirt. And I don't want to take off my shirt."

"She won't make fun of you—"

"Right. She'll pity me. And that's worse." Meret folds her arms across her chest like they are wings, like she can disappear behind them. "You don't understand *anything*," she says, and she runs upstairs.

I scrub my hands over my face. "Jesus."

Brian follows me into the kitchen. "It was just an octopus."

"You didn't know."

I take the chicken breast out of the oven, cut it into thirds, and separate it onto plates. Then I spoon rice on each, and a few slices of tomato and mozzarella. We both look up the stairs. "You want to call her down?" I ask.

Brian shakes his head. "Not for a million bucks."

I cover the plate with foil. "I'll bring it up in a little bit."

He dances around me to the cabinet, a choreographed routine, pulling glasses and silverware as I carry the food to the kitchen table. There's a beauty in the way we revolve around each other in that tight space, a moon around a sun. I am just not sure which of us is which.

Without Meret as a buffer between us, the air becomes tinder, and any rogue word might make it combust.

"How was your day?" Brian asks. Neutral. Safe.

"Good." I swallow a bite. "How was *your* day?"

"I talked to the people who organized the conference. They asked me to present in October instead."

"Good."

"Yeah."

I look up to find Brian watching me. "When did this all get so hard?" he asks softly. He has the grace to blush. "Not just this," he says, gesturing between us. "But all of it." He glances up the staircase.

I settle my fork against my plate. I've lost my appetite. Maybe I will tell this to Meret. The best diet plan is waking up one day and wondering how the hell you got here. "Can I ask you something? How many tickets did you buy for that MIT lecture?"

Brian tilts his head. "Is this a trick question?"

"No. Just curiosity."

"Two," he says. "You usually see clients on Saturday and I assumed—"

"You assumed," I interrupt.

He is genuinely confused. "Do you want to see the octopus? I'm sure I can get another ticket—"

"This isn't about the octopus," I say. "Why didn't you even ask if I wanted to go?"

Brian rubs his forehead. "Can we . . . not fight?" he sighs. "Can we just . . . eat?"

I nod. I pick up my knife and fork and start cutting my chicken into tiny pieces. And again. I wonder how small I can get them. I count to one hundred as I do this. I push the tiny bites around on my plate.

"Dawn."

Brian has been watching me the whole time. His voice is wrapped in batting, so soft I can barely hear it. It is a broken bone of desperation, and it won't set.

I meet his gaze over a tabletop that is suddenly so vast we might as well be on different continents. We might as well be my mother in Boston, squinting to see the coast of Ireland again.

"Tell me what you want from me," Brian begs.

I should dive in and start swimming, but I'm already sinking here on dry land.

"I shouldn't have to," I say.

# LAND / EGYPT

. . .

TECHNICALLY, WYATT CANNOT hire me to work at his dig site. It's a Yale concession; I have no connection to Yale anymore. The graduate students and colleagues who fall under the umbrella of the university each season have work visas and have been vetted by the Egyptian government for their credentials in the field of antiquities.

I don't know why I asked Wyatt for a job. I blurted it out, instead of all the things I really want to say. But asking for a job is simpler, and will buy me the time I need for the rest.

"There must be someone you can ask," I beg. "Someone who can bend the rules."

Out of the blue I remember that, back when I left, Westerners were not supposed to travel on the Desert Road between Minya and Cairo. Hasib—Harbi's father—had given Wyatt directions to the airport with this warning to stay off that thoroughfare. *Unless,* he had said, *you are brave of heart.* Which meant, when we were stopped at a checkpoint, Wyatt had played dumb, saying he had no idea about the restriction, until we were waved through.

Wyatt sinks down onto the arm of a battered chair. "Forgive me, but I assume that you haven't been in the field for the past fifteen years?"

I feel a pang, realizing that he has not been keeping tabs on my life, and what became of me, but then why should he have? I was the one who walked away without looking back. I force myself to meet his gaze. "No."

"Why, Dawn?" he asks quietly. "Why now?"

I hesitate, considering how to tell him the truth without garnering his pity. "Do you know how, if you chop down a tree, you can look at its rings and be able to tell the moments where everything changed? Like, a forest fire. Or a plague of bugs. A year where there was a drought, another year where something fell against the trunk and made it grow in a different direction?" He nods. "This would be one of those moments."

"You've been blown pretty far off course if you landed in Egypt," Wyatt says.

"Or I was blown pretty far off course when I left."

His eyes narrow. "Look. I'd like to help you but I can't just—"

"Wyatt," I interrupt. "Please."

"Dawn, are you all right? If you're in trouble—"

"I just need a job."

Wyatt sighs. "There's a chance I can pull strings for next January. This isn't even our dig season."

"But you're here. Working. I mean, that's a sign, isn't it? That you're here, and I'm here . . ." I swallow. "I know you need the help. You don't have to pay me. You just have to give me a chance. And then . . ." I falter. "Then you'll never have to see me again."

Wyatt looks at me. His eyes are still the blue of the heart of a flame, the blue of the sky when you have been staring too long and close your eyes and still find it painted there. His fingers tap a tattoo on his thigh. I can almost see ribbons of thought and reason being fed through the machine of his mind. "I know I made you a promise a long time ago," he begins, and in that instant I realize he is going to tell me what I do not want to hear.

I brace myself, knowing I made a mistake. *What if* cannot trump *what is*.

"I can't make any guarantees, but I'll see if I can get you a temporary permit."

My head snaps up. "You will?"

"Isn't that what you want?"

"Yes," I breathe. I take a step toward him, and then that strange and shifting invisible wall between us reminds me to stay where I am. "Thank you."

"Don't thank me." Wyatt stands. "I haven't done anything yet, and if you do get to stay, you're going to be worked to the bone. Let me introduce you to everyone, and then we can drive into Minya to the antiquities office this afternoon." He starts out of the library, expecting me to follow. I can hear the house humming, the Arabic chatter of Harbi and his family preparing a meal; the pipes clearing their throats as water rushes through them.

Suddenly, Wyatt stops so abruptly that I nearly crash into him. He turns around so that we are frozen in the hallway, eye to eye. "One more thing?" he says. "I don't know why you're here. I don't know what you're hiding. And you may well be out of practice." Then a smile ghosts over his lips, a challenge. "But I unearth things for a living."

UNTIL RECENTLY, EGYPTIANS who graduated from college were guaranteed jobs by the Egyptian government, which meant there was a glut of government employees and not a tremendous amount of work to do—one study suggested that the average government employee only actually performed about a half hour of labor per day. Because of this, working with the Yale concession was a plum occupation, and Harbi's father and the others I had known fifteen years earlier were so good at their jobs that it became a family affair, passed down over generations. Wyatt introduces me to Mohammed Mahmoud, son of the Mohammed I knew when I was last here. He works now with Harbi, Abdou, and Ahmed to prepare food, clean the Dig House, and labor on site. In between dig seasons, he and his family live in Luxor.

Wyatt introduces me as an old friend to those who weren't here before. Some call me *doctora*, like Harbi did. "It's just Dawn," I say cheerfully, but I am aware of Wyatt's eyes on me the entire time. When he leads me out of the kitchen, I ask, "What happened to Harbi's leg?"

He props a shoulder against the stucco wall. "How come you didn't finish your degree?" When I don't respond, he shrugs. "Think of it as currency. You want an answer, you have to give one."

"I got an MSW instead," I say. "Academia wasn't going to pan out."

Wyatt regards me, as if he's trying to figure out if I am telling the truth. "Harbi's leg broke when a ladder gave way in a tomb shaft about five years ago. Never set right."

I suddenly see a ladder tangling under my own feet in the tomb of Djehutyhotep II, Wyatt catching me and breaking the fall. I remember how he smelled like the sun baked into his clothes and also butterscotch. How, weeks later I would learn that he kept sweets in his pocket, for himself and to give to the barefoot children who waited for him in the blistering heat at the entrance to the *wadi* as we left for the day.

"Come on," he says. "Let me show you what we're working on."

In the main room of the Dig House, there is still swing music playing. A young man with tightly cropped hair is bent over a table, sketching Paleolithic flints, which are lined up in neat rows. Wyatt picks one up and passes it to me; I run my finger over the scalloped edge. "Joe," he says, "this is Dawn." Joe pushes his glasses up and nods to me, waiting for an explanation from Wyatt that isn't forthcoming. "He's the only grad student here this late in the year," Wyatt explains.

"I'm hoping for a trophy." Joe laughs. "Or at least a grave marker: Here lies Joe Cullen, dessicated in the desert."

"Are these flints part of your dissertation?" I ask.

He nods, scratching numbers onto a tiny metal label. "Yeah, I'm all about how ancient Egyptians worked with their hands. These are all primitive tools; I'm recording the season number, the date, and the location found."

"These used to be paper tags," I murmur.

Joe glances up, surprised that I know this. "There was a European expedition working in the south that was storing potsherds in palm-rib crates in their magazine at Aswan, and they got termites and basically were left with an unmarked pile of broken sherds. This system saves us from two things that are hard to avoid in Egypt: fading and bugs."

I set the flint down gently on the table. "That's a scraper," he says. "We've found a huge number of them, which suggests that there was a lot of hide preparation in the deep desert."

"That's really inter—"

"Don't encourage him," Wyatt jokes. "Or he'll pull out his hand axes." He leads me to the other side of the room, where a man in his thirties has his dark head bent over a computer screen. "Alberto, did you get it up and running again?"

He nods, looking up to notice me for the first time. His face, thin and sharp-nosed, changes when he smiles, white teeth flashing. "You did not tell me we were having company. Beautiful company."

I feel myself blush. When was the last time I did that?

"She's not company. She's working here." Wyatt looks at me. "Maybe." I glance at the computer screen, on which a three-dimensional model of a rock-cut tomb pivots. "Alberto's a digital archaeologist from Italy."

Fifteen years ago, that job didn't exist.

Wyatt laughs when he sees that expression cross my face. "I know. We're old."

"You draw digital models of the site?" I ask.

Alberto shakes his head. "I do photogrammetry and geomatics. Digital mapping in 3D, instead of the linear measuring that used to be the standard."

Wyatt hits a few keystrokes, zooming in on the model on the screen, until I can read the hieroglyphs on the wall. It's almost like being there. "Amazing, right?" Wyatt murmurs.

"It's incredible," I say. "How does it work?"

"I take a photo of a site and enter it into software, and—how is it you say?—*bam*, we have a 3D model with topography."

Wyatt points to an icon on the desktop. "Show her this one."

He hands me a set of gaming goggles and I fit them over my head, waiting as a picture loads before my eyes. I draw in my breath, suddenly transported to a *wadi* I know well: a rock overhang; a quiet, dark hollow beneath. I stretch my arm out as if I might touch it, but of course, it's only digital.

"Turn left," Wyatt instructs, and I do, leaning forward to simulate walking, until I am close enough to read the painted hieratic rock inscription we had found years ago.

It's so different from the way we used to do things. The Mylar we used attracted dust and melted in the brutal heat and there were constantly shimmers of light caught in the plastic so I'd be forever correcting my image against the actual carved sign. This—this is nothing short of revolutionary.

"The sites we excavate are in situ in a landscape," Wyatt says. "They're meant to be viewed there. This is about as close as you can get, without flooding Middle Egypt with tourists and their fanny packs. The way we used to do it, you lost half the information—*why* the inscriptions were put in that particular place, instead of somewhere else."

I lean forward again, moving closer to the virtual rock wall. "Epigraphy must take half the time."

"You have no idea," Wyatt replies. He tugs the goggles off me and hands me an iPad. "Alberto makes a flattened ortho image based off the high-def 3D image and sends it here. Then I can trace the hieroglyphs like it's a coloring book. You can manipulate the color and change the contrast if the stone itself is busy, like limestone, and you need to tell what's aspect of the stone and what's part of the carving."

"Then after he traces everything, I can put it back into the 3D image of the site," Alberto adds.

"It means we can get a final drawing even within one part of a given field season."

"And it's incredible for sites like the one we are working on now," Alberto says. "Instead of having to decide whether you'll put a section through this way or that way, and instead of destroying layers with each excavation, you take a 3D photo before you start, another photo after you clear the first layer, another photo after the second layer—*e così via*—it is like having a birthday cake you can slice and unslice and reslice any way you want."

"The only downside," Joe pipes in from across the room, "is that the iPads overheat and the batteries die and my tender ears are subject to curses in a variety of languages."

For a moment, I think that maybe I am years too late. That there's no way to continue where I left off. Then Wyatt takes his iPad from my hands, tapping a few icons until a new three-dimensional image appears. "Djehutynakht's tomb," he says, and he offers it to me.

As a grad student I had read up on the excavation of the Djehutynakhts whose coffins were in the MFA—but this doesn't look familiar. Instead, there is a tomb chapel, and a shaft in various stages of excavation.

"Not Djehutynakht II," Wyatt clarifies. "Djehutynakht, son of Teti."

I pinch at the screen, trying to get closer.

"It's not published yet," he says quietly.

In other words: I am the first person outside of his team to see it.

There is nothing—*nothing*—like being the one to discover a piece of the world that has gone missing. Your pulse races, your heart pounds, you forget to breathe. You go still, wanting to hold on to this moment, when it is just you and your miracle, before everyone else intervenes. I was lucky enough to have had that experience, once, with Wyatt. The closest I ever came to it, again, was giving birth to Meret.

"I'd heard you'd found it," I murmur. But reading that tidbit and seeing this on the screen are two very different things.

I don't realize I've said this aloud until I find Wyatt looking down at me, his face inscrutable. "It's even better in person," he says. "Let's go to Minya."


WYATT ASKS ME if I want to change before heading back to the city. When I tell him I didn't come with luggage, he narrows his eyes. "You flew to Egypt without a suitcase?"

"Yes."

"Planning to work at an archaeological site."

I raise my chin a notch. "Yes."

"Without any appropriate clothing."

"It was," I say, "sort of a last-minute decision."

He opens his mouth as if to say something, and then snaps it shut. "Alberto," he calls, "I need your help."

I hear their voices, muffled and argumentative. The only words I can make out are *unqualified* and *daily*. Wyatt says, "I'm still the director." In Italian: *Avere gli occhi foderati di prosciutto*. Then footsteps recede.

Ten minutes later, I am wearing a pair of Alberto's pants. Of the archaeologists at the Dig House he is the one closest to my size, slim-hipped and only a few inches taller than I am. I belt the waist tight and roll the cuffs, and then Wyatt gives me one of his own long-sleeved cotton shirts. It's fresh from the laundry, but it still smells like him. "Here," he announces unceremoniously, and he dumps a pair of boots in front of me as I am still fixing the sleeves of his shirt so they don't hang over my fingers. They are women's boots, size eight, a perfect fit. I wonder whom they belong to, but I do not have the right to ask.

From a table near the doorway, Wyatt grabs a hat—battered, with a stiff brim that won't bend in the incessant wind. "Take one," he says, gesturing to the collection: panama hats and bucket hats and baseball caps with long tails to keep the sun from blistering the back of your neck. I grab a straw cowboy hat and jam it on my head, hurrying to match Wyatt's long strides as he walks to a Land Rover that is covered in a film of grit. It feels strange to sit in the passenger seat; as a graduate student, I always had to walk. I watch Wyatt expertly shift gears as we jostle over the pitted road that leads from the Dig House into the desert.

The local office of antiquities is in Mallawi, but the main permissions are processed in Minya, so we drive back exactly the way I have come. The ride is bone-jarring, dusty, sweaty. The cracked leather seat is so hot it feels like the sun is a cat curled between us. I keep leaning forward to peel my sweaty shirt away from my body. Behind us, a billowing cloud of dirt erupts like a plume.

After about fifteen minutes of silence, I offer an olive branch. "I didn't know if I'd find you here in August."

"And yet here you are," Wyatt said.

I turn my attention to the road again, unsure of where to go from there.

"Alberto and Joe seem nice."

I once read an article about the differences between how men and women converse—how men prefer side-by-side conversation, because face-to-face feels confrontational; how women prefer talking face-to-face to read all the nonverbal cues. The article suggested broaching difficult subjects with your husband in the car, instead of over the dinner table, for this reason.

The author of this article clearly had not ridden in a Land Rover with Wyatt.

He glances at me, his wrist balanced on the steering wheel. "I'm sorry, are we doing small talk now?"

"I'm just trying to have a conversation."

"You didn't seem to be eager to have one earlier."

"It's hard for me—"

"Do you not think this is hard for me, too?" Wyatt interrupts. His words feel like knives being thrown, pinning me back against the seat.

I close my eyes. "I'm sorry."

Even without looking, I can feel him staring at me. The air feels heavier. And then, as if someone has broken the glass of a window during an inferno, I can suddenly breathe. Wyatt is once again facing the road, his features smooth. "The reason I'm here when it's hotter than hell is because the semester ended in May," he says, as if half our conversation hadn't taken place. "Then there was Ramadan, and I've got to excavate this tomb before classes start back up again mid-September."

There's additional information he isn't sharing—maybe it has to do with funding. Maybe he can't get any more without the proof that he has found a new tomb with an intact coffin. "You're lucky you didn't go into academia," he adds. "Although I imagine social work isn't a lark, either."

He says it gently; it's a peace offering. "I'm not a social worker," I say. "I'm an end-of-life doula."

"A . . . what?"

"I take care of people who are terminal."

"So your clients are dying to meet you," Wyatt replies.

I laugh. "You could say that. It wasn't as huge a transition of career as I figured it would be. In a way, I've been studying death since I was eighteen."

He glances at me. "Likewise," he says frankly.

"And you? Still focused on the Book of Two Ways?"

Wyatt nods. "The translation we used to use? It fell by the wayside in 2017 with a new publication. Turns out there are mostly two independent Books of Two Ways, and even when the spells overlap, there are big variations in the text."

Now he is talking to me not like an enemy, not like a refugee, but like a colleague. I catch my breath, feeling something I haven't in a long while: the popping in my brain that used to happen when I listened to a stellar lecture or when I cracked a puzzle in translation.

"So the old translation was wrong."

"Well, it wasn't *right*," Wyatt answers. "Oh! And remember how you were always livid because the Pyramid Texts that were found in the coffins were never printed in the Coffin Text publications?"

"*Livid* is a strong word . . ."

"They finally were. Two thousand six. Did you see it?"

"In 2006 all I was reading was *Goodnight Moon*." I laugh.

Wyatt looks at me. The spare air in the truck is suddenly gone. "That's a children's book, isn't it? You have children?"

"Child," I say softly. "A daughter."

"Presumably, she has a father," Wyatt replies, his gaze fixed on the road.

I swallow. "She does."

I look down at my hands, folded in my lap. I twist my wedding band around my finger as silence settles between us.

"I did think about you, you know," Wyatt murmurs. "I wondered how someone could disappear into thin air."

There is so much I want to tell him, *need* to tell him. But the words jam in my throat, dammed behind fear: fear that he doesn't have time to babysit a middle-aged woman who wonders what else her life might have been, fear that he will send me packing, or that he will laugh at me. Or—maybe worse—that he is indifferent. That he'll treat me like an amateur—the way we did, as Yale grad students, when we met someone who had read a little about pyramids as a kid or was obsessed with Brendan Fraser in *The Mummy*—polite but dismissive.

And me? Had I thought of Wyatt? I would be lying if I said no. I didn't pine for him; I loved Brian. But there would be times when I would be comfortably immersed in my daily life and he'd pop into my head. When we went to Greece for my thirtieth birthday, and on the cobbled streets, I watched children sort through broken potsherds. Putting on eyeliner and regarding the tilted wing in the mirror, and picturing Wyatt trying—and failing—to sketch the kohl-rimmed eyes of a nomarch's wife on a sheet of Mylar.

"I thought of you when the FBI cracked the case about the severed mummy head in the MFA," I tell him. "Remember how Dumphries didn't know if it belonged to the male mummy or his wife?"

I had read the story in *The Boston Globe*—how doctors had done a CT scan of the mummy's head and noticed that there were mutilations to the mouth and jaw area, all the parts that would have been involved while eating. Immediately, I had known why—the Opening of the Mouth ceremony, performed on the deceased so that they could eat and drink in the Netherworld. But they still didn't know who the mummy was, definitively, and so the FBI was called in to extract DNA from a tooth.

"I think I read that, too. Wasn't it—" Wyatt starts, as I begin to speak.

"Mr. Djehutynakht," we say in unison. Then we both burst out laughing.

He looks so at home here, his skin tanned and hair curling where beads of sweat rise on his temples. I wonder what would have happened if our roles had been reversed: if I had stayed, and he had gotten the call that changed the rest of his life. If he'd be awkward in a three-piece suit, working in London in finance or government. Then I remember that he was destined to become a British peer, doing whatever peers do. I conjure up a new image of Wyatt, playing polo. Sitting behind a mountain of paperwork at a heavy mahogany desk older than my entire country. Smiling up at his wife, who is named Pippa or Araminta, and who learned to ride before she could walk.

"Are you a marquess now?" I blurt out.

"Ah. Actually," Wyatt says, "yes."

"I'm sorry." I know that would mean his father had died.

"The title is utter rot. I'm here, or in New Haven, anyway. I don't actually stand on the ceremony of it. Much to the dismay of my mother." His lips twitch. "But since you didn't bother to call me *my lord* when I was an earl, perhaps you should start now."

"I'd rather swallow my tongue," I say.

He grins. "I admit I've never heard of a death doula before."

"It's a different model of care. It's . . . richer, if that makes sense. A doctor spends about seven minutes on average with a patient in traditional medical care. I become a part of the family, if that's what the client wants. I'll show up and sit vigil, but I also have the distance to ask the hard questions of the medical team and caregivers, and I don't mind calling the DMV fifteen times if that's what has to get done." I hesitate, thinking through my responsibilities and trying to see them from the perspective of an outsider. "I guess I give people time at the moment they need it the most."

"Is it depressing?"

"I mean, I cry sometimes." I shrug. "The first time I cried in front of a client I beat myself up, but then that night her brother called to thank me. Seeing me cry made him realize that his sister wasn't just a paycheck to me. So yeah, there's sadness. But there are also moments of beauty."

"Evidence?" Wyatt barks, and I bite back a smile—this is what Dumphries used to say to us, when we were in the field and made a hypothesis for which he wanted support.

"I had a trans client once, and just before she passed, her mother said, 'I gave birth to a son, but I'm burying a daughter.' And just like that, my client let go. It was almost like she needed to hear that before she died."

"What have you learned?"

It's such a professorial question I have to hide my grin. "Everyone's surprised by death, which is kind of ridiculous, when you think about it. It's not exactly a spoiler. But I think that what really shocked me is how many people can't see the shape of the life they've lived until they get to the very end of it. You know?"

Wyatt nods. "Sure. It's not until you start building your tomb that you realize you're going to be the one inside it."

"Life and death are just flip sides of the same coin," I say, and I turn to find him staring at me. "What?"

"I was just thinking that maybe you never really stopped your studies after all."

We pass by the giant El Minya sign, wedged incongruously into the rock cliffs like the Hollywood sign in Los Angeles. As Wyatt tries to find a parking spot, I watch two men holding hands, walking down the street. It doesn't mean what it does back home. Here, it's just a sign of friendship. Legally, in Egypt you cannot be gay.

Wyatt finds a spot in front of a small shop selling ice cream. "Hungry?" he asks. "My treat."

I am starving, in spite of the meal Harbi fed me. I walk up to the glass case, frost delicately etching the window. Strawberry, chocolate, orange blossom, coconut. I point to the Norio flavor—the Egyptian cookie knockoff of Oreo. Wyatt orders for me, the Arabic flowing easily off his tongue. The round hums and soft els make the words sound as if they are made of honey.

He hands me a cone, and suddenly I am back in my tiny bedroom at the Dig House, fifteen years ago. Wyatt had snuck inside when everyone else was asleep, brandishing a pack of Norios. "Where did these come from?" I asked, already tearing into the packaging.

"Don't look a gift horse in the mouth," he said, and he kissed me. "Sweets for my sweet."

I rolled my eyes, intent on separating the cookie from the cream. I looked up to find him biting into a cookie, intact.

"Who does that?" I asked, truly shocked. "You're supposed to split them apart."

"Says who? The cookie Gestapo?" He popped another cookie, whole, into his mouth.

"That's pathological," I said. "Downright sociopathic."

"Yes, I eat my Norios like a caveman, and I also am sewing a skin suit made out of undergrads I've murdered."

"I don't know if I can love you anymore," I told him.

He stilled, a smile spreading, morning chasing night. "You love me?" he asked.

Now, I blink to find him holding out a napkin. "You're dripping."

"Thanks," I say, and wrap my cone.

"I miss real Oreos," Wyatt opines, starting down the street. "And having ice in my drink. And baths. Damn, it's British as hell, but I miss baths."

I fall into place beside him. *I miss this,* I think.

THERE IS A sign on the door of the antiquities office stating that the director is temporarily indisposed—which can mean he is out touring sites, helping curate museum collections, or doing general cultural heritage work—but that he will return, *inshallah*. The note does not, however, give a return time.

"Now what?" I ask.

"We wait," Wyatt says. He steps into the shade thrown by the lintel of the doorway and squats down, tucking himself out of the sun and leaning his back against the locked door. He gestures to the spot beside him.

I rub the back of my neck. "Wyatt, no. You have a thousand things to do. You can't just spend an afternoon sitting here till God knows when. We don't even know if this guy is coming back." I force myself to exhale. It's one thing to ask Wyatt to try to get me clearance. It's another to waste his time. "You tried, and I cannot tell you how much I appreciate that. But—"

"Dawn." He extends a hand to me, shading his eyes with the other. I look down and have a crippling moment of déjà vu. "Stop talking."

I reach for him, his fingers sliding around mine, dry and strong and so familiar that my chest squeezes. How can you go for over a decade without holding someone's hand, and still have the feeling of it imprinted on you so firmly?

He tugs me down to a sitting position, shoulder to shoulder. "Firstly . . ." Wyatt winces. "Who says *firstly*? God, I sound like a complete wanker." I smother a laugh, and he shakes his head. "I *do* have a thousand things to do. But I've been working around the clock and I'm the director and if I decide I need an afternoon's break, so be it. Second"—he hesitates—"-ly: I don't consider this a waste." He traces a crack in the pavement with his thumb. "I owe you, Dawn. I would not have discovered this new tomb without you. So believe me when I say that if showing you my thanks means sitting on my arse for a few hours in downtown Minya, it is a small price to pay."

I think about the citation he left me in his thesis. "I'm pretty confident you would have eventually found it whether or not you'd ever met me."

"Wrong. It all started with that dipinto."

I remember that afternoon. It had been so still that the world seemed to be in suspended animation, and we had been standing in a shaded hollow beneath a rock wall of the *wadi* where we did not have permission to be. I remember dusting the stone gently, and Wyatt running his finger beneath the hieratic, translating the bits of the inscription that he could read—including the mention of a tomb that had never been found at the Bersha site, in hundreds of years of excavation.

I remember Wyatt's hand catching mine, squeezing so tight that it hurt, and me squeezing back just as hard.

"I looked for that tomb from 2003 till 2013," Wyatt says. "And I found absolutely nothing. Dumphries let me do it, but I think it's because he wanted me to realize I was on a fool's errand. He had me nearly convinced that even if there *was* a Djehutynakht who was a distant early relative of Djehutyhotep II, there was enough damage to the rock inscription to cast doubt on whether his tomb was actually part of this necropolis, or somewhere else."

The thing about archaeology is that it's like baking a cake, one layer on top of another, with the most recent layer first and the oldest layer at the bottom. Your number one goal is to figure out what got put down when. You cannot be misled by someone who dug a hole into an older layer and pitched something into it. When you excavate, you aren't finding brilliant, clear lost hieroglyphic text. You're moving masses of mud. You're finding broken pottery. You're looking for the needle in a haystack of desert sand.

"It was 2013. I was standing at the top of Djehutyhotep II's tomb, where we spent that last season. I was looking around, trying to figure out what the hell I had missed. And I thought about Howard Carter."

"As one does," I joked.

"Well, as one does when searching for ten years for something one can't find."

Carter had systematically looked for Tutankhamun's New Kingdom tomb for a decade, to no avail. In 1922, his benefactor, Lord Carnarvon, said he was going to pull the plug on financing. Carter begged to check one last area—even saying he'd fund it on his own. Lord Carnarvon agreed to a final season, and Carter went to the tomb of Ramesses VI, which had been excavated a while back. He started to dig past the workmen's huts associated with that tomb, on top of other debris, and found the steps to a second tomb buried beneath it.

"*'At last, wonderful discovery in the valley,'*" Wyatt murmured, quoting the wire that Carter sent to Carnarvon when he found the corridor sealed with the stamp of the necropolis—a jackal over bound enemies. He then had to cover the buried steps and wait for Carnarvon to arrive, so the benefactor could see the tomb being opened, the fruits of his investment.

I look at Wyatt, understanding what he is trying to tell me. "Wait," I say. "Really? Djehutynakht's tomb *was right beneath us* all that time?"

He nods. "I'd looked everywhere, except where I was literally standing. So I dug down two feet from the entrance of Djehutyhotep II's tomb and found the top of a lintel. There was enough autobiographical inscription on it for me to see the glyphs for Djehutynakht. A couple of weeks later, I'd uncovered the entry— painted with faux red-and-green granite and a seal of a giant scarab on the door. By then I'd read enough inscriptions to know that this was Djehutynakht, the son of Teti. He's five generations removed from Djehutyhotep II, and one or two generations older than the Djehutynakhts in the Boston MFA. And he's been referenced in nine other restoration inscriptions he left behind at different tombs in Middle Egypt."

My jaw drops. "So he's truly the granddaddy of the necropolis?"

"Most likely. He's probably from the First Intermediate period, Eleventh Dynasty. He may be the immediate predecessor of Ahanakht I, the first known nomarch to have a rock-cut tomb at Bersha."

"Evidence?" I demand.

He laughs. "We don't have anything substantive, but I'm not the only one who thinks it. Given the dates of their existence as nomarchs, it fits. And we know for a fact that Djehutynakht liked going around Middle Egypt to other necropolises to fix up other people's tombs, so it's entirely plausible that he would start *this* necropolis area for his own family."

"It also would explain why his name was written on the dipinto, as a sacred place officials might have come to spend the night before a festival," I say.

"And," Wyatt adds, "if there's a Book of Two Ways in that coffin in the burial shaft, it would give him the earliest known version."

"Wait. You still haven't gotten into the burial chamber? In all these years?"

He runs a hand through his hair. "I started excavation in 2013, and it took three seasons to clear the material from the front of the tomb and record it all in order to even *reach* the burial shaft. One year we lost our funding and I had to find a new benefactor—which I did. But I'm still full-time at Yale, which means that I only get two to three months in the field here each year. Which brings me to Minya, in the beginning of August." Wyatt turns, leaning his shoulder into the wooden door, facing me. "So maybe you came to Egypt on a whim," he says. "Or maybe the universe knew you belonged right here, right now."

Brian would roll his eyes at that and say it's just the laws of physics splitting you into many different versions of yourself, each of which thinks that the path you're on is unique and providential.

In one world, I'm in Boston.

In another world, I am with Wyatt when he opens that coffin, and sees the Book of Two Ways.

In yet another world, the antiquities director refuses me a permit.

A shadow falls over us, and I squint up to see a man whose edges are lit by the sun. I cannot make out his face as he points to me. "Don't I know you?" he says.

MOSTAFA AWAD, THE director of antiquities, had—in 2003—been an inspector who came to the dig site to record anything Dumphries and the expedition discovered. He had been young then, and eager to learn about his country's own history. I remember Wyatt teaching him the signs of the ancient Egyptian alphabet; him waving his hands and laughing and crying uncle when the grammar reached nominatives and pronouns and complications that were over his head. Now, he is twice as big around the middle as he was fifteen years ago, and his hair and beard are peppered with gray.

He serves us tea in his air-conditioned office. Wyatt leans back in a chair too small for his frame, sips from his cup. "I completely forgot you knew Dawn."

"I never forget a face," Mostafa says, winking at me. "And yours, I saw for three seasons."

I smile back at him. "How long have you been the director?"

"Well. Let's see. In 2009 I did my two years of military service, and then I got this position, *Alhamdulillah*." Praise be to God. He turns to Wyatt. "I admit to being startled when I saw you in the doorway, like a vagrant. I am coming out to your site tomorrow, after all."

"Yes, well, there was something that couldn't wait," Wyatt begins, sliding a glance toward me. "I'd like Dawn to work with the Yale concession."

"Ah." Mostafa gets up and rattles through a desk, searching in files. "I have the forms for next December's permits right here—"

"I beg your pardon," Wyatt interrupts. "Actually, I meant *now*." He levels a look at Mostafa. "Tomorrow."

Mostafa sinks into his desk chair, steepling his fingers. "I see." He looks at Wyatt. "Are you asking me as the director of antiquities?"

Wyatt starts to nod, but Mostafa cuts him off. "Because of course, as the director, I could never compromise the high standard for which Egyptian archaeological excavations are known. You can imagine what might happen if word got out that I made an exception for one concession. How others might come begging for a favor, too."

My hands grip the arms of my chair. "Of course," Wyatt says smoothly. "Which is why I am asking you as my *friend*."

A wide smile breaks across Mostafa's face. "Now *that* is a different story. If you happened to have a visitor that you brought to the site—a personal guest—I might not be looking in her direction if she does more than just observe."

He holds out his hand to me. "Welcome back, Dawn."


ANY ANCIENT EGYPTIAN would tell you that words have great power. There were myths in which knowing the true name of a god could give you dominion over them. There were gates in the Book of Two Ways that could not be passed through unless you knew how to address their beastly guards. The tomb itself, where the *ba* soul reunited with the corpse each night, was also fueled with words. Visitors to the tomb would read the written spells, a *peret kheru*, a going forth by voice. There were lists of fish and fowl, beer and boats, bread and oxen, everything someone would want or need in the Netherworld, and when you spoke them out loud, they magically appeared for your loved one.

That's what I'd been thinking about one afternoon in the tomb of Djehutyhotep II, during my first dig season, as Wyatt and I attempted to trace different sections of the inner chamber. It was nearly lunchtime, and I was starving—having been awake since 4:30 A.M. Staring at a giant palette of painted food, I listened to my stomach grumble.

"I heard that," Wyatt murmured.

I was sketching, on Mylar, a roast goose. It looked more like a turkey, but there were no turkeys in Ancient Egypt. Even in modern times, it was called *dik rumi,* for Roman chicken.

When my stomach rumbled again, Wyatt glanced up from his own work. "If you don't stop that, we're going to be ambushed by those bats."

I glanced up to the ceiling of the tomb, which rippled like a dark curtain. "They don't even know we're here."

"Last season we had a postdoc here who said they wouldn't hit us if they started to fly, because of echolocation. Then one smacked him in the face."

I squinted at them, watching one bat detach itself from the rest to crawl to a clear part of the tomb ceiling. As if it had torn open the corner of a grain bag, a spill of black followed it. I took out my mirror and tried to bounce light upward, so that I could see how many there actually were.

Wyatt caught my wrist. "For God's sake, don't do that. They'll go everywhere."

I shuddered.

"There must be a word for an angry group of bats," Wyatt said. "You know, like a bloat of hippopotamuses. Or a business of ferrets."

"You made up that last one."

"Swear to God. There's also a conspiracy of lemurs."

"A coven," I announce. "That's what a bunch of bats should be."

"Hey, can you look at this damage?"

I crawled toward the right-hand wall in the inner chamber. Wyatt was scrutinizing a section that had, centuries ago, been hacked away or disintegrated. He pointed to the remnant of a hieroglyph. "It's a bird," I said, after a moment.

"Thank you, Sherlock," he said. "But what's the shape of the back of its head? Is it an *aleph* vulture or a *tiw* buzzard . . . ?"

"It looks like an *aleph* to me."

Wyatt grins. "Then, no offense, but it's probably a *tiw.*"

I didn't pretend to be as good at epigraphy as Wyatt was, but if I were the one drawing that vulture, it would look a lot better than what was materializing on the Mylar in front of him. I turned away, staring at a long line of Djehutyhotep's family and retinue. The skin colors ranged across all different tones, but the women were usually painted yellow, and the men red. If you were a well-paid official in Ancient Egypt, your wife worked indoors and not in the fields. Even back then, there was privilege connected to being light-skinned.

Below a line of well-dressed ladies was a row of seal bearers carrying everything from a bow and arrows to spears and shields and axes and a litter. With them walked a spotted, curly-tailed basenji, scaled not to the other figures but larger than life, to signify his importance to Djehutyhotep.

Wyatt saw what had grabbed my attention. "Did you know that the Ancient Egyptians gave dogs the names of people, but all cats were just called 'cat'?"

"Seems right," I said.

The dog's name was clearly marked over his back: the hieroglyph for "life"—*ankh*—and the quail chick that represented the letter *u*. "Ankhu," I murmured, smiling. "Do you have a dog?"

"It was my brother's."

"He didn't share?"

"He didn't have to," Wyatt said, cryptic. He sat back, dropping his Sharpie and massaging his hand. "You know what Ankhu means?"

"Living one."

"Yes. But it has the same root as the word for concubine: *ankhet*."

"Is that all you think about?" I said. "Sex?"

"Looks like it's all our boy Djehutyhotep thought about." He pointed to the left of the image, where the image of Djehutyhotep had been hacked out or eroded, leaving only a general large blank spot with a remnant of a painted kilt. Facing him was a female figure—his wife, Hathorhotep. Then came a parade of eleven women—some who were labeled and some who weren't.

"We know this is his wife because of the inscription above her," Wyatt said, pointing all the way to the left. "And this is likely his mother, Sat-kheper-ka. There's a sprinkling of daughters, a sister or two . . . but these three were his concubines, nestled for eternity right between his wife and children. How cozy."

"You can't know that for sure."

He grabbed a book from his knapsack—Newberry's publication of the tomb from 1895, and scrolled to a page. "There's a block in the Cairo museum that's been attributed to this tomb by Fraser."

I leaned over his shoulder, listening to him translate a column of hieroglyphs. "The *Ankhet,* his beloved one . . . who wins his praise . . . daily," Wyatt read.

I stared at the signs in the book, then took the Sharpie from his hand. With the cap on, I drew in the dirt floor of the tomb.

"You're saying this means *courtesan,*" I said, redrawing the hieroglyphs for *Ankhet:* the ankh, the *n* of water, the *kh* of placenta, the *t* of the bread loaf.

"But we know for sure these hieroglyphs aren't always crystal clear." I held out my hands as scales. "*Aleph* vulture?" I offered as an example. "Or *tiw* buzzard?" I bent down to the dirt again. "So let's say that Newberry made a tiny error transcribing the sign in 1895."

I wiped away the third sign, replacing the third *h* with the very similar *niwt,* the sign for city.

"If you make one little artistic correction, the whole meaning changes," I said. "It's a female citizen now. A married woman who has a town council position. The opposite of a concubine, basically."

Wyatt looked at me, nonplussed. Then he burst out laughing. "Well done, Olive. If only the status of women today could be elevated due to a grammatical error."

In the distance we could hear the muffled loudspeaker of the midday call to prayer, vying for dominance over the Coptic church bells. He rolled to his feet, extending a hand to pull me up. "Come on. We're going to miss all the gourmet offerings."

The moment we stepped out of the tomb, the light and heat shrank around us like a second skin. I wrapped my scarf around my head as we picked our way down the necropolis to the *gaffir*'s hut. Hasib had packed a field lunch of bread, peppers, and tomatoes, and some of the other grad students already sat with Dumphries. "Thought we'd lost you in there," he said, as I sat down cross-legged. I took a pita and began to mash a Laughing Cow cheese onto it as Dumphries passed me his coveted personal stash of Asian five-spice. My first bite was full of sand, as usual.

I watched Wyatt spread peanut butter on a pita. "Professor Dumphries," I asked, "what's the word for a group of lemurs?"

"Why do you—oh, hell, I don't care," he said. "It's called a con-spiracy."

Wyatt looked up at me and grinned.

ON THE WAY back to the Dig House is the Rameses Café, a little open-air hut set like an oasis in the middle of the desert, with picnic tables beneath a thatched, patchy roof. There is a cat yowling on the elbow of the road in front of the restaurant, faded framed advertisements for Egyptian beer on the corrugated metal wall, and absolutely no customers. Wyatt suggests we stop for lunch, and then laughs when he sees my face. "It's fine," he insists. "I've eaten here many times on my way back from Minya, and I'm still stand-ing."

I sit across from him at one of the tables, resting my elbows on the sticky red-and-white checked plastic tablecloth. Wyatt takes off his hat and sets it beside a roll of paper towels and a basket of cutlery, then squints up at the thatch. "Once," he says, "I was here with Dumphries, and there was a cat on the roof with diarrhea."

"I do *not* want to know how that story ends," I say.

"Neither did Dumphries," Wyatt replies.

"I once read that he taught his dog how to read Middle Egyptian."

"That's true. But only the twenty-four uniliteral signs," Wyatt says. "And yes, she was a basenji. She always messed up *k* and *t*."

In all fairness, they were quite similar.

"The obituary you wrote in the *Yale Alumni Magazine* was perfect," I tell him.

Wyatt studies me. "So the alumni association was able to track you down."

I hear all the words he is not saying: *He* couldn't. Or maybe he never tried.

Lightening my tone, I shrug. "I think Yale would call out the CIA to find alums, just for the capital giving campaigns." Then I look up at him. "It must have been hard for you. When Dumphries died."

"I spent a lot of nights wishing for his position," Wyatt admits. "But I've spent more nights wishing that I'd had several more years to learn from him first. I was thirty-six when I took over as the head of the department. It's been seven years and there's a good percentage of the Egyptology community that thinks I'm still cutting my teeth in the field."

"Publishing the new tomb should shut them all up."

Wyatt raises a brow. "Such loyalty."

"I'm trying to impress my new boss."

He laughs. "You know, there was a time when you would have gotten on the first plane rather than let me give you orders."

He has no idea how close to the bone his words strike. I force myself to meet his gaze. "I know you went out of your way for this. For me." I hesitate. Now is the moment of reckoning; now is when I need to tell Wyatt why I am here. But it feels like the truth is at the top of a mountain, and I am standing at the bottom.

I am saved by the arrival of a waiter, who approaches us impatiently, as if we are the ones who kept *him* waiting. Wyatt asks for a Coke, and the waiter turns to me. "Can I have bottled water?" I ask.

The waiter shrugs dispassionately. "Why not." He walks to a

cooler and takes out a bottle, hands it to me. As Wyatt orders baba ghanoush and hummus, I twist the cap and accidentally spill water all over the waiter. He drops his pen, looks at me sourly, and heads back to the kitchen to place—and probably cook—our order.

Wyatt mops up the table with a paper towel. "An Egyptian would say if you spill water on someone, you won't speak to them again."

"I'm ninety-nine percent sure that waiter didn't want to speak to me again anyway."

"Are you still superstitious?" he asks. "Like your mom?"

Surprised, I glance at him. "I can't believe you remember that."

"I remember everything." His voice is low, soft. It pulls at me. "Dawn. Ghosts don't reappear after fifteen years. What's going on?"

People do not get to rewind their lives, to rewrite the outcome. We make our beds, and we lie in them. Literally, in my case.

I have had a good life. I have loved, and have been loved. I have helped people. I've found a career—maybe not the one I intended, but one that has been rewarding all the same. If I die today, I would be able to say with honesty that I left this world a tiny bit better than how I found it.

I have had a good life. But, maybe, I could have had a great one.

How do I tell the man I left behind that I think I might have made a mistake?

"I'm not here to finish my dissertation," I confess.

Wyatt nods, his eyes never leaving my face. "Then why come to Egypt?"

*Because*, I think. *You're here.*

*Because I didn't get to see how this might have turned out. How I might have turned out.*

*Because if there is a garden of maybes, you are the invasive plant I can't ever get rid of.*

But instead, I shake my head. "I don't know. My life is chaos."

Wyatt is silent for so long that I think I've offended him. Maybe I seem like a whiny woman in the throes of a midlife crisis, or a bored housewife. Then Wyatt idly picks up the pen that the waiter left behind. "Does he know you're here?"

I know who he is talking about. I shake my head.

Wyatt begins doodling on a folded piece of paper towel. "Chaos isn't such a bad place," he says, and he excuses himself to go to the bathroom.

On the napkin, he has drawn the hieroglyphic signs that write *nun*.

*Chaotic waters,* I translate, surprised that I can still decipher this. It could be referring to rain, or it could be referring to inundation. It can be positive, like when the Nile floods and waters the crops. Or it can be devastating, and demolish a city. Ancient Egyptians believed that the first and most necessary ingredient in the universe was chaos. It could sweep you away, but it was also the place from which all things start anew.

BECAUSE THE DIG House is not full of grad students as it would be during a true season, there is space for me. Harbi sets up a room down the hall from where I stayed fifteen years ago. When I step inside, there is a clean Disney Princess mattress on the bed frame, and a stack of folded white sheets. A flat pillow sits, thin-lipped, at the head of the bed. Someone has found me a tiny tube of toothpaste. The clothes I arrived in are folded neatly on the nightstand.

"Thank you," I tell Harbi. I sit down as he closes the door behind himself, and run my palm over Cinderella and Prince Charming, Beauty and the Beast, Aurora and Prince Phillip, Ariel and Prince Eric. All these happily ever afters.

I snap the fitted sheet over the mattress, erasing them. A small cloud of dust rises as I make the bed, and I cough a little as I lie down and stare at the ceiling.

There's a water mark in the shape of Ohio, and I wonder if the pipes burst at some point. When I had been here during the season, we'd trudge back to the Dig House and race to be the first to take a shower before the electricity cut out, gingerly stepping into the stall because the water was so brutally hot—you could actually see the fire when the heater turned on in the boiler. Shaving my legs had been physically painful, and I could remember waving the razor in the air to cool it down before setting it on my skin. The water spread all over the floor, so you'd have to squeegee it to the drain before relinquishing the bathroom to the next person.

Then I would sit with the pottery specialists as they sifted through buckets of curated sand, talking to the younger grad students who tried to put broken sherds together like a three-dimensional puzzle; or I'd pass time with the bone specialists going through the huge backlog of material in the magazine. Excavation is often fast, but analysis is slow.

Since there was no television, in the evenings Dumphries would do dramatic readings aloud from a Jackie Collins novel. I remember how it wasn't until I came to Egypt for a dig with him that I began to think of him as human, rather than as a demigod. In close proximity, you couldn't help but see someone's eccentricities and flaws—the way Dumphries took six sugars in his morning coffee or snored loud enough to wake Osiris, or how he giggled when he read the word *erection* in *Hollywood Wives*.

When I came to Egypt each season, I'd brought the fattest books I could find, hoping to make my entertainment last. My first season was Russian lit, my second season was David Foster Wallace. In 2003, I was reading fantasy.

One afternoon, Wyatt poked his head into my room as I was lying on my bed with one of my novels. "What are you doing?" he asked.

I didn't even let my eyes flicker from the page. "Skydiving," I said.

"Science fiction?" he asked, looking at the cover.

"Fantasy."

"There's a difference?"

I didn't answer, hoping he would just go away.

"What's it about?" Wyatt asked, coming in and sitting on the edge of the bed.

It was a love story, but I wasn't about to give Wyatt that weapon.

"Two brothers," I told him. "One who is raised to be a king, and one who finds out *in this chapter* that he's the true heir." Wyatt didn't take the hint. Instead, he plucked the book out of my hand. "Hey!"

He scrolled through it, his eyes lighting on the paragraphs I'd underlined. I always did that in books, when authors found ways to say the things I never could. " 'You can plan for something your whole life, and still get taken by surprise,' " he mused. " 'And you can experience an earthquake and deal with it like you were born to have the ground vanish beneath you.' " He cut me a glance. "I guess that's the moral of your story. You never know."

He had tossed the book lightly at me, but it was so thick that when it landed on my belly, I grunted. He was gone before I could ask him what he meant.

Now I don't have any novels for diversion. I could finish reading Wyatt's dissertation, I suppose. Given the fact that he's just hired me, it wouldn't be a bad idea.

I pad through the Dig House, which is dark and empty. I can hear tinny radio music in the personal living quarters of the Egyptians, and smell the faint scent of smoke. In the library, the stack of books I had set on the floor is exactly where I left them. I slide Wyatt's bound dissertation under my arm.

"What are you doing?"

The unexpected voice makes me jump. I turn around to find Alberto staring at me, his hands in his pockets.

"Finding something to read?" I say, but even I hear the question mark in my own words, as if I'm guilty of something.

Alberto's eyes are dark and assessing. He looks at the book tucked under my arm and then back at my face. "So you're on the payroll now."

"Well. Sort of. I mean, I don't expect to get paid. That's not why I'm here."

*Then why are you?* He doesn't say it. He doesn't have to.

There is something unsettling about the silence he's wrapped me in, like the unwitting fly caught in the spider's web. I know he's uncomfortable with me being here. I just can't figure out why, unless it's because he thinks I will slow down their progress.

Well. If that's the case, then the best thing I can do is to prove to Alberto I'm a hard worker. I produce a smile. "Big day tomorrow. I'm off to bed."

I can feel him watching me as I make my way back down the hall to my room.

I reach for my clothing on the nightstand and fumble for the phone in the pocket of my cargo pants. I turn it on, but there is no signal.

There's a soft knock, and the door opens before I can respond. Wyatt leans in, his face limned in shadows, his eyes an abiding blue. He sees me holding the phone.

I feel my cheeks flush with heat. "Guess I should have upgraded to an international service plan," I murmur.

"You have everything you need?" he asks politely.

I nod.

"Harbi will knock at four-thirty. Breakfast is at five in the main room." He hesitates. "I'm not going to go easy on you."

"I know."

His fingers tighten on the doorjamb. "I hope you also realize that choosing to hide from the world in a tomb that's bound to become a media circus may not be effective."

"Noted."

He glances at the book sitting beside me. "If you're looking for something to pass the time I have far better material. There's still some Jackie Collins around, I'm sure. Joe loves manga. Or you could try one of my later publications, after I succumbed to the joy of the Oxford comma."

"That's okay. I want to read this one."

He inclines his head. The moon, spilling through a window in the hallway, silvers his hair and deepens the lines that bracket his mouth. For a moment, I can see his future.

"Sleep well, then."

He says the words, but he doesn't leave. It's almost as if he doesn't know how to put himself on the other side of the door. Years ago, when he snuck into my room, he would wedge the desk chair under the knob for privacy, barricading us in, together.

"Wyatt?" I say, my throat dry. "Thank you. For the citation."

He looks up at me with such wonder that it is clear he included that footnote as an emergency flare, an SOS across continents and oceans. Finally, against all odds, it had found its recipient.

"You're welcome, Olive," he says, and he closes the door behind himself.

# WATER / BOSTON

. . .

HARVARD SQUARE IS dissected by roads, an ill-fitting puzzle. The university is sprinkled across the sections, with a cluster of Georgian brick buildings in the main yard. This summer, Brian is teaching at their extension school. It's good money and easy work, since the topics he covers are layman-friendly versions of the ones he gives to physics students during the academic year.

I slip into the rear of the lecture hall just as he puts up his first slide, and try to see him the way the others do.

Brian has jet-black hair, with silver threads only just starting to show. He's tall and lean and rangy, and I know that at least one undergrad wrote an ode about his eyes—something that included a shaft of sunlight falling through a forest, and about which I'd teased him for weeks. He wears a professor's uniform: wrinkled button-down shirt, rumpled blazer, khaki pants, Oxfords. He is the kind of guy whose collar you want to fix, whose jacket you want to smooth, whose hair you want to push out of his eyes, just so that he will look down at you, sheepishly, with a shared secret and a stealth smile that feels like a jolt to the heart.

I look around the lecture hall. Since this is an extension class, it's not just college-age kids. There are elderly couples, women in yoga pants, professionals whose schedules allow them to take a long lunch break. "According to quantum mechanics," Brian says, "you may well be immortal." He reminds me of a tiger as he paces in front of an audience that knows he is toying with them. "A very controversial proposal was put forth by Max Tegmark—from that physics department down the street." He means MIT, and that makes some of the audience laugh. "It's called 'quantum suicide.'" He clicks a remote in his hand and a slide appears: a ket bracket with pictures of an electron, a gun, and a kitten inside. "You remember the quantum state of the electron that spins both ways at the same time? The one that both killed and didn't kill Schrödinger's cat? Let's take that a step farther. Let's say that in this ket, we have that spinning electron, and a trigger, and a gun . . . but now, *you* take the place of the cat. If the electron spins clockwise, the trigger goes off, the gun fires, and you're dead. If the electron spins counterclockwise, the trigger doesn't go off, the gun never fires, and you live. We're playing Russian roulette with an electron."

A new slide appears on the screen. "We know that the laws of quantum mechanics say that as a result of this experiment, you'll be split into two versions: one who gets killed, and one who does not. In one universe, you leave your physics lab and go pick your kid up from summer camp and have a beer on the back porch and watch an episode of *Fleabag* on Amazon Prime. In the other universe, everyone's coming to your funeral."

He spreads his hands. "Here's where it gets really interesting. The dead version of you has no experience of where you are and what's happening. Because, face it, you're dead. On the other hand, the live, conscious version of you bears witness to the fact that you've survived the experiment. So the *only* outcome you will ever perceive, if you run the quantum suicide experiment, is the one where you live. You can literally run it a thousand times, and every single time—a statistical near impossibility—you will survive . . . because that is the only version of you that *can* experience anything."

He raises a brow. "Ironically, for those of you who are still doubting the concept of a multiverse, this experiment might actually prove to you that parallel universes exist. If there actually is only a single universe, you should expect to die half the time you run the experiment. But . . . if there truly are multiple universes, and you perform the quantum suicide experiment a few dozen times and *always* come out alive, you can't help but admit that multiple worlds or timelines *must* exist."

I sink back into the wooden chair, wondering if another version of myself is in a world where her husband catches her eye just then and smiles to see her there.

If it fixes everything between them.

When Meret was ten we took her to Disney World. I was most excited about Space Mountain—a roller coaster in the dark. But in the middle of our ride, our little car screeched to a stop. A voice came over a loudspeaker, asking us to remain seated, while a technical difficulty was addressed. And then the lights came on.

If it had been exciting in the dark, it was terrifying well lit. I could suddenly see how tight the curves were, how little space existed between the tops of our heads and the tracks. It was absolutely shocking, in its transformation. What I thought I'd been looking at was something else entirely.

Now, staring at Brian, I have the same sensation. As if the home we have created, the marriage we've settled into, the life we have, has had the lights turned on, and now I can see the grinding gears and steep drops and near misses that constitute it.

"You can take it one step further," Brian says. "If we assume that cancer, and heart attacks, and Alzheimer's, and anything else that might kill you is the compilation of a ton of cellular—and therefore subatomic—events, that spinning electron may or may not launch a gene that causes a reaction that will lead to your death. Die-hard quantum immortality buffs will say that we are all, in some universe, the oldest living person on the planet—having dodged all these genetic and literal bullets.

"So," he continues, "should you go and commit quantum suicide? I wouldn't advise it, for the same reason I personally have issues with Tegmark's hypothesis. Every time you run the experiment and survive, there are people who will see you survive, and who will think you're the luckiest bastard on the planet. But every time you run the experiment and die—there are people who will see that, too, who will grieve and bury you and come visit your grave. From *their* point of view, in the vast majority of universes, you're guaranteed to die. Here's the problem with quantum immortality: it's subjective, not objective. Even if you can prove it exists, you'd only be able to prove it to yourself—not to anyone else. To them, you'd just be a really stupid dead person."

He turns off the projector and faces the students again. "Questions?"

A young woman raises her hand. "How do I get to the universe where Hillary Clinton is president?"

Brian grins. "Unfortunately, you can't. You're stuck here now. The door is closed."

*You're stuck here now.*

If that's the case, if Brian is right, then I have to make my peace with the spot that Brian and I have occupied for fifteen years. There has to be value in comfort. When you reach into your closet, do you grab the new, stiff, unwashed jeans, or the pair that feels like pajamas?

"There's a philosophical component to that question," Brian continues, and I startle, thinking he has heard my thoughts out loud. "We don't get to choose the universe we're in, so no matter what kind of positive thinking or voodoo you do, you don't get to land in the timeline of your choice. The laws of physics say you just plod along and then there's a branch point, and you get funneled into one universe or the other. In other words, it's not free will. It's chance, based on however that electron happens to be spinning."

Suddenly Brian looks right at me. Until this moment, I thought that he hadn't seen me slip into the rear of the lecture hall. As it turns out, he's known I was here all along. He gives me a half smile, rueful and self-deprecating, as if I have caught him in the act of something embarrassing, rather than his livelihood. "Keep in mind: physics says that if something terrible happened to you, there would still be another version of you somewhere else. A version that realizes how lucky you are to have a second chance. So, we could become devotees of quantum immortality," he says. "Or we can live every day like it's our last."

Brian dismisses the class to a smattering of applause, but I hardly hear it. I swim upstream against the students who are dispersing. He is gathering his notes, and all the while, he keeps glancing up at me. He steps away from the lectern, to meet me halfway.

*This is how it happens,* I tell myself. *This is how we start over.*

I can take this first step.

Finally, I am standing in front of Brian. Silence bunches between us.

"Hi," he says finally, softly.

I open my mouth, but before I can answer I see a movement from the corner of my eye. A young woman with a dark braid, thick as a fist, hovers at the edge of our conversation. She is holding Brian's battered leather briefcase like it's the Holy Grail. "If you're late to the department meeting again, I'm not going to take the fall for you," she says to him. It is as if I'm invisible.

All I can smell is roses.

BRIAN'S GRANDMOTHER LEARNED English by watching *Gone with the Wind* over and over at a movie theater. I tried to imagine what it felt like to wind up in a country where you could not speak the language. After being in Egypt for the season, immersed in my doctoral research, coming back to Boston to watch my mother die wasn't all that different.

On our first date, Brian told me that his grandmother had survived the Nazi occupation of Poland, a work camp called Pionki, a sorting line at Auschwitz, and typhus in Bergen-Belsen. I watched him tear a sourdough roll into quarters and sipped from my second glass of wine as he told me stories about her. "At Pionki, there weren't supposed to be children. It was a labor camp, and children weren't strong enough to do the work. But there was one couple from her village who had a little five-year-old, Tobie. They couldn't stand the thought of being separated from her, so they smuggled her in. My grandmother knew that if Tobie was found, she and her parents would be punished, and probably killed. And she wouldn't let that happen."

"Jesus," I breathed. I tried to reconcile the tiny, birdlike skeleton in the hospice bed with this flesh-and-blood younger version being painted for me by Brian.

"My grandmother spoke fluent German, and because of that, she got to do office work instead of physical labor. This meant she could see the Nazi supervisors coming and going. So she made Tobie play a game—if my grandmother hung a white scarf outside the office, Tobie had to promise to hide herself so well her own parents couldn't even find her. She couldn't come out until the white scarf—and the Nazis—was gone."

I leaned forward. "What happened?"

Brian shrugged. The flame of a candle danced between us. "She got moved to Auschwitz and lost track of Tobie and her parents."

"That's a terrible ending," I told him.

"Who said I was finished?" Brian said. "Fast forward to 1974. The war's long over, and my grandmother's visiting my mother in New York City, who's pregnant with me—"

"Aww." I settled my chin on my fist and looked at him. I was a little drunk, which was the loveliest alternative to how I'd felt for the past two weeks at my mother's deathbed.

"My mom dragged my grandmother to Saks to buy maternity clothes. But my grandmother got tired, so she sat down in the shoe department to wait for my mom to finish shopping. She was just minding her own business when she saw a woman staring at her. And staring. And staring."

Like I was, now. Brian was not handsome, he was cute. He had edges that needed to be smoothed, and a smile that was crooked. Looking at him was not like stepping outside, unprepared, into a heat that took my breath away. It was more like being able, finally, to exhale.

"The woman came up to her and said, *Forgive me . . . ?*"

I blinked. *Forgive me.*

Suddenly I was not in a little Italian restaurant; I was not holding the stem of a wineglass. I was in a place where the atmosphere had a pulse, where there were stars I could not see in Boston.

I was with someone else.

But Brian, of course, knew none of this.

"The woman asked my grandmother if she had been in Pionki. My grandma said yes, but she didn't recognize the woman."

"It was Tobie!" I said, shaking myself back into the conversation.

"Yeah. But she wasn't five anymore, obviously." Brian smiled at me. "They've stayed in touch all this time. She visited my grand-mother about a week before you came to the hospice."

I took a long drink of my wine and focused on Brian. "So you noticed when I showed up."

"September fourth, just after ten A.M.," Brian said. "Which sounds way creepier out loud than it did in my head."

I wondered what it would be like starting over in Boston, after Egypt. I wondered if Brian's grandmother had woken up for years after her liberation, panicked and bitter as memories of her prewar life grew harder and harder to recall.

When Alzheimer's came at the end, was it actually a blessing?

Suddenly I wanted to cram my brain with details that had nothing to do with the Book of Two Ways or what Wyatt Armstrong looked like when he was asleep, and a dream was chasing him.

"What's your middle name?" I demanded.

"Rhett." Brian laughed. "My grandmother didn't just love *Gone with the Wind*. She got my mom to love it, too."

"Look at the bright side," I said. "You might have been Ashley."

Brian grinned. "Brussels sprouts. Yay or nay?"

"Yay," I told him. "But God save me from celery."

"Who doesn't like celery?"

"It's what *sad* people eat. It has no taste and it's hard labor for your jaw," I insisted. "First pet?"

"Komodo dragon," Brian said.

"Why am I not surprised?"

"In a world full of elementary school kids with hamsters, I was an original." He narrowed his eyes, thinking hard. "Theme song you know by heart?"

"*M\*A\*S\*H*," I replied. "Used to watch reruns with my mom. How about you?"

"*The Facts of Life*," Brian said. "Don't judge me."

We kept this up through the main course, a shared tiramisu, and a second bottle of wine. I learned that he could tie a cherry stem into a knot with his tongue. I told him I could whistle through my thumbs. By that time, the room was soft at the edges, and we were the only diners left.

"When was the last time you sang?" I challenged.

He ducked his head, smiling a little. "To my grandmother. She's the only person who thinks I'm a decent baritone." Brian drained his wineglass. "Okay, what's your best cocktail party random fact?"

"When the mummy of Ramesses II was sent to France in the 1970s, he got his own passport, and the occupation was listed as *King/Deceased*."

Brian burst out laughing. "That is so, so good."

The waiter appeared with the check. I couldn't imagine how expensive it was; I never ordered bottles of wine, only glasses. But I reached for the little leather folder anyway, only to be stopped by Brian, who grasped my wrist. "Please. My treat," he insisted, but he didn't let go, and his fingers tangled with mine.

I nodded, accepting his offer. "Well, don't leave me hanging," I said. "What's *your* fact?"

Brian stroked his thumb over the back of my knuckles, watching, as if he were certain I would vanish beneath his touch. "M&M's stands for Mars and Murrie," he said quietly. "My grandfather Carl's pension came from Mars, and as a kid, I used to think that was amazing—that he got checks from outer space." He took a fan of twenties out of his wallet and set it on top of the bill. "If you could go anywhere when you blink your eyes," he asked, "where would you be?"

"Egypt." The answer came as easily as my next heartbeat. "How about you?"

"Wherever you went, when you blinked," Brian said.

I felt as if I had been transformed. When was the last time I had smiled, laughed, had a normal conversation? Waiting for my mother's death was like a slow suffocation; I had been holding my breath for weeks. In this moment with Brian, I could escape. I wasn't a girl whose mother was dying. I wasn't a grad student whose future had been upended. I hadn't left a relationship halfway across the globe.

I was just someone who needed to forget the real world for a little while.

In retrospect, I was probably not being fair to Wyatt *or* to Brian. I was not thinking clearly. In fact, I was actively trying *not* to think.

We went back to the house he shared with his grandmother, who of course was not there. His room was painted in shades of gray and his sheets were charcoal. Then we were facing each other, naked, tangled at the ankles. His palms bracketed me, and I thought of his physicist's ket, the quantum state of how a thing is. "I've never done this before," Brian confessed. "Does that matter to you?"

"I have," I told him. "Does that matter to *you*?"

He smiled his sideways smile, then. "Well, one of us should know how to steer this thing," he said, and he rose over me. His hair, like the feathers of a raven, fell onto my forehead as he kissed me.

When he arched like a bow I wrapped my arms and legs around him, as if he could carry me with him as he fell. It was too fast for me, though, and so I held on. I held him.

"Worth the wait?" I whispered.

He blushed all over his body. "No physicist worth a damn would run an experiment once and give his conclusions."

I smiled. "Tell me more about this scientific method."

"Lectures are overrated. I'm more of a hands-on researcher."

I remember that night. His touch was so different that where it should have felt awkward, it was a revelation. When I should have cried, I cried out. Brian traced my body, mapping me as if I were a new constellation, and his destination depended on navigating by it. That giddy thrill of falling, I realized, was rivaled by the discovery of a soft place to land.

I knew Brian would say quantum mechanics didn't support it, but I had jumped timelines.

I fell asleep with him curled around me, and dreamed of my mother and the tide pool exhibit she manned at the Boston aquarium. *Hermit crabs,* she used to say, *are too soft to survive on their own. To protect themselves, they find a shell that fits. They'll tuck themselves inside, for protection. They'll carry it with them, wherever they go.*


THE FIRST NIGHT Brian and I made love, I woke up in the middle of the night, slipped out of his bed, and wandered through the little house. I opened the medicine cabinets and read the pill bottles. I scanned the contents of the refrigerator. I picked up every photograph I could find, learning Brian's history by seeing him in a T-ball uniform, in a prom photo, at graduation. I touched tiny knickknacks on shelves: glass fashioned into the shape of an acorn, a brass mortar and pestle, bookends made of a stone that glittered as if it were weeping.

I looked at the books, too.

There was a full set of Hardy Boys mysteries and Isaac Asimov novels. *War and Peace* and *Anna Karenina*. Poems in their original Polish by Szymborska and Miłosz.

There was one book bound in tattered green cloth, a worn collection of Polish fairy tales. The spine fell open to a horrific pen-and-ink drawing of Jędza, skeletal, clawed, living in a house made of the bones of children she had eaten. She stole babies from their mothers, put them in cages, planted them till they grew plump, devoured them. I read the story of a young boy who was told to lie down on a pan, so that she could roast him. He told her that he didn't know how, and when she showed him by doing it herself, he stuffed the pan into the oven and ran away.

I thought of Brian's grandmother, reading him these stories after his parents had died. Of her liberation from Bergen-Belsen, when she was too weak to stand for the American soldiers who came to her rescue. I imagined her in the shoe department at Saks, as timelines crossed.

I thought of my mother, lying so still that when I walked into her room at hospice, I had to rest my cheek on her chest to see if she was still breathing.

Then I went back to Brian's bed and folded myself back into his arms before he even realized I'd ever gone.

In every fairy tale, the only way out is to keep running forward. To never look back.

BRIAN CATCHES UP to me as I turn the corner of Harvard Square where a long escalator leads underground to the T, like a passage to hell. He catches my arm, spinning me around. We are suspended in time at the point of JFK Street and Brattle, in front of the Curious George store, where I used to take Meret when she was little. I stubbornly refuse to look at Brian, staring instead at an enlarged cartoon image of the little monkey and the man in the yellow hat. "What was his name?" I say.

This throws Brian off. "What? Whose name?"

"The man in the yellow hat. Who writes an entire children's series and never names the main character?"

He shakes his head, as if that can clear the space between us. "Why did you come to my lecture?"

I force myself to meet his eyes. "You ought to be asking why I left."

The tips of his ears pinken. "Dawn. She was there because it's her job. She's a postdoc, working under me."

"That seems to be exactly what she's hoping for," I say. To my surprise, I feel tears sliding down my cheeks. "She talks to you like you're the only two people here who speak the same language."

Brian seems nonplussed. "She told me I was about to be late for an appointment. That's not a state secret."

"It's not what she said. It's how she said it." Like the verbal equivalent of straightening his tie before he took the stage, or wiping a crumb away from his lips. Like she had the right to lay claim to him.

He lets go of me, as if he has only just realized that we are standing in the middle of a crowded public place. "Can I ask you something?" Brian says. "If I *had* slept with Gita . . . would you be treating me even worse than this?"

When I was an undergrad at U Chicago, I'd gone out once with a guy to a movie. Afterward, we went to a bar, and then he invited me back to his dorm room. We lay on his twin XL bed, kissing, his hand sliding under my shirt. When it started to move lower, I sat up and said I was heading home.

He was at the door before I could open it, holding it closed and trapping me against it. He smiled, as charming as he had been the whole night. *You don't really mean that, do you?*

I don't know what it was that made my amygdala kick into high gear, seeing this as a threat, instead of a lazy invitation. But I was painfully aware of how much bigger than me he was, how much stronger, how I was caged by the brace of his arms.

I kicked him in the balls and I ran and I never spoke to him again.

I have not thought about this incident in over twenty years, but even now, I could tell you the color of the sweater he was wearing, what I had for dinner that night, his name. I could not tell you the movie we saw, or the name of his dorm building, but that fuzzing of the edges of the memory does not make the incident any less real. And yet, when it happened, I stayed silent. My friends didn't know. I didn't go to the administration or tell my mother. I was one of the lucky ones, after all. It could have been so much worse.

I gaslit myself.

Now, it is all I can do to force the words through my jaw. "You act like nothing happened," I say to Brian. "But something *did*. You made a choice to hire her. You made a choice to go to her apartment. You could have been with us that night. You *should* have been. I can't unthink that."

I leave him in front of a mural of Curious George holding the hand of the Man in the Yellow Hat. Stockholm syndrome, I think. How else could you be stolen from your natural home, and still call a kidnapper your best friend?

THERE WAS A three-week period where my mother faded away more and more each day, until there were times when I swore I could only see her outline against the sheets of her bed. It was during that three-week period, too, that the hospice social worker helped me to sort through my mother's financial statements.

During those three weeks, the spring semester started again at Yale. I received official word that I could take a medical leave of absence for the term. And I learned that we were in debt.

It wasn't just my education—although that was a large part of it. It was the mortgage on our house and credit card bills and the car we'd had since I was in high school.

I also learned that my parents, who certainly acted like they were married, never actually were. I had no idea why not, and my mother at that point was too unresponsive to tell me. What it meant, though, was that any military benefits we might have received after my father died while serving did not go to us.

I was almost twenty-five years old, I was $150,000 in debt, I was about to become the guardian of a thirteen-year-old, and I couldn't afford a funeral for my mother.

When someone is about to die, they spend more time *elsewhere* than in the sickroom—lost in memory, processing the tapestry of their lives, or unconscious and dreaming. I spent as many hours as I could sitting next to my mother. I told myself that even if she wasn't conscious, she knew I was there. What I really meant, though, was that when I looked back on those last few weeks, I would know that I had been there.

Egypt, at that point, seemed so foreign and far away I could barely envision it. There was here and there was now and even those moments were a senseless blur.

I did not see Brian very often. He never intruded on my privacy. But when I came out of my mother's room to get a cup of coffee, he was in the kitchen with a snack for me because I had forgotten to eat. When I needed to cry, he was there to hold me. When I left to go home to Kieran, he walked me to the car.

My mother died on a Tuesday. One moment, the world was a place where I had a parent, and the next, it wasn't. I remember feeling like something elemental was wrong, like I'd woken up and found the sky green and the grass blue, and was expected to pretend this was normal. She was cremated, and Kieran and I took a boat out to the Isles of Shoals. We scattered her ashes on the sea, and I like to think the tide swam her back to Ireland.

I began to settle my new life around me like a costume. I put the house on the market and circled rentals that would allow Kieran to stay in the same school district. I baked oatmeal cookies and took them to the staff at the hospice as a thank-you. When the director floated the idea of having me work there, I burst into tears in her office.

Then I asked her about Brian's grandmother, how she was. How *he* was. "She died two weeks before your mom," the director said, surprised. "I thought you knew."

I shook my head, thinking of all the times that I had run into Brian in the kitchen, in the halls; the way I had slipped out of my mother's room craving a moment with him, where I could breathe again. How every time I needed someone, he was there. "That doesn't make sense," I said. "He's been at the hospice this whole time."

The director raised her brows. "For *you*," she said.

IT IS VIRTUALLY impossible to put a price on a good death. Right now, death doulas are for people who can afford them, because Medicare doesn't have the good sense to cover our services the way they cover hospice care. That means I set my own rates—and they vary. It's hard to figure out whether to charge a flat fee or an hourly rate. If I charge a flat fee for an Alzheimer's patient who is ninety-four and whose sleeping and breathing habits have been changing, she may live for another two weeks . . . or she may live for another two years. If I charge $1800 and spend two years with her, it's not cost effective for me as a business model. But if she dies in two weeks, it's a reasonable income. I try to base my fee on the illness, the prognosis, and some gut sense of how much the client will need me at the end of life—but the truth is, I win some and I lose some.

I know it feels crass to talk about death in such mercenary terms, but that's the very problem with death in the first place. We don't know how to talk about it. We use euphemisms and discuss pearly gates and angels while glossing over the fact that we have to die to get there. We treat it like a mystery, when in fact, it's the one experience all of us are guaranteed to share.

I'm also painfully aware that having someone with you when you die should not be a privilege but a right. This is heart-centered work, and you don't go into it to become rich. I would do this work for free. I *have* done this work for free. I've bartered services. I took care of a nail stylist's mother and received manicures for a year. I got a side of beef from a farmer whose wife died of ALS. I have the luxury of doing this work because in spite of the fact that I run a business, I still have Brian's professor's salary to support us.

At my second visit with Win and Felix, they have iced tea sweating in glasses and small almond cakes. I hope they did not go to this trouble for me; I am supposed to make their lives easier, not more cluttered with things to do.

I've decided to take her on as a client, if she is similarly inclined to work with me. I keep telling myself it fits into my schedule well—I have several long-range clients with illnesses that will keep them alive for years, rather than weeks—but I know that there is more to it than this. There is something about Win that I cannot tear my eyes from. *There but for the grace of God,* and all that.

Felix is staring down at his notes. I know, for many caregivers, this blunt conversation is the first time they really, truly understand that the person they love is going to die. Not even the doctor's diagnosis is as frank. "Do we . . . have to sign something?"

I wait for him to look at me. "No. But I do have a secret handshake I'm going to have to teach you." His eyes widen and I smile. "I'm kidding. Yes, there's paperwork. But we don't have to worry about that yet. I'm as good as my word, and I am assuming that you are, too."

I pull out a small notebook and write Win's name at the top of a blank page. By the time Win dies, this book will be filled—with notes from our visits, memories, requests, medication logs. This is the paper trail she will leave behind. "If you're feeling up to it," I say to Win, "I'd like to ask you a few questions to start. Have you had a conversation about a DNR yet with anyone from hospice?"

She tilts her head. "DNR?"

"Do Not Resuscitate. There's a form for the hospital and one for out-of-hospital. It's something you sign if you don't want anything done, should you stop breathing."

"Like what?" Felix asks.

"Resuscitation. Calling 911."

"So you mean . . ."

"Allow natural death to happen," I say. "Yes."

Win puts her hand on Felix's arm. "Baby, that's the finale here. No matter what."

"I know. I just . . . I mean, what if there are other options—"

"On average, people who code and get CPR do live another eighteen months. But you'll be doing that with cracked ribs, because once compressions are started, by law they have to continue until you're resuscitated or you are pronounced dead. So . . . if you do survive, you'll be in pain, and we also won't know how long your brain was denied oxygen."

"And if I don't want that?" Win asks.

"Then you sign the DNR."

She looks at Felix and nods sharply.

I ask her about feeding tubes, ventilators, defibrillators—all life-sustaining measures—confirming that she doesn't want any of those. I talk about medical power of attorney, and financial power of attorney, about sedation, about antibiotics for comfort during UTIs or other infections. I talk about cultural traditions and funeral planning, whether she wants music as she's dying, or religion, or neither. Who she'd like to be with her at the end, and who she doesn't want to see. Just because someone is dying doesn't mean that they can't call the shots. As I tick off the items, Felix seems to draw further and further into himself, until finally I turn a bright smile toward him. "Do you by any chance have some coffee?" I ask.

He goes into the kitchen to brew some, and as soon as the door swings closed behind him, Win meets my eyes. "Thank you," she says.

I nod. "He's not the first husband to be overwhelmed by details."

"There are times I think this is harder on him than on me. I mean, I get to leave at the end. He's stuck here, reliving these weeks."

"I will make sure he's not alone. I'm here for him, too." I can hear Felix banging around in the kitchen. "Plus, this next part would have probably put him into a fetal position. Have you thought about what you'd like to happen to your body?"

"You mean like burial or cremation?"

"Those are two options," I tell Win. "But there are green burials. And aquamation—you put the body in a vat of alkaline solution, like lye, and all the muscles and fat and tissue dissolves, and then the bones are ground up and given back to the family."

"That sounds like how the Joker died in Batman," Win murmurs.

"It's not legal in Massachusetts yet, but it is in Maine."

"That's okay. I'm not dying to try it."

I raise a brow. "I see what you did there," I say. "There's also a living forest."

"Where I'm buried and a tree grows over me?"

"More like the cremains are used to mulch the trees. The hot new thing is recomposition—human composting. It's being pitched for urban centers where there isn't space for cemeteries."

"What about donating my body to science?" Win asks.

One of the things I notice most about talking to those who are dying is that they're eminently practical. They know they have a checklist to tick off, and many people are ready and willing and able to discuss it with objectivity, a weird dual state where they know they are the one who will be gone, but they also want to make sure they have the agency to decide how that is going to happen. One of the other things I notice most about talking to people who are dying is that this conversation rarely happens in front of a loved one, as if one of the last acts of grace you can perform with your death is to protect your spouse from the nuts and bolts of the process.

"Donating to science is definitely an option," I tell Win, "but you need to be aware that if you do that, a lot of stuff may happen to your body that you're not thinking about. True, you may wind up as a med school cadaver. But you're just as likely to become filler for lip and butt implants, or be a crash test dummy, or decompose on a farm in Virginia for students of forensics."

She shudders. "I do not want to wind up in someone's ass crack."

She means it as a joke, but that's not how I hear it. "When people say that sort of stuff," I begin delicately, "it tips me off that they think that body and spirit are one. That a part of you is still going to be here, after you die."

She raises her face to mine, and I see it: the awareness that the road just . . . ends. That there's no promise of anything coming after, at least not as far as we have proof.

"It's a bummer, if not," Win says. "I'd like to go to my own funeral. Eavesdrop on who's saying nasty shit about me."

"I had a client who wanted to be at her funeral, so she held it before she died. People gave eulogies and she clapped along with everyone else. She danced and she drank and she had a phenomenal time."

"You can *do* that?" Win says, shocked.

*"We,"* I correct, "can do anything. There's no template."

"I used to joke around and tell Felix I wanted Snow White's hermetically sealed glass case, until I went to the British Museum and saw the mummies. I don't think I'm enough of an exhibitionist for that, even if I looked good for being four thousand years old."

The last mummy I had seen was in the Egyptian necropolis of Tuna el-Gebel; the body of a wealthy girl named Isadora, who lived during the Roman reign of Egypt in the second century C.E. She fell in love with a soldier from Antinopolis on the east bank of the Nile, but her father didn't approve. She wanted to elope, but the boat overturned while she was going to meet her soldier, and she drowned. According to Ancient Egyptians, anyone who drowned in the Nile was automatically made *hesy,* or *the blessed dead.* Her devastated father built an elaborate tomb for her in the desert, a small stone building with crumbling steps. Inside the tomb were ten lines of Greek elegiac couplets: *To tell the truth, they are the nymphs, the water nymphs, who raised you, O Isidora.*

Isadora was preserved at the site in a glass case. I remember the smooth, resined bulb of her skull; the gap of her open mouth and the glint of her teeth, the pinch of a nose. The narrow neck, rising from the modest white sheet that covered her from collarbone to ankle. Her toes peeping out.

When I visited her tomb, Wyatt was with me.

I shake my head, dislodging his name, and force my attention back to Win. "Egyptians didn't get mummified just to look good," I say. "It was a way to control decomposition of the *khat,* the corpse. In order for an Egyptian to reach eternal life, the body had to last forever and house the soul. It mirrored the path of the sun god Re, who became one with the corpse of the Osiris every night before he was reborn the next morning."

"How did they do it?" Win asks.

"Priests would remove the organs—and put them in canopic jars that got buried with the body. There were gods who watched over them—Qebehsenuf, the falcon, guarded the intestines; Hapy, the baboon, had the lungs; Imsety, a person, protected the liver; and Duamutef, the jackal, had the stomach. The brain was taken out through the nose. The heart was left in place, because to the Ancient Egyptians, it was the seat of all personality and intelligence. Then the body was packed with natron, a kind of salt, and padded with linen, before getting wrapped in hundreds of yards of the stuff. Sometimes amulets and prayers and spells were tucked inside or written on the bandages. The wrappings were coated with resin, and wrapped again, and the last layer was a shroud. The whole thing took seventy days."

"To dry out?"

"Yeah, but also because of a star, Sothis, which disappeared from the sky for that amount of time before coming back during the annual flooding of the Nile. Death, rebirth, you get it. Then a *sem* priest—usually the eldest son—performed the Opening of the Mouth ceremony, which let the deceased eat and drink and speak and have sex in the afterlife. The mummy was put in a coffin or coffins, and the burial chamber was sealed shut. That is, until some archaeologist decided thousands of years later to move it to a museum."

The mummy room in the Cairo Museum is always the most crowded. There are tons of pharaohs there—from Ramesses II, to Hatshepsut, to Seti I, whose body is in such good shape that he looks like he's taking a nap. There's a mummified king who died in battle, who has a hole above his eye that matches a foreign ax blade. The whole thing always felt creepy to me—a stream of tourists who were basically Peeping Toms. "So much about Egyptian tombs was meant for people to explore and to celebrate their lives—but they never intended for us to see their mummified bodies," I say. "That was private."

When I finish, I realize that Win's been listening to my diatribe with increasing wonder. "What came first? Death or Egypt?"

I blink. "What?"

"That's your thing," she says softly.

"My what?"

"Your thing. Egypt. That's what made your heart beat. Mine was art." She leans back against the couch. "Do you know who Marina Abramović is?"

I shake my head.

"She's a performance artist. She and her partner, a man named Ulay, worked together. For one installation, they crashed into each other over and over again for an entire hour. They braided their hair together and faced away from each other for seventeen hours. In 1977 they inhaled and exhaled the same square of air until they passed out. In the 1980s, when I was an art history student, they did a piece where they sat across from each other and stared in silence for seven hours."

"I've never understood why that's considered art."

Win looks surprised. "What's love, if not art?" she asks. "In 1988, Abramović and Ulay came up with the performance to end all performances. They were going to start walking from opposite sides of the Great Wall of China and meet in the middle, and get married. They called the piece *The Lovers*. But while they were planning it, Ulay told her that he was having an affair with another woman. They broke up, but they decided to still do the Great Wall walk. Their relationship hadn't turned out the way they expected, and what was more real than *that*? So they started, almost six thousand kilometers apart from each other, with Abramović still holding out hope they might get back together. Three months later, they met up. But he wasn't walking toward her the way they had planned. He'd stopped and waited at a spot between two temples, because it was a perfect photo opportunity for when they reunited. That's when she realized she didn't want him back." Win shook her head. "Relationships aren't about photo ops. They're about scaling mountains and crossing deserts, about getting to where you think you belong, about having your partner's arms around you, and realizing that you don't fit into them. *That's* why it was art."

"Wow," I say, breathless. "You've convinced me."

I stare at her, thinking that there is so much more of this woman I need to know, and so little time in which to do it. I wonder what will happen, when we meet in the middle.

"Some pair we are," Win muses. "Love and death."

Felix walks in at that moment, holding the cup of coffee I hadn't really wanted. "What did I miss?" he asks.

WHEN YOU ARE waiting for someone to die, time is unrecognizable. Hours bleed into days; days are suddenly weeks. You might go several days without realizing you have not showered; you forget to eat. You sleep and worry and sit vigil in a world with no circadian rhythm.

After my mother died, I was so sick that I could not keep food down and couldn't sleep. I thought that I had grieved myself into some kind of autoimmune disease until I had blood drawn and a doctor told me I was pregnant. That's when I realized that while my mother was in hospice, when I had given myself permission to find mindless peace with Brian, I had not been using birth control with any regularity.

I thought about how to tell Brian I was pregnant, until I was knotted up so tight I could barely function. Every time I practiced what I would say, I could see my mother crossing herself superstitiously. *Go to a funeral pregnant,* she warned me, *and you'll raise sadness right inside of you.*

In the end, when I told Brian I had something important to talk to him about, I took him out to Boston Harbor, and we sat side by side throwing bits of Italian cookies we'd bought from Mike's Pastry to the seagulls. I said I was pregnant.

I didn't know, back then, how he would react. It's one thing to find comfort in someone else's body when you are both grieving. It's another thing to have a baby.

But Brian was incandescent. I watched the knowledge settle in him, the wheels turning in his mind.

For one awful, terrifying moment, I thought he was going to ask me to marry him.

I still thought about Wyatt, of course. And I had betrayed him, for sure, no matter that he didn't know it; no matter that I could justify my behavior as physical release and escape and a Band-Aid slapped over a deep sorrow. Yet with Brian, there was respect. And *like*, if not *love*.

But when I thought about Wyatt, he was further and further away, like an island with no bridges leading to it. Even if I'd entertained the thought of reaching out to him, finding out I was pregnant decimated that intention. I honestly had no words to describe what I had done. Why I had needed to do it.

"Dawn," Brian said soberly. "We're good together, don't you think? If anything positive could come out of losing your mother and my grandmother . . . maybe it's this." He reached for my hands. "Move in with me."

I let out the breath I had been holding. Brian was providing me with a way out. Blinders, so that I could see only forward, and not back.

"I already have a place you can stay. And I can help you take care of Kieran."

A practical arrangement, then. This would start slow. There were eight more months, after all, to figure this out.

I did not realize at that time that when you plant seeds, you also get roots.

He looked down at my abdomen with wonder. "Are you sure? Are we really going to . . ."

I had entertained the thought of going back to finish my Ph.D. Maybe not right away—maybe not for *years*—but in the back of my mind, it was still how I defined myself: as an Egyptologist, albeit on hiatus.

But Brian said *we*.

He was offering me a lifeline before I even realized I was in way over my head. So I grabbed on with both hands. I wrote Yale and officially withdrew from the Egyptology program.

I had not written Wyatt. He would have been back on campus by then. *I needed you*, I imagined saying, *but you were not here*. Never mind the detail that he might have wanted to be; that I hadn't asked.

There was no way to explain my actions without hating myself; there was no way the consequences would not involve Wyatt hating me. So every day, I put off composing that letter. And every day, it got easier to do just that, until I stopped thinking about composing it at all.

I moved Kieran and me into Brian's house. I bought a bassinet at a garage sale.

The next day I saw blood in my underwear when I went to the bathroom.

Not even a week had passed, and I was stunned at how fast an unsurmountable problem had transformed into something I wanted viscerally. When the radiologist at Brigham and Women's shrugged and told me that spotting was normal, I stacked the odds. I told myself my good fortune would not come at the expense of any bad fortune. I apologized to my baby for equivocating, even for a hot second. I slipped a newly minted penny in each shoe. I slept with a knife under my mattress, to keep away evil spirits.

I went into labor two weeks early, but all my superstitious behavior paid off. Meret was born plump and perfect. Her lungs were fully developed, and even when I stayed awake for hours to watch the rise and fall of the tiny cage of her chest, it was steady and infallible. *You see,* Brian told me, already in love with his daughter. *You had nothing to worry about.*


MERET IS IN her bedroom, bent over some kind of science experiment with swabs and vials, when I return from Win's house. "Do you want to take a walk? The humidity finally broke."

It's funny, you think as a mother that the very act of giving someone life should be enough to bind you to them. But just because you love someone unconditionally doesn't mean you don't have to work at it. I remember how, when Meret was first born, she would turn to the sound of my voice as if it were a lodestone. Since every conversation I had while I was pregnant was a soundtrack to her, that instant recognition was guaranteed. On the other hand, Brian started at a disadvantage. He had to spend hours talking to her, not like she was a baby, but like she was a very tiny adult. He carried her around in a backpack as he mowed the lawn; he fed her strained peaches as he described what he was doing in his lab. He saw the distance between them and he coaxed and beckoned and engaged until she came closer.

What I did not realize at the time is that every step she took toward him was one further away from me.

Do not get me wrong—I would not erase the bond Meret and Brian have, not for the world. But I have made a career out of being with people who, by definition, are going to leave me. Sometimes I wonder if I am destined for that in all my relationships.

She looks at me suspiciously. "You want to take a walk."

"Yeah. I've been sitting for hours. And you've been at camp, so we haven't spent a lot of time together." I hesitate. "I miss you."

"I don't see how. I'm pretty big to overlook."

Her words fall like an ax. "Meret—"

"We could go to a movie. Or start a mother-daughter book club. There's a lot we could do that doesn't involve me exercising so you don't have to look at your disgusting, fat pig of a daughter—"

"Meret!" Hearing her break her own heart is breaking mine. "Stop it!"

When I was pregnant with Meret, she would kick so fiercely that sometimes I had to lean against a wall or take deep breaths. I used to tell Brian she clearly wasn't comfortable in my skin. She still isn't, in her own.

"I love you," I tell her fiercely, and I hope it's every bit as loud as she's screaming, silently, that she hates herself. "Please. Tell me what's wrong."

For a second, I feel her soften. I feel her on that threshold, deciding what would happen if we weren't squaring off, but side by side. Then she turns away, her attention focused on the vial in her hand. "Why don't *you* tell *me*?" Meret says. "You're so good at it."

THERE IS A guest bedroom in our house that doubles as my home office. I keep my laptop there, and files on my clients, and a futon couch. When I am with someone who's very close to the end of life, and my hours are round-the-clock or inconsistent, I move into the guest room so that I don't wake Brian up by crawling into bed in the middle of the night.

Tonight, though, I take my pillows and some extra bedding and settle myself in there just because.

I'm not sure what my endgame is here. Getting rid of Gita won't erase her; it's like the way the television burns like a phantom behind your lids even after you turn it off. It's possible, too, that Brian is telling the truth—he was on the committee to choose postdocs, but he may not have the individual power to remove one.

Or maybe this isn't about Gita and Brian at all.

Maybe this is about me and Brian.

Meret stomps her way through a silent dinner, where she picks at her food but doesn't seem to eat any of it—which makes me wonder if she'll sneak down to binge in the middle of the night, which makes me embarrassed to admit I was wondering. Brian doesn't come home and doesn't text. The house is quiet as a tomb.

In four years Meret will be at college and Brian and I will be rattling around here, forced to have conversations when there is nothing left to say.

Once I had a client whose husband had had an affair, yet they'd stayed married for thirty-five years afterward. She was ready to leave him but he swore if she stayed, he would do anything she asked. She thought it over and told him she needed to be able to ask him, at any time of the day, *Where are you?* and to have him answer. That was the only way she could get reassurance, and without that bridge, she couldn't reach the far shore of forgiveness. There were some days she asked him twenty times. There were other weeks where she didn't ask at all.

Although I am so tired I expect to fall asleep right away, I find myself staring at my watch as it ticks past midnight, 1:00, 2:00 A.M. At 2:30, when I hear the front door click open softly, I get out of bed and stand like an avenging angel at the top of the stairs. Brian looks up at me, purple shadows beneath his eyes. He hesitates, and then starts to climb, as if daring me to block him.

I don't. I fall away, like mist.

"Where have you been?" I hear myself say.

He doesn't turn around. "Does it matter? Aren't you going to believe what you want anyway?"

He sees the light on in the spare bedroom and his step falters almost imperceptibly. When he reaches our room, he closes the door.

I lean against it, palms pressed flat. I try to pretend that on the other side, Brian is doing the same.

MERET IS WAITING for me in the kitchen the next morning. She doesn't meet my gaze but bashfully asks, "Do you want to go for a quick walk?"

She needs to get ready for camp. I have a pounding headache from lack of sleep. But I turn in to her enthusiasm like a flower finding sunlight. "Yes," I say. "*Yes!* Just let me get my sneakers."

As we start along the reservoir, I hold up my end of the conversation, wondering what precipitated her change of heart. We talk about what we'd do if we won a million dollars in the lottery. Meret chatters about Sarah, about how their STEM contraption meant to shield an egg from a two-story fall won a competition, about a rumor that one of the counselors was related to Princess Kate. I tell her the story of Marina Abramović and the Great Wall.

"So what happened?" she asks.

I shrug. "They hugged. And that was that."

"That is *so* sad. I mean, you go all that way for nothing."

I look at her. "Do you think she should have taken him back?"

"No," Meret scoffs. "He cheated on her."

"You believe it's that black and white?"

"Don't *you?*"

Apparently, I do, because I'm still not speaking to Brian.

"I wouldn't walk three thousand kilometers for a guy," Meret says.

"I'm glad to hear that."

When she turns back to me, her cheeks are flushed, her chestnut hair is unraveling from its braid. Her eyes are gray, nearly silver, sometimes blue, storming along with her moods. "Mom," she says, biting her lower lip. "I'm sorry I was such a bitch."

In elementary school, when Meret was throwing tantrums at home, Brian and I went to a parent-teacher conference. We expected the worst, but we were told that Meret was the model of good behavior; never a problem in class. *Well,* Brian said, *if she has to have a meltdown, I'd rather it be with us.*

There's something to be said for being someone's safety zone. Even if, sometimes, it means a kick or a punch or a rush of angry words.

I slip my arm around Meret's shoulders. "Bitch away," I say lightly. "I can take it."

She starts walking again and looks at me from under her lashes. "I want to ask you something but I'm scared to say it out loud."

"You can ask me anything, baby."

"Are you and Dad going to get divorced?"

Well. That answers the question of how much she has overheard. I realize how silly I was to assume that, under this roof, she might not know that Brian and I have been fighting. I wonder if this is the reason Meret has been pushing me away, and then pulling me back, as if she can't decide between the two extremes. Is she so scared of losing me that she thinks letting go would be less painful?

I want to ask her how much she knows. But I can't do that without throwing Brian under a bus, and that wouldn't be fair.

I stop walking and put my hands on her shoulders. "Meret. I'm not going anywhere."

"But you left."

*You knew?* I think.

"Your father and I had a fight," I tell her. "But everything's going to be fine."

She scrutinizes me, as if to divine whether or not I'm telling the truth.

"Was it about me?"

"No!" I blurt out. "Never."

"Then what?"

I hesitate. "Money," I lie. "Married couples argue. And they get over it. You'll see, one day."

She ducks her head. "I doubt it."

"In the near future there are going to be suitors lined up around the block for you," I tell her. "I know these things because I'm your mother."

Meret stifles a smile. "You may be *slightly* subjective."

"Then remind me to say *I told you so*."

We walk back home in silence. Our arms swing at our sides, back and forth. On one of those pumping motions, I brush Meret's hand accidentally, but she catches my fingers.

She holds on tight.


WHEN WE GET back home, Meret goes upstairs to shower and get ready for camp.

I am at the counter, cutting strawberries, when Brian walks into the kitchen. "I'm sorry about last night," he says. "I wasn't with her."

"I didn't ask," I reply.

He nods. "I know."

There was a time when Brian and I had so much to say to each other—we would talk through dinner and over the television set at night and we'd lie in the dark with our legs tangled, recounting the bits of our day that the other had not been privileged to witness firsthand. I wonder if this new unsettling silence is a result of everything becoming a minefield, or if we have just, after all these years, run out of things to say.

The knife slips and I jump, startled, as a gash opens up on my thumb.

"Goddammit," I say, tears springing to my eyes. I suck at the wound, then hold it at a distance, watching the welling blood.

"Shit!" Brian says, reaching for a dish towel and wrapping my hand in it. "Hold your hand over your head."

I lift my hand obediently.

"Stay here," he orders, and he runs upstairs. It is a deep cut; I can feel my heartbeat in my thumb. I peek under the dish towel but blood wells fresh. I press my other hand against it.

Brian clatters down the stairs holding a box of Band-Aids, gauze, Neosporin, bandage scissors, Bactine, Ace bandages—armfuls of equipment. "What, no tampons?" I ask.

"What?"

"Well, you brought down everything *else* we have in the bathroom," I say. "Brian, it's just a cut."

He reaches for the dish towel and unwraps it. We both watch the blood rise again. I press the cotton down harder, feeling a little queasy, and he covers my hand with his own to slow the bleeding. "Maybe I need stitches," I suggest.

"It's messy, but I don't think so." He smiles crookedly. "And I'm a doctor."

"You have a *doctorate*," I clarify, a grin pulling at my lips. "Not the same thing."

"Dawn." He meets my eyes. "Don't you trust me?"

We're not talking about a knife accident anymore.

With all the attention of a surgeon, he spreads Neosporin on my cut and then wraps it with gauze. This he covers with a length of self-adhesive tape. When he is finished, my thumb looks like a snowball is perched on its tip.

I do trust him, I realize. I trust him to take care of me. I always have.

He positions my elbow on the kitchen table, higher than my heart, and gently holds my wrist so that it stays in that position. Which is how Meret finds us.

"Are you guys . . . arm wrestling?" she asks.

"No," Brian replies, as if this is ridiculous. "We're holding hands."

Which is equally ridiculous.

All three of us start laughing, and even though I am still bleeding and my thumb is throbbing, I can't remember the last time I have felt this good.

. . .

MY FIRST EXPERIENCE with death involved a dog, a black and white springer spaniel named Dudley my parents had before I was born. Dudley wasn't happy unless he was pressed along the length of you, his nose burrowed into your elbow or neck or belly. He was my playmate when I didn't have anyone else, and I would string ropes of plastic pearls around his neck and clip earrings onto his long ears, dressing him up for tea parties where I served him water in a tiny, tiny cup he struggled to lap with his long pink tongue. He slept at the foot of my bed and he waited for me at the front door, his entire body shimmying like a tractor trailer going sideways when he saw the school bus pull up to the curb. I made him birthday cakes out of peanut butter and rice every year. When my father was deployed, I sobbed into his fur, so that my mother wouldn't have to hear me. He was the kind of dog whose heart was too big for his own body, and so he continuously offered it up to me.

When I was eleven, I woke up one night to find Dudley standing in the dark on the carpet in front of the bed, just peeing. He knew better; I could see in his eyes that he didn't even quite understand what was happening to him. I mopped up the mess and didn't tell my mother. I knew, even then, that I probably wouldn't like what she had to say.

She found out on her own, by stepping into a wet patch when she was putting away my laundry. When I came home from school that day, she had already taken Dudley to the vet. I burst into tears. *It's okay to be scared*, my mother told me.

When we found out that he had bladder cancer and a massive tumor blocking his urethra, I asked my mother what would happen to him. I asked if I could come when she brought him back to the vet to be put to sleep. The vet did a double take when he saw me waiting in the car with Dudley. I sat in the backseat while Dudley snuggled close enough to get under my skin, and I fed him a cookie while the vet gave him a sedative. He fell asleep forever with my fingers combing through his fur.

My mother didn't try to rush me. For once, there were no superstitions to obey. She waited until I nodded at her, and then she let the vet carry Dudley's body inside. Instead of getting into the front seat of the car, though, she slipped into the back with me. *It's okay,* she said, *to be sad.*

The thing about death is that we're all terrified of it happening, and we're devastated when it does, and we go out of our way to pretend that neither of these things is true.

THAT DAY, WHEN I go to visit Win, she has a surprise for me. Sitting across her lap is a piece of framed Egyptian art on papyrus. "I've had this forever," she says, "but I have no idea what it actually means. I just liked the guy with green skin."

*Osiris.* "It's from the Book of the Dead," I tell her. "The Egyptians called it the Book of Going Forth by Day, which makes much more sense. It's all about how the deceased can get to the afterlife. This painting is a reproduction of one found in the tomb of Ani, in the New Kingdom."

The Book of Going Forth by Day contained two hundred spells, many illustrated, but tombs and papyri could curate selections, from only a few to as many as the tomb owner could afford. It was sort of like picking your favorite Bible verses to be buried with. They were written on the linen shrouds of mummies, on bandages, coffins, scarabs, *shabti* statuettes, tomb walls, and papyri. Some were straightforward. Some were specific—like Spell 100, which stated that the words were to be pronounced over a certain design to be drawn on a clean unused sheet of papyrus with a powder of green clays mixed with water. Only *then* could the deceased enter Re's solar bark in the afterlife.

"This scene is Spell 125, and it's really famous," I tell Win. "It's where Ani's heart is being weighed."

In the image, the deceased is being led into the Hall of Two Truths to have his heart balanced on a set of scales against the feather of Ma'at—truth. This scene—Judgment Day, really—was the one spell that was never found in the Book of Two Ways. There were definitely snippets of Middle Kingdom Coffin Texts that evolved into the New Kingdom's Weighing of the Heart, but I hadn't stayed in the field long enough to find that connective tissue.

"Why is he green?" Win asks, tapping on Osiris's white crown.

"He has a whole mythological history of regeneration after his death—it's a long story. His green skin represents fertility and rebirth. He's got a divine beard—see that curve at the bottom?—and he's mummiform. The lady behind him is Isis—you can tell by the throne on her head. She's Osiris's wife, and she resurrected him after he died, and protected his heir, Horus. She also helps the dead make that transition."

"So she's like you."

I laugh a little. "Well, I mean, maybe. But I have no plans to weigh your heart."

"What happens after it's weighed?"

"Those who are true of voice—innocent—get eternal life."

I run my finger over the hieroglyphs, reading from right to left, the direction in which they face. The spell starts in red—it's called a rubric—and the signs themselves are in cursive. "Spell for entering the Broad Hall . . ."

Win looks stunned. "You can read those?"

I touch each of the signs, translating as I go. "The red mouth is the letter *r*, and it means *spell*."

Suddenly I am back in a desert, grit on the nape of my neck as I carefully ink hieroglyphs onto a slippery curl of Mylar.

"The bird plus hill plus walking legs is *aq*, which means to enter."

I imagine Harbi scrambling to set a ladder up for Dumphries, who is complaining about the heat like a baby. I see Wyatt standing on the other side of the tomb, his teeth flashing in a smile over the shared joke.

"The quail chick, folded cloth, circle with lines, and loaf are *wsḥ.t—wesekhet—*which means *broad hall*."

The ladder Harbi sets up comes crashing down, and as I block it from falling on me with my hand, a piece of wood slivers into my skin.

"The two ostrich feathers, *m3ꜥ.ty*, are the two truths."

Standing outside in the blistering sun, Wyatt reaches for my hand. *Stop fidgeting*, he says. *You're going to make it worse.*

"Above the feathers are phonetic signs that say the same thing."

His hand is warm. He digs a needle beneath the pad of my thumb, rooting for the splinter. There is a bead of blood on my thumb. Wyatt lifts the wound to his mouth and sucks it away. He doesn't take his eyes off mine.

I stare down at the bandage from this morning's knife injury, as if it has started bleeding fresh.

Win interrupts my reverie. "You are *wasted* as a death doula," she says. "You could be teaching college classes!"

I shake my head, smiling. "I'll be a lot more useful to you this way than I would be as a professor."

"Do more!" She gestures toward another part of the painting, where a table behind Osiris has the names of the gods of the tribunal, and the hieroglyphs are in retrograde—they face to the right, but are read from left to right, in reverse, like some other religious spells from the Coffin Texts and the Book of Two Ways. "This part is the negative confession," I tell Win. "The deceased denies forty-two ways he might have screwed up in life." I point out the red arms with the palms facing down, the sign for negation, and the sparrow—which the Egyptians called 'the bad bird,' and which was a determinative for wrongdoing. *I did no wrong. I did not tell lies. I didn't fornicate with the fornicator.*

"And here I thought the Egyptians were so sexually progressive."

"Well, they were okay with premarital sex," I say. "There's no word for virgin in Ancient Egyptian."

"How egalitarian."

"Yeah, but there were conditions. You couldn't have sex with someone married. Infidelity was grounds for divorce."

"So that was the deal breaker," Win muses. She flattens her hand on the edge of the artwork, tracing the border. "Would it be one for you?"

For a moment, I wonder how she has seen past the façade I've presented, to know so much about my private life. I haven't even told her Brian's name.

"I think there are lots of ways to be unfaithful that don't involve fornicating with the fornicator," Win murmurs, before I can even respond.

"That's why there are forty-one other negative confessions," I reply.

Win sets the frame down beside her on the couch. "So that was it? You said your confessions and you got through to the next round?"

"No. You said four times: *I am pure, I am pure, I am pure, I am pure.* And then you had to be given a lot of detailed knowledge, like how to answer the floor about the names of your feet before it would let you walk across it, and the titles of the doors in another room. There were instructions about what to wear during the judgment, too, and what to offer and where and to whom. But if you did all that, and answered all the questions right, and had a heart lighter than the feather of truth, and you were nice to the really snarky Divine Ferryman who transported all the souls, you could wind up in the Field of Offerings, where you were given back everything you'd left behind—your loved ones, your pets, your backyard. Your souvenirs. The view from your favorite window. Everything that brought you joy during your life, but for eternity."

"That sounds . . . nice," Win says. She traces Osiris's crown. "What about the people whose heart was heavy?"

"They got eaten by a monster that was part crocodile, part hippo, and part lion."

"Jesus Christ."

"No, not for another couple thousand years," I say.

Win stands. I automatically catalog how steady she is on her feet, how frail her arm looks as she braces against the side of the couch. "So, Dawn Edelstein," she says, "a lot of people go through an Egypt stage as kids, and build pyramids out of blocks and wrap their little brothers up in toilet paper as mummies. But something tells me you never grew out of that. Are you going to tell me *why* you know all this?"

"I used to be an Egyptologist, in another life."

Win's eyes narrow. I get the sense she is taking stock of me just as thoroughly as I am taking stock of her, and for a moment I wonder which of us is in charge. "Do you *believe* in other lives?" she asks.

I picture Wyatt walking away from me, the heat rippling through the air to make him seem like a mirage, a figment of my imagination.

"I want to," I say.

# LAND / EGYPT

. . .

IN MY DREAM, Brian is trying to open the door to a parallel universe. In a gleaming lab, he sets up his experiment. He is going to send a beam of subatomic particles down a tunnel, past a giant magnet, into a wall. If he does it correctly, some of those particles will become mirror images of themselves, and will go right through the wall, proving that there's a shadow world cozied up beside the one we live in.

I see him flip the switch of the particle accelerator. I am close enough to notice his square-cut nails, the scar on his thumb from when he hit it with a hammer putting together Meret's big-girl bed. Then the knocking starts, like the metallic heartbeat of an MRI machine. I feel an enormous pressure, a thunderstorm caught in my ribs, and suddenly I realize why I am close enough to witness all this: I am trapped in that beam of particles. *Wait*, I try to tell Brian. *There's been a mistake.*

But he is too focused on his work to notice me. There is so much heaviness; my chest is caught in a vise. I remember Brian's voice: *We're all made up of molecules, like those electrons. If you zoom in and zoom in and zoom in, everything we do is explained by quantum mechanics.*

And then I am light, I am air, I am speed, I am nothing. I brace for the impact but there isn't any. I find myself on the other side of a mirror, pounding hard, my knocks drowned out by the steady rap of the particle accelerator. All I can hear is the banging.

*Whack. Whack. Whack.* And then: "Dawn?"

My eyes fly open. I am lying on a twin mattress in a room I do not recognize. I squint at my watch: 4:30 A.M.

I scramble to the door and open it a crack; I'm wearing a T-shirt and underwear, since I have nothing else to sleep in. I find myself blinded by a beam of light, and for a moment, my dream comes rushing back to me.

The light switches off. It is pitch black, but I can make out the shape of Wyatt, the white of his teeth, a headlamp on his brow. "The electricity's out," he says. "Here."

He pushes a spare headlamp into my hand. Immediately I am flooded with muscle memories of moving around in the dark every time the electricity failed during the dig season, which was often. I slip it onto my head, turn on the switch, and Wyatt frowns.

"You need pajamas," he says, and he turns and walks away.

It's cool this early in the morning, which is why we start work, as Dumphries used to say, at "the ass crack of dawn" (before looking at me and adding, "No relation."). The Dig House feels like a voles' burrow—dark and hushed, with scurrying in all its corners as everyone gets ready for the day. Without electricity, there's also no water, which means no shower. I find a wet wipe in the bathroom and drag it over my face, under my arms.

By the time I get to the table, Joe is already seated. Wyatt and Alberto are deep in conversation, but when I walk in, they abruptly stop. I wonder what Wyatt has said to them about me. I wonder why Alberto lifts his cup of juice as if it is the most interesting thing in the world and refuses to look at me. "Good morning," I say evenly, and I sit down as Mohammed Mahmoud brings food to the table that doesn't require a stove: bread and jam, honey, cereal. No coffee, because there's no hot water. The condiments get passed around, and I try to figure out people's morning personalities based on how they interact. Joe is chatty and cheery; Alberto silent. Wyatt scrolls through his phone.

Suddenly, the phone rings. Wyatt answers the call, stepping away from the table. "Omar's motorbike is broken," he announces. "He'll be late."

"Who's Omar?"

"The antiquities inspector," Joe says.

*"Per piacere, il sale?"* Alberto mutters.

"He doesn't do English till he's caffeinated," Joe explains. He passes me the salt, but I set it on the table somewhere between me and Alberto.

"You can't pass salt," I say. "It's bad luck."

Wyatt catches my eye and raises a brow.

I eat a piece of bread with honey, feeling too queasy to put anything else in my stomach. I have effectively begged or bullied Wyatt into letting me work at the site. But even if I manage to not make a fool of myself, so much has changed with technology that I might be completely in over my head.

"Dawn? Hello?"

When I hear his voice, I realize he's been speaking to me. For a while. Everyone else is staring.

"We leave in five," Wyatt says, all business. "Be ready."

I nod, my face burning. Alberto rolls his eyes, making no move to lower his voice. *"Santo cazzo Madre di Cristo,"* he says, and I don't need a translation.

Abdou, Mohammed Mahmoud, and Ahmed emerge from the annex where they live and begin to load up equipment, under the direction of Abdou, the *reis*—or head workman. I am wearing the same borrowed clothing I wore yesterday, the same borrowed hat. I stand awkwardly near the Land Rover, not sure what I should bring. Joe comes up beside me, handing me a pack filled with brushes, a ruler, a mirror, a flashlight, an iPad, and a portable charger. "You can use some of my stuff," he says. He takes a military *keffiyeh* and drapes it around my neck. I wind it around my nose and mouth to block out the sand.

Wyatt walks out of the Dig House and swings into the Land Rover. Abdou is driving and the back is filled with equipment. Alberto, Joe, and I follow its tracks. The sun comes over the horizon, bloodying the desert, as if the moon was massacred overnight.

. . .

THE TOMBS IN the necropolis look like kernels of corn, evenly spaced and lined up in a row along the *gebel*. The tomb of Djehu-tynakht sits slightly below the rest due to the infrastructure of the hill itself. As we get closer, I see the split in the rock face near the new opening, which must have prevented the other tombs from being built on the same level. Instead, the later tombs—like Djehu-tyhotep II's—were dug above it on an intact ridge of stone.

Seeing it now, I wonder how we never noticed it fifteen years ago. At the same time, I know exactly why: it was buried, because of all those later tombs. Their excavation hid the entrance of this earlier tomb from view.

As we get closer, we start climbing the stone steps that are washed with sand. I viscerally remember doing this when I was here as a grad student, and every time, it felt futuristic, as if I were the last human on earth, instead of peeling back years to be part of an ancient civilization. The Land Rover has already been parked and un-packed by the time I reach the tomb. Joe has told me that the main work of this season has been excavating the shaft and shoring it up so that Wyatt and the workers can descend safely. In addition to Harbi's family from Luxor, there are Coptic and Muslim hired men clearing debris from the shaft in a bucket brigade, passing the mate-rial from rubber *maqtaf* to *maqtaf*. The sand they bring out of the tomb becomes part of a giant pile that two men shake through giant sifters, to make sure there's nothing of note in the debris. "Have they found anything?" I ask Joe.

"A few barley seeds," he says.

They'd be picked out with tweezers, and put in a Ziploc for later archaeobotanical analysis.

Wyatt calls to Joe from inside the tomb. "The boss beckons," he says, and he flashes me an apologetic grin as he leaves me behind. I stop at the entrance to the tomb, suddenly close enough to see the hieroglyphs.

I touch my fingertips gently to the lintel, and stumble through the transliteration of the text.

*ḥry-tp ꜥꜣ n wn.t ḏḥwty-nḫt*
*Nomarch of the Hare nome, Djehutynakht.*

The last datable hieroglyphic inscription was written by a Nubian priest visiting Philae in 394 B.C.E., because even when the Byzantine emperor closed all the temples, he still let the Nubians come worship Isis. Then the entire language was forgotten for fifteen hundred years—until the Rosetta stone was found in 1799. Written in demotic, hieroglyphs, and Greek, it's an incredibly boring text about tax benefits and temple priests—but because it bore the same message in three languages, it provided the code needed to crack the meaning of Ancient Egyptian writing. In 1822, Jean-François Champollion published the first translation of hieroglyphs.

What he must have felt, being able to step into history and understand what was being said four thousand years ago . . . well, it's how it feels right now, to hold my hand up to carvings in stone, just like the artist who had set them there, wondering who would read them in the future.

The tomb is a hive of activity. I slip inside, staring around at the brightly painted walls. This is what people never understand about Egyptology—when a tomb is left untouched for thousands of years in a desert, it's not found bleached and faded and crumbling. It can be just as vibrant as the day it was sealed, if it is preserved well. The blood reds, the aqua blues, the mustards, the creamy whites—it takes my breath away.

One full wall is a hunting scene. There are fish in a cobalt pond, and more in a delicately wrought net. Hippos frolic in the water and on the shore, a lion is eating a gazelle as two crocodiles mate. There are ibises in the bush and geese flying overhead. Djehutynakht and his wife are off to one side; he's holding a throw stick—a boomerang-shaped piece of wood used for hunting. Turning, I step closer to another scene—this one with harpists and lute players, women clapping a beat, men dancing, and a dwarf spinning on his head to entertain them. Beside this are women spinning and weaving, picking and pressing grapes for wine, grinding grain between stones and baking bread in molds. To the far right are two donkeys rolling in dust, beside a *yuyu* dog, with its long tail and greyhound body. There's another scene with fighting—soldiers with shields and arrows, vanquished dead enemies with blood pouring from their foreheads. There's an elaborately painted false door for the *ba* soul to come and go.

The wall closest to the tomb shaft opening is a depiction of the offerings being carted in for Djehutynakht, and a scribe recording them on his scroll. The *peret kheru*—the offering formula—runs the length of the array of foods and gifts. Djehutynakht stands in all his glory in a garden of lotuses beneath a portico with faux painted granite pillars, with servants holding the nomarch's sandals and his parasol. Beside him are his wife, three daughters, and two sons. One holds a fat basenji with a bell on its collar. Rusty, I try to make heads or tails of the hieroglyphs, murmuring to myself.

"*iri-pᶜ.t ḥȝty-ᶜ* . . . something . . . *mry nṯr imi-r ḫȝs.wt iȝb.wt mȝᶜ-ḫrw ḏḥwty-nḫt sȝ tty* . . ."

*A noble and mayor . . . something . . . one whom the god loves, overseer of the eastern foreign lands, true of voice, Djehutynakht, son of Teti.*

"*smr-nswt*," I hear behind me. Wyatt is standing with his hands in his pockets, watching me stagger through the transliteration. "Friend of the king," he deciphers. "It's pretty amazing, right?"

I nod. "I remember seeing some of these themes before in other tombs at this necropolis."

"Well, it's like when you move to the suburbs and everyone has the same furniture because they're all keeping up with the Joneses."

"Or the Boston Djehutynakhts," I suggest.

He laughs. "Ready to earn your keep?"

He's already moving through the tomb, expecting me to follow. My eyes land on a hieroglyph beside Djehutynakht's wife, Kem.

*mry. Beloved.*

"You'll be making a paleography of the hieroglyphs near the burial shaft. They've been blocked by debris until now," Wyatt tells me. He turns to Alberto, who is setting up his camera equipment. "She's got Joe's iPad; can you send her the photographs?"

"Already done," Alberto says, his voice clipped.

I wonder again why he was so friendly when we first met, and now is formal and stiff.

Wyatt is already opening up the iPad and scrolling through photographs from different angles of the wall of the tomb in front of me. He unclips the Apple pencil and traces one of the hieroglyphs, just like he showed me yesterday in the Dig House. "After you finish, Alberto will digitally create a 3D model of the wall, with your drawings included. Don't forget to save your work."

Again, I'm amazed at how much has changed since I was last working in a tomb at Deir el-Bersha. In 2003, after we traced on Mylar, we would photocopy the drawing on a slightly reduced scale, and then correct all our mistakes by checking the black and white copy against the actual inscription. It took several seasons to finish a single inscription, and Wyatt and I had to compare notes to make sure our art was correct: *What do you think might be in this damage? What do you think is the shape of this sign?* To have the iPad, where a tracing can be immediately corrected, is a gift.

I wedge myself into a narrow space between the wall and Abdou, who is speaking in Arabic to a worker inside the tomb shaft who hefts one of the rubber baskets full of debris. "Any questions, ask Alberto," Wyatt says.

I make a mental note to not have any questions.

Abdou edges past me to climb down the ladder into the shaft. A moment later, I hear him calling for the *Mudir*. "Duty calls," Wyatt says. He sets a foot on the first rung of the ladder, turning back to me at the last minute. "Make sure you notate where each inscription is in the whole of the tomb," he instructs, and he disappears into the tomb shaft.

Wyatt never cared about the location and placement of inscriptions before, in relation to the entirety of the tomb. It's another reminder that now, he's signed on to my theories.

I touch the tip of the digital pencil to the iPad screen and watch a black line materialize. When it's too thick, I can redo it with the touch of a button. I enlarge the photographs to the point of graininess, and begin to etch pixel by pixel.

The first few hieroglyphs are rough. But then, instinct takes over. I find my fingers moving of their own accord, like the planchette of a Ouija board, demarking the beak of a cormorant and the ears of the Hr face. The language pours through me, water in a rusty pipe, coming clearer.

I lean back, rubbing the bones of my wrist, aching and electrified.

It is painstaking.

It is glorious.

I remember my mother telling me that when she was a girl, she dreamed in Irish. She would imagine herself under the sea with kelpies and merrows, and their silent conversations winged from mind to mind in the same ancient language that her grandmother used to speak. I thought she was lying until, during my last season at the Dig House, I began to dream in Middle Egyptian. I was always walking through the desert at night desperate for the sun to rise, my eyes straining to see the person in front of me. *Don't turn around*, I would say, in the ancient tongue. *Trust me. I'm still here.* But he never heard. Or he did not speak the language.

When my fingers cramp, when I lose feeling in my foot and need to shift my weight, I peek down the hole of the tomb shaft. I watch Wyatt, part of the parade moving rock and sand. I listen to his quiet orders. I see how he commands respect; how authority sits on his shoulders the same way the sun tangles in his hair, as if that's exactly where it belongs.

DURING THE SEASON, Professor Dumphries's wife would come stay at the Dig House for a week. We called it the Conjugal Visit, and it was a time of celebration. Bette Dumphries brought with her a case of French champagne and boxes of HoHos and sugared American cereal. When she was here, Dumphries was as happy-go-lucky as a demanding, mercurial genius professor could be. For the duration of Bette's visit, we put a plastic tablecloth on the scarred wooden table where we took our meals. We fought to sit next to her so that she could tell us incriminating stories about Dumphries—the time he was afraid of a bat that got into the bedroom; the way he once started a fire in a microwave and shorted out an entire apartment building.

On Bette's last night at the Dig House in 2003, Dumphries set a record player up on the roof of the Dig House, and we all drank Taittinger and watched him whisk his wife through a fox-trot. It felt gloriously old world, as if we had spiraled back to the 1930s, and we were no longer students but expats in Egypt, re-creating a slice of home beneath the stars.

It was after midnight. The other graduate students had slowly drifted down to their bedrooms. The unwritten rule to all this celebrating was that you could stay out as late as you wanted, but you were still expected to be up at 4:30 A.M. to work. That left Dumphries and his wife, still dancing to tinny Big Band music, and Wyatt and me.

There was no way I was leaving before he did. Even when you

didn't think you were being tested as a student of Dumphries, you were being tested—and I didn't want to look like a quitter. Plus, Dumphries had a habit of expounding on *everything* when he'd finished a bottle or two of wine. What if, in a moment of weakness, he revealed a new idea he had for publication and invited Wyatt to be part of the research? If I wasn't there, I couldn't reap the same benefits.

I poured Wyatt another glass of champagne. "You're empty," I said.

He narrowed his eyes. "Since when are you the consummate hostess?"

I shrugged. "Since the booze is free."

Wyatt must have decided that his suspicion wasn't worth the trouble, because he flopped down on an orange satin pillow and pointed up at the night sky. "Lepus," he said. "The rabbit."

"There is no rabbit constellation," I insisted.

"Of course there is. It's what Orion's shooting at." He looked at me as if I were an utter idiot. "Why do you think it's called the *Hare* nome?"

I faltered, because I didn't really have an answer to that. I was a little tired and a lot drunk and I didn't want to show any vulnerability in front of Wyatt or Dumphries—who was dipping Bette gracefully.

Suddenly Wyatt was on his feet, his hand extended. "Come on, Olive. Let's show them how it's done."

I blinked at him. "I don't dance."

"I'll do all the work," he said. "As usual."

He grabbed my wrist and yanked me up so fast that I had to clutch on to his shoulders or else smack directly into him. One hand bracketed my hip, one caught my fingers, and I was a phrase caught between those parentheses. When Wyatt started to move to the melody, I stumbled, and he immediately tugged me so close that I didn't have the space to falter. I had never danced with someone who was so good at it—strong, commanding. I couldn't *not* follow him. I spun where he spun. I stepped into the spot he vacated. He pulled me in his wake like a tide.

When the last strains of music hung in the hot air, the ghosts of the notes still vibrating in the dark, Dumphries bent over Bette's hand. He kissed it and she laughed, curling her fingers around his and squeezing in the kind of silent communication that comes with longevity in relationships. "To the young, we leave the night," Dumphries said, sliding an arm around his wife's waist. "And the remainder of the champagne."

They disappeared down the staircase that led inside the Dig House. "Well," I said. "We should go to bed, too."

Wyatt grabbed the last champagne bottle and popped the cork. "Why, Olive," he said, pretending to be affronted. "I'm not that kind of guy." He lifted the bottle to his mouth and took a long swallow, then held it out to me. "We could go to bed . . . or we could enjoy this fine vintage."

It was a challenge, and I was not going to back down from a gauntlet thrown by Wyatt, so I settled on the floor again. I took a long drink of champagne. "Where did you learn to dance?"

"The lovely Eleanora DeBussy," he sighed, looking up from beneath his lashes. "She taught me everything from body rise to the Carolina Shag." I rolled my eyes, and Wyatt laughed. "Eleanora DeBussy was seventy-five and smelled like tinned sardines."

"Why didn't you just say that?"

"Because it's much more entertaining to ruffle your feathers."

"I'm completely unruffled," I insisted. "I don't care what rises or who you shag."

Wyatt reached for the bottle and took another drink. "Just think. Right now, Dumphries is probably doing a slow striptease for the missus."

I squeezed my eyes shut. "I can't unsee that."

"Just goes to show you, there truly is a lid for every pot." He leaned back on the floor, staring up at the night sky. "Do you think they role-play? *You be Isis, and I'll be Osiris.*"

"Ew," I muttered. "Stop. Talk about *literally* anything else."

Wyatt passed me the bottle. "Poor Olive. So easily shocked."

"Piss off."

He rolled over, bracing his head on his crossed arms. "Make me."

I couldn't help it; I laughed. "You definitely bring out the kindergartner in me."

"Then let's play a game," he suggested. "Truth or dare."

The evening was pleasantly fuzzy, the stars burning holes in the blanket of the night. I could imagine at least ten dares I could give Wyatt, all in varying degrees of humiliation. "Deal," I said, passing him the bottle again. "Truth."

"What was your first impression of me?" Wyatt said.

"I thought you were an arrogant asshole. That was my second impression, too." I leaned back on my elbows. "Truth or dare?"

"Truth," he said. I passed him the bottle again.

"Craziest thing you've ever done while you were drunk?" I asked.

Wyatt was silent. Either he had passed out or he was going to forfeit. But just as I was about to tell him he had to spend the night sleeping next to George, the mummy, in the magazine, he said, "I brought a new car into Eton—which is forbidden—and crashed it into the burning bush."

"The *what*?"

"It's a lamppost. I convinced the head man it had been done by a bloke I hated. He got sacked and I never got caught." His teeth gleamed white in the darkness. "Truth or dare?"

"Truth."

"Last time you looked at porn online?" he said.

"Never."

Wyatt sat up. "My God, Olive. You're missing out."

"Maybe *you're* the one missing out, if you need to get off via computer. Truth or dare?"

He laughed. "Truth."

"How many relationships have you ended?" I asked.

"All of them. Because then I can't be left behind."

He seemed to realize, at the same time I did, that he had not meant to say the second part out loud. He ducked his head, running his thumbnail through a groove in the wooden floor, bright spots of color on his cheeks. "Truth or dare," he said.

"Truth."

"What's your deepest, darkest secret?"

*That I can't stop looking at you.*

Even when I didn't want to. Even when he was being a dick. Even when I was resolutely trying to ignore him—I was always aware of where Wyatt was, in proximity to me, in the desert, in the Dig House, in my thoughts.

The truth stung at my lips. "I changed my mind," I said. "Dare."

"You don't get to renege."

"Sure I do. American rules."

"That's BS."

"You're going to back down from a chance to give me a dare?"

He considered this for a moment. "Eat a bug," Wyatt decreed.

I got to my feet unsteadily, bobbing along the half wall that lined the roof of the Dig House. I found something crawling along the railing and without thinking too hard about it, I plucked it off and popped it into my mouth. "Mmm. The crunchy kind."

Wyatt gaped at me. "You just ate a fucking beetle."

I shrugged. "Tell me something I don't know."

"In addition to dancing, I can tell the difference between a dessert fork and an oyster fork and I know that you only pass to the left at a dinner table." It hadn't been an official question in the game, but I didn't interrupt Wyatt as he answered me. "Eleanora DeBussy taught dance, and also etiquette. And she drummed *Debrett's Peerage* into my head."

"What's that?"

"A very archaic and bullshit book about the titled gentry in the United Kingdom."

I remembered his friends calling him Mark, short for *marquess.* When I thought of titles, I pictured Jane Austen and gilded ballrooms and fat men in tails with quizzing glasses. Wyatt was frowning, lost somewhere inside himself, and he looked so miserable that I wanted to break him free. I felt an ache under my ribs, a shifting surprise at feeling more for him than just annoyance. "Hey," I said. "Your turn. Truth."

Wyatt cleared his throat. "Worst day ever?"

"My father was killed on duty. He was in the army."

He scooted to sit beside me, so that our shoulders were bumping up against each other. "That's truly terrible," he said.

"That wasn't actually the worst day," I admitted. "It was like three years later, when I realized my mother was never going to get over it."

I tilted my head back, because I didn't think I could bear to see the pity in Wyatt's eyes, and goddammit, I saw the rabbit constellation he had been talking about.

"My older brother died of Hodgkin's lymphoma when I was twelve," Wyatt said softly. "He was the Earl of Rawlings, not me. I was the bonus child and perfectly happy doing my own thing. It was the only time I've truly felt tied to anything noble. I mean, imagine being the child of a king who dies, and being named the new regent at the very moment all you want to do is burst into tears. My father has made it quite clear that I'm to get over this childish fascination I have with Egypt, to quit being Indiana Jones and come home and work in an investment bank and make gobs of money. But I never wanted that life. I want my own." Wyatt huffed out a self-deprecating laugh. "My God, *that* took a turn," he said. "What was your *best* day?"

I was dimly aware that we had emptied the bottle of champagne. "Every summer my mom would take my brother and me to Newburyport for an afternoon. There's a bird sanctuary out on Plum Island, and at the very tip of it is a beach. They only let a certain number of cars out there, so it always feels deserted. We'd watch the plovers nesting or walk along the water—it's so cold there, you can't feel your ankles after a few minutes. We'd collect the things that get thrown back from the sea—a boot, a fishing lure, once a whole plastic shipping container filled with canned tuna." I hesitate. "It doesn't sound so amazing, talking about it. But it was just the three of us, in a place where I only ever remember being happy, and I don't have too many of those places."

When I looked up, Wyatt was staring at me as if he'd never seen me before, and maybe that was true. Maybe I hadn't let him. "Truth or dare," he said. "Take the dare."

My teeth sank into my bottom lip, and Wyatt flinched.

"Dare." The word fell dry from my mouth like an autumn leaf. "Forgive me, Olive."

I felt a prickle of fear, the sixth sense you have when you know your life is about to be cleaved into *before* and *after*. "For what?"

"This," Wyatt said, and he leaned forward and kissed me.

The night tightened around us, a noose. Wyatt's hand slipped under my braid, curving around the nape of my neck. I tasted champagne and butterscotch and shock. Somehow, Wyatt was just as surprised as I was.

My hand settled over his heart, as if I could weigh it against a feather of truth.

Then I pushed him away, stumbled to my feet, and ran like hell.

BY THE TIME we break for tea at 10:00 A.M. I feel like I've been awake for days. My muscles ache as I stretch them, leaving the shaded comfort of the tomb for the blaze of sun outside. The *gaffir*, a painfully thin man with the face of an apple dried in the sun, brings us tea and pours it into small glasses. You would think that drinking a hot beverage in the desert is like striking a match on the surface of the sun—superfluous—but it turns out to be just the opposite. Somehow, the hotter the drink, the cooler your body becomes. "*Shokran*," I say, as he hands me my glass, and he ducks his head and offers a smile missing multiple teeth.

Wyatt is the last one to the tent, accompanied by the inspector, Omar, whose motorbike has been fixed. "Ah," the inspector says, his eyes lighting on me. "*This* is the one." I wonder what Wyatt has told him. He gives a little bow. "I am pleased to make your acquaintance."

He turns to Wyatt, resuming a discussion about how much longer it might be before they are ready to open the burial chamber. I try not to eavesdrop, but I realize Joe and Alberto are doing the same thing. When Wyatt says that they'll likely be able to get into the burial chamber tomorrow, and that Mostafa Awad—the head of antiquities—is coming, a current of palpable excitement whips between us.

"We've been at this for weeks," Joe murmurs to me. "Guess you're the lucky charm."

Alberto grunts and leaves the *gaffir's* tent.

In ancient tombs, there were public parts, and private spaces. The public space was where visitors could mill. The private part was where the deceased was actually buried. A shaft was dug perpendicular to the floor of the tomb, and then a small burial niche was carved out horizontally at its base. After a coffin was lowered down the shaft and tucked into the burial niche, a limestone slab or blocks would have been placed in front of the entrance to the chamber. Then the shaft would have been filled with sand and dirt, and another limestone slab would have capped it, sealing off the entrance to the private part of the tomb.

That slab was moved aside weeks ago; if Wyatt is confident that we'll be entering the burial chamber tomorrow, it means that the shaft is very nearly clear as well.

From the corner of my eye, I watch him down the glass of hot tea in nearly a gulp, and then clap Omar on the back. Abdou ducks into the tent, apologizing for the interruption, and hands Wyatt a stack of papers. "Three more hours and we'll probably quit for the day," Joe tells me. "It's too fucking hot to be here after two P.M."

"*Inshallah,*" I answer, and he grins.

"You ready?"

"To bend myself into a figure eight under a natural rock ledge? You bet," I say. "There's a reason grad students are your age, and not mine."

I'm following Joe out of the tent when I hear Wyatt's voice. "Dawn. A word?"

Joe raises his eyebrows: *Good luck with that.* The *gaffir* takes the glasses and teapot outside, leaving me alone with Wyatt. He is seated, and from where I am standing, I can't read his expression. Then I realize that he isn't holding a stack of papers.

"That's my iPad," I say, stupidly.

"Technically," Wyatt answers, "it's *mine.*"

Immediately my heart starts hammering. Was I supposed to bring it with me to the *gaffir*'s tent, lest it get stolen? Did he look at my work, and find it lacking?

Is this the moment he sends me home?

I watch him flip it open, scroll through the work I have saved. He enlarges one of the areas I have been tracing, one with considerable damage. In the back of his throat, he makes a small sound. "I can do better," I blurt out.

"No, you can't," Wyatt says, and everything inside me turns to stone.

He flips down the magnetic cover and hands it to me. "I have never seen anyone as good as you are at drawing hieroglyphs," he murmurs. "It's like you're a scribe yourself."

I feel blood rush to my cheeks. "Thanks."

"Clearly it's going well," he says.

"I'm glad I can be helpful."

"Likewise," Wyatt replies, tipping back the brim of his hat so I can see his eyes. "Although I still am not quite sure what I'm helping with."

Desperate to avoid this runnel of conversation, I clutch the iPad to my chest. "Sounds like *all* the work's going well. Do you really think you'll get to the burial chamber by the end of today?"

He nods. "We may even get some of the men to dislodge the stone blocks at the bottom. Although then I have to technically wait for Mostafa to get here before I can go inside and see what's what, and that may very well kill me."

"Technically," I repeat, and I know that Wyatt is thinking exactly what I am thinking—of another discovery, another inspector. Of rules that were broken.

"Have you found anything in the debris?" I ask.

He beams at me. "Nope."

All the sand and dirt that is cleared from the shaft has been sifted by the workers, in case an amulet was dropped, or if there is a discarded floral collar or a broken *shabti*. The fewer funerary finds in the rubble, the more likely it is that this tomb has an intact burial—a coffin with a mummy that was never violated by grave robbers.

"Wyatt," I say quietly. "That's . . ."

"Fucking amazing. I know."

I imagine how quickly his academic profile will rise, if this discovery pans out. I wait for jealousy to wash over me, but it doesn't. This isn't the life I chose to lead.

I find Wyatt staring at me like I am a crossword he cannot finish, even though he's read all the clues three times over. I glance toward the tomb, where a line of local men are back to excavating buckets of sand, the white sails of their *galabeyas* like the sails of a fleet crossing an ocean.

"You know," Wyatt muses. "To anyone else, the mystery would be the mummy eighteen feet under the ground. Not the woman who showed up in Egypt fifteen years late."

I swallow. "I better get back to work."

"No," Wyatt says, the word striking like flint. Then he takes off his hat and grins. "I mean, I'll put in a good word with your boss."

Unsure of what he wants me to do, I sink down to the ground, cross-legged. He is sitting on a little folding stool, as if he's the teacher and I'm the preschooler. "I guess this isn't quite your usual workday," Wyatt says.

"Yeah. And no," I reply. "I mean, it's not that different. The whole point of all this"—I wave toward the notched rock of the tomb—"was to prepare for a good death, right?"

"Amazing to think that's become a cottage industry."

"Why?" I ask. "Think of all the people who were employed building this tomb."

"So you build twenty-first-century tombs," Wyatt says. "They're just not made out of rock."

"Yeah. I suppose they're made out of stories and conversations and relaxation techniques and wills. Obituaries. Social media passwords. Did you know that you can designate someone to cancel your social media accounts when you die so they don't just keep telling everyone when it's your birthday year after year?"

"This is why I'm not on Facebook."

"I noticed," I say, and then clap my hand over my mouth as if I could stuff the words back inside.

A smile plays along the edge of Wyatt's mouth. "*Did* you," he murmurs.

"Everyone knows how to die," I say, shrugging. "But that doesn't mean you can't use a little support."

Wyatt glances toward the tomb again. "Let me play Devil's advocate, though. You don't need a death coach—"

"Doula."

"*Doula.* Not any more than you need a rock-cut tomb to become one of the blessed dead. If you couldn't afford to have texts painted in your coffin, you could borrow papyri. Did you know that I found dozens of soul houses in Middle Kingdom cemeteries, right next to graves of the poor that are basically pits in the ground—a little model of a house and a few offering vessels, maybe with an onion or a loaf of bread. The point is that *anyone* could reach the afterlife, too. All you really needed to do was live morally."

"Nothing's changed in four thousand years," I tell him. "The way to have a good death is to have a good life."

"So, Olive?" he asks quietly. "Did you?"

My mouth seems filled with ash. "I'd like to think it's not over yet," I say lightly.

Wyatt looks away, so that his eyes aren't pinning me anymore. "Well, as long as someone remembers you, you never really die." I think of the names on the calendar in my phone—the phone that doesn't work here. The litany of the dead I run through, daily, recalling one tiny detail of each of their lives: her perfect French manicure, his collection of foreign stamps, a beloved dachshund for whom she sewed bow ties. "Djehutynakht probably started building this tomb the minute he became nomarch," Wyatt says. "He's lucky it was ready by the time he took his last bow."

"Every beginning is already the start of the end," I reply. "I sound like a fortune cookie."

"You always did see the big picture."

"Wyatt Armstrong. Is that a *compliment*?"

He slaps his hat against his thigh. A tiny cloud of dust rises between us. "You were right. About the coffin, being a microcosm of the universe."

"I know you finally realized that. I read your dissertation." I lean down and pick up a flat piece of rock. "But still, could you etch that in stone for me?"

Wyatt laughs. "What you were saying all those years ago—it's just the tip of the iceberg." He stands, reaching out his hand to pull me up. "It's crazy to think about, isn't it? What might have happened if you and I had been working together back then, instead of against each other?"

I let myself go there, for the span of one breath: a perfect translation of the Book of Two Ways, with imagery and text interwoven. An understanding that the way to get to the afterlife wasn't just about the inscriptions, but also about where they were placed in relation to the deceased.

A map with two paths; a key we both crafted.

"Let me walk you back," Wyatt says. "We're not being paid to drink tea."

"Who *is* paying?" I ask. "Yale?"

He shakes his head. "They cut off my funding years ago. We've got a private benefactor now. Rich as fuck," he admits, "but that's sort of the way it's always been, all the way back to Howard Carter and Lord Carnarvon."

We walk out of the tent into the heat; it feels like stepping into someone else's mouth. "Aren't you sort of Lord Carnarvon in this equation?"

"Not if you're going by a bank statement," he admits. "The one thing that the Athertons have excelled at is gradually squandering the family fortune."

"Good thing you have Dailey," I say. The benefactor's name. When Wyatt looks at me in surprise, I shrug. "Joe talks a lot."

He sees one of the workers flagging him down, and his eyes flicker over my iPad. "Back to it, then."

I watch him disappear into a knot of workers, crouching down to look at something in a sieve. Instead of heading into the tomb, I double back, walking into the *wadi*. In the desert, this is the best you can do for privacy when you need to use the bathroom. I shimmy my borrowed pants down my legs, squat, and finish. I'm pulling them back up when my phone falls out of my pocket.

I pick it up and notice that, in this vast wasteland, there is a faint roaming signal.

I think of all the times I've told Meret to stop texting at the dinner table. I imagine her phone vibrating beside a bowl of mashed potatoes and her water glass.

*Home soon,* I type. *I love you.*

*Tell dad I will be back soon.*

I start toward the tomb, hesitating in the last shadow of the *wadi.* I think of what I've been tracing all morning. The last message left by a nobleman, who is now no more than dust.

I add: *Forgive me.*

THE DAY AFTER Wyatt kissed me was a Friday, and the reason I remember this is because we always had Fridays off. Dumphries was taking Bette to the airport in Cairo, and the other graduate students were driving to Tell el-Amarna to see the tombs of Akhenaton and Nefertiti. Normally, I would have gone with them—part of the joy of a dig season was using our few moments of freedom to explore other parts of Egypt—but Wyatt had announced at breakfast that he had to catch up on work. And no matter how much I wanted to see Amarna, I wanted to talk to Wyatt more. I wanted to tell him that whatever last night had been, it was never going to happen again.

He worked alone in his room all morning. I sat at the table in the common area, trying to figure out the three blank spots on a crossword someone else had already attempted, but mostly just waiting for Wyatt. When he did emerge from his room, it was shortly before noon, and he completely bypassed the common room. Instead, he banged out the front door.

By the time I got to the front steps of the Dig House, he was gone. I walked down the path that led to the Nile, passing small raised patches of barley and broad beans, but there was no sign of him. The other direction headed west into the desert, where we went when we were working. I frowned—he wasn't allowed to visit the site alone, on a day off—but jogged lightly into the ripple of sand and heat.

By the time I got a glimpse of Wyatt's white shirt in the distance, I was sweating and red-faced, cursing the fact that I hadn't grabbed a hat. I called his name, but the syllables were snatched by the wind.

"Hey," I yelled, as he tracked into a dry valley east of the necropolis. *"Hey!"*

Wyatt whipped around to face me. His eyes darkened, as if I were the last person he had hoped to see. "What are you doing here?" he asked.

"What are *you* doing here?"

"Taking a walk," Wyatt said. "I wasn't being productive."

"I don't believe you."

He smirked. "As charming as your faith is in my efficiency, I was falling asleep over the text. I needed some fresh air."

It was high noon in the desert; this was not fresh air. "I want to talk about last night," I said.

"Well, I don't." Wyatt spun on his heel and started off into the *wadi* again.

"I don't want you touching me again," I called out.

"Perfect." Wyatt tossed back over his shoulder. "Since I don't want to touch you."

I stood, watching him stride deeper into the desert. "Where are you going?"

"Wherever you aren't," Wyatt said.

His words set a fire in me; I immediately remembered what an arrogant dick he was. I didn't have to worry about what had happened between us last night because I was never going to get close enough to him for it to happen again.

Suddenly Wyatt stopped moving. He pivoted, his hands in his pockets. "I apologize for taking the liberty of kissing you," he said, so formal. "I could blame it on the alcohol, or I could say that spending all this time in tombs makes me atypically horny, or I could just chalk it up to an egregious mistake. Take your pick."

I didn't disagree with him, but I didn't particularly like being called an egregious mistake, either. Yet I'd wanted to get him to admit to that, didn't I?

And if he had, why was I still standing here?

"But right now, Olive, I have a hangover the size of Russia with a side order of self-loathing, and I'd appreciate being left to my own devices. Run along home."

For a moment I just stared as Wyatt turned and walked deeper into the crevice of the *wadi*.

*Run along home.*

Like I was a child, not a Ph.D. student. Like I was not equally as qualified to be hiking through this goddamned parched desert as he was.

"Fuck you," I said, fuming. "Fuck you, you entitled, condescending asshole." I ran until I had caught up to him, furious, hating that last night, for even a millisecond, I'd been fooled into thinking that he deserved compassion, that we were a team instead of rivals.

Wyatt turned, stumbling backward as my rage rose over him like an angry djinn spinning out of the sand.

I poked one finger at his chest, driving him deeper beneath a rock ledge. "I am just as smart as you are. I am just as capable as you. And I am—" My voice broke off, and I fell forward, brushing my fingertips against the granulated limestone beside his left shoulder. "Wyatt," I breathed. "Look."

In the little worn groove of the *wadi,* beneath a natural rock shelter that was shielding us from the punishment of the sun, there was a dipinto—faded ink on stone.

My heart thumped, out of beat. I thanked God for the class we'd taken on Middle Kingdom papyri—and all the Twelfth Dynasty hieratic we'd had to translate as part of the course. Unlike hieroglyphs, which could be read in either direction, hieratic was always read right to left. Wyatt spun around, his arms braced over me as I crouched, reciting the transliteration. He translated haltingly over my shoulder. "Regnal year 7, fourth month of Peret, day 14 under the majesty of the king of Upper and Lower Egypt Kha-kau-re, living forever and ever . . ."

I knew that the nomarchs of Deir el-Bersha had left commemorative inscriptions at quarries to the north of the necropolis at Hatnub. They'd been used by scholars to reconstruct family histories. It wasn't unlikely that, thousands of years ago, nomarchs might have stopped here, beneath this rock ledge, to celebrate something.

I scanned the next part of the dipinto, but it was fainter than the words at the beginning.

"On this day, the count, hereditary noble, and nomarch of the Hare nome . . ." I murmured.

". . . Djehutyhotep," we said in unison, having seen those signs dozens of times in the tomb where we worked.

This was the ancient equivalent of *Kilroy was here*. Except it was the nomarch whose tomb we had been copying meticulously for the past three dig seasons.

Wyatt rubbed his jaw. "*Spd.t*," he said, pointing. "He came to this mountain to see the rising of Sothis."

Other words jumped out at me: *Peret, day 15. Priests. Tomb.*

"I'm missing a few bits," Wyatt said, "but I'm pretty sure the gist of it is that he came here to party and stayed overnight in the necropolis, in someone's tomb."

"Djehuty . . . nakht?" I translated, touching my fingertip to the name of the tomb owner. "The ones from the Boston MFA?"

"No. A different Djehutynakht. Born of Teti." He read carefully. *"We spent the night in the forecourt of the tomb of Djehutynakht, born of Teti, which is . . . cubits from . . ."* Wyatt rubbed his hand over the back of his neck. "There used to be a measurement here."

We couldn't read the numbers, the damage of four thousand years was too severe. I turned to Wyatt. "Still. A tomb in the necropolis . . ."

". . . that hasn't been found yet."

The gravity of this—not just the discovery of a painted rock inscription but one that might point to a new, undiscovered tomb—knocked the breath out of me. Suddenly, my feet flew off the ground as Wyatt wrapped his arms around me and spun me around. "Oh my God," he cried, as I laughed. Then, just as quickly, he dropped me. "We can't tell anyone," Wyatt said.

"What?"

"It's illegal to be here without an inspector. We have to figure out a way to bring Dumphries here and pretend to discover this all over again." His eyes pinned me. "Are you with me?"

It would have been far easier for Wyatt to throw me under the bus—tell Dumphries I'd been off exploring where I shouldn't be, and take all the credit. Instead, he was offering me a partnership.

"I thought you hated me," I said carefully.

Wyatt ducked his head. "I *wanted* to. I *tried* to," he admitted, his words slick with frustration. "You waltz in here from U Chicago, and of all the things you could be studying, it's *my* thing."

I bristled. "You don't hold the monopoly on the Book of Two Ways."

"I *know* that," he said. "But still. Hardly anyone focuses on Middle Egypt."

"That's why I like it."

"That's why I like it, too," Wyatt snapped. "And I was good at it. The best, even. It was like being the only child, the golden boy. But then you arrive with your crazy microcosm ideas and suddenly Dumphries decides he wants *two* TAs that year, instead of one. He invites you to come on the dig, even though first-year grad students never come. Fast-forward to now, when he's grooming you to be his little protégée—"

"What are you *talking* about?" I exploded. "You're so far up his ass you've probably built a condo."

"Because I can't risk ceding any more ground to *you*," he argued.

I was roiling with the shock of learning that Wyatt was just as jealous of me as I was of him.

"Haven't you noticed that when visitors come to the dig site, you're the one he asks to give them a tour? Or he asks me to haul *maqtaf*s while you get to trace inscriptions? He notices you, when he's supposed to be noticing *me*. And fuck it, Olive," he said angrily. "I can't help but notice you, too."

As aggravated as Wyatt's words were, his touch was the opposite. His hand came up to my hair, rubbing a strand between his fingers. His eyes were the sea. *This is how people drown*, I thought.

This time, when he kissed me, I kissed him back.

IT WAS A rare feeling, being allied with Wyatt instead of being at each other's throats. We walked together to Djehutyhotep's tomb, trading whispers, trying to come up with a way to rediscover the dipinto and make it look completely happenstance *and* net us equal credit for the find. We tossed out a variety of scenarios, but ultimately decided the best way was to replicate exactly what had happened: Wyatt wandering off, me spotting the ink on stone.

The next morning we worked in the outer chamber, tracing on Mylar in uncharacteristic silence. At one point, Wyatt snuck up behind me. "That's not right," he announced.

I pivoted, glaring at him. "Yes it is."

"It's a triliteral sign," he said. "Not a scepter."

I hesitated. I was used to Wyatt's transliteration being better than mine, but I was confident about this interpretation. "You're wrong—"

"I know," Wyatt murmured, and suddenly, quickly, he winked. "I just thought we should act like our normal selves."

"In that case, stop being a dick," I replied.

He laughed. I watched him walk back to another wall of the tomb, where he was working, wondering how he could keep so calm. Every time I looked at the inspector chatting with Dumphries, I broke out in a sweat.

When we broke for a snack, the *gaffir* served mint tea. I sat beside Wyatt, imagining what it would taste like on his lips. Dumphries regaled everyone with a story about an excavation at Hierakonpolis that revealed five-thousand-year-old animals like leopards and hippos and elephants buried with their owners.

Then Wyatt bumped my knee with his own. "Nature calls," he said, rising to his feet, striking out behind the *gaffir*'s tent. Our makeshift toilet facilities were in a *wadi* near the necropolis that had been carefully checked for antiquities before being designated a bathroom area. Wyatt would be striking out to a different spot, one closer to the Dig House. We were both hoping that the excitement of the discovery would eliminate any questions about why he had walked that far to relieve himself in the first place.

We were also counting on the timing working in our favor—as Dumphries announced that our break was over, I walked back into the tomb with the other grad students and specialists working alongside us. I must have stared at a *d*-hand sign on the right wall of the outer chamber for five minutes, waiting for Wyatt to return. And then, he burst into the tomb entrance, calling out for Dumphries.

We trekked behind Wyatt to the spot he'd allegedly just found. Mostafa, our inspector, was with us. There was the rock ledge, just like the day before. I was careful not to look at Wyatt, but instead kept my eyes on Dumphries as he crouched down and picked up a sherd from a broken beer jar.

"What are we looking at, Armstrong?" he asked.

"I think it might have been a popular site during the inundation festivals," Wyatt said.

"Because of a beer jar?" Dumphries said. "We find those in tombs, too."

I wandered into the crevice of shade, just like we had planned. The dipinto looked different, the light striking it in a way that bleached it out. "Professor Dumphries?" I said. "I think you should take a look at this."

Dumphries came up beside me, Wyatt flanking my other side. He began to translate the hieratic, showing off, which was completely in character. "It *was* a festival," Dumphries said, excitement painting his voice. "This is like the dipinti at Hatnub." He crouched, reading the text aloud twice. Then he stood and slapped his dusty hands against his thighs. "Sometime during the reign of Senwosret, Djehutyhotep II stopped here and slept overnight in the tomb of his ancestor Djehutynakht. We know from a graffito in Sheik Said that there was a Djehutynakht who made a point of caring for earlier tombs, but no one knew where he fit in the family tree, or where *he* might be buried."

He looked at Wyatt and me, and a smile broke over his face.

"Until now, my chickens."

Behind his back, Wyatt met my gaze. The secret was caught between us like a star, its edges sharp, its seduction blinding.


DUMPHRIES CELEBRATED WITH bourbon. A *lot* of bourbon. We sat on the roof beneath the same constellations that pharaohs had seen, and our mentor toasted us. "To Wyatt's bladder and Dawn's eagle eyes," he said, "which have transported this dig season into the realm of something truly spectacular." He declared that we would use the rest of our brief time in Deir el-Bersha to split into two teams: one that would continue the work at Djehutyhotep's tomb, and one—led by Wyatt and me—that would copy the newly discovered dipinto and get it ready for publication. But because we had twice the work to do in the same amount of time, now our celebration ended by nine o'clock.

When I left, Wyatt was doing shots with some of the younger grad students. Dumphries and I went down the staircase, shoulder to shoulder. At the spot where we'd part ways to go to our individual rooms, he put his hands in his pockets and rocked back on his heels. His eyelids were at half-mast. "Dawn," he told me, "I am quite glad U Chicago relinquished you to us." Then he gave me a little bow and walked away. Drunk on bourbon and on this unexpected praise, I made my way back to my own room. The walls of the Dig House slanted, and the floor tipped beneath my feet. I closed my door and tumbled onto the bed, still fully clothed when I fell asleep.

I woke up tangled in a cocoon of darkness, with someone's hand over my mouth. I thrashed against the sheets, my eyes going wide, and then as they adjusted to the darkness, I saw Wyatt. He was sitting on the edge of my bed, outlined in moonlight. He let go of me and put a finger to his lips. *Shh.*

"Come on," he whispered.

My mother had told me that people are born leaders, or they are born followers. *Be the first, Maidan,* she would tell me, *or all you will see is the back of someone braver than you.* I had always believed that I was a trailblazer, but the truth is, I would have followed Wyatt anywhere that night. If he'd walked me to the edge of the earth, I would have stepped off right behind him.

Instead, he held up a full bottle of bourbon from Dumphries's private collection. "Did you steal that?" I whispered, and he just grinned.

We slipped out of the Dig House, and Wyatt's hand curled around mine. His palm was warm and a perfect fit—so necessary pressed against mine that I wondered how I hadn't noticed, all this time, that something was missing.

The desert at night was a world of shapes and shadows—the rough, undulating tongue of a beast beneath my feet, the eye of the moon peeking out from a veil of clouds, the sky as wide as a scar. I would not have been surprised to see a basilisk rise in our path and turn its stone stare on us, to have a sphinx block our way with a riddle. We didn't speak, as if words might break the spell.

Wyatt didn't turn on the flashlight he carried in his other hand until we reached the *wadi.* Almost by instinct, we navigated to the rocky ledge that shaded the dipinto. In the dark, it was a smudge of color. He opened the bottle of bourbon and drank from its neck, then passed it to me. "To Djehutynakht," he toasted. "We're going to find him."

"We?" I asked.

He nodded.

Dumphries had not mentioned searching for this lost tomb. He was already busy with his work in a different tomb, and going on a wild goose chase for Djehutynakht without actual directions or a starting point didn't seem like a smart use of time. But just because Dumphries was too busy or too close to retirement to take on a challenge didn't mean we had to let it fall to the wayside.

We would be a team, McDowell & Armstrong, and we would unearth the tomb of Djehutynakht. Our work on the Book of Two Ways would be seminal, thanks to a new version found at the bottom of an intact coffin we could only dream about right now. Little girls who never pictured themselves as archaeologists would know my name. We'd cochair an Egyptology department at a university—Wyatt focusing on philology, while I specialized in iconography and imagery. We would be interviewed by every foreign press about what we'd found underneath a rock ledge.

A dipinto. A tomb.

Each other.

I glanced at Wyatt from the corner of my eye. He was sitting against the rock wall, underneath the dipinto. "How?" I asked.

He understood immediately what I was talking about. "I don't know. Of all the parts that were damaged, it *had* to be the numerical distances." Without the actual directions once given in cubits in that text, it was going to be a struggle to find Djehutynakht's final resting place. The necropolis had been excavated for nearly two hundred years by Egyptologists; how could all of those archaeologists have missed a tomb?

"Well," I said. "If it was easy, then someone else would have probably found it by now."

"True. We have a lot of work to do." Wyatt reached for the bourbon again. "But tonight, Olive . . . we celebrate."

We drank, sitting in the quiet, muddled joy that was still left over from the day, much like the heat that the sand retained. I thought of how perfect it was that we were drinking, here, just like Djehutyhotep had thousands of years ago.

"What are you thinking about?" Wyatt asked.

*That your long eyelashes are criminally wasted on a guy.* "What it would have been like here during the Sothic rising," I said.

He took my hand and brought it to his lips. Such a courtly gesture, and so British, and still, when his mouth touched my skin I shivered. "One unique is the sister," he murmured. "Without her equal, more beautiful than all women. Behold her like the star, having appeared in glory at the beginning of a good year."

Wyatt was quoting Ancient Egyptian love poetry. Festivals were social get-togethers, among the few places to meet someone outside your village and hook up. To that end, poems would be exchanged to attract someone of the opposite sex. "Shining of excellence, luminous of hue," he said. "Beautiful of eyes when glancing, sweet her lips when speaking . . . for her no word is excessive."

His voice was a river, and I was stone, and every syllable reshaped me. "Long of neck," he said, leaning closer to kiss a spot beneath my ear. "Luminous of chest." His teeth, on my collarbone. "True lapis is her hair." He tugged loose the tie of my braid and unraveled it with his free hand, sliding his palm up to my shoulder. "Her arms putting on gold . . . her fingers like lotuses." He finished where he'd started, kissing my hand, his tongue a quick brand between my knuckles. "*Now* what are you thinking about, Olive?" he whispered.

At that point, I couldn't answer. I couldn't form words.

Wyatt laid me down on the ground beneath the dipinto, cradling the back of my head. My hands fisted, sand spilling through them like through an hourglass.

"Maybe once, instead of admiring your brain," Wyatt murmured, "I could admire your body?"

He hesitated, a breath away, and I realized that he was waiting for me to say yes.

Instead, I reached up and started to unbutton his shirt. His skin was hot and smooth under my palms, and muscles shuddered when I touched him, as if my fingertips were made of electricity. He didn't seem to know what to say anymore, either, so he kissed me instead. He tasted of smoke and sugar.

I rose up, tidal, my arms holding him together. Somehow we switched places so that he was spread on the sand, his discarded shirt and pants beneath him. When I came up on my knees beside him, granules bit into my palms and rubbed me raw.

He was naked except for his socks and I was still fully clothed and

I could not stop shaking. My hand slid down his stomach; he twitched in my fist. "Olive," he groaned. "You're killing me."

I touched the very tip of him. He was circumcised, which was one of the ways you could culturally become Egyptian, if you were a foreigner. There was actually a stele where a captive man talked about being inducted into the Egyptian army with a hundred and twenty other men and—

Suddenly Wyatt's hand closed around mine. "Stop picturing that stele," he gritted out, and my eyes flew to his as he finished my sentence. *"I was circumcised with 120 men. I struck no one; and no one struck me. I scratched no one; and no one scratched me,"* Wyatt recited. "I know what you're thinking." In one fast, grating move, he flipped us over. "And frankly, if you're still thinking, I'm not doing this very well."

His thighs bracketed mine, but he was careful to not rest his weight on me. He unraveled me, pulling back the edges of my shirt and shucking my pants as if they were lotus petals, *she loves me, she loves me not.*

She loves me.

He poured bourbon on me and licked me dry, his mouth moving from one breast to the other. Sand scratched between us when he fitted his body against mine. Pain and pleasure; somehow that seemed right. We had been enemies and now I couldn't remember the war we had been fighting.

"Dawn," Wyatt whispered.

A name was once seen as part of the soul, and now I understood its magic. It's why cartouches were surrounded by *shen* rings, for eternal protection. It's why a king would hack out the name of his predecessor. It's why, as long as someone held your name on their lips, you were alive.

I stared into his eyes when he sank inside me. We moved together, a chord of music I could never sing out loud, but would never stop hearing.

Somewhere in time, others drank and danced. A star flashed green on the horizon.

We were ancient.

. . .

HIS HANDS TANGLED in my hair.

Brushed sand off my belly.

Scrapes, cuts, teeth, elbows.

Wyatt curled around me like Mehen, the protective serpent that encircled the sun god in the Book of Two Ways, protecting him from chaos.

I lost track of the number of times we came together, or slipped apart. And even then he touched me or I touched him, until the distance between us was like the line between sea and sky, so hazy it was impossible to see where one stopped and the other started.

We fell asleep wrapped in a blanket made of night, and when it became threadbare, I knew Wyatt was just as awake as I was. "What are you thinking about?" I asked, and his arms tightened around me.

"Sakhmet," he said.

Sakhmet was the flip side of Hathor, a sky goddess and a consort to Re. As Hathor, she represented joy and creativity and beauty and love, and she was depicted wearing a sun disk headdress between cow horns. But as Sakhmet she was a lioness goddess, a fierce hunter who protected pharaohs and led them into battle. Hathor on a rampage, with PMS, was Sakhmet. Sakhmet, pacified, was Hathor. And during the Sothic rising, Sakhmet/Hathor was Sothis, the daughter of Re.

In New Kingdom tombs, like Tutankhamun's and Seti I's, there was a text called the Book of the Heavenly Cow. In it, mankind rebelled against Re, who decided to retaliate by destroying them. He ordered Sakhmet to do it. But the night before the deed was to be done, Re had a change of heart. The problem was—he had already dispatched Sakhmet. How did you stop unstoppable destruction?

The answer: You made men brew beer and women grind red ocher. At the end of the night, they took the tinted beer and spread it all over the fields. When Sakhmet came to destroy humanity, she saw all the red beer and mistook it for human blood. Bloodthirsty, she lapped it all up and got so drunk she couldn't destroy a fly, much less mankind.

At the inundation festivals, when Egyptians drank the night away, they were imitating Sakhmet—soothing her anger with beer, so that she would swallow up the overflow of the Nile when it ran red with silt from upstream, threatening to wash away settlements.

I turned slightly in Wyatt's embrace. "You're thinking about a drunk girl with bloodlust?"

Against the back of my neck, I could feel his smile. "I'm thinking that *you're* the drunk girl with bloodlust."

"I like you *so* much better when you're not talking."

Wyatt laughed. "Do you know the Tale of the Herdsman?"

It was a story from the Middle Kingdom, but I'd never read it. I shook my head.

"The narrator meets Sakhmet in the marshes before she's changed back into Hathor," he explained. "She's a wild animal, and he's scared shitless because he thinks she's going to eat him. But the next day at her festival, she's all woman and ready for the new year."

He buried his face in the curve of my shoulder. I could smell him on my skin.

"I'm thinking that I came to the desert with a lioness," Wyatt said softly, "and ended up with a goddess in my arms."

Together we watched the sun rise—my namesake, gilded in pinks and oranges; the universe being born again.

WE CREPT BACK to the Dig House then, to snatch a few minutes of sleep before the day officially began. But I woke up alone with the sun streaming into my room, panicking because I had slept through the morning's work. I jumped out of bed, already wondering how much trouble I was going to be in.

The Dig House was empty because everyone was at the site. Or so I thought until I heard something crash in the magazine. I padded down the hall to find Wyatt picking up pieces of pots and setting them into a box.

A thousand thoughts cycled through my head: if he was here, and we were alone, he should have come to my room. Unless he didn't want to. Unless there was a piece of him, like me, that believed last night didn't happen. Or shouldn't have.

"Tell me that was already broken," I said evenly, and he jumped.

"Jesus, Olive!" He turned around. "You're going to give me a heart attack."

"That may be the kindest way to die after Dumphries figures out we slept in."

"Relax," Wyatt said. "I told him we were both hungover. Apparently, finding a new dipinto and a potential tomb allows us one grace period of fucking up."

"Speaking of that." I swallowed. "This thing. Us."

"What about it?"

It felt like knives in my throat, but I said what had to be said. "We had a lot to drink."

He stared at me. "Are you saying you took advantage of me?"

"I'm saying maybe we took advantage of each other." *It was the most earth-shifting moment of my life.* "We were celebrating. It was . . . bound to happen."

Wyatt slid his hands into his pockets. He was quiet as he walked deeper into the magazine, trailing his hand along the box where George, the mummy, rested. "You think last night was a mistake."

I tried to say yes. Really, I did. I had a hundred reasons why this was not a good idea, starting with the fact that we didn't really like each other and ending with the reality that two graduate students would not be taken seriously for this discovery if we weren't acting the part. But, still, I couldn't say it.

Wyatt moved so fast that I didn't even see him coming. He backed me up against a row of shelves, whose contents rattled with the force of my weight. His mouth was a bruise. He ripped the seam of my pajama bottoms, lifted my hips, and drove into me. I wrapped myself around him, the source of the flame, and set myself on fire.

"My God," he said, shaking in the circle of my arms when I finally slid along the length of his body and let my toes touch the floor. "Did that feel like a mistake?"

But just because we were combustible didn't mean we belonged together. Just because we'd made history together didn't mean we were a team. "Dammit, Wyatt," I said. "I'm trying to let you walk away."

"Who says I want to?" he blistered. "Olive, you're the only person I've ever met who gets the joke without me having to explain it. I was so busy trying to figure out what made me better than you that I didn't pay attention to what we had in common. Every time I looked five years out, there you were. I thought it was a threat. But what if, all this time, it's because you're supposed to be wherever I am?" He stepped away from me, breathing hard. "Stop bloody trying to save me from yourself."

Then he pressed a broken piece of limestone into my hand. "This is why I came down here, you idiot." He turned and walked out of the magazine.

The stone was a lopsided triangle, and he had written on it in hieratic with a Sharpie. I recognized the writing from Ostracon Gardiner 304, about which I had once written a paper, comparing this poem to the Song of Songs in the Bible.

Both texts were exchanged as tokens of favor during harvest festivals. Both had nothing to do with politics or religion—just intimacy.

Both were about lovers who aren't married.

The original poem had been scrawled on a limestone flake. Since papyrus was pricey, limestone or potsherds had been used as cheap writing surfaces. Wyatt had given me the Ancient Egyptian equivalent of a Post-it note.

*I shall kiss [her] in the presence of everyone,*
*That they might understand my love.*
*She is the one who has stolen my heart—*
*When she looks at me it is refreshment.*

That piece of limestone was the only thing I took with me from Egypt, when I left.

# WATER / BOSTON

. . .

I GREW UP knowing that love came at a price. My mother would tell me the story of Tristan, who journeyed to Ireland to bring back beautiful Iseult to his uncle, the king, only to fall in love with her himself. His uncle sentenced them to death—Tristan by hanging, Iseult by burning. Tristan escaped and rescued her, and brought her back to the king out of honor. Years later, when Tristan was married to another and was struck by a poisoned lance, he sent for his first love. He didn't know if she would come. If she said yes, the ship bearing her response would have white sails. If she said no, they were to be black. Iseult rushed to be with her old love, and the sails flew white. But Tristan, too weak to leave his bed, couldn't see the ship. He asked his wife what color the sails were, and jealous, she lied and said black. He died of grief, and when Iseult saw his body, she died of a broken heart. After they were buried, a hazel tree grew from Tristan's grave, and a honeysuckle from Iseult's, and they twined so tight they couldn't be pulled apart.

The moral of this story, my mother told me, was to plant your honeysuckle far from your hazel.


IN FRONT OF Meret, Brian and I act as if nothing has changed. And there are moments where, when we are together, I forget that we ever argued. But then, there are times I am furious at him for being stupid enough to upset the balance of our relationship. At night, I sleep in my office, and sometimes I wake up with the memory clenched between my teeth.

The truth is that it is easier to spend time with a woman who is dying than in a relationship that I am struggling to bring back to life. Win quickly becomes my primary client. I visit her three times that first week, and four times the next, and I tell myself that spending so much time with Win has nothing to do with the fact that it means spending that much less time at home with Brian.

One day, Win and I take the T to the MFA. A collection of Manet paintings is on loan from the Met, and she wants to see them. We wander through the exhibit, stopping to sit when she gets tired. Eventually we end up in a room full of contemporary art.

"I don't understand modern art," I tell her, when we are standing in front of Picasso's *Rape of the Sabine Women*. I tilt my head, looking at the geometric warping of figures, the distorted bodies being trampled by horses, the eye of the naked soldier painted on his sword.

Win laughs. "You're not supposed to understand it. You're supposed to feel it."

"They don't even look human," I say.

"That's the point. That's what war does to people. It makes them into killing machines, where a weapon might as well be a body part. And it makes the victims bleed into each other, indistinguishable."

I stare at her, blinking. "Did you ever teach?"

She laughs. "No. I just listened really well in class." Win fumbles for her phone and pulls up a picture of a beautifully rendered painting. A woman reclines naked on a bed, while a Black servant brings her a bouquet of flowers. "This is Manet's *Olympia*," she says. "It's widely considered the start of modern art. See how she's staring right at you? That was so upsetting to people that when Manet displayed it in Paris in 1865, he was critically crucified. The painting had to be guarded so it wouldn't be destroyed. He wasn't glorifying a goddess or a religious icon. He was showing you a real woman— a sex worker—who was daring the viewer to look her in the eye instead of pretending she didn't exist." Win shrugs. "All those fancy rich dudes at the salon were screwing prostitutes, but they sure as hell didn't want to be reminded of it."

I take the phone from her hands, touching the image to enlarge it.

I look right into the woman's eyes. I look at how her hand presses down on her thigh, the dimple in the flesh. "I'd like to see this one in person."

"Go to the Musée d'Orsay," Win says. "It's glorious."

I try to imagine traveling with Brian to Paris, spending time wandering around a museum. I can see myself doing it. But beside me is just an empty space. Brian is wary of art, of film, of anything meant to manipulate emotions. If it can't be quantified, it isn't legitimate.

We have turned the corner into a room full of canvases that remind me of the paintings Meret used to bring home from nursery school: drips of paint that look like they belong on a drop cloth, giant blocks of gray and brown sitting on top of each other. "This is what I mean," I tell Win, gesturing to a Rothko. "Even I can do that."

"Ah, this is abstract art," she explains. "It's all about universal expression. And believe it or not these artists were influenced by the Renaissance masters, too."

"I'm not seeing it."

"They knew that a great painting could pull emotion out of a viewer. But the world's different from how it was during the Renaissance, when beauty was as necessary as oxygen, and when religion was an entry point for art. So they tried to figure out what it would take to inspire that same flood of joy or grief or awe today. It's what feeling would look like, on canvas, if it was in its most raw form."

I stand in front of the Rothko—the dark, muted blocks of color. "This just depresses me," I say.

"Yup. How you react tells you something about your emotional state, and you can unpack where that comes from."

"Canvas as therapist," I muse.

"Exactly."

"What's your favorite painting?"

"*Sunday Afternoon on the Island of La Grande Jatte*," Win says without hesitation. "By Georges Seurat."

"Isn't that the one made up of dots?"

"Pointillism. Yeah. It represents the two sides of art that I love—on one hand, it's just beautifully rendered because the artist made sure every inch of the canvas was pulsing with life. But there's a whole other side of it—pointillism is a metaphor for society and politics. Painting dot by dot stands in for the industrial revolution and how it was filtering into leisure time in society. I could write a whole paper on it." She smiles. "I *did*."

"Sounds like a perfect marriage of skill and significance," I say.

"A perfect marriage," Win repeats. "Yes."

We stop in front of a Pollock mural. Win stares at it, silent, and I look, too. It is full of swirls and sharp edges, yellows and blues and crimson flicks that remind me of blood spatters from a *CSI* show on television.

"I like the blue in it," I say.

"Yes," she breathes. "The blue."

"So when you painted, was it like this, or like Manet?"

"Neither." Her lips are bloodless, white. I watch her shrink within her own bones. "I don't feel well," Win says. "We should go home."

Immediately I give her the strength of my body. I wrap an arm around her waist, holding up her slight weight. As we walk through the galleries, I feel a prickle at the back of my spine, a magnet that twists my gaze to the right.

Through the entryway I can see the wooden models that came from the tomb of Djehutynakht and his eponymous wife. If I take three steps in that direction, I will be able to see the coffins, nestled into the case against the wall. The wavy lines of the Book of Two Ways drawn against the wall of one of them.

*I wonder who looked at that and first thought it was a map.*

Then I see him, crouching in front of the glass.

I gasp, and the man stands up. Younger, then. Less blond. A stranger, not a ghost.

"Dawn?" Win says, her voice a frayed thread.

"I'm right here," I reply, and I help her move forward.


You CAN ARGUE that all fear is related to death. Fear of spiders? You're really afraid of being bitten and killed. Fear of heights? Falling to your death. Fear of flying? Crashing. Snakes, fire—you get it. Jerry Seinfeld even says that people are more terrified of public speaking than dying, so if you're asked to give a eulogy, the person inside the coffin is better off than the one giving the talk. Why are people so afraid of dying? Well, that's easy. Because it's hard for us to conceive of a world without us in it.

As Win's health deteriorates, she becomes more anxious and she can't sleep. Felix tells me she is eating less, and I can see her fear eating away at him, too, like termites at the foundation of a house.

"What did you do before to relax?" I ask her.

"Every now and then I'd take a Xanax," Win answers. "But I'd rather not sleep away the limited amount of life I have left."

"We can try magnesium, if that doesn't interfere with your meds," I suggest.

She grimaces. "No more pills."

"How about more holistic methods? Meditation, aromatherapy, massage, sound bath—"

"You know what?" she interrupts. "I want to get stoned."

Pot is legal in Massachusetts, which makes it simple. I have a choice of weed, lollipops, CBD pills, even milkshakes. In the end, I bring gummy bears.

I have no plans to partake, but Win—who has, amazingly, never tried pot—is so anxious about the possibility that it is negating all the benefits. I finally say I will be right there with her, and she makes me chew the gummy bears in front of her like she is Nurse Ratched from *One Flew Over the Cuckoo's Nest*. I settle down next to her on the couch, letting the corners of the room go pleasantly furry, feeling my eyelids grow heavier.

"How long have you been married?" Win murmurs beside me.

I slide my glance to her. Her arms are crossed over her chest, in the archaic position of death. I decide not to mention it. "Fourteen years," I say.

"Why did you get married?"

That follow-up makes me blink. Usually, you ask how or why someone fell in love; how you knew he was the one. I'm reluctant to answer, not just because I don't feel like poking at an open sore, but because in this relationship with Win, I'm supposed to be helping her, instead of the other way around.

Then again, I'm getting stoned next to my client.

"It was right. At the time," I reply. Trying to steer the conversation onto neutral ground, I add, "Did you know that modern Egyptian women pinch the bride for good luck?"

"That's unfortunate."

"There are all kinds of superstitions around weddings. Veils protected the bride from evil spirits. Bridesmaids confused the Devil, if he came to snatch the bride. And a long train made it harder for her to run away."

"Wow. Those are some grooms with seriously low self-esteem."

I laugh. "The reason we 'give the bride away' was because she used to be a property transfer."

Win twists her wedding band around her finger. "When Felix and I went shopping for this, Felix asked the difference between platinum and white gold. The saleslady said that as it got older, platinum would go a little gray at the edges. Felix pointed to me and said, *Oh. Like her?*" Win looks down at her hands, as if she does not recognize them as being part of her own body. "I'm not going to get gray at the edges, am I," she muses. "I'm not going to last that long."

I sit up, aware that there are people for whom pot does nothing; there are others who feel paranoid instead of relaxed. I don't want this backfiring for her. "Win," I begin, but she interrupts.

"I've been trying to figure out what this disease is teaching me," she says slowly.

"About death?"

"No. About life." Win runs her hand over the couch, making the nap of the suede stand on end. "I mean, life is supposed to make us grow, right? To become better? If that's the case, what is death going to do to me?"

"Death doesn't just *happen* to us. In fact, there's no passive voice in the English language for it. It's an action verb. You have *to die*." I shrug. "Three hundred sixty thousand babies are born every day while a hundred and fifty thousand people die. On a micro level, the body's sloughing off skin and brain cells while we're still alive. Even after the heart stops pumping, the cells still have enough oxygen to be considered alive for a little while, even after the doctor pronounces us dead. Life and death are heads and tails. You can't have one without the other."

"Maybe in order to grow and become better, part of us has to die to make room for that new thing," Win says slowly. "Like a broken heart."

I turn to her. She has tears in her eyes.

She dashes them away with her hand, giving a little embarrassed laugh. "Here's some breaking news: it's harder to face the death of someone you love than your own. Go figure."

I thread my fingers through hers and squeeze. "Win. I will make sure that Felix has all the grief counseling he needs. I will be with him through the funeral, and I'll check in with him afterward. I swear to you, he will not be on his own until I know he's doing all right."

She glances up, surprised. "That's good to know. But I was talking about Arlo."

*Her son.* The one who died.

"I'd like to hear about him, if you feel up to it," I say.

She sinks deeper into the cushions of the couch. "What can I tell you? He came a month early. His lungs weren't strong enough, and he had to be in the NICU for weeks. But he came into this world laughing. I know they say babies can't do that, not for weeks, but he did. He laughed all the time. When he pulled himself up in his crib; when I gave him his bath; when I sang to him. And, honestly, my singing makes most people cringe." A smile ghosts over her lips. "He laughed all the time, until he started to cry. We didn't know what was wrong. Neither did Arlo. It was too hot, or too cold. The tag on his shirt hurt. The teacher didn't understand him. The other kids didn't like him." She hesitates. "It was always someone else's fault. There were some days when he would crawl into the closet and sob until he fell asleep. And then there were other days when he broke every window in the house with a baseball bat."

She draws in a breath. "We took him to a psychologist. Family therapy, the whole nine yards. Arlo was diagnosed with oppositional defiant disorder. You know what that is?"

I had heard the term before, applied to a little girl in Meret's elementary school class who had been adopted from an orphanage in the Ukraine, and who just never seemed to settle into her new family. She bit and scratched and sobbed. "Doesn't it have something to do with not being able to form an attachment?"

Win swallows. "Yeah. Imagine how *that* made me feel. It was three weeks in the NICU, and I was there every day. *Every* day. No one loved Arlo like I loved him." She leans forward, elbows on her knees. "Nothing worked. Not reward systems, not time-outs, not even—I'm sorry to admit—spanking. I used to pretend that my real boy had been taken by faeries; that this . . . this creature I didn't understand . . . was just a temporary replacement. I know, ridiculous. But it was easier than admitting that there were times I wished Arlo had never been born. What mother can admit that, and still call herself a mother?

"Then one day my pediatrician told me about holding therapy. It's pretty controversial. There were conferences where you could take your kid and be taught how to do it, but we couldn't afford that. So I read books, and I tried to do it myself. Whenever Arlo had a meltdown, Felix or I held him. I held him *so* tight, for hours. The rules were that he could scream and shout, he could curse me, he could say terrible things, but at the end of the two hours he had to look me in the eye. That's it. And I'd release him," Win says. "It worked. Until he was too big to hold." Her face becomes a lantern. "Arlo still had bad days, but he *came* to me when he did, you know? I wasn't the enemy. I was fighting *beside* him. *I* was his safe place. And then, one day, I wasn't." She knots her hands together. "I don't know the first time he used. I don't know who gave it to him. It was easy, and cheap, and when he was high, he was happy." Win glances at me. "He laughed again. Like, all the time."

I know how terrible addiction can be. I had a patient in hospice who had come home from the hospital with a fentanyl patch on his body, which his grandson peeled off and boiled in alcohol, so that he could use the drug. Even now, if a client dies and there are opioids in the house, I destroy them by mixing them with cat litter or bleach.

"I begged Arlo to go to rehab. He went and relapsed. He died of an overdose six days before he turned sixteen." Win buries her face in her hands. "And it's all my fault because my body couldn't hold on to him—not before he was born, and not long enough, after."

"No, Win. You can't blame yourself because he was in the NICU, and you can't prove that was the source of his anger. And you certainly can't blame yourself for not being able to save him."

"I prayed that Arlo would be put out of his misery," she says flatly. "And he was."

Suddenly she gets up, weaving a little. "I want to show you something."

I jump to my feet, steadying her. Win walks up the stairs, stopping at an antique desk to pull from a drawer an old-fashioned key on a yellow ribbon. She leads me to a locked door at the end of the hallway.

The room is small and octagonal, part of the turret of the Victorian house. Heavy velvet curtains cloak it in darkness until Win walks toward a window and yanks it open. Dust swirls in the stale air like magic. She goes to the other two windows and pulls back their drapes as well, and light fills the bowl of the room.

The only furniture is a stool and a squat table spattered with paint. An empty easel.

Lining the hitched walls are dozens of canvases, stacked and balanced. Some face away, with a handprint of color smudged onto the wood stretchers offering a backward glance. Others boldly stare me in the eye.

I crouch down to examine one painting. It features a brown boy with an explosive halo of white hair, holding a dandelion with a matching crown. The technique makes me think of the Impressionists we saw at the MFA—slurry, drugged, color hinting at an object but no defined edges. Win's lines are wavy and rippled and in some places the paint is caked thick enough to stand away from the canvas. It reminds me of the way the world looks when you sink to the bottom of a pool and try to find the sun. To really see this picture, you can't be close to it. You have to step away and let your mind fill in the rest.

It isn't just a painting of Arlo. It is a picture of a wish, the moment before you make it. The moment before you risk being disappointed.

I sort through the canvases, seeing more pictures of this boy—clearly her favorite subject—but also a study of hands that might belong to Felix and a landscape that looks like Maine. I'm filled with grief—not just for Win's loss of Arlo, but for the forfeit of her art. For all these beautiful moments of a life, which are rotting away in a locked room.

"I would love to bring some of these downstairs," I say.

"I wouldn't," Win replies, and that's that.

She brushes her hand over a palette, her thumbnail picking at a splotch of black that looks like an eye passing judgment. "Did you know that the origin of art is a love story?" she asks. "Pliny the Elder says that the daughter of Butades was upset her boyfriend was leaving town, so she traced the outline of his silhouette on a wall while he slept, and that was the first line drawing. The thing is, when she drew him, he was already gone. You can't look at your subject and at what you're drawing at the same time. She was only sketching his shadow." Win looks at me. "Art isn't what you see. It's what you remember."

She sinks down to the floor, touching her fingers to one of the paintings. Arlo is older in this one, floating in an inner tube at the horizon, as if he could sail off the edge of the world.

"I want the blanket from Arlo's bed with me when I die," Win says.

"I'll make sure you have it," I promise.

I make a mental note to ask Felix where to find the blanket. While Win steeps in her memories, I riffle through a stack of canvases on the other side of the room.

One looks nothing like the others.

For one thing, it's classically rendered, a nude. It's so real that I can see the indentation of the teeth where they bite into the lower lip; I can feel the heat of the sun pressing its cheek to the window in the far corner of the piece. One hand is flung across the subject's eyes, the other moves between her own legs. The pose reminds me of Manet's *Olympia*, but with such excruciating detail that it may as well be a photograph. The artist's rendering is so accurate that I can hear the hitch in the woman's breath.

It is Win. Back when she had hips and breasts instead of hollows and angles; back when she was whole and healthy and in love. In spite of what she has just told me, I can almost feel the tickle of the brush on her skin as the artist brought her to life, and not just her memory.

"Who painted this?" I ask.

For a moment, Win doesn't answer. She gets to her feet and pulls the canvas out of my hands. Her face flushes. "That shouldn't be here." She turns it away from sight, jamming it into the back of a stack of art.

My watch vibrates against my wrist; an alarm I've set. "It's time for your medicine," I tell Win, and she looks so relieved that I feel guilty. She locks the door behind us, and instead of slipping the key back into the desk, she puts it inside her bra.

It isn't until after I bring her the dose of medication that Felix measured out and left in the kitchen that Win speaks again. "Do you think Arlo will be . . . wherever I'm going?"

"I don't know," I admit.

"I'd like that. Seeing everyone I've lost."

It isn't until much later that I consider the word she used. *Lost.*

Someone does not have to die for you to miss them.

WE ARE WATCHING a terrible Hallmark movie when the CBD gummies finally kick in, and Win drifts off to sleep. I sit with her for a while until I hear Felix's car pull into the driveway. I watch him for a moment from the front door: checking his rearview mirror, putting on his parking brake, collecting his belongings from the passenger seat. I wonder what it would be like to be cared for by someone whose profession was all about safety.

When he sees me waiting, he walks faster. "Is everything okay?"

"Fine." Well, as fine as it can be when your wife is dying. "She's sleeping."

His shoulders relax as he realizes that he is not about to hear the news he dreads most. "Oh. Oh, good."

I follow him into the kitchen and give him a quick rundown of the medications Win has taken, of her food intake and her urinary and bowel movements. This is the caregiver passing of the baton. "Win showed me her paintings today," I say.

He pauses in the act of getting a pitcher of water from the refrigerator. Then he pours a glass, drinks it, and sets it down empty on the counter. "Did she?"

"We talked about Arlo," I tell him. "She wants his blanket with her when she dies."

Felix flinches when I say the word *dies*.

"Do you know where it is?"

"In the attic," Felix says, waving his hand toward the ceiling. "Somewhere. All his stuff is there. At first Win made me promise not to change anything in his room, and then I came home one day and found her tearing apart the sheets and ripping his clothes up and smashing his computer—" His voice falls from a cliff. "I boxed everything up. Just in case she needed it one day."

I meet his gaze. "I know this is hard—losing Win, when you lost your son not so long ago."

Felix blinks. "Arlo wasn't my son," he says. Then, chagrined, he ducks his head. "I mean, he was, in the way I loved him. But he was already six when I met Win."

I think about the portrait of her in ecstasy. "She didn't mention that," I reply.

WHEN I GET home, Brian is pacing in the kitchen. "You're here. Thank Albert."

He doesn't believe in God, but he does believe in Einstein.

For a moment I panic, wondering what appointment I almost

missed. And then I remember: Meret is going to a dance at camp, and we are having dinner at the home of the dean of the faculty.

Normally it's hard to make social commitments, due to the nature of my work, but this means a lot to Brian. A promotion to chair might be riding on it. I promised him I would be there. He promised me that Gita would not.

"I just need to throw on a dress," I tell him. "Is Meret ready to go?"

"She's changed her mind."

I stop on the stairwell. "Why?"

"I don't know." Brian looks at his watch. "She's old enough to stay by herself. And we can't be late."

She may be capable of staying home, but that doesn't mean she *should*. If Meret gives in to her social anxiety, it only feeds the beast. Her friends will have fun without her, will not call, will not text. She will sit here all night and think: *See, I was right not to go. No one missed me anyway.*

I run up the stairs and rap on Meret's door. There is music pulsing; it sounds like the inside of a headache. When she doesn't answer, I turn the knob and find her lying on her bed reading in sweatpants and a T-shirt, oblivious to the noise. The bass thumps so strong my pulse adjusts, a new moon and its tide. "Hey," I say, deciding to play dumb. "What time are Sarah's moms picking you up?"

"I'm not going," she snaps.

"To the dance?" I cross to her laptop and hit the volume key, bringing down the decibel level. There's no melody, just a beat and freestyling. I wonder if every generation is destined to find a style of music that is completely incomprehensible to the previous one.

Meret doesn't answer. She lifts the spine of her book so that she breaks our line of sight.

"I don't understand. You were looking forward to this."

She was, a few days ago. Sarah had come home from STEM camp with her and there were whispers and hidden notes and at least once I caught a name: Todd. I wonder who he is. If he said something, did something, to hurt her.

Primally, I want to hurt him back.

"It's not even a dance. It's a bunch of kids grinding against each other."

"Well," I say lightly. "Friction *is* STEM."

She puts down the book. "You did *not* just say that."

I squeeze her arm. "Maybe it will be better than you think. Besides, what's the alternative? Dad and I have a work thing."

"I don't need a babysitter."

"Meret," I say softly, "if you won't even try—"

"Then no one will think I'm a loser," she explodes. She turns onto her side, away from me. "I don't have anything to wear."

I get up and open her closet, pulling a dress from a hanger. "How about this?"

"I wore that to a *funeral*."

"Jeans?" I suggest.

"Mom. It's a *dance*."

I pull her up from the bed. "Come on. We're going to find something."

Reluctantly, she lets herself be dragged into the master bedroom, the walk-in closet. I remember vividly how, as a little girl, she would sneak in here and try on my dresses and jewelry and come downstairs to give us a fashion show. I pull out a sequined blouse she used to love that was way too expensive for her to be playing in. "Here," I say.

Meret's eyes go wide. "Really?"

"As long as you don't grind in it."

She smirks and yanks her shirt over her head, turning her back to me. I help her unzip my blouse and settle it over her head. As she pulls it down, the stitches strain under the armpits.

"You know," I say, "this was always cut weird. Try this." I yank out a boxy tunic, which floats over Meret's shoulders with room to spare, and spin her in front of the mirror.

"I'm wearing a tent."

"A *designer* tent," I amend, but she *is* swimming in it.

I go back into the closet, ripping through the hangers. I have a lot of black in my wardrobe, I realize, but then again, I go to a lot of funerals. I hesitate at a couple of dresses, but worry that the zippers might not close. "You know what?" I realize. "These are old-lady clothes."

Meret blinks up at me.

"But I have killer shoes."

I reach down into the recesses of my closet. My hand brushes the seam of spackled wall. When I was growing up, my mother hid a baby shoe in the insulation, to ward off evil. I thought it was ridiculous, and then when I moved into Brian's home, I did exactly the same thing. Still, even when you plaster over something, you know it's there.

I know we are both a shoe size eight. I hand Meret a pair of heels that are probably too high for her.

She takes them, looking down at the shoes instead of at me. We both know that this is a concession. *Don't say it,* she tells me in silence.

I will take her shopping. I will buy her clothes that make her feel beautiful. I will show her what I see when I look at her. But none of that helps in this moment.

"Maybe jeans are okay," Meret says, and it breaks my heart. She turns to go back to her room, her shoulders rounded. Diminished. It seems impossible that someone so worried about her size can make herself so small.

"Wait," I say, and I take her hand. I draw her into the master bathroom and sit her down on the closed toilet seat. I pull out foundation and eyeliner, shadow and rouge. When Meret was little, she would watch me put on my makeup, and beg me to make her match. I'd lean into the mirror, swooping the mascara wand over my lashes, and then I'd cap it and pretend to do the same to her. Blush on her cheeks. Lipstick and gloss.

This time I do not pretend. Meret is my canvas. Except I am not creating anything; I am only tracing art that already exists.

I used to hold up a hand mirror when I was finished, and Meret would turn her little face left and right, as if she could truly see that invisible difference. *Mommy,* she would ask. *Am I beautiful now?*

I would kiss her forehead. *You already were,* I said.

. . .

THE DEAN OF the faculty, Horace Germaine, lives in a brownstone on Mass Ave that still has its Halloween decorations in spite of the fact that it is summer. Or maybe it's because his wife, Kelsey Hobbs, is rumored to be descended from a family whose daughter was tried for witchcraft in Salem. Either way, I like her more than I like him. While Brian is sucking up to whoever it is that makes departmental chair appointments, I stand in a corner, nursing my third glass of white wine, feigning interest in a discussion about traffic in Cambridge.

"So, Dawn," says the husband of an economist. "What do you do?"

"I'm a death doula," I say.

"A what?"

"I'm contracted privately by people who need end-of-life care."

Another wife nods. "Like nursing?"

"Everything *but* nursing," I explain. I give a nutshell description.

I can see it, the moment their demeanor changes. Tell someone you work with the dying, and you are suddenly a saint. "It was so hard when my mother passed," another spouse offers, touching my arm. "You're an angel."

Here is what I wish I could say: No, I'm not. It's important work, but I am much less Mother Teresa than I am a pain in the ass. Just because I get close to something that makes a lot of people uncomfortable doesn't mean I'm special. It just means I am willing to get close to the things that make people uncomfortable.

Here's what I do say: "Thanks."

The fact that I can still censor myself proves I'm not as drunk as I thought I was.

The husband of the economist sways closer, lowering his voice. "Anyone ever ask you to . . . speed up the process?"

We've all heard the stories about so-called mercy killers, upping a morphine dose so that a patient never awakens. The closest I've ever come to that was a Catholic client on heart medication. If she stopped taking it, she asked, was it suicide? I told her I didn't think so—there's a difference between actively ending your life versus letting a disease progress in a way it would without treatment.

She kept taking her heart medication, and died of a stroke two weeks later.

"My grandmother was hit by a foul ball at Dodger Stadium," a young woman says. "Dropped like a stone."

"That must have been incredibly difficult for you and your family," I say.

"I heard that on Mount Everest, there are bodies that have been frozen so long they're used as trail markers—"

If you are an expert on dying, people believe you are also an expert on death. Suddenly, Kelsey Hobbs slips her arm through mine, as if we are long-lost friends instead of spouses introduced only a half hour ago. "Dawn," she says, "I must show you some memento mori I have in the library."

Death memorabilia. I wouldn't have taken Kelsey for a collector. But her bright blue eyes widen, and I realize that she's sending me a message. "Oh, of course," I reply, letting her unravel me from the knot of people and pull me down a hallway.

I do not expect there to actually be a trinket, but I am wrong. A photograph hangs on the wall across from a massive bookcase, and in it, a couple poses on either side of a young girl. The couple is hazy; the child crystal clear. I know that in Victorian times, photography was a popular way to commemorate the dead. The reason the girl's parents are blurry is because of the long exposure time. The dead, on the other hand, don't move.

"Who is she?" I ask politely.

"Who the fuck knows," Kelsey answers. "She came with the house. For years I thought the parents were ghosts and that's why they were fuzzy. Then I did a little research." She reaches into the top drawer of a massive desk and takes out two cigars, offering me one. "Smoke?"

"No, thanks." I think Kelsey Hobbs may be my favorite person at Harvard.

She lights her cigar and takes a deep drag. "It felt like you needed rescuing. Just a guess, but I'm thinking if you spend the whole day with people who are dying, it's not your first choice of conversation topic when you're off the clock."

"Actually, I don't mind talking about dying. But there's a limit to what I know about death, having not experienced it myself."

"Imagine the business you could start if you *had*." Kelsey narrows her eyes. "Is it depressing?"

"Sometimes," I answer honestly. "Mostly, it's humbling."

She stabs the cigar into an ashtray. "Well, I'm going to die sooner rather than later because of these things. Maybe I'll hire you."

I smile. "Maybe you will."

The door opens, and Brian's head pokes through, followed by Horace Germaine's. "There you are," Horace says to his wife. "You're doing a terrible job of hosting a party."

"They're all horrible people," Kelsey says. "Besides, I'm hiring Dawn to help me die."

Brian's smile freezes on his face.

"Is there something you're not telling me?" Horace asks pleasantly.

"We're all dying," I say cheerfully.

The dean of faculty raises his brows. "That's grim."

"Not really."

"Dawn—" Brian's face flushes.

"Really, it's okay to discuss it," I add, warming to the topic. "Talking about sex doesn't make you pregnant, and talking about death isn't going to kill you—"

"No one wants to talk about dying at a faculty meet-and-greet," Brian grits out.

"Why? You talk about dead cats all the time."

"Why don't we get you a drink?"

"I have a full glass."

"Then why don't we get you another one?" Brian grabs my arm and tugs me toward the door. He turns at the last minute, addressing Horace. "I am so, so sorry."

I stumble behind him like a child who knows that the worst of the punishment is yet to come. When we are in a hallway somewhere near the bathroom, Brian faces me. He is so upset that for a moment he can't even speak. "You knew how much tonight meant to me," he finally says.

"I talked about my job. Would you prefer that I introduced myself as Brian's wife?"

"Don't twist my words."

"*I'm* twisting *your* words?" I say. "I came to a cocktail party. You abandoned me."

It's saying this out loud that makes me realize that this isn't about Gita—and maybe never was. She is the symptom, but not the illness. I had always believed that Brian would be there for me. It's why I fell in love with him—slowly, second by second, depending on him for strength and comfort until I couldn't remember what it was like to exist without that. But then came the moment when Brian *wasn't* there for me. And if that was possible, then maybe I'd been lying to myself for years. Maybe our entire relationship was on shaky ground.

*You abandoned me,* I think again, and I wonder if I'm angry at him for that, or angry at myself for taking him for granted.

There's a flush, and the bathroom door opens. A woman with a thick rope of seed pearls looks from me to Brian and then edges past us, murmuring an apology.

The room is swimming, and I don't know if it is because of all the wine I've drunk, or because I'm crying. Brian reaches for me, but I am faster. I run through the hallway, past the woman who was using the bathroom, into a kitchen, where a hired chef is filling the trays of four bored servers. I nearly crash into a table with stemware on it, and fly out the door like the Devil is at my heels.

Outside, in the cool, quiet patch of a Cambridge backyard, I walk the perimeter of the fence until I find a latched gate. I let myself out and walk down the street, stopping under the glow of a streetlamp at the corner to wipe my eyes and kick off my heels. Two college kids walk by, arguing, too caught up in their own drama to notice mine.

Love isn't a perfect match, but an imperfect one. You are rocks in a tumbler. At first you bump, you scrape, you snag. But each time that happens, you smooth each other's edges, until you wear each other down. And if you are lucky, at the end of all that, you fit.

Two weeks after I moved in with Brian, we went out to dinner at an Olive Garden. He was so excited about the doggy bag he took home—a whole second chicken parmigiana that he was going to eat for lunch the next day. At a stoplight was a homeless man who waved, and without saying a word, Brian rolled down his window and gave him the doggy bag. I thought: *He's so* good. I wanted to be like him. I hoped he would rub off on me.

Even now, sitting on the curb with mascara running down my face and a terrible wish to rewind the past twenty minutes, I cannot imagine what my life would have looked like without Brian in it. I don't know who would roll his eyes with me at the concept of pine-apple on pizza. Who would know which song to turn up on the radio, without me having to ask. Who else could possibly know me well enough to wound me.

The car slows as it approaches, its bright yellow eyes blinding. It pulls to a stop; the door slams. Brian sinks down beside me on the curb. His hand rests beside mine, on the concrete.

I cross my pinkie finger over his.

"I don't mean to be such a bitch," I say.

"I'm sorry," Brian murmurs. "I wish I could take it all back."

My throat tightens. "Me, too."

It strikes me that we may not be talking about the same thing.

I rest my head on his shoulder. "When you're department chair," I say, "we're serving better wine."


WE ARRIVE HOME in the soap bubble of a fragile peace. "I . . . could take a shower," I offer.

That's code for: *Let's have sex.* I know there was a moment in our relationship where sex was totally spontaneous. But at some point, it became more structured *because* we cared about each other. Brian would shave so that his beard growth didn't scratch my thighs. I'd bring a washcloth and tuck it under the pillow so that when we finished, there wasn't a wet spot.

Brian squeezes my hand. "Maybe you need someone to wash your back," he says.

"Maybe I do."

The door opens, and we jump apart, as if this is not our house, as if we are not married. Meret slips inside, just as surprised to see us there as we are to see her. She is barefoot and carrying my shoes. Her face is streaked with mascara, and she is struggling to hold back tears.

"Baby," I breathe. "What happened?"

A battering ram of *the worst* hammers at my mind: she was date-raped, she was in an accident. Her face twists as she holds out my heels. "I broke the strap," she sobs, and then she runs upstairs.

I look at Brian, bewildered. His hands clench and unclench; he has never done well with a tidal wave of emotion. "I'll go," I say.

In Meret's room, I sit down beside her on the bed. I rub her back, waiting for the sobs to stop. "Do you want to talk about it?"

She shakes her head, but the story bleeds out.

The dance, under twinkle lights, at a camp on a lake. A DJ playing "Cotton-Eyed Joe." Meret and Sarah, sitting to the side on a redwood picnic table, when two boys came over. Todd and Eric were not like a lot of the other boys in camp—they weren't geeks. They were on the soccer team, doing STEM to boost their college résumés.

They had a flask.

Sarah took a drink, and so did Meret.

Todd came up with the idea to steal the rowboat, even though the waterfront was off-limits. It would only be for a little while. It would be romantic, Sarah said. So Meret went with the others, and it *was* fun. It was messy and dirty and forbidden and she was in on it, instead of standing on the sidelines.

Eric got into the boat and helped Sarah in. But before Meret could climb inside, Todd stopped her. *She'll sink it,* he complained, and Eric laughed.

*Don't say that,* Sarah said.

Meret looked at her, so so so grateful.

Sarah smiled at the boys, and added: *If she falls in, she'll float.*

They were laughing as Todd climbed in, as they rowed Sarah into the middle of the lake like a princess. They were talking scientifically about whether fat makes you sink or rise, when Meret ran away.

I grab Meret's shoulders and I look her in the eye. "You are not fat," I say slowly.

Her eyes spill over with tears. "Mom. Don't lie to me, too."

I want to ask how she got home, but I am afraid. I want to swaddle her in bubble wrap. I want to hunt down those asshole children and blister them.

She finally falls asleep, lashes damp and spiky, her hands curled over her chest.

When Meret's breathing evens, I go to our bedroom. Brian is already in bed with the lights out. I give him the abridged version.

He is hurting for her, too, I know. But he swipes with that sore paw: "I told you she should have stayed home."

Whatever hopes I had of being with him tonight are gone. His words are a sword in the middle of the bed, cutting the sheets to ribbons. I take my pillow and sleep in my office.


*Scene from a marriage:*

> BRIAN (ENTERS KITCHEN): I overslept.
> DAWN: There's coffee.
> BRIAN: Last night—
> DAWN: I don't know what time I'll be home.
>      (He pours coffee into a travel mug.)
> BRIAN: Is Meret—
> DAWN: She's not going to camp today. Or ever again.
>      (A beat.)

BRIAN: I'll bring in something for dinner.
(He exits.)
(End scene.)

THINGS YOU SHOULDN'T do when someone is dying:

Don't talk about when your aunt or your grandmother or your dog died. This isn't about you, and the sick person shouldn't have to comfort you; it should be the other way around. There are concentric circles of grief: the patient is at the center, the next layer is the caregiver, then their kids, then close friends, and so on. Figure out what circle you're in. If you are looking into the concentric circles, you give comfort. If you're looking out, you receive it.

Don't say things that aren't true: *You're going to beat this cancer! It's all about a positive outlook! You look stronger!* You aren't fooling anyone.

Don't overact your happiness. It's okay to be sad with someone who is dying. They've invited you close at a very tender time, and that's a moment of grace you can share.

Don't think you have to discuss the illness. Sometimes, a sick person needs a break. And if you ask up front if he wants to talk about how he feels—or doesn't—you're giving him control at a time when he doesn't have a lot of choices.

Don't be afraid of the silence. It's okay to say nothing.

Don't forget: No one knows what to say to someone who's dying. Everyone is afraid of saying the wrong thing. It's more important to be there than to be right.

Win and I have reached the stage where we can sit in quiet, without a background noise of NPR on the radio or the television murmuring. That's an important part of the process. I know that Win is turning over memories as if they are treasured jewels. I am going over everything Meret told me the night before, and trying to pick a path forward through comfort and courage.

Win is figuring out how to die; I am figuring out how to live.

She is having a bad day. She hasn't eaten. For the first time, she didn't try to get out of bed. There's a point in the process of dying when it really hits you. You have the diagnosis, you know that your body isn't acting the way you want—but one morning you wake up and realize that you really weren't sure that you *would* wake up. You understand that there's a curtain you cannot see behind, and your toes are brushing the edge of it, and you aren't able to reverse course.

Win clears her throat, and I immediately offer her a glass of water with a straw in it. She sips, wets her lips. "What's the strangest request you've ever had?"

"To make someone's ashes into a diamond. There's a company called LifeGem that does it."

"Of course there is," Win murmurs.

"My client's widow wore it until she died, too, and then she was buried wearing the necklace." I glance at her. "Why? Do you want to make Felix a piece of jewelry?"

"Weave me into a hair shirt instead," she says. She is listless, tired.

"Maybe you should close your eyes for a bit," I suggest.

"I'm afraid if I do, I may not open them again."

"And that makes you anxious?"

"Shouldn't it?" She raises her brows. "I just wish I could get a peek at what's coming. Other than a whole mess of fear served up with a side of who the hell knows."

"People fear different things about death," I tell her. "Pain. Not finishing something you're working on. Leaving someone you love. There's even real FOMO, fear of missing out, of the world going on and you not being here to see it."

"I can't decide if missing the 2020 election is terrible timing, or excellent timing."

"It probably depends on who wins," I say, smiling a little.

"The not knowing. That's what's killing me," Win murmurs.

"Well. That, and cancer." She glances at me. "I'm okay with dying. I really am. But I don't want to do it wrong, you know? Does that sound ridiculous? I just wish I could know what's going to happen. How I'll know it's time."

I have not thought about my failed doctorate in a long time—at least not until I was reading Win those hieroglyphics. But I remember that what fascinated me most about the Book of Two Ways was how comforting it would be to have a map to reach the afterlife. Even the Ancient Egyptians recognized that knowledge was the difference between a good death and a bad one.

"I don't know how long you have," I say carefully, "and I don't know what the process is going to feel like. But I can help you understand what happens to your body."

Guided death meditation is something I usually do with healthy people who want to understand how to help those who are terminally ill. But I think it might help Win a little; bring her some peace. The meditation was developed by Joan Halifax and Larry Rosenberg, based on the nine contemplations of dying—written by Atisha, a highly revered Tibetan monk, in the eleventh century.

Win says she'd like to try it, so I help her out of bed and have her lie on the floor in corpse pose. I sit next to her, legs crossed. "If anything I say starts to stress you out," I tell Win, "raise a finger."

She looks at me and nods.

"Just listen to my voice," I say, and I begin, pitching my tone even and soft. "All of us will die sooner or later. No one can prevent death; it's the outcome of birth. It's inevitable. Not a single sentient being—no matter how spiritually evolved, or powerful, or wealthy, or motivated—has escaped death. Buddha, Jesus, Mohammed did not escape death, and neither will you or I. All the gifts of your life—education and money and status and fame and family and friends—will make no difference at the moment of death. In fact, they can make it harder, because we hold on to them. What are you doing right now that will help you die? Hold your answer in your head. On the inbreath, think: *Death is inevitable*. On the outbreath, think: *I, too, will die*."

I move on to the second contemplation, rising up on my knees to dim the light beside the bed. "Your life span shortens every second you live. There is the moment of your birth, and the moment of your death, and your movement toward death never stops. Every breath you take in and release brings you closer. Appreciate what you have now, because there may be no tomorrow. If your life span is decreasing every day, what are you doing now to appreciate what you have left? What gives your life meaning?"

Win's finger twitches and I wait, but she relaxes.

"Every word you speak, every breath you take, moves you closer to the end of your life. On the inbreath, inhale gratitude for the additional seconds you have been given. On the outbreath, think of the seconds that have passed in your life."

I watch her chest rise and fall. "Death will come whether or not we are prepared. Of the one million three hundred thousand thoughts we have each day, precious few are about how to meet the challenge of death. Can you listen to me, now, as if there is no tomorrow? Are you ready to die?"

I work through the other contemplations: that death has many causes; that the body is fragile and vulnerable; that loved ones can't keep you from dying. I ask her to imagine herself on her deathbed, growing weaker, picturing her house and her clothing and jewelry, her paintings and her bank account and her wine collection—all the comforts she has worked hard for, now useless. "Dying means letting go of everything," I tell her. "Picture everything you have being given away to friends and to relatives. Some of it may wind up in a thrift store or a dumpster. You can take nothing with you. On the inbreath, think about this. On the outbreath, let go of everything that is yours."

I end on the body, the very thing that is failing her. "You've spent so much time working on your physical self. Feeding it, watering it, exercising, dressing and undressing, soothing pain, feeling pleasure. You've spent hours looking in mirrors, trying to feel beautiful. You have treasured your body. You have despised it. And at the moment of death, you lose it. Imagine the moment before you die. You have already contemplated the fact that you are losing your money, your loved ones, your status, your identity. You will also lose the shell it all comes in. What can you do to acknowledge this? To prepare yourself?"

Then I lean closer to her, urging her to tense and release different muscles and limbs and thoughts. "Imagine your organs are shutting down, now," I murmur. "You have no more desire to eat or to drink. Next is your central nervous system. You can't move. You lose your connection to your limbs. Your eyes may roll in your head, you may not be able to keep them open. Finally, your respiratory system will slow down. Breath won't come easily or naturally." I sit in the quiet, feeling the absence of noise press against my eardrums and my skin. "Your legs. Your hands. Your head. Your brain. Your abdomen. Your kidneys and liver and intestines. All the big and small muscles and bones. They are gone. Consciousness is moving toward your heart, your center. You're shrinking inward to a point of light. Your breathing is getting shallower. Your energy is draining. Your body temperature drops. You can't feel the floor beneath you because you are weightless. You are aware now that you are dying, but that is the only consciousness you have left." I pause. "You're opening and opening and opening into consciousness. You're part of all that ever was, and all that will ever be. You let go. Finally."

I look down at Win with tears in my eyes. "You are safe," I say. "You're looking down at this body on the floor, with no more breath in it. You see people standing around your body."

I wait a beat. "It's a few days later, now, and the body is naked and cold."

I count to twenty. "A few months later, there's decay. Gases fill the body and it decomposes."

Win doesn't move. "A year has passed," I whisper. "There are only old bones."

I look down at her and imagine a world without her in it. "Fifty years. There is just dust. You are not here anymore. But you're safe."

We inhabit that dark, small truth for a long time.

Finally, I bring her back—first with a shallow breath, then with a stretch, then lengthening her muscles, then feeling her bones shift and her organs pump and process and her blood moving through her heart and the air filling her lungs and awareness sprawling to the tips of her toes and the roots of her hair. "What do you feel beneath you?" I ask. "Can you feel the carpet on your palms? What do you hear—pipes as water moves through them? Your own heartbeat? What do you smell? The lemon in the shampoo you use, the detergent in your bedding? What do you see?"

Win's eyes blink open. "You," she says. "I see you."

You would be surprised at what people wish they'd done when they get to the end of their lives. It's not writing a novel, or climbing to Machu Picchu, or winning a medal in ice dancing. It's having an ice cream sundae, or watering the houseplants more. Playing cards with a grandson. Catching up with an old friend.

My mother's dying wish was, likewise, simple. She wanted to see the ocean one more time. That wasn't something the residential hospice could do, but I was determined to make it happen. I talked to the doctors and priced out a transport vehicle. I bought my mother a floppy sunhat at Goodwill and sent a note to Kieran's school saying that he would be absent the following Tuesday. But the day before we were scheduled to go, my mother took a turn for the worse. So instead, Kieran went to school, and I went to the North Shore. I filled gasoline jugs with ocean water. I shoveled sand into a Ziploc bag. I collected shells and jammed them into my pockets.

At the hospice facility, the nurses helped me get my mother into a sitting position. I wedged pillows beneath her knees and set her feet in a basin of the water. I poured sand into emesis basins, and placed them on each side of her chair, burying her fingers in beach. I told her to close her eyes, and I moved a gooseneck reading lamp closer to her face, so she could feel its warmth. Then I placed shells from her clavicles to her belly button.

But.

I could bring her the memory of the ocean, but I couldn't take away the sound of the heart monitor.

I could give her the coastline, but only as much as could fit in a room.

I could make her a mermaid, but she couldn't go back to the sea.

That's why I'll move heaven and earth for my clients. To make sure they get that last heart's desire. That there's nothing they haven't had a chance to finish, before they leave.

TWICE DURING THE day, I've called Meret to see how she is doing. The second time, she told me to stop treating her like one of my clients, and I nearly cheered. I will take an angry daughter any day over one who is weeping, or—worse—silent and blank.

Win starts running a fever after dinner and complains of pain urinating; she likely has a bladder infection. I wait for the hospice nurse on call to show up and confirm the diagnosis and give her antibiotics before I leave. It is nearly 11:00 P.M. by the time I get home.

The house is dark. Even the light in Meret's room is out. I open the door as quietly as I can, to find a small candle flickering in the entryway, set right in the middle of the floor. In the near distance—at the juncture of the entryway and the living room—is a second candle burning.

I blow out the first flame and move to the second. From there, I can see another candle pointing toward the staircase, and then three dotted like lighthouses all the way up.

The last candle burns just outside the closed master bedroom door.

Inside, the four posts of our bed have been strung with Christmas lights. They provide the only light in the room, but it's enough for me to see that hanging from the ceiling are photographs. They twist on short lengths of fishing line, buoyed by the currents of air-conditioning. There's a picture of Brian, holding the stuffed monkey that he shoots from a cannon to explain vectors to freshmen. One of Kieran—still lanky and young, holding a lobster he'd taken out of a trap. Meret as a toddler, wearing a lopsided strawberry hat—the one and only item I've ever knit. There's a picture of Meret as a newborn, and another of her at an elementary school holiday concert in a red velvet dress. There is a photo of Brian standing next to the sign announcing the top of Mount Washington, and another of him in a tuxedo. There is the last picture I have of my mother, smiling from a hospice bed.

I see a movement from the corner of my eye, and Brian steps forward from the corner, where he has been watching me. "What's all this?"

He doesn't answer directly. "You don't see black holes, you know." His voice shakes, as if he is nervous. "They just pull you in. No light escapes, so you wouldn't either. They say if a person actually approached a black hole, he'd be torn apart, because the gravity is that great."

I sit down on the edge of the bed.

"Since astrophysicists can't actually see black holes, they had to figure out another way to find them. They look at how planets and other matter moves and reacts around them. They see things falling in, or at the brink."

Images pirouette above my head. "There aren't any pictures of me."

"No." Brian steps forward and pulls me up, positioning me in the dead center of the room. "That's because you're our star. You hold us together. Without you, there's no life. No gravity. No me." He hesitates. "No us."

I realize that he is trying to communicate in a language he knows and understands. That for him, this is crystal clear.

"You think you know the edges of your world," Brian says. "And then it turns out there's all this dark matter out there. I fell out of orbit, Dawn."

I look at him, the familiar planes of his face, the level of his chin, the sickle-shaped scar that cuts through his eyebrow. He is trying to find his way to me again; I can meet him halfway. So I put my hands on his cheeks. "How do we get back on track?"

In response, he sways forward. He stops before we touch, I inhale what he exhales. It makes me think of Abramović, the performance artist, and her lover, fainting in the same square of air. "Is this . . ." he asks. "Can I . . ."

I rise up on my toes and press my lips against his.

For a moment, he goes still. His heart, flush against mine, kicks hard. Then he grabs me tighter, his palms skimming from my shoulders to my waist, as if loosening his grip means I might float out of reach.

We kiss like we haven't in years—like that is all we are going to do, like we could taste the world in each other. We lie down on the bed and stay like this for hours, for centuries. I move against him, wanting more, but he holds my hands flat on either side of my body. He kisses his way along my jaw, scrapes his teeth at the base of my throat. When I manage to reach for his shirt and try to pull it over his head, Brian darts away. Instead, he skirts his fingertips over me. Brian has always been a scholar, and I have become the subject.

I'm completely undressed, and Brian isn't. I arch against him and try to cage him with my legs. Instead, he crawls off the bed, leaving me to ache. I come up on my elbows, thinking he will finally take off his clothes, but instead he kneels. He bows to me, sliding his hands from my knees to my thighs, and his mouth closes over the core of me.

This. This is what it means to be alive.

It feels like lightning when I come, so stark that I look down at my hand against the sheet, expecting a burn. "I'm sorry," I gasp, and Brian looks up at me, surprised. "I wanted us to be together."

I realize, with an aftershock, that I mean it.

With a strength I didn't know I have, I pull Brian down to me and roll so that he becomes my feast. I taste each patch I uncover. He catches bits of me as I move—a wrist, a shoulder, the underside of a breast—but I am everywhere at once. I rock on him, over him. I look into his eyes.

I can't remember the last time we did that. Usually, we hide in our own pleasure. We use each other to get where we need to, in our own little hedonistic bubbles. It's safer than peering through the windows of his eyes and glimpsing something I might not want to see.

Or letting him peer through mine.

When he swells inside me, when neither of us blinks, I wonder if this is what it's like for the moon when she pulls the tide and changes the shape of the world.

We don't have a washcloth. Brian's beard has scratched me raw. His hands are broad and restless on my spine, and my hair is damp against my face. "We're going to have to clean the comforter," I whisper.

"Worth it," Brian grunts.

I squeeze him with my legs. "That is my new favorite sport," I whisper.

He buries his face in the curve of my neck. "Imagine the gym memberships you could sell."

I laugh and feel him slip out of me. There is wetness and mess and I don't even care. Brian cradles me, my back to his front, idly playing with my hair. I look up at the ceiling, at the starry string of lights, at the absence of me. "Can't you get too close to the sun?" I murmur.

"Not in my metaphor," Brian says.

"Tell that to Icarus."

He yawns. "Who?"

Brian's breathing evens, a bellows behind me. I think he has fallen asleep, when I feel his words on the back of my neck. "I need help," he confesses.

*So do I,* I think. I catch his fingers with my own, ceding the space and the silence.

"I managed to hurt the person I love most in the world. And I want to ask my best friend how to fix it," Brian says. "But they're one and the same."

I am not sure what he is apologizing for. A single act, or many. I don't want to know. I realize I should apologize to him, too, but maybe that is the problem in my marriage—that we have been tethered too long to our past, and we need forward movement.

I don't want to slip back. I was a student of history; I know this. The shadow of a thing doesn't exist without the original to cast it. A dry bed was still once a river. A bell unrung is still a bell.

IN THE MIDDLE of the night I get a call from the hospice where my mother died, where one of my longer-term clients—a woman with

Parkinson's—has taken a turn for the worse. I slip out of bed, telling Brian that someone is dying. I drive to the facility and talk to the nurses about Thalia—the forced respiration, the mottling in her limbs. Then I go into her room and assess for myself that she is actively dying.

She's been unresponsive for a few weeks, so I knew that it was coming. I take my phone out and cue up a playlist of Broadway songs. Thalia had been a showgirl, a Rockette. She was married for sixty years to a producer, who died in 2012. They never had any children; she's outlived her friends. In Amsterdam, if you have no one to survive you, a poet is hired to write and read a few lines at your funeral; this is obviously not the case in America. Thalia hired me so that she would not have to die alone.

I sit down beside Thalia and reach for her hand. The skin is paper-thin, the veins a purpled map. Her hair, a white tuft, has been brushed back and secured with a pink ribbon. Her cheeks are sunken and her mouth hangs open. A tabby kitten—a generational offspring of Cat, I imagine—curls at the foot of her bed.

The last time Thalia was conscious, she told me how, as a kid, she would sneak down her fire escape when her parents were fighting and make her way to Broadway. The curtain rose at 7:00, which meant at 8:30, everyone came outside to smoke. Ushers didn't check tickets on the way back in, so she would blend in with the crowds and hover in the rear of the theater, scoping out the empty seats. Every now and then a wealthy couple would eye her—a teenager—oddly, but who was to say she wasn't the child of a couple in the row in front of them, or off to the right? She never got caught, and she saw the second acts of over a hundred shows for free. "I used to wonder," she told me, "why *do* those Sharks hate the Jets so damn much?"

"Thalia," I say, aware that hearing is the last sense to go, "it's me, Dawn. I'm here with you." I gently squeeze her hand.

Her breath is wet and thick. The cat's tail flicks. Soon, then.

I don't sleep; I bear witness. Broadway scores run on repeat: *Kiss Me, Kate* and *West Side Story* and *Showboat* and *A Chorus Line. Kiss today goodbye.*

My phone dings once; a text from Brian. *Bed is too big without you.*
I start to type a reply but cannot figure out what to say.

After a few hours of vigil, my eyelids feel gritty and my mouth feels full of chalk. Nurses move in and out of the room in regular intervals, checking vitals, asking me if I need anything. Just before the sun rises, Thalia opens her eyes. "Are you here to take me?" she asks.

It is not the first time I've been mistaken for the angel of death. When it gets this close, clients have one foot in this world and one foot in the next. Some see a light. Others see people who've died. I had an elderly client once call out to a man named Herbert, who turned out to be a high school boyfriend that died in World War II. A college kid with an inoperable brain tumor saw a stoic, silent man in suspenders and boots sitting on the edge of his bed. *His name was Garmin,* the boy said, *and he said he was supposed to watch over me.* When I told my client's father this, he went white and said that Garmin was the name of his grandfather's brother, whom he never knew and never met because he'd died in a mill accident in his twenties.

I don't know what makes people see what they do before they die. It may be dopamine, or oxygen deprivation. It may be meds. It could be brain cells firing one final time or a short circuit between synapses. Or maybe it's a way of saying that you may not know what comes next, but it's still somehow going to be all right.

I don't tell Thalia that I am here for her, but I lean so close that my breath falls like a blessing. "Rest," I tell her. "You've done what you need to do."

When Thalia dies, it is like an old filament bulb that glows for a moment after it's turned off, and then loses its vibrance and its light. She is there, and then she's not. There's a space in the world the size of her small body, but she is gone.

The cat jumps off the bed and slinks out the door.

I wait a moment before I go to tell the nurses. I hold Thalia's hand and look into her face. When you look at someone whose life has just ended, you don't see horror or pain or fear. You see peace. Not just because the muscles relax and the breath has left—but because there's a deep satisfaction, a conclusion. It never fails to move me, what a privilege it is to be at this moment, to be the bearer of their story.

I take out my phone, open my calendar, and start to read.

Manoy Dayao, who waited nineteen years for a winning lottery drawing to get to the United States from the Philippines. Three months after he and his wife arrived, he was diagnosed with cancer. I was hired when he was already unresponsive. He didn't speak English, and I did not speak Filipino, so I asked his wife for his favorite song. "New York, New York," she told me. Frank Sinatra. When I started to sing the first line—*Start spreading the news*—Manoy suddenly opened his eyes and belted, *I'm leaving today*. And he did, three hours later.

Savion Roarke, who had perfect color—like perfect pitch—and could hold any hue in her head and match it to a sample.

Stan Wexler, who worked for Western Union for forty years, and whose great-grandson was teaching him to text. In telegraph code, he told me, *LOL* used to mean *loss of life*.

Esther Eckhart, whose son was a singer on a cruise ship in the middle of the Atlantic, who died with him crooning to her on speakerphone.

I type in one more name.

Thalia O'Toole, who never knew that Maria married Captain von Trapp, or that Harold Hill was a shyster, or that Eliza Doolittle wasn't to the manor born.

ONE MORNING, ON my way to see Win, I take a few moments with Felix. I've noticed a decline, and I am sure he has, too. Win is sleeping more, engaging less. She only eats a meal a day. She has stopped putting on makeup.

"How long do you think she has?" he asks me.

"If I knew that, Felix, I'd be a millionaire."

He smiles and hands me a cup of coffee. I have become part of the household. I have my own assigned mug and Felix buys me a vanilla creamer that I like. I keep a toothbrush and a pair of sweats in a reusable grocery bag in the mudroom, in case it's a late night. When we sit at the table together for dinner, I have a usual spot.

I slip into it now, and wait for Felix to sit across from me. "How are you doing?" I ask.

He sips his coffee and raises a brow. "I mean," he says.

"Are you sleeping all right?"

"No," he admits. "Every time I hear a sound—even if it's a bug hitting the window—I jump out of bed to make sure she's okay."

We have moved Win to the guest room, to a hospital bed provided by hospice. There's a wheelchair nestled up against the side of the refrigerator now, too. Caregivers are so busy trying to stay afloat, to remember medications and dosages and to be brave and compassionate and hide their own fear, that they don't even see the water level rising.

"She's not okay," I say. "She's dying."

"I know that," Felix snaps, and then his eyes widen. "I'm sorry."

"Don't be sorry. It sucks. You are allowed to be angry, sad, frustrated, whatever."

He rubs his hands over his face, making his hair stand on end. "The whole time we've been married," he says, "we never said goodbye to each other. I know that's weird, right? But when I left for work, or if she went out with friends, we just waved and went off, because we *knew* we were going to see each other in a few hours. It's kind of our little superstition." Felix looks up at the ceiling, as if he can see Win. "Now I have to say it. I have to say goodbye."

I reach across the table and hold his hand. "I know."

A sob folds him at the waist. "I love her. I love her to death."

"You love her *through* death," I correct gently. "You don't stop loving someone just because they're not physically with you."

One of my favorite concepts from Ancient Egypt was *kheperu*, or manifestations. An individual was much more than just the *khat*, or body. You were made up of the *ib*—a heart; a *ka* soul—a familial legacy; a *ba* soul—your personality and reputation; *shuyet*— a shadow; and *ren*—your name. After death, while the *ka* stayed earthbound in the mummified corpse, the *ba* soul winged its way to Re, the sun god. There is an 18th Dynasty tomb in Luxor that shows a procession carrying all these different pieces of the deceased. The physical act of death affected only one of those, and the afterlife was where all the parts came back together.

"She'll be here," I tell Felix. "In the way your living room is decorated. Or the bulbs that come up next spring. The way you remember how it rained every day of your honeymoon."

"She told you that?" Felix murmurs, blushing.

"She said you found other ways to pass the time." I smile at him. "If you wind up remarrying, she'll be there, too. Because she's the one who taught you how to love someone."

"I'm not going to fall for another woman."

"Okay," I say, privately thinking otherwise. The good ones often do, because they remember how it feels to be happy. It's not a replacement; it's more like an echo.

Then I hear Win's voice behind me. "You can get remarried, Felix," she says. "Just wait till I'm gone."

There is a smile threaded through her words, and she looks better than she has all week. She has a bright scarf wrapped around her head and is wearing a sundress. Her eyes are dancing, illuminated. With the exception of bruises in her arms from where blood has been drawn, she doesn't even look sick.

Felix stands and wraps an arm around her. He kisses her temple. "Don't joke about that."

"So," she says, "I'd love to get some fresh air."

Felix rises from the table, ready to do her bidding.

"Oh, baby," she says, touching his arm. "You were up all night with me. I thought you could get some rest while Dawn and I take a walk."

She looks good, but she doesn't look *that* good. I hesitate, but Win interrupts. "I meant *you* could walk, and I could be pushed." Then she crosses to the refrigerator and lowers herself into the portable wheelchair. "It's beautiful out."

Honestly, it isn't. It's so humid that my skin feels rubbery; it's stagnant and hot, and the sky is threatening rain. But Win hasn't wanted to leave the house for some time. If she feels like getting some fresh air today, we're going, even if a freak blizzard hits.

I grab my purse and an umbrella. Then I push Win outside and ease her chair backward off the porch. "Where to?" I ask.

She points. "That way," she says, tilting her chin toward the sun.

I push her several blocks, until we are sitting outside a small dog park. There is an insane Chihuahua barking orders at a mastiff, and a mutt humping its owner's leg. "He should get a dog," Win announces.

"Felix? Does he like dogs?"

"I don't know. I'm allergic, so it never came up." She nods more definitively. "Yeah. A dog."

"I'll make a suggestion," I tell her.

"What about a wife?" Win asks.

"Instead of a dog? Or in addition to?"

She smirks. "Do you think he'll get married again?"

"How would that make you feel?"

Win considers this for a moment. "Fair," she says softly.

I wonder what she means by that. Does she feel like he deserves a partner, because she is leaving him? Does she feel that, if Felix were the one dying, it is what she'd want for herself?

"I want to be remembered," Win announces.

"Felix and I were kind of talking about that today," I tell her. "I don't think that's going to be a problem for him."

"I wasn't talking about Felix," she says.

"Is there a charity you support?" I ask. "Maybe there's a way to have an art scholarship in your name—"

"No art," Win interrupts flatly, cutting me off.

I let the heat fan off the sidewalk, rippling toward me. "We could do a legacy project," I suggest. "Something you can leave behind that's a reflection of who you are."

"No art," Win says again.

"Okay, okay!" I hold up my hands in surrender. "It doesn't have to be art. I've stuffed Build-A-Bears with the T-shirts of a client so her grandkids would have them. I've made recipe books and written down oral histories. One woman was a master quilter with rheumatoid arthritis who couldn't finish a project, so she dictated instructions for her daughter to finish. I even had a client with dementia who was a master gardener, but he started forgetting the names of plants, so we made a picture book and he'd flip through and try to remember. He got frustrated sometimes, but man, the joy on his face when he got it right—" I break off, realizing that Win is somewhere deep inside herself.

"There was an artist in Seattle, Briar Bates, who was dying of cancer," I say carefully. "She wanted her art to outlive her. So she choreographed a water ballet for her friends to perform as a flash mob after she was gone. She sewed the costumes and organized the synchronized swimming and they all came together to do it in a fountain after she died. She wanted her friends to grieve together and for it not to be sad, but joyful."

"So . . . a way to leave a shadow in the world, even when you're not in it."

I nod. "That's a beautiful way to say it."

We watch a puppy race to the fence, turning on a dime to grab a tennis ball. "Felix would be terrible at water ballet," Win says after a moment.

"But he'd do it for you."

"I know," she says, on a sob. "That's what's even worse."

She lifts the hem of her dress and wipes at her eyes. I stand, rummaging for a tissue.

"You asked me why I don't paint."

I give her the tissue and then sit down with my back against the chain-link fence so that I am facing away from the dog park, but looking at her.

"When you're an artist," Win says, "it's because there's something inside you that you can't keep from spilling out. Maybe it comes in the form of sentences, or a grand jeté, or a stroke of a paintbrush. The end result can be a million different things. But the seed, it's always the same. It's the emotion there isn't a word for. The feeling that's too big for your body. To show someone your soul, you have to bleed. People who are comfortable—people who are content—they don't create art."

"You stopped painting because you stopped hurting."

She nods.

I reach for her hand, hold it between mine. "But you're hurting now, Win."

"I know. But not because there's too much inside me." She sucks in a breath. "Because there's nothing left."

I shake my head. "I don't buy that. I know you. I *see* you."

"You see what I've let you see," she scoffs.

A dog owner hurls a ball, which bounces high enough to jump the fence. Win catches it before it can crash into her. She holds it up, as if surprised to find it in her hand. She turns it over like it is a Fabergé egg.

"Did you ever wonder who you would have been, if you hadn't become who you are?"

I take the ball and lob it over the fence. "You mean like a center fielder?"

"No," she says. "You *know* what I mean. I know you do."

There are moments that feel more like spun sugar than time. A summer evening on a stretch of grass, when your tongue is blue with the heart of a Popsicle. A heartbeat when a hummingbird stops moving long enough to look you in the eye. A first kiss. A star flashing once in the sky before the sunrise. A goodbye. Blink, and it's like it never happened.

"What if I want to be remembered by someone who may not remember me?" Win asks.

I wait for her to continue.

"I grew up in New York City. I was a good painter; I already knew that. When I was a freshman at NYU, a gallery owner saw my work at a student show and wound up representing some of my paintings. When I was a junior I went to study for a semester in Paris. I took an art class, and the professor was constantly standing behind me, criticizing this line or that intention. He said I was too technical, as if that could be a thing. I went to his office hours to tell him he was an asshole, and he brought me back to the studio. He tied a rag around my head like a blindfold, and told me to paint how he made me feel." She twists the fabric of her dress in her hands. "I didn't know how to do what he was asking, and he wouldn't shut up, so I picked up the palette and threw it across the room. He ripped the blindfold off, and he was smiling. *Now we're getting somewhere,* he told me.

"What I drew that night—I'd never done anything like that before. It wasn't just art. It wasn't measured or literal. It was like being a medium, and having spirit pour out of you. I started spending all my time in the studio. I met my professor for coffee. We were inseparable, even though he was twice my age. He took me to the Louvre; we'd have a scavenger hunt for the artist who was most in love with his subject, or for the mangiest dog, or ugliest Madonna. He taught me how to copy the masters and then to deconstruct them. And one day he asked if he could paint me.

"He set up the studio and locked the door. He sat me down near a window. First he did sketches, and we talked about stupid things— how the prime minister was caught with his mistress, where the best falafel could be bought. He couldn't get it right. He was more and more frustrated. He asked me to close my eyes. I heard him get up and move, could smell the coffee on his breath. Then I felt the lightest stroke on my forehead. Down my nose. Over my cheek and chin and lashes. I opened my eyes, and he was painting me, just like he had asked. But with a dry brush. Tracing my ear and my jaw and my throat and my lips."

She holds her breath, lets it out in a rush. "You know where this is going," Win says. "I got pregnant. I was going to tell him, but then I found out he was married. And his wife was also due to have a baby in a couple of months. So I left."

I look down between my bent knees.

"You're judging me," she says.

"No."

"I like to believe I loved him so much that I couldn't make him choose. But mostly, I think I was afraid to find out who he'd pick. I came home and wore baggy clothes until I couldn't hide it anymore. I told my parents I was dropping out of school to have the baby, and that the father was a one-night stand I'd met in a club in Paris. A few years later, I married my driver's ed instructor. Clearly, I have a pattern, falling for authority figures."

"Felix," I say.

"Yeah. I loved him. I *love* him. But I never forgot about Thane." She stares directly at me. "I want him to know that. I want him to know that Arlo . . . *was*. I want that before neither of us is in the world."

Win reaches up and pulls the scarf from her head. She runs her hand over her smooth scalp. "There's so little left, already," she says. "Before it's all gone, I want him to remember me."

My lips feel stiff. "Why are you telling me this now?"

"A legacy project," Win says. "I want to write Thane a letter. I want you to find him and deliver it by hand."

I stare at her, silent.

"I've thought a lot about what my life would have looked like, if I hadn't left," Win says. "Even though I was the one who made the decision."

I feel a wash of heat. "What about Felix?"

The corners of her mouth turn up. "I don't think he'd really be up for that errand."

"You can't hide this from him. He loves you so much."

"And I love him," Win insists. "Enough to not hurt him any more than I already am by dying." She pulls at my sleeve. "Please?"

*No*, I think. *Too close.* This is crossing a line; this is unethical; this is wrong.

But I also hear the very words I spoke to Felix minutes ago: You don't stop loving someone just because they're not physically with you.

I get up and face the dog park. Two mutts are chasing each other in circles. "I can't give you an answer right now."

One dog nips the other's tail. He yelps and scurries away from a friend who became an enemy. "Dawn," Win begs. "Isn't there someone in your life who got away?"


IT TAKES ME hours to sort through the boxes in the attic. At one point Meret comes up, sees a bin full of baby clothing, and exclaims her way through it—reliving a dress with a giant squirrel on it, and a onesie with bumblebee stripes. We find Brian's mother's wedding gown, yellowed in a sealed box. There are yearbooks from Brian's college years, his ears sticking out like saucers and his hair too long.

"What are you looking for?" Meret asks.

"I'll know if I find it," I tell her.

She leaves not long after, which is good, because I cannot explain to her what I am searching for.

It is so hot in the attic that sweat pours off me, streaming down my neck and soaking my tank top. I wipe my face with the back of my arm. It is hotter than hell in here. It might as well be Egypt.

I find it buried under a crate of books: Gardiner's *Egyptian Grammar* and an early translation of the Book of Two Ways and thick volumes in German and Dutch and French that I used to be able to read for research. Wrapped in a dish towel with blue edging is a limestone flake, almost triangular, its edges ragged. One side of it has been crushed under the weight of the tomes, but the writing is mostly intact, scrawled in black marker. I do not remember all the hieratic, but I don't have to, because I know the translation by heart.

*I shall kiss [her] in the presence of everyone,*
*That they might understand my love.*
*She is the one who has stolen my heart—*
*When she looks at me it is refreshment.*

# LAND / EGYPT

. . .

AS IT TURNS out, Wyatt is not ready to excavate the burial chamber the next day, or the day after that. The first delay has something to do with the integrity of the shaft and shoring up the sides. The second delay has to do with the schedule of Mostafa Awad, the director of antiquities who has to be present before the chamber is opened. This means that Wyatt prowls around the Dig House and the site like a wounded bear, finding fault in everyone and everything. Joe says that when Professor Armstrong gets like this, it's in everyone else's best interests to get very, very absorbed in their own work.

I have had only two moments of interaction with Wyatt privately. The first was at the end of my very long first day, when he was unloading the Land Rover and handed me a tripod to carry back to the Dig House. "How did it go?" he asked, and I smiled broadly and told him it was great. The second was when he knocked on my door at 4:30 A.M. and unceremoniously tossed two pairs of women's khakis and two long-sleeved linen shirts on my bed, along with some white cotton underwear and wool socks. "Thank you," I said, wondering who had been dispatched to get me a change of clothing, if it had been Wyatt's directive. He had merely grunted, "I want my shirt back."

It wasn't until I began sorting through the clothes that I realized he had also bought me a burner phone, the cheap kind sold at street stands in Cairo, which had international service.

After the end of my second day in the tomb, I finish drawing the hieroglyphs closest to the shaft entrance and give them back to Alberto to input digitally. He is the only person in the Dig House who is cool to me, even though I try to be as cheerful and amenable as humanly possible. That afternoon, while we are all back at the Dig House avoiding the blister of afternoon, I find him at his computer. "Hi. I was wondering if you finished my file?"

"I'm kind of in the middle of something."

"If you teach me how to do it," I suggest, "then maybe I won't even have to bother you."

He glances at me. I watch his hands flying over the keyboard, and then I hear the ding on my iPad that lets me know the file has been sent back to me. *"Prego,"* he says flatly. *You're welcome.*

Joe, who is cataloging his flints, catches my eye and shrugs.

Suddenly the air changes in the room. Wyatt stalks into the communal work area with his cellphone pressed to his ear. "I don't give a damn," he fumes. "If you want the paperwork, then you have to *provide* the paperwork—"

He streaks out the doors onto the porch and the doors close behind him.

I walk to the window, watching Wyatt pace and rant on the porch. It strikes me how lucky we had it, fifteen years ago—to be Dumphries's pawns, instead of the *Mudir,* the director in charge of everything. It makes me wonder: while we were trapped in our own story, what was the one Dumphries was living? Did he know, then, that he was sick? That he was racing against time to publish his work before he stepped down from his post at Yale?

Wyatt looks regal and demanding, the sun anointing him, frustration billowing out behind him like royal robes. He jams the phone back into his pocket and braces his arms on the stone balcony. For a moment, he bows his head.

I am filled with the overwhelming desire to step out there, touch his arm, rub his shoulders. To take some of the responsibility away just long enough for him to breathe again.

I tell myself that it's because of what I do for a living—I'm used to helping people. Wyatt does not need my support; it's the other way around.

But when he turns, his eyes find mine through the window with unerring accuracy, as if he knows I've been there all along.

· · ·

AFTER THE SUN sets, Wyatt brings a bottle of cognac up to the roof and holds a meeting, explaining to his team how the excavation will be done, step by step. Wyatt, of course, will be the first one inside. Joe is in charge of making sure the generator is working—since it will be dark in the burial chamber, we need portable electricity for lighting. Alberto will be on hand to photograph everything in situ, before it is removed. "Dawn," he says, "you'll be with me." Before Alberto can open his mouth to complain, he adds, "She's smaller than the rest of us, and given how tiny the chamber seems to be, she may very well be the only one who can maneuver around the coffin."

No one is brave enough to contradict him.

Alberto gets up and lights a cigarette, then tosses the match off the roof.

"My mother used to say you should never light three cigarettes off one match," I murmur.

Wyatt turns to me. "Another superstition?"

"No, actually. It came from her dad, who was in the war—if you kept a match lit that long the enemy would see the flame and shoot you."

Wyatt refills his glass. "Here's to the knowledge that keeps us alive."

I shake my head. "If being a death doula has taught me anything, it's that we know nothing about life. At least not till it's too late."

"Evidence," Wyatt barks.

"Well, you have to be near death to understand why life matters," I say slowly. "Otherwise, you don't have the perspective. You believe you have the time to put off that phone call you haven't made to your mother. You let an old argument fester. You fold down the page in a travel magazine and tell yourself one day, you'll get to Istanbul or Santorini or back to the town where you were born. You have the luxury of time, until you don't—and then it becomes clear what's most important."

An awkward quiet settles. "Wow," Joe says after a moment. "You must be a real hit at cocktail parties."

I look at him. "What keeps you up at night?"

Joe frowns. "Climate change?"

"Something more personal," I ask.

"I'm a pretty chill guy—"

"You rub the lamp and the genie says, *I'll answer one mystery for you and only one mystery*. What is it?"

"Why did my dad leave?" Joe blurts out.

"You're not going to know that on your deathbed," I say gently. "Not unless you use your life to figure it out."

Alberto narrows his eyes. "Is that why *you're* here?"

I pin him with my gaze. "I know why my dad left," I reply, deliberately misunderstanding. "He was deployed, and then he died in a helicopter crash."

Alberto grinds his cigarette beneath his boot. "Maybe what you know isn't as important as what you *don't* know, right?" He gives Wyatt a pointed look before he walks downstairs.

Joe stands up. "Guess I'm gonna go figure out what I did to make my father disappear," he mutters, and he leaves.

"I should apologize to him." I bend my knees, groaning. "I'm an idiot."

Wyatt shrugs. "No, actually, you're quite bright. But your sense of tact could use a polish."

"Sometimes it's hard for me to remember not everyone spends all day with people who are dying."

"True," Wyatt says. "Some of us spend all day with people who are already dead." He nudges my shoulder. "Besides, you're not wrong. It's why the Coffin Texts even existed. What's the point of life, if not to accumulate knowledge?"

I glance at him, surprised. "That's absolutely *not* the point of life. It's who your existence snags on. Who changes, because they knew you. There's not a single tomb without art that represents a relationship—a father and his children, a man and his wives, even a noble and his citizens. *What* you know isn't nearly as important as *who* you know. Who will miss you. Who you will miss."

Wyatt studies me. "Who misses you?" he asks quietly. "Whom do you miss?"

Since that first day, we have not talked about Meret, but suddenly I miss her so fiercely that everything in me aches. I look at Wyatt, while the call to prayer runs over us like a river.

I imagine Re ducking underground, slipping into the corpse of Osiris as if he's wrapping himself in a blanket.

I think about why I came here.

I think of all the people whose hands I have held while they step off a cliff, into the unknown. Each time, I am floored by the bravery of humans. Each time, I am aware of what a coward I am.

"I miss lots of things," I say lightly. "Food without sand in it is at the top of the list, right now."

"Ice cream."

"Air-conditioning." I laugh.

"Well, there are some lovely hotels in Egypt. Or so I hear."

"I didn't come for a vacation."

"Right," Wyatt says, tightening the trap he's laid. "What did you come for?"

I hesitate. "Clarity."

He tilts his head. "I may be completely off the mark here, but my guess is that you left a comfortable home with a daughter and a husband who love you to prove something to yourself."

"You're partially right," I admit, hedging. "I wanted to be an Egyptologist ever since I was little, and I fucked that up."

"There's a host of things I wanted when I was a child that never came to pass," Wyatt counters.

I give him a sympathetic glance. "Friends?"

He whacks me on the shoulder. "No. But . . . French fries."

"You never had French fries?"

"Not the kind you get from a drive-through," Wyatt says. "Mine were pomme frites. And I wanted the kind of birthday cake with little sprinkles in the batter."

"Funfetti?"

His face lights up. "Yes. I saw it once on a television show."

I burst out laughing. "Are you really complaining because you had a private chef?"

"Grass is always greener, right? I truly think I missed out on a childhood rite of passage because I never had a cake that came out of a box."

"I forget you were born with that silver spoon up your—"

"Come to think of it, I don't think I ever had a proper party. My birthday was always during the school term," Wyatt says. "I think once my mother had a cake shipped to me. From Fortnum's. But that was because she canceled a visit to see me to go to France instead." He shrugs. "That's the thing about being obsessed with the past. It keeps you from having to notice the present."

He is speaking lightly, words running like mercury, just like mine were when I didn't really want him to look too closely at my responses. Even so, I'm reminded of who Wyatt truly is, and not what he projects into the world.

"You're the marquess now," I state. "So why haven't you gone back to England?"

"Turns out being the director of an Ivy League program is a much more acceptable profession than being a fledgling Egyptologist."

We both stare over the lip of the balcony at the cheek of the horizon, and the blush of the moon. "Your father, was he alive when you took over at Yale?"

"He was," Wyatt says. He fishes his phone out of his pocket and cues up the voicemail. "He called me and left a message. Honestly, I think he probably had to get my number from my mother, since he'd never done that before. I didn't answer—not because I was busy, but because I didn't know how to have a conversation with the man."

"What did he say?"

"I don't know. Never listened."

"You—*what*?"

He looks down at the glowing green screen. "I couldn't," he says softly. "At first because I was afraid I might still be a disappointment. And then—after he died—because I was afraid that maybe I *wasn't*."

I know how something in you changes when a parent dies. You go about the rest of your days just like you have before, pretending you are fine, knowing it is all a lie. It isn't until you lose a parent that you become an actor in the play of your own life.

I hold out my hand. "Give it to me."

"No," he says.

"I'll listen for you."

Wyatt's eyes widen. "*Absolutely* not."

"Why? Is this all some scam for pity? Is the message really from a restaurant in Cairo confirming your reservation on Friday at eight?"

Scowling, Wyatt passes me his phone. I press the little paused arrow and hold the phone up to my ear.

The voice is much like Wyatt's, but deeper and grained, like old wood. *I hear congratulations are in order.*

A beat.

*Well.*

*Well done.*

*Son.*

I realize that his father could have simply left out that last word, and it would have been enough.

I hand Wyatt back the phone. "Your father wasn't disappointed in his child," I say. "Trust me."

He slips it into his shirt pocket and fiddles with a button at his cuff.

"Like, how much of a not-disappointment?" Wyatt asks. "On a scale from one to Jesus?"

"You'll just have to listen one day if you want to find out."

"It's pathetic, isn't it. Forty-three years old and I'm still looking for a crumb of approval. Clearly that's why I suffered under Dumphries for so long."

I blink, and I can see Dumphries doing the fox-trot again with his wife. "Did he know? That he was sick?"

Wyatt glances at me. "I think so. But he didn't tell me at first. I don't know if it was because he was private, or because he wanted to make sure I was qualified for the job before he handpicked me to succeed him. Ironic, isn't it? All that time he pitted us against each other, and in the end, he would have been better off served by you while he was dying by degrees."

"I wasn't a death doula then," I point out.

"No," he says. "You weren't."

"I wish I'd known. I would have liked to let him know what he meant to me."

Wyatt turns so that he is facing me. "I tried to tell you."

"Dumphries didn't get sick until years after I left."

"But I wrote you," Wyatt says. "Daily, at first. They all were returned undelivered. When I was in New Haven again, I emailed you through Yale's server—and they bounced. After that, once a year, I'd go to the alumni network and see if they had any forwarding information for you. But it was the damnedest thing. It was almost like Dawn McDowell never existed." Wyatt stares at me. "I know why you left. I just don't understand why you didn't come back."

I can feel all the blood rushing from my head, making me dizzy. Snail mail from Egypt was spotty at best, but even if it had reached Boston, I was at the hospice with my mother, too consumed by her illness to pay attention. When I moved in with Brian, he had patiently gone through a Rubbermaid tub of bills and junk mail and had paid whatever was outstanding and tossed out the rest. Were letters from Wyatt in there? Had Brian deliberately thrown them away?

By then, I was pregnant. Everything had felt so fragile—loss, love, life—that maybe he had just shoved aside whatever might have threatened the equilibrium.

I swallow. "I never got your letters."

Wyatt takes my hand. He turns over my palm as if he is a special type of soothsayer who can read the past, if not the future. His fingers are scarred, warm, gentle. "I thought," he says, "that you were avoiding me."

I remember sitting at the airport with Wyatt, windshield wipers racing between us like a shared heartbeat. I remember thinking, *I have to get out of this truck,* and not moving. I remember running into my mother's room at hospice, twenty hours of travel collapsing down to the head of an arrow as I ran to her bedside. I remember being in Boston, thinking that one of us should get to grab the brass ring of the life we wanted, and if it couldn't be me, then at least it could be Wyatt.

*Don't do it,* I tell myself.

*Don't.*

But my thumb closes over his knuckles and my fingers curl around his. Every word I speak is ballast. "I didn't know you were looking."

I close my eyes and pull my hand away and stand.

"Big day tomorrow," I say, and I do what I do best.

I leave him behind.


IN MY TINY room, I lie in my underwear on the princess mattress. It is still so hot, even at midnight, that the room seems to breathe with me. A fan wheezes on an overturned milk crate, blowing a tongue of faded yellow ribbon in my direction.

Whenever I've thought about my life, it has been before and after, scored on different fault lines: Egypt. My mother's death. Meret. It's like there is one Dawn who inhabited the space on one side of the division, and a different Dawn who inhabits the space on the other, and it's hard for me to see how one evolved from the other. I wonder if this is a new fault line. I wonder if you can erase an old one, by going back to the spot where everything changed.

I have heard Brian expound upon this theory enough to realize that the answer is no; that we get no do-overs and whatever consciousness we are in negates the consciousness of any other timeline we might have traveled down. But surely that isn't the case. The World War II vet who winds up getting his college degree fifty years late; the man who marries his elementary school sweetheart seventy years after they shared a peanut butter sandwich; the boy in a developing country who is orphaned by Ebola gets a medical degree, and goes back to his homeland to cure the disease. In all of those cases, Fate was fulfilled eventually. But even so, the recipient wasn't who he had been at the beginning—wide-eyed and full of promise. By then, he'd *lived*. And when he was holding his diploma or his wife's hand or his stethoscope, you can bet he was thinking, *Well*. That *took forever*.

Maybe Wyatt is not the only one who's wrong about the point of life. Maybe it's not about accumulating knowledge or accumulating love. Maybe it's just about collecting regrets.

I can't sleep, and find myself twisting my wedding band around my finger. I got married on a Tuesday afternoon, a little less than a year after my mother's death. I did not actually ever tell Brian I would marry him. At the time, Meret was a few months old, and Kieran was used to seeing Brian as a father figure. His home had become mine: I no longer had to ask where the extra linens were kept or which drawer held the tiny screwdriver set for eyeglasses. When he casually suggested that we should make it official, because of things like taxes and health insurance, it made sense. We had settled into a comfortable routine; it wasn't as if a piece of paper was going to change much of my daily life. By then, Wyatt was so distant in my mind, he might as well have been something I dreamed.

I did not know much about modern marriage. My own parents, after all, had never managed to tell me they never officially tied the knot. I wondered if there had been a reason for that, beyond my father's family's wariness about an Irish girl who spent so much time longing for the sea, she was only a shadow onshore.

Ancient Egyptian marriage, though, was not all that different from what Brian was offering. We have no record of what the ceremony was like, but scholars know it was an economic partnership: finances were combined, and the resulting house and children were the products of that merger. It was so professional, in fact, that as terms of endearment husbands and wives sometimes called each other "brother" and "sister"—not because of the incestuous overtones, but because in legal and financial terms, they split holdings equally. Even in divorce, Egyptian women could take a third of the property and full custody of the children. In fact, divorce law was so fair to women in Egypt that Greek women took Egyptian names, preferring to marry and divorce under Egyptian law.

A week after Brian brought up the idea of getting married over a pot roast and mashed potatoes, we sat in the waiting room. I held Meret, and Kieran sat between Brian and me. If the other people in the grotty, gray waiting room of the town hall were judging me, they had their own issues: there was a couple that didn't look old enough to procreate, much less marry; and a woman in a sleek white suit who was holding a bouquet of sweet peas and whispering to a man old enough to be her grandfather.

Brian took one look at her and turned white. "I'll be right back," he said, and he bolted.

"Nice job," Kieran said. "You scared him off."

As it turned out, Brian had run down the street to a convenience store, because he realized that I should have flowers. He came back with a Cheeto-orange rose glued to a little plastic sign: GET WELL SOON. "It was all they had," he apologized.

He also got me a scratch ticket.

We had agreed that we would write up something simple—vows that would make this seem a little more special than just signing a piece of paper on a Tuesday afternoon. But when it came time, Brian turned pink from his neck to the tips of his ears. "I didn't . . . I didn't think we were going to say them out loud . . ."

*What else do you do with vows?* "That's okay," I told him. "It doesn't matter."

Really, no one else's words mattered but my own. I smiled at Kieran, who was juggling Meret in his arms while Brian and I held hands. I looked Brian in the eye and promised to honor and cherish him. When we walked out into the waiting room after the ceremony, people cheered. It was like the DMV of Love.

Afterward, we went to an Italian restaurant. We took turns going to the bathroom so that Kieran wasn't left alone at the table. In the restroom, I took out the vows I had written but not spoken during the ceremony—in hieroglyphs, and in English. From my Yale class notes I had copied a piece of a New Kingdom poem called "The Flower Song":

*Hearing your voice is sweet as pomegranate wine!*
*I live but to hear it!*
*If I could gaze upon you with every glance,*
*It would be more beneficial to me than eating or drinking.*

I threw them out with the towel I used when I washed my hands.

When Brian went to the bathroom, I used a dime to rub off the scratch ticket.

We didn't win.

That night after Kieran went to bed, Brian touched me as if I were made of glass, as if moving too quickly or holding me too close would make me disappear. Afterward, while he lay on his side and stroked the parabola of my shoulder, he gave me a piece of paper.

"These are my vows," he said.

"I thought you couldn't write them."

"I couldn't *speak* them," he corrected.

$$9x - 7i > 3(3x - 7u)$$

I was used to Brian talking about scientific concepts way over my head. It didn't look familiar, like the vector for acceleration or the theory of relativity. "Am I supposed to know what this is?"

"Solve for *i*."

I sat up, letting the sheet fall away from me. I rummaged in the nightstand, where I couldn't find a pen but did manage to unearth a crayon.

$$9x - 7i > 3(3x - 7u)$$
$$9x - 7i > 9x - 21u$$

"Now what?"

Brian reached over and wrote $-9x$ on each side of the equation.

$$-7i > -21u$$

*Solve for* i, I thought.

$$\frac{-7i}{-7} > \frac{-21u}{-7}$$

Then I smiled.

*i <3u*

Just before I fell asleep in Brian's arms, I asked, "Do you ever wonder if the reason your grandmother had to die, and my mother got sick, was so that we'd find each other?"

He hugged me closer, speaking against my skin. "I would have found you, no matter what."

I had fallen asleep on my wedding night wondering what might have brought a physicist to Egypt, had my mother not died, and if Brian had to cross paths with me there. Or what might have made an Egyptologist seek out a physicist to learn more about the past.

Now, in the heat of Egypt, I pull out the burner phone that Wyatt has given me. It is almost 7:00 P.M. in Boston. The service is spotty out here in Middle Egypt, but Brian picks up on the first ring.

"Hello?" he says in the flat voice he saves for telemarketers, for phone numbers he does not recognize.

"Brian, it's me."

"Dawn," he breathes. "*Dawn?* Are you all right? Where *are* you—"

"I texted Meret. I told her to tell you I was okay." I wince, realizing how stupid this sounds. "I didn't want you to worry."

"Jesus Christ, Dawn. It's been *days*. You said you'd be back soon . . . I thought you meant *right away*."

I swallow. "I thought I meant that, too."

There is a scuffle, and then quiet, as if Brian has shut himself inside a closet. "I don't understand," he says, his voice running the ragged edge of panic. "Please. Come home."

I rub my temple. "I can't, yet."

There are tears pushing behind his words. "Is everything okay?"

My throat feels hot and swollen. If being here is right, then why does it hurt so much to listen to Brian?

There is a soft knock just as I say *Yes* into the phone.

The door of my room opens. "Dawn," Wyatt says, unraveled. "What you said upstairs—" He stops, seeing the phone pressed to my ear, realizing that my response was not to him.

"Who is that?" Brian asks.

I do not take my eyes from Wyatt's face. From the stiffness of his body, I know he has guessed who I might be talking to.

"It's nobody," I whisper, and Wyatt's expression shutters.

"I have to go," I say into the phone, but the connection has been lost.

Wyatt and I are frozen in a sick tableau, unsure of what either of us is supposed to say or do now. He came to me because he couldn't sleep. I called Brian for the same reason.

What does that even *mean?*

I slide the phone under my thigh. "I was . . . calling home," I tell him.

"I'm sorry to disturb you," he says, with a formality that feels like the moat around a castle. He bows his head; the door closes with a click.

*I was,* I think.

I am.


WYATT IS ALREADY gone by 4:30 A.M., having left for the site to greet Mostafa and to organize the day's work. I wonder if he slept at all.

I wonder if, like me, he was running the lines of last night's conversation through his head.

The atmosphere is silent, but electric. The rest of us rush through our breakfast and pack our gear and hurry to the tomb. Today is the day no one wants to be late.

At the site I see Wyatt almost immediately, standing in the glow from a generator-powered lamp. He is bent over paperwork that Mostafa holds, but he looks up when he hears us all enter. "It's about time," he says shortly, even though we are fifteen minutes earlier than usual. He begins to bark out orders, reinforcing the jobs he outlined last night. My name is the last one he calls. "Dawn," he says. "You're with me."

I give a quick nod to Mostafa and fall into step behind Wyatt, who is already moving. He doesn't look back at me, doesn't speak.

All business then, as though last night never happened.

But this is not the time or the place for that conversation, and anyway, I am the one who cut Wyatt off last night. If he is treating me like a research assistant, like a grad student lucky enough to be in the distant orbit of this discovery, I have no one to blame but myself.

Wyatt stops near the safety fence that has been constructed around the mouth of the shaft. Several local workmen are speaking rapidly in Arabic, pointing and arguing over the best way to secure the ends of a long rope ladder. The rungs curl into the dark pit like the tongue of a viper. Because of the low ceiling of the tomb chapel, it isn't possible to angle a metal ladder down the shaft, and this is the alternative. Wyatt easily climbs over the wooden barrier, bracing his hips on the inside. I watch him tug on the rope and then hook one boot and the other, heading down. When his head is level with the floor of the tomb chapel, he glances up at me. "Problem?" he asks.

I shake my head and climb over the safety fence.

I wait until the rope ladder goes slack, which means Wyatt has reached the bottom.

His voice floats up to me. "The chamber seems undisturbed," he says.

I step onto the first rope rung, feeling it swing under my weight. I look at the two men who are holding the stakes in place. The shaft leading down to the burial chamber is about eighteen feet deep, and fairly narrow. I take a deep breath and begin to crawl beneath the surface of the earth, willing them to not let me fall.

It is like sliding down the parched throat of the world. The deeper I go, the darker it is. Wyatt's headlamp flickers at the base of the shaft, a pinprick I'm driving toward. As the light falls away above me, I imagine the walls are contracting, that I'm being swallowed.

Maybe halfway down, the ladder slips.

I give a small shriek and grab on to the rope and feel my shoulder scrape against the shaft. Wyatt yells in Arabic, and the rope goes taut again. *"Ana asif!"* I hear above me—a fervent apology.

My shoulder is bleeding, I think. I don't even have enough room to bend my arm and touch it to see.

"Dawn?" Wyatt calls.

"Yeah," I say, my heart hammering, my palms slick. "Be right there."

But I don't move.

The shaft at this level is only slightly wider than my hips. What if the ladder falls completely? What if there isn't enough air for both me and Wyatt by the time I get to the bottom? What if—

"Dawn," Wyatt says, "I want you to listen to me."

"All ears," I grind out.

"Take one more step down."

I give a tiny shake of my head, and my boot slips. I hear loose limestone rubble strike the bottom of the shaft, Wyatt curses as grit hits his face.

"Did you ever hear about Archie Hall?" he asks.

"No," I say. I force myself to set my foot down one more rung. I wait for Wyatt to respond.

"He was one of the epigraphers for U Chicago in the sixties or seventies," Wyatt says, as if we are chatting over coffee, instead of practically being buried alive. "Actually, I can't believe you've never heard of him. What kind of Griffin are you, anyway?"

Another shaky step. "Phoenix," I tell him. "Our mascot was the Phoenix."

"Of *course*. Anyway, Hall was transcribing an inscription in a temple—Karnak, or maybe Medinet Habu, I can't remember. Instead of climbing up and down the ladder to move it to the next spot on the wall he needed to read, he'd hold on to the top rungs and hop it horizontally, like a giant pair of stilts."

Step. And step again. The toe of my boot nudges the stone, and some more limestone powder falls.

"Dawn?"

"Still here," I say.

"So. Hall didn't realize the ladder was set up on a column, and at one point when he hopped, the ladder dropped a foot."

I pause in my climb. "Why the hell would you tell me this right now?"

"Hall broke both heels crashing through the rungs of the ladder," he says blithely.

I feel like I'm breathing through a reed.

"What's the punch line?" Wyatt asks.

"I don't know."

I take one more step, and feel his hand close over my calf. It is sure and steady and warm, and I let him guide me until I am on solid ground.

Wyatt angles his headlamp so that it doesn't blind me. "The punch line is: What was he doing wearing his heels in the temple?"

There's barely enough room for us to both fit. "All right?" he murmurs.

"All right," I say.

We are pressed up against each other from chest to ankle. Awkwardly we shift until I am behind him, my front to his back. If he crouches down, there is a little more space—this is the bit that had to be reinforced with timbers over the past few days. Beyond that is the burial chamber itself, which is blocked at the end by loosely stacked limestone blocks.

"I need light," he orders, and I do my best to shine my own headlamp in his direction as he crouches down and curls his fingers around the edge of the limestone. He grunts, and his shirt pulls tight across his shoulders as he struggles to dislodge the block. I watch his spine twist, his back flex with effort. I am just about to suggest we call up for a crowbar when the rock gives an inch. Thousands of years breathe toward us, a hot, dry gasp.

He makes a hole big enough to accommodate his own body, adjusts his headlamp, and begins to crawl through the narrow rock tunnel. I follow at his heels. Stones bite into my palms and my spine scrapes along the top of the channel. It is tight and, blessedly, short. Wyatt stops moving, filling my line of sight. "Can you see anything?" I whisper.

For a long moment, Wyatt is silent. Then he responds, the words a nod to Howard Carter, when he had first peeked into the burial chamber of Tutankhamun, and was asked the same question by Lord Carnarvon. "Yes," he says. "Wonderful things."

"Is there a coffin?"

He nods. "And it's intact."

He crawls from the tunnel into a slightly larger room of the rock-cut tomb. His headlamp illuminates the wooden box, taking up nearly all the floor space. Its surface is pale with years of lime dust. Three models sit on top of the wooden planks, equally dusty, with bright paint peeking through underneath. There seems to be a line of decorative hieroglyphs on the lid of the exterior coffin beneath the light fall of powder—symbols that justify the fifteen years of Wyatt's search:

Djehutynakht.

I AM DYING to know what's in that coffin, as is everyone else, but documenting the architecture of the tomb is the first task. Using classical methods—like the ones done when I was in grad school—would take a significant amount of time. The antiquities director gets a peek inside, and then Alberto and I swap places in the tiny tomb so that he and Wyatt can come up with a basic planimetry. Using a laser distance meter and goniometers, they draw the plan on an iPad. Alberto runs the scans while Wyatt, above, calculates the depth and orientation of the tomb on a map. For several hours, I serve as the runner between Alberto and Wyatt whenever there's a glitch, and at the end of our work, we have a full three-dimensional reconstruction of the burial chamber. Only then can individual pieces be moved by the Egyptian conservator, Safiya, who logs and packs them to be lifted out of the burial chamber. It's painstaking, celebratory work.

The ceiling of the burial chamber is only about 1.5 meters high. The space between the coffin and the wall of the chamber is so narrow that I'm the only one who can squeeze to the far end to see it and to brush off the limestone powder.

In addition to a lid, the exterior coffin has five sides—two long, two short, and the floor. The sides are beveled and fastened with dowels and copper ribbons; the top edges are pressed flush in a butt joint but the bottom is notched in a rabbet joint, and secured with more dowels and copper through the battens. There's a reason it's lasted four thousand years. The wooden box has one horizontal line of brightly painted hieroglyphs on all four sides, which gives all of Djehutynakht's titles. The only other paint on the exterior is a pair of *udjat* eyes facing east, although there may well be more detailed art on the interior walls that we can't see yet, with the inner coffin nestled tight inside. There isn't a treasury of gold, but there are offering figures and models stacked on top of the exterior coffin. The canopic chest has fallen off a limestone shelf onto the floor.

I spend hours huddled in the back of the chamber, looking at the models—the wooden carvings of a funeral procession led by a man in a kilt and followed by three slender women carrying wine, grain, and a black-and-cream painted offering box; a large funerary boat carved from a single piece of wood, its rowers attached by pegs and its oars remarkably intact; a kitchen boat that would have sailed with an official up and down the Nile on government business. The coffin is all about Djehutynakht's death, but these models are life as he knew it—his work and government responsibilities; the family and friends who would grieve him.

I realize with a little shock that this snapshot of Djehutynakht is no different from the clients I have now, who want to make sure they're ready for what comes next, but also want to remember who they have been.

THREE DAYS AFTER the burial chamber has been opened, the models have been removed and the coffin can be opened. The local workers scamper up and down the rope ladder, setting up extension cords and lights that run from the generator outside the tomb. Its noise is deafening, and I watch Wyatt cover his ears. "My mother used to say if your left ear rings, it means someone you love is talking about you," I shout. "If it's your right ear, someone wishes you evil."

"What if it's both ears?" Wyatt asks.

I grin. "Then you have a migraine."

We are standing at the top of the shaft, drowned out by the noise of the generator as Alberto moves around the burial chamber by himself taking photographs of the coffin from multiple angles. Omar, the inspector, trusts him enough to be there alone. His light source is a battery pack that flashes every time he takes a picture, and with each snap, the photograph instantly appears on the iPad that Wyatt holds.

I glare down the dark shaft. There's another burst of light, and a photo blinks onto the iPad screen. "Why is it taking forever?"

"Do you know how long it took Carter to clear out Tutankhamun's tomb?" Wyatt says. "Ten *years*. He numbered everything. Photographed everything. Drew everything." He smirks. "I've been at this for fifteen years. If anyone deserves to be impatient, it's me."

The tomb is still crowded—but there's one person conspicuously missing. "Dailey," I say, reaching into the corners of my mind for the name Joe once told me. "Why isn't your money person here?"

I cannot imagine funding an expedition and not wanting to be present when the actual discovery is made. Wyatt's head snaps up, and his cheeks flush. "From what I've been told, because of an airline workers' strike in Italy."

"Your benefactor's Italian?" I ask, but before Wyatt can reply Alberto calls up to us. It is finally time to open the coffin.

We shimmy down the rope ladder in quick succession—first Wyatt, then me, then Safiya the conservator, and finally Omar. There is virtually no room in the chamber with all of us, plus half a dozen workers having an in-depth discussion with Wyatt about the best way to lift the top of the outer coffin, so the inspector offers to wait at the top of the shaft again. Sweat pours off my face and under the collar of my shirt; it is easily a hundred degrees in this tiny stone room, and the air does not move inside it. Fans to improve air circulation are, of course, forbidden. What has been a blessing for preservation makes our work a living hell.

Abdou comes up with the best plan, and the workers and Wyatt lift the massive lid of the exterior coffin and muscle it sideways. In the weak, splintery light that the wheezy generator provides, I can see an inner coffin made of cedar nested inside, much like the ones we had gazed at in the Boston MFA as graduate students. I cannot make out any of the individual markings; I can only tell that the paint is even more vibrant than that on the outer coffin.

It takes nearly an hour for the cedar lid to be removed, and it requires a human Jenga of positioning as we bunch together to make room for the wood to be gently rested on its side. Alberto darts between and around us as we jostle, so that he can continue snapping his photographs.

Wyatt wipes his brow with the sleeve of his shirt. "That was such great fun," he says. "Let's do it again." He gestures to the inner coffin, and curls his fingers under the seam of the lid.

It's not as heavy, but it is still unwieldy and there is very little space in the burial chamber for the sheer number of bodies needed to open and lift it. I am at the far end of the burial chamber, squeezed between the rock and the short end of the coffin.

When it opens, there's no smell of death. Just resin, heady and sharp. Djehutynakht's dessicated mummy lies on his side facing east, the shape of his body hidden beneath tight layers of linen. The light flickers over a funerary mask, and the outer layer of wrappings has been bored into by insects. The mummy is draped in a shroud with a fringed edge. Opposite him are lines of spells from the Coffin Texts, as well as a vividly painted false door through which his *ba* soul could come and go. The mummy is flush against the other interior wall, but above his hip and head I get a glimpse of a colorful offering frieze with sandals, jugs of wine, haunches of meat. For a moment we stand in awe, as Alberto captures our reverence with his camera.

"Right," Safiya says, jerking us all back into motion. "Let's get started."

She scrambles out of the chamber and up the ladder, calling orders to workers to bring padding and ropes, which will be used to secure the mummy as the open coffins are lifted in tandem. Alberto follows her, because once everyone descends on the burial chamber to pack up the mummy for excavation into the main tomb chapel, space will be at even more of a premium.

Wyatt starts after them but turns back when he realizes I am standing with my hands lightly balanced on the wooden edge of the inner coffin, staring at Djehutynakht's mummy.

"The answer is: *I don't know*," he says.

"What's the question?"

"Is there a Book of Two Ways under him?"

I glance down, where a thick layer of dust lies on the interior coffin floor.

"For your information, that *isn't* what I was thinking about."

"No?" Wyatt says. "Taking mental notes for a Halloween costume, then?"

"You have to admit this is not an average Thursday," I reply.

I look down at the funerary mask. It appears to be embellished in gold leaf, but the features are detailed—one nostril larger than the other, corners of the eyes dotted with red. They would have mirrored the features of the nomarch in a stylized way, so that his soul could recognize his mummy as part of its daily resurrection.

It makes me think of the death masks that were taken of kings and scholars and artists from the Middle Ages to the Civil War, from Henry VIII to Napoleon to Nikola Tesla, displayed at funerals and then in museums. "Have you ever heard of *l'inconnue de la Seine*?" Wyatt shakes his head. "She drowned in Paris, in the 1880s. Someone at the morgue made a death mask of her face, and it's . . . beautiful. She looks like she fell asleep smiling, even though it was probably a suicide. She was compared to the Mona Lisa, and rich people had copies of the mask on their walls as art. In the 1960s, it was used as the face of the first CPR mannequin."

Wyatt slips his hands into his pockets. "Irony, in a nutshell."

"It's pretty amazing, to think that you could go so peacefully into death." I look down at Djehutynakht. "Do you think it worked, for him?"

"What?"

I wave my hand at the spells written on the coffin. "All of this. All the preparation. Do you think he got where he wanted to go?"

Wyatt shrugs. "I sure as hell hope so, because it was a shit ton of work to get him in here, and it's going to be a shit ton more work to get him out."

He turns and I hear the groan of rope as he starts to climb the ladder. I take a last look at the mummy. I know, philosophically, that the only way to learn more about the way people lived in the past is to do just this: pick apart what they believed to be their final resting place. From an academic standpoint that justifies our work. I also know that religion is what we make of it. But what if Djehutynakht—and the others—were right? What if, when the sun goes down tonight and his *ba* soul returns to his coffin, the corpse he needs to reunite with is gone?

What if the piece of you that's missing is the critical one?


I HAVE HEARD that love and hate are two sides of the same coin, which is the only explanation I can give for why I fell so hard for Wyatt, so fast. As a grad student I'd been in a two-person race with him, trading places every now and then. I'd spent so much time trying to surpass Wyatt that it was a revelation to stand on equal ground and stop running long enough to truly see him.

He was not the persona he projected—an arrogant, quick-witted Brit used to being the smartest one in the room. That, I learned, was an act. He had nightmares that made him thrash in my arms. He was mischievous, leaving me dirty hieroglyphic messages that would steam up in the bathroom mirror when we were showering. He touched me as if I were made of gold or mist or memory.

It was hard to hide a romance from eight people living in a single small household, but we were determined. We had to work together at the *wadi* on the newly discovered dipinto, so we continued to snipe at each other and generally act as if we could not stand to be in close proximity, when—in fact—every time Wyatt passed me he'd slide his hand along the shallow of my spine, and when we were sit-

ting beside each other at dinner, I'd hook my pinkie finger with his
and draw his hand onto my thigh beneath the table.

When the household napped in the high heat of the afternoon, I
would listen for Wyatt's footfall outside my bedroom door. There
were two loose tiles that rocked, no matter how quietly you moved.
I'd count to a hundred, and then I would follow. Sometimes I would
have to sneak past Hasib, Harbi's father, sleeping in the shade of the
courtyard underneath the bright flags of laundry flapping on the
line. As soon as I was outside the gates of the Dig House, I'd look
down at the dust, shading my eyes from the glare of the sun. Wyatt
would have left me a handful of stones in the shape of an arrow, or a
line carved along the edge of the path that led to the bank of the
river. I would be halfway to the Nile when I saw him waiting. Or
he'd spring from a crop of corn planted by a farmer and wrap his
arms around me from behind.

We stole those hours for ourselves. The sun never bothered us,
even when our cheeks pinkened and our hair bleached lighter. We
would walk the narrow paths between raised garden beds, kissing
amidst the sharp smell of wild onions. We lay on a bed of hay, Wyatt
painting me from nape to navel with a brush made of timothy, as a
donkey rolled in the dust and sang for us. We would sit on the edge
of the river and talk—about his father, who had managed to deplete
the family fortune on a series of terrible business investments, but
still insisted on sending his sons to Eton to keep up appearances;
about my mother, who worked two jobs to pay off my student loans.
What it would be like to see our names in print together. How it felt
to get lost in time by getting lost in time.

At night, I'd count off the number of people who headed to the
showers, waiting until I was second to last. Then I'd wander into the
bathroom and Wyatt would follow—which wasn't odd, because
there were multiple stalls—except that we'd wind up in one together. He would lift my hips and pin me against the tile wall. Or
he'd sink to the tile floor and feast on me until my own knees gave
out. I remember his head thrown back in the steam; his fingers leaving bruises on my thighs. I remember being so close to him that
even the water couldn't slip between us.

. . .

WHEN HOWARD CARTER found the mummy of Tutankhamun and attempted to lift it out, he didn't realize the innermost coffin was solid gold and the entire operation nearly collapsed. For Djehutnakht's mummy, Safiya has set up a winch, positioned over the burial shaft on long wooden legs. The conservator has already removed the two coffin lids to the main tomb chamber, and has padded the mummy where it lies and bound it tightly so that it doesn't move as the nesting-doll coffins are hauled up by local workers. From there, she will move the mummy into a wooden crate that breathes. Mummies are not unwrapped anymore, but given CT scans instead. Wyatt has teamed up with a hospital in Minya for that sometime in the future, but he's not a physical anthropologist, so it's not the focus of this discovery. I know that everyone equates Egyptology with mummies, but the truth is, they don't really tell us all that much. Yes, someone died thousands of years ago. Always good to confirm. But it's what's underneath him in that coffin that might help us understand how Djehutynakht lived, what he believed, what he hoped for.

The tomb chapel is once again packed with people—Mostafa Awad is back, and there are antiquities directors I've never seen before, plus Safiya has brought a team with her to assist with the transfer of the mummy from coffin to crate. We all technically have work we could do in the tomb but this is one of those days we will be telling the story of for years to come, and Wyatt doesn't seem inclined to order anyone back to copying texts on the walls. We mill around, listening to the call of the foreman at the winch and the coordinated shouts from the workers below as the pulley system is engaged. Inch by inch the coffins are lifted, until finally from my vantage point behind Wyatt, I can see the cedar lip of the coffin emerging from the burial shaft.

It takes the better part of the morning for the entire coffin to clear the shaft and balance beneath the winch over the hole. Three more hours for it to be gently removed from the pulleys and ropes and set on padded splints in the tomb chapel. We work past lunch, when the sun is bleaching the sand and the rock around us and the heat becomes a living thing, because no one wants to leave before seeing this through.

Finally, the wooden coffin is settled and the conservation team can do their work. They gently lift the mummy from where he rests on his side and place him on his back in the waiting crate. Like a transplant surgeon waiting for the handoff of the organ, Wyatt then takes his place at the center of the action. Alberto seems to be everywhere at once, photographing the transfer of the mummy and the golden funerary mask and the reveal of the interior coffin.

The transfer of the coffins has dislodged more limestone dust, as has the removal of the mummy. Wyatt waits impatiently for Alberto to finish documenting the inside of the narrow cedar box and then takes a clean brush from his pocket. He leans way down, stretching to reach the bottom, gently brushing away the powder to get a better look at the floorboards of the coffin, which were previously obscured by the mummy.

With a whoop of delight, he drops the brush onto the stone floor of the tomb chapel, lifts me off my feet, and swings me in a circle. I stiffen, aware that everyone in the vicinity is staring at him. At us.

But then he sets me down and I completely disregard their raised eyebrows. Because there on the bottom of Djehutynakht's inner coffin is a wavy line of blue, a rolling stripe of black, a narrow red rectangle. Egyptology's newest discovery is the world's oldest version of the Book of Two Ways.

THE SEASON WE had a hidden relationship, Wyatt would come to my twin bed every night, and to fit we'd flatten our bodies together. I got so used to falling asleep beside him that I couldn't do it on my own, which is why one night when he didn't come to the shower or to my bedroom, I found myself headed to his room instead.

I collided with him in the hallway in the dark. He steadied my shoulders, dropping the comforter he carried. "Change of scenery," he whispered.

I knew he was headed to the *wadi* without him saying so. There was a guard stationed there at night now, but we would tell the *gaffir* that we wanted to look at the inscription with glancing light, which you sometimes did after dark. Wyatt gave me a headlamp, and we struck out, two shooting stars.

Underneath the inscription, Wyatt spread the comforter and then gestured to it. "After you, my queen."

I stretched out. "Queen?" I said. "How come I can't be a king?"

He laughed. "Like Hatshepsut?"

She had been the daughter of Thutmose I, and became queen of Egypt when she married her half brother, Thutmose II. When he died, she acted as the reigning queen until her stepson, the baby Thutmose III, got older. But because she had all these other remarkable qualifications like bloodline and ritual training, she decided she shouldn't limit herself. She became co-king around 1473 B.C.E., taking on male royal titles.

"She was pretty damn ambitious," Wyatt said.

I came up on my elbows. "How come when a woman takes power it's ambitious? And when a man does it, it's the natural order of things?" I frowned. "Being politically motivated and being female aren't mutually exclusive. For all we know, she was in the middle of a family crisis. Like maybe someone was threatening to take the throne from her stepson and she had to figure out how to save it. That's just being a good mom."

"Mommy dearest, maybe. After she died, Thutmose III smashed all her monuments and erased her name—"

"Not till it was time for his own kid, Amenhotep, to take over. Being a woman was literally the least important thing about her. She didn't hide it. In art, she wore a *nemes* headdress and a male kilt and was topless—but you could still see she had breasts."

Wyatt unbuttoned my shirt. "Do tell."

"Even when she was a king, her name was still written as Foremost of the Noble Ladies. And all the royal texts describing her have female pronouns."

He nuzzled my neck, tugging down my pants. "I love it when you get all feminist."

I swatted him. "She also built Deir el-Bahari as a huge memorial temple and she led a trading expedition to Punt that was huge—"

"You know what else is huge?"

"—but none of it had anything to do with her gender. It would be like having a female president and saying that any of her achievements were because she was a woman, not because she was a leader."

"Hatshepsut definitely got shit done," Wyatt said. He framed my face and kissed me.

By the time we broke apart, I was fighting for breath. "You have a problem with smart, ambitious women who get shit done?"

He rolled me on top of him, so that I straddled his body. "You know what they say," Wyatt murmured. "Beneath every powerful woman is a very, very lucky man."

I loved that we could fight about Egyptian kings and queens in the middle of the desert at night. I loved that I didn't have to explain to Wyatt who Hatshepsut was. I loved the physics of our relationship: that we could argue with the same intensity that we came together. I loved how every minute with him felt like a storm, the moment before it happened.

I loved Wyatt.

I think the reason I remembered that one night so clearly was because it was the first time I admitted this to myself, and instead of feeling panic or confusion I just felt this soft, flannel blanket of *right*. It was like staring out your bedroom window the morning after a blizzard and seeing the hills and slopes of a landscape that seemed unrecognizable, but that you knew you could still navigate by heart.

The other reason I remembered that night was because we overslept in the morning. We yanked up the comforter and raced through the desert to get to the Dig House before anyone else could wake up. But when we stumbled into the kitchen, the five other grad students and Dumphries were already sitting at the table, tucking into their breakfast. "Thank the gods," Dumphries said, without looking up from his coffee. "Now we can all stop pretending we don't know you two are getting it on."

I flushed so deeply that I thought my face would melt. Wyatt mumbled something unintelligible and handed off the comforter to Hasib, slinking into the chair beside mine. We didn't touch. We barely even breathed. "You're not the only one who can hear a loose tile," Dumphries said, and he turned to me. "Pass the creamer?"

THERE IS A water main break at the Minya antiquities magazine, which means that the coffins cannot be moved there as planned. Fortunately, no artifacts already inside were harmed, but the building itself is hard to get in and out of, so the decision is made to transport everything to the Dig House magazine for more detailed study, and to station extra police guards there for protection.

It also means that Wyatt and I will have round-the-clock access to the coffin. I could literally roll out of bed, and study the Book of Two Ways. But if I had any dream of my head bent beside Wyatt's as we pored over the image on the coffin floor together, it vanishes as I realize that this discovery only means there is even more work to be done, and I am not the one who decides what we get to analyze first.

Fifteen years ago, I'd been writing my thesis on how the coffin was a microcosm of both the tomb and the universe itself. At a basic level, each funerary text contained information the deceased would need in the afterlife. But zoom out a bit, and the coffin itself became a miniature of the cosmos, from the sky painted on the lid to the map of the Book of Two Ways on the floor, to the mummy that filled the space in between. Zoom out again, and the tomb itself—with its superstructure of a public chapel space and underground burial chamber and the coffin contained within—was another symbolic representation of the layers of the universe.

But here, in the Dig House magazine, we are deconstructing even further. Set on separate sawhorses, the inner coffin and the exterior coffin are both intact and quite large, with walls over a meter high. We've set up scaffolding so that we can climb up and look inside, but even so, the text is small and distant enough for it to be a struggle to see. Instead, we rely on Alberto to photograph, his camera affixed to a long pole.

I have already started copying the art in the coffins, tracing it on my iPad so that Alberto will be able to input the images into a three-dimensional digital representation. Wyatt has directed me to start with the paintings on the inside of the exterior coffin, which are so breathtaking that I cannot do them justice. On my screen I can see the brushstrokes of the artist, the shading and detail that leap off the cedar in white and sienna and blue directly across from where Djehutynakht's head would have faced. There is the head of an ibex, its horns grooved and its ear patterned. A huge ceremonial wine jar in terra cotta is given dimension with a white highlight on one side. There are tables groaning with fruits and vegetables and meat and cones of bread, the haunch of a steer with spotted skin, a coiled rope with individually articulated fibers and strands, and one stunning goose whose broad wings are painted with mottled feathers in every shade of gray. The most intricate artwork is the ornately drawn false door through which the *ba* soul can slip between the Netherworld and the tomb. Above it is a text asking for offerings from the king and Osiris on festival days, with a handy list of suggested items on the far right side of the wall.

My eyes are burning after an hour of painstaking work on the iPad. I rub them, and glance at Wyatt. He is deep into his own iPad images, his mouth silently moving as he murmurs transliterations of texts that Alberto has already photographed on the sides of Djehutynakht's inner coffin. There are 1185 individual spells within the Coffin Texts; he has to figure out which ones Djehutynakht included.

He isn't paying attention to what I'm doing, so I glance at the inner coffin. As on the outer coffin, there are *udjat* eyes on its outside front panel. These line up with a matching pair of *udjat* eyes on the flip side of the wood, painted above a false door, as if the mummy would have been able to peer through both sets of them to see through the wood and look at all the gorgeous artwork I've been copying from the inside of the exterior coffin. On the floor of the coffin is the telltale wavy map of the Book of Two Ways. I flip through the digital files until I find the photographs Alberto has taken of it.

When I first studied the Book of Two Ways, I didn't start with Egypt. I began with maps—Anaximander's world map from Greece in the sixth century B.C.E., Fra Mauro's medieval map, the Atlas Maior, maps of Atlantis and Middle-earth, maps of what the United States would have looked like if the South had seceded and Europe if D-Day had never happened. Maps don't have to be literal. They don't have to be to scale, or to be tangible. They might be drawn to depict the real world, to dream a fictional space, or to inspire a symbolic one—like medieval maps of cathedrals that moved from door to nave to altar in a journey toward Christ. In that sense, the map mirrors the belief system of its maker—just like the Book of Two Ways. Middle Kingdom artists sketched a graphic image of how to walk through the afterlife, complete with entry points and impassable gates and lakes of fire. Crossing this landscape successfully was like winning the best ever season of *Survivor,* with an eternal home in the same neighborhood as the gods. Here in Deir el-Bersha, there have been four published generations of coffins with the Book of Two Ways in them. Wyatt's will precede them all.

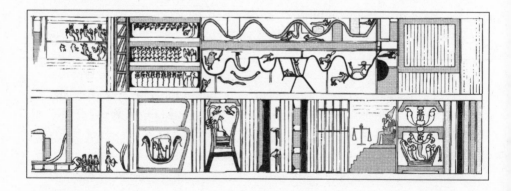

Djehutynakht's coffin contains the long version of the Book of Two Ways, 101 spells, which cover two long bands on the cedar floor, and which are broken into segments. It begins at sunrise as Djehutynakht sets sail on the sun god's solar bark. The distinctive geographic map—the upper blue water route and the lower black land route—comes next. The trails are divided by a red band, the "Lake of Fire of the knife-wielders." Text fills the rest of the space, describing mountains and fields and rivers and shrines and the names of armed monsters trying to knock the deceased off course. In the loops and hills and valleys, there are tiny, faint pictures of these beasts. Finally, the deceased gets special clothing and accessories to show that he's conquered this part of the journey, and has made it to Rosetau, the place of hauling, where a coffin would have been moved into a tomb.

In the next section, things only get harder. There are three chambers with fiery walls guarded by "watchers." If the deceased survives this hurdle, he gets tossed into the paths of confusion on the flint walls in Rosetau, where illustrated tracks crisscross. Beyond that are demons with heads made of scarabs, and demons who hold snakes and lizards, who must be defeated before the deceased reaches Osiris and can live forever.

There is a shorter version of the Book of Two Ways that usually ends here, but in Djehutynakht's coffin, there is more: an appeal to the god Thoth, patron of this geographic region; and then a thick block of text with no stories or descriptions of the afterlife. Instead, it is a justification of the life of the deceased, meant to prove him worthy of sailing with Re. Then seven gates are shown, each with a more terrible guardian. Finally, the deceased channels his immortality, and is compared to both Re at sunrise and Osiris in the underworld.

This map was the way an Ancient Egyptian reached the afterlife. But it also shows us what Ancient Egyptians *thought* of the afterlife. This wasn't all pearly gates and cherubs playing harps. The gates were on fire, and the creatures were terrifying—chimeras with human heads and animal torsos and knives, snake bodies and wings and claws. In this Book of Two Ways, I find a baboon-snake chimera wielding a knife in the water route, and a leopard-bodied monster with a cow head and divine horns.

There's another image, too. I scroll lower on the photograph, zooming in on it. A seated man, a white crown, a crook and flail in his hands. This is no monster, but a classic Middle Kingdom image of Osiris, seated on a stepped platform, with Thoth as a baboon above him—a direct allusion to the Judgment Hall of Osiris in the much later Netherworld Books. Beside him are empty scale pans. It's drawn in the part of the Book of Two Ways that is usually solely text, no illustrations.

Scrambling up the side of the scaffolding, I check the photograph against the actual art in the coffin. This can't be right. I've never seen a Book of Two Ways with Osiris and scales in it before. In fact, the only place you ever see that is in Spell 125 of the Book of Going Forth by Day, where the heart of the deceased is weighed against the white feather of truth.

Except that text will not exist for another four hundred years.

"Wyatt," I say, "I think you should come look at this."

He glances up from his iPad and frowns at me. "You're supposed to be working on the exterior coffin," he says, but he climbs up beside me on the scaffolding.

"I may be rusty," I tell him, "but I think this is the Hall of Two Truths."

"From the Book of Going Forth by Day?" he says. "It can't be. That's New Kingdom."

"What if something in the Coffin Texts evolved into it?"

I could see Wyatt reaching through the vast store of knowledge in his mind. "Coffin Text 47 comes closest," he says. He starts flipping through the images Alberto has downloaded for us. His finger passes over the hieroglyphs, reading so much faster than I ever could, until he finds the text in question on a photo of the inner coffin's western-facing wall: *"As for any god, any spirit of any dead person who shall oppose themselves against these dignities of yours . . . they shall be crushed as the confederates of Terrible of Face. Your seat shall be spacious within the disk. You shall measure in the scales like Thoth. Your reputation shall be recognized by He who is in his Disk as that of a god who is beside him. You shall eat bread in the Broad Hall. You shall be given meals just like Re, by those in charge of the storehouses of Heliopolis. Your heart belongs to you. It shall not be stolen by the guardians of the roads . . . Raise yourself to life forever!"*

The deceased, weighing his own heart. The immortal result of a passing grade: keeping company with Re. The Broad Hall of Two Truths. Heliopolis—beneath the neighborhood now closest to the

Cairo Airport, and the chief cult place of Re. It's all there, the ingredients of what will become Spell 125 in the New Kingdom. But until now, there hasn't been an image in the Middle Kingdom to connect the two.

I lean down to find the placement of the actual text inside the coffin and notice something strange. I can match a string of the hieratic, but it's bisected by a split in the cedar that isn't reproduced on the iPad image of the text. "Where's the break in the wood?"

Wyatt tilts his head, baffled. His eyes scan the coffin, narrowing. "The spell's duplicated on *both* sides of the coffin."

"Is that normal? To repeat?"

"Sometimes," he says. "In this case, it could be intentional. The Hall of *Two* Truths."

From where we are on the scaffolding, we are just too far away to accurately read it. I scroll through Alberto's photos for the opposite wall, and look for Coffin Text 47. Wyatt and I hold our iPads side by side, so that we can read the matching spells on both the eastern- and western-facing walls.

Except they don't quite match.

*As for any god, any spirit of any dead person who shall do evil against your soul . . . you are justified within the Hall of Two Truths. You are pure! You are pure! You are pure! You are pure! Your purity is the purity of He who is in his Disk. No evil can happen to you in the land, in this Hall of Two Truths, because you know the names of the gods who are in it. Raise yourself to life forever!*

"*This* one's almost verbatim Spell 125 of the Book of the Dead, except it's in the second person, like the rest of the Coffin Texts—"

"Wyatt," I interrupt. "Look." Using the tip of a pencil to reach, I point to the spot on the eastern-facing wall where this spell is painted, and then the board directly opposite it. I imagine the mummy as he was found, lying on his side. If you drew a line from one spell to the other, it would most likely have passed through Djehutynakht's heart.

If I ever wanted proof of how inextricably linked text and location on the coffin were, this is it.

"Dawn," Wyatt says. "I think we just found the missing link."

. . .

NOT LONG AFTER our relationship was outed by Dumphries, Wyatt and I were tangled together in my twin bed one late afternoon. He was naked, the fan cooling the sweat on his spine, his profile obscured by that tangled beacon of hair. The sun gleamed at the window, a peeping Tom. This was the time of day when everyone else in the house usually napped, and Wyatt had drifted off after making love. For some reason, I couldn't fall asleep. I sketched my finger over his shoulder as if I were drawing a map of the world where I wanted to live.

We had come together like a conflagration, as usual, like there was not enough time and we had a terrible need to consume each other. My bra was looped around the base of the fan, where Wyatt had thrown it. His pants were caught in the bedding. One of his shoes was upside down.

My mother would have said that's bad luck; that it needed to be turned right side up. But I couldn't do that without pulling away from him.

Wyatt mumbled something, swatting at his neck, then catching my hand with his own. "Let me be, wench, you're going to kill me." He rolled over, his eyes slitted, a smile already playing at his lips. "But what a way to go."

"Wench?" I pinned him to the mattress. "You misogynist pig."

He reached for me, pulling me closer. "Talk dirty to me."

My laugh was caught between us, passed back and forth in a kiss. Wyatt flipped me onto my back and licked my throat. My skin cooled as it dried, as he traced a trail down the middle of me.

At first, we didn't hear the knock on the door. Then, when we did, Wyatt yelled out to whoever was on the other side of it. "Piss off . . ."

"Dawn." Dumphries's voice was grave.

I looked at Wyatt and grabbed his shirt from the floor. Pulling it on so that it fell to my thighs, I waited for him to wrap himself in the sheets, and then opened the door.

"There's been a message," Dumphries said.

Back then, I didn't have a cellphone with international coverage. Very few people did, but Dumphries was one of them. It was the emergency number we all left for our families at home. He held out the phone. "You should call your mother."

He left me with the phone, with Wyatt. When the door closed, I dialed the country code and my home phone number. While I waited for the connection to be made, I stared at Wyatt's upside-down shoe.

Wyatt curled himself around me as I sat on the edge of the bed, his arm around my waist, as if he knew in advance that I was going to need something to anchor me. "Mom?" I said.

When she started to talk, when she told me about the cancer, I went still. I thought maybe if I stopped moving, I could stem the flow of words. But they kept coming: *ovarian . . . hospice . . . weeks.*

I don't know if Wyatt could hear her speaking, but he knew something was very, very wrong. I felt his fingers thread with mine, squeeze.

She was still talking, recounting the chemo that had not worked, explaining why she hadn't told me earlier, insisting that I not interrupt my life for her death. "I'm coming home," I announced. I stood, letting go of Wyatt.

THE TEXTS THAT Wyatt and I have found in the interior coffin are all about morality—namely, being able to stand up to the gods after death and say with honesty that you haven't done anything wrong. But what does it really mean to be good? Is it finding a calling that helps other people? Is it running to the bedside of someone who is dying? Is it putting someone else's needs before your own? You could argue, I suppose, that any of those actions are about not selflessness, but martyrdom. Driven not by ethics, but guilt.

For that matter, what does it mean to be *im*moral? Is it pursuing your own dreams at all costs? Is it lying to others, or lying to yourself? Is it falling in love with a person when you are supposed to be in love with someone else? Does it matter if you only have the feelings, and tamp them down?

I know this much: morality is meant to be a clear line, but it's not really. Things change. Shit happens. Who we are is about not what we do, but why we tell ourselves we do it.

Wyatt misses dinner because he is on the phone with the dean of graduate studies at Yale, and then with their communications department, working through the messaging that will be sent out tomorrow morning after the Ministry of Antiquities puts out the initial press release. It's not nearly as thorough as what will be revealed when he publishes the coffin, but because that is months away, this will give him—and Yale—a bump of recognition in the academic archaeological community.

When everyone in the Dig House has turned in for the night, I stay on the roof balcony, too keyed up to fall asleep. I know Wyatt will put my name on the paper he publishes. Long after I've left, my work will remain in the canon for future Egyptologists. It is what I told Wyatt I wanted, the reason I gave him for coming here.

I watch a mayfly hop along the balustrade before it is joined by two others.

"There you are," Wyatt says. "I thought I'd lost you."

*I thought I'd lost you.*

I turn, a bright smile pasted on my face. "Finished with your calls?"

"For now," he says.

"Did you get in touch with Dailey?"

He frowns a little. "Why do you ask?"

"I just assume that the benefactor would want to know about a major discovery."

"I don't really want to talk about Dailey," Wyatt says, leaning against the balcony. He swats at one of the flies.

"No, don't," I tell him.

"Please tell me you haven't become one of those people who carries a spider outside in a paper cup so it can live out the rest of its life . . ."

"Mayflies have the shortest life span on earth. Like, twenty-four hours. Wouldn't you feel terrible if you caused an even more untimely death?"

Wyatt looks at the fly. "What rotten luck. Well, mate, I hope you've had the best of days."

*I did,* I think.

He pauses. "What *do* flies do?"

"Dance in groups and get it on with each other."

"Clearly more evolved than we are, then," Wyatt replies. "If you only have a little time, make the most of it."

I cannot even meet his eyes.

"Olive," Wyatt says quietly, balancing his elbows on the balustrade. "What really happened?"

There is no point in pretending I don't know what he's referring to. I lean back against the railing, so that we are facing in opposite directions. Which, I realize with a sad, smothered laugh, is just right. "I didn't have a choice. My mother had cancer, and she'd kept it from me as long as she could. She was going into hospice."

"I know why you left," Wyatt says. "I want to know why you never came back."

So this is what it feels like, a reckoning. When you have to push at the scar you try to keep hidden under scarves and coats and layers, and in doing so, you remember exactly what it felt like at the moment of injury. I feel gently along the fissure, the crack that separated my life from what I thought it would be to what it would become. *What if, what if, what if.*

"I had to be there for my mother." My words ring with conviction, and I think again of Djehutynakht in the Hall of Two Truths, justifying the acts of his life. "And then I had to be there for Kieran."

"Your . . . brother," Wyatt says, pulling at a thread of memory.

"Yeah. He became a doctor," I answer proudly. "A neurosurgeon."

Wyatt shifts, so that he is looking at me. "And meanwhile . . . you . . ."

"Became a death doula," I finish. "You know that already."

But we both know that wasn't what he was asking. His real question is about what I *didn't* become. A doctor, myself. An Egyptologist.

His.

For years I told myself that this was about Brian, because of Brian. I told myself I was too ashamed to admit to Wyatt that I had turned to someone else so quickly. But this was never about Brian. It was about *me*.

"If you had gotten my letters," Wyatt asks softly, "would you have come back?"

I face him, staring into those bright blue eyes that have always been the pilot light inside me. "I couldn't."

"Then I would have come to *you*."

There was a world, maybe, where this worked. Where Wyatt finished his degree and got a job at a university and went off on digs a couple of times a year, thriving in a career I couldn't have. In that world, I might have come to resent him for something that was never his fault.

In that world, I had not turned to another man—a good, kind man who made everything feel easier, rather than more tangled. In that world, I was not pregnant with that man's baby.

In the real world, I chose safety and security over Wyatt.

My throat is throbbing, I try to explain all this, but I can't. "You asked me why I'm here: because I thought this would be my life, and it wasn't, and I needed to know what it would have been like. You, me, a dig site. A discovery. I know it was my choice to give it up. But I wanted to see, just once, what I was missing."

I don't even realize I'm crying until I feel Wyatt's touch on my cheek, wiping away a tear. He rubs together his thumb and forefinger, as if my sadness could seep into his skin. "Maybe we *did* take the same path, in spite of it all," Wyatt says. "You get close to people who inevitably leave you. The difference is that *you* call it work. *I* call it love."

He walks downstairs into the Dig House. I don't know how long I stand on the balcony, beneath the stars in a feverish sky. Long enough to stop crying, to be able to draw in a breath without feeling like I'm breaking apart.

The Dig House is still and silent. The only light in the main workroom comes from Alberto's computer, a geometric screen saver that twists like a Möbius strip in the throes of pain.

I sit down at his desk and open a new browser tab. It takes a few minutes for my Gmail to load, and another ten seconds to filter out the messages in the mailbox I reserve for family.

Because I am a coward, I read Kieran's first.

*Dawn, Brian won't tell me where you are. What the fuck?*

It makes me smile; he doesn't beat around the bush.

*Dawn. Everyone's freaking out.*

*Dawn. If you're in trouble, just tell me.*

When I open Meret's messages, I start crying again.

*Mom, Dad swore you're okay but if you were really okay why wouldn't you have come home by now?*

*Mom, if you're really visiting your aunt in France like Dad says you are then send me a postcard because I think he's lying. Also, I texted you a hundred times, why aren't you writing me back?*

*Mommy. Did I do something wrong?*

At that, I lose it. I bend over the keyboard, thinking that my sobs will probably short-circuit all of Alberto's fancy software and that I don't give a damn. I imagine Meret typing this on her laptop, the glow reflecting on her face.

I can't remember the last time she called me "Mommy," but I do remember the first time she called me "Mom." I had picked her up from school in fourth grade, and she was bringing home a friend. Up until that point, she would reach for my hand every time we crossed the street, as if she didn't know how to move forward without me. But that day when I reached for her hand to cross the parking lot, she tugged away, embarrassed. *Mom*, she said. *I'm not a baby*.

Except it doesn't work that way. She will always be my baby, even when she has children of her own. I will never stop wanting to keep her safe. But I can't do that when I'm half a world away.

The last email from her doesn't have any text. It's a photograph she has scanned of the two of us. I don't even know where she's found it—some album, I suppose, up in a box in the attic. Meret is maybe two, standing next to me on the beach. She is holding a starfish in her palm and looking up at the sky. *Did it fall?* she asked, just before Brian took the picture. I remember feeling my mother there, and if you look carefully in the photograph, there is a halo of spray that looks a little like the profile of a ghost.

It is not impossible that Meret was right about that starfish. I would have given her the heavens and the earth. I *still* would.

Finally, I take a deep breath and I open Brian's messages, from oldest to newest.

*Where are you?*

*Seriously, Dawn.*

*You probably think it's enough to send some cryptic bullshit about you being fine and needing space and time and whatever but honestly, Dawn, this isn't only about you anymore.*

A day later: *I didn't mean that. I was angry. I take it back.*

Then: *I've been thinking that maybe you're waiting for something, and that if you're waiting for something, it's probably for me to say I'm sorry. So, I'm sorry. But also, I'm sad. I'm confused. I'm scared.*

*Did you lie when you told me you love me?*

There are several days with no messages, and then the last one:

*I know you think I don't listen to you half the time, that I'm in my own world, but you're wrong. I do listen. And I've been thinking a lot about what you said before you left—that sometimes the past matters more than the present. Assuming that's the hypothesis—it still can't matter more than the future. Because otherwise, scientifically, we'd regress instead of evolving. Look. I'm not good with words. Or with noticing that things aren't right. But I do know this: your state and my state are entangled.* $|me> = |us>$ *The quantum state of* me *is us. Please, Dawn. Come home.*

I curl my hands so that they are poised over the keyboard.

The first person I write back is Meret.

*I miss you like crazy,* I type.

I hesitate. *I didn't leave because of you, Meret, but you're why I'm coming home.*

Then I write Kieran just three simple words: *I am fine.*

I send another email to a social worker from the hospice, asking about a client.

Finally, I start an email to Brian. I type: *I'm sorry,* but then erase it. I'm not sorry.

I type: *I didn't mean to hurt you.*

That sounds like a goodbye, so I backspace until the page is blank again.

I don't know what to say, so I answer the question he asked me.

*I never lied when I told you I love you.*

I press send, watch the words fly from the screen. And I think: *I just never told you the whole truth.*


WHEN I LEFT in 2003, it was in the middle of a desert storm, which Ancient Egyptians called a *neshni*. Wyatt drove me all the way to Cairo through the insane bumper-to-bumper traffic. Puddles on the highways became wading pools, and cars swam through them beside braying donkeys struggling to yank their carts through the mud. Vehicles were abandoned; drivers got out of their cars to shout at each other in the driving rain. I was sick to my stomach with grief and fear and had to keep the window open a crack. "I should be going with you," Wyatt muttered, as he squinted through the downpour.

But we both knew that this was too new, too raw. That to put value on the connection between us instead of the actual timeline that we had been a couple—several weeks—was insane. What had happened between us was intense and unexpected, much like the weather.

My mind had already begun to separate into *before* and *after;* even sitting close enough to Wyatt to see the stubble of his beard, I was thinking of my mother lying in a bed that wasn't her own, of the hands of strangers wiping down her skin and washing her hair. I was thinking of how odd it was that the things our parents do for us when we are young are what we do for them when they are old.

"Jesus," Wyatt said. "Another roadblock?"

The sheer number of motor vehicle accidents had left us a circuitous, lengthy route to the airport. "I may miss my flight," I murmured, checking my watch.

"*Inshallah*," Wyatt murmured. *God willing*.

In spite of the fact that the universe seemed to be conspiring to keep me in Egypt, we finally pulled up to the airport curbside drop-off. Neither of us made a move to get out of the car. In front of the windshield, a man in a hazard-yellow vest gesticulated wildly and angrily; we were taking up space and blocking the flow of cars.

I looked Wyatt in the eye. "I'll be fine," I said preemptively.

"Olive. If you need anything . . . ever. Dammit. I will do anything for you." He caught my hand with his own. "Anything. Anytime. No expiration date."

The truck began to fill up with words we hadn't had time to say, fogging the windows and raising the temperature. I could feel myself being pulled toward Wyatt, and toward Boston simultaneously.

He raised my palm to his lips, kissed it, folded my fingers tight. "I love you," Wyatt said.

I knew if I said it, I would never be able to leave: the transaction would be sealed, a vow given and a vow received. So instead I opened my hand like a star and let his words drift away, instead of keeping them. "I know," I whispered, and I left without turning back.


WYATT DOESN'T SLEEP with his door locked. When I slip inside, he is flung across his bed, the sheet tangled at his waist, his chest bare. The moon has painted him gold, as if he is her favorite model. I stare for a moment. Of course I've seen the gray threaded into his hair and noticed the fine lines at his eyes, but there's something about seeing him like this that hammers home how many years have passed since I last saw him undressed. How he's changed. How *I* have.

He bolts upright with a start. "Dawn? What's wrong?"

"I love you," I blurt out, and realize that it also accurately answers his question.

Wyatt seems to realize that he's not wearing clothes, that some-one who might as well be a stranger is standing in his bedroom. He gathers the sheets more tightly against his middle and looks up at me. "I know," he says, and he narrows his eyes. "That's the next line, isn't it?"

"I should have told you fifteen years ago. But I thought if I did, I'd never be able to leave."

"Why tell me now?"

I hesitate. "Because I don't want to get to the end of my life and be sorry I never did."

His eyes fly to mine. "Are you well?"

"I'm not dying anytime soon," I say. "At least not that I know of."

Wyatt relaxes. "Well. At least there's that." He pats the bed be-side him, and I sit down. His words come slowly. "Fifteen years is a long time, Olive."

"Yes," I agree.

I stare down at the white sheet, where our hands are inches apart. His fingers brush mine, and I feel myself shiver.

Wyatt has touched me in the weeks I've been here. He's passed me instruments and directed me with a tap on my shoulder and even helped me down the rope ladder. But this is the first time we have touched in a more deliberate way. I feel him looking at my face, ask-ing what he cannot put into words.

Before I can think myself out of it, I kiss him.

It's quick. And startling. A press of lips that is a prelude, an over-ture. He still tastes like butterscotch. I pull back before he can.

"You have another life," Wyatt says.

I hesitate. "What if, for a night, I want this one?"

His palm curves around my hip. "Then I'm the luckiest mayfly ever." Wyatt shifts, pulling me closer, and still giving me time to change my mind. Then his mouth touches mine.

All it takes is a brush of a match in the right environment to start an inferno. That is what I think when I taste him, and I am whisked backward through time, to another twin mattress and another stolen moment and the same arms around me. Wyatt is everywhere at once, setting fires. Unlike with Brian, this isn't comfortable—it's the wild plunge of the roller coaster, rather than the hand that holds yours as you go.

"Olive," Wyatt scrapes against my throat. "Jesus." We are a tangle of arms and lips and buttons and sleeves. But when he is about to pull off the last of my clothing, I grab the edges of my shirt together. Immediately, he goes still. "Second thoughts?"

I shake my head. "I don't look like I used to, Wyatt."

"You look magnificent," he says.

"You're saying that because you want to get into my pants."

"That, too." Wyatt grins. "But it happens to be true."

"I've had a baby. I'm old—"

"I'm three years older than you." He cups my face in his hands. "Dawn. If it will make you feel better, I could show you my appendix scar, and where I think I'm going bald, and you could point out your stretch marks and wrinkles. But I'd much rather pay attention to all the bits of you that are glorious."

I pull on his hair. "I don't have wrinkles. And you're not going bald."

"Thank God," Wyatt says, and he peels off my shirt. His hand skims up my side, beneath the lace of my bra. My heart beats under his palm.

I pull away the sheet and grab hold of him, stroking, watching the tendons in his neck stretch as he arches back. "Not yet," Wyatt murmurs, and he flips me onto my back. He kisses me, long and slow and lovely. *"Entirely as a god have you come into being,"* Wyatt quotes. *"Your head is Re. Your face is the Opener of Ways, your nose is the divine Jackal . . ."*

He brushes a kiss over my closed eyes. *"Your two eyes are the two children of Re-Atum. Your tongue is Thoth. Your throat is Nut. Your neck is Geb."*

His hands close over my arms; his tongue circles my breast. *"Your two shoulders are Horus. Your breast is He Who Pleases the ka-spirit of Re."* He glances up. "Side note: It also pleases me a good deal."

I feel him sliding his palms up my thighs. *"Your two sides are Divine Utterance and the Divine Scarab . . . your stomach is the Dual*

*Lion . . .*" He spreads me wide, bending my legs so that he can settle between them. *"Your bottom is Isis and Nephthys,"* he whispers. *"No part of you lacks in divinity."* His mouth closes over me.

In that moment, I feel every second I've missed with him. He breathes life into me. When Wyatt lifts his head and moves up and slides into me, I wrap my arms and my legs around him, as if that is all it would take to keep him there.

After, I lie on my side, with Wyatt curled behind me, and he laughs when I yawn. "We used to do that three times a night," I say.

"Maybe we *are* old," he concedes.

I test myself, poking through my thoughts for regrets—but I don't find any. There is no guilt in me, no rush of shame.

But what happens, now that it's done?

Wyatt spreads his hand over the round of my belly, the five pounds I cannot ever lose. "I would have liked to see it, you know."

"Me getting fatter?"

"You having a baby," he says.

I press his hand flat and close my eyes so tight that it hurts. Then I turn in his arms, so that we are face-to-face. "I want you to think of me *when*," I say. "The second before a kiss, when you're so close you can't see clearly and you can feel your pulse in the air. Then."

Wyatt leans in by inches. "Now?" he whispers.

"Now." I nod.

I kiss him until I feel him stirring against me, until I smell him on my skin, until I can see him when my eyes are closed. When we finally break apart, Wyatt is smiling at me, lazy. He tucks my hair behind my ear. "Where are you off to, that I'll have to remember you?"

I kiss him again, so that I can swallow my answer.


NEHEH DJET. Time in a circle, time in a line. Ancient Egyptians believed the world was structured both ways. Lying in the arms of the man I used to love, and maybe never stopped loving, I am painfully aware that ages have passed—and at the same time, it feels like yesterday.

I wonder what will happen to me now, if I have to stand in the Hall of Two Truths and defend my actions. If I'll qualify as *akhu,* the blessed dead, or if I'll just be damned, *mut,* gone. If I've done something unforgivable, or if I've moved closer to the person I was meant to be with.

In the Netherworld, the blessed dead and the damned share the same space. In the New Kingdom's Book of Gates—a later funerary text—there is a lake, which is cool water for the blessed dead but feels like a lake of fire for the damned.

I fall asleep fitfully, thinking of fire and drowning, and wake up when the door to Wyatt's room bursts open. I jackknife up, forgetting where I am for a moment, and Wyatt has the grace to throw the sheet over me. Sunlight floods the tiny room, and I think maybe we have overslept, but then I remember it is Friday, our day off. Alberto is standing in the doorway, and my stomach flips, thinking that I have finally given him a reason to hold me in contempt. But he doesn't even seem to notice me. "Dailey's here," he bites out.

"Fuck." Wyatt leaps out of bed, grabbing clothes from where they've been draped on his desk chair, hopping into his boots. He scrubs his hands through his hair, trying to rake it into a semblance of order. "Fuck, fuck, fuck, *fuck,*" he mutters, streaking through the hallway and leaving me behind.

Alberto blinks at me in Wyatt's bed. "You'd better get dressed."

I wonder if Wyatt has told his benefactor that I asked to work at the site, if he is going to be in trouble for hiring me without getting approval first. "Is Dailey going to be upset to find me here?"

"Yeah," Alberto replies. "You could say that."

I gesture to the door, rolling my eyes so that he'll close it, and then hop up and throw on my clothing from last night. I'm still tying off the bottom of my braid when I burst into the kitchen area, determined to make sure that Wyatt doesn't take the fall for something I asked him to do.

Sitting at the kitchen table is a woman with raven-black hair piled onto her head, wearing a light linen shirt and the kind of torn jeans that are so artfully ripped you know they cost hundreds of dollars to look ragged. She is facing Wyatt, and they both hold cups of tea.

"Is he gone already?" I ask breathlessly.

The woman turns. She wears crimson lipstick and has amber eyes and perfect posture and is quite possibly the most beautiful human being I've ever seen. Wyatt, on the other hand, has gone bright red, and is pulling at his collar, which is already unbuttoned. "Anya," he introduces, "this is Dawn. She's working under me."

I hear a snort, and realize Alberto is standing behind me.

Wyatt pushes up from the table. "Dawn, this is Anya Dailey. She's footing the bill for the expedition. She came to see the coffin."

Anya rises and slides her arm into Wyatt's. "Among other things," she says, smiling.

I look down at her hand, resting in the crook of his elbow. At the vintage diamond solitaire on her finger, put there by the fiancé who leads her past me and out of the room.

# WATER / BOSTON

· · ·

ABIGAIL BEAUREGARD TREMBLEY got interested in the business of death when she was visiting Indonesia the summer of her college sophomore year and ran out of money. She was hired, by the hour, to cry at funerals. On those days she would put on the only black dress in her suitcase and walk through the streets behind a funeral procession, wailing and weeping with a throng of others. "It didn't feel dishonest," she told me years later, when we both were hospice social workers. "For some religions, the louder your funeral is, the easier it is to get to the afterlife. Some people just have fewer mourners. Some people outlive their friends or family. Shouldn't they get to have a good send-off, too?"

Abigail had been working at the hospice when my mother died. I became a social worker because of her. There was no one I trusted more when I had a professional question, or needed to process a client's death. Today, when she comes into Perkatory—the coffee shop where we try to meet at least once a month just to catch up—I am already on my second pour-over and a slice of banana bread. "I know, I know . . . I'm late," she says, sliding into a chair across from me and dumping her giant purse on the ground. "Professional hazard."

I laugh. "Did you order yet?"

"Girl, I called my soy chai latte in from the road." As if she has channeled it, the barista sets it down in front of her. "It'll do, but what I really need is straight vodka."

"I've had a few of those days myself."

"Yeah, I heard you were with Thalia when she died. Sweet lady."

"She was," I agree, and we both sit in the memory for a moment. "So what's making you wish you were drinking?"

"I have a patient whose wife couldn't handle his death."

"Sudden diagnosis?"

"No, believe it or not. ALS. It's been a long time coming; reality just sort of hit her like a ton of bricks. I am not exaggerating when I say that I've spent more time preparing her for the inevitable than I have him. Today I go for my visit and I find them curled up together on the bed, OD'd with morphine. She dosed him and then dosed herself. Goddamn Nicholas Sparks and his goddamned *Notebook*." Abigail sighs. "Here's the kicker. *She* died. *He* didn't. So now I have an ALS patient with no caregiver."

"That's terrible."

"I know." She looks at me over the lip of her mug. "So. What did you call the emergency powwow for?"

"I have a client who wants to make a deathbed confession."

"Okay," Abigail says.

"It's one that could hurt people who are left behind." When I have a confession like Win's, which could rock the world of someone else in her orbit, I think hard about what should be revealed, what my responsibility is.

"I once had a thirty-eight-year-old patient tell me that he had killed his best friend," Abigail says. "It had happened twenty-five years earlier. His friend had been drunk, on a bridge, when he slipped and fell. He thought his buddy would swim, so he didn't jump in after him—but actually the kid had hit his head on the beam as he fell, and he drowned. My patient never told anyone, because he was afraid he'd get in trouble for underage drinking."

"What did you do?"

"After my patient died, I traced down the kid's family and I told them the truth. I had to, so that I could sleep at night."

"That's what I'm worried about," I tell her. "Sleeping at night."

"Is your client a serial killer or something?"

"No. Nothing illegal." I look up at Abigail. "She wants me to do something for her. Something that might hurt her husband pretty badly after she's gone."

"Client trumps caregiver."

"I know. The thing is . . . helping her makes me think about things I buried a long time ago."

"Things?" Abigail says. "Or people?"

I look at her and raise my brows.

"Buried literally," she asks, "or figuratively?"

"Figuratively," I reply, smiling faintly.

"Dawn. What's the first rule of hospice work?"

*It's not about you.*

I pick at the banana bread, and a random thought pops into my head. Back in the eighteenth and nineteenth centuries in the United Kingdom, when someone died, a piece of bread would be placed on their chest to soak up their sins. Then, the village sin-eater was paid to consume it—taking on the guilt and the shame and the lies, leaving the soul of the deceased light enough to go to heaven.

"What are you going to do?" Abigail asks.

I take a bite of banana bread and think of Win Morse and her missing lover. I wonder what happened to sin-eaters when they died, when there was no one left to absolve them. I wonder if, with every bite, they tasted poison.

BEFORE WE LEAVE, Abigail asks how Brian is doing.

This morning, when he came downstairs smelling like fresh shampoo and soap, his hair still slicked back, I handed him his travel mug of coffee. This is a scene so common for the two of us that by now, it should have caused a repetitive motion injury. But today, instead of distractedly taking the mug and collecting all the things he needs to bring to the lab and leaving without saying goodbye, he stopped in front of me. "My grandmother used to say that cooking was love," he said. "I don't know if coffee counts as food, but still . . . thanks. For the cup of love."

He blushed when he said it, and the tips of his ears went red. It was so un-Brian I almost laughed, but something held me in check.

Maybe this would be the new *us:* appreciating what we have, instead of expecting it. "You're welcome," I said.

"Brian's great," I tell Abigail.

SINCE MERET REFUSES to go back to STEM camp, I find a new summer program. This one isn't just science-oriented, but takes a Renaissance approach to gifted-and-talented education, marrying technology and the classics and Latin and phys ed. Meret is cautiously excited about the idea, about beginning fresh. We picked out an outfit last night, a top whose color turned her eyes an otherworldly blue.

At the end of the day I drive to the school where the program is housed and wait near the front entrance. When I see her exit the building, I wave. The girl she is walking with says something and smiles. Meret is a mirror, reflecting that same smile back at her. *Okay,* I think, letting out the breath I hadn't realized I was holding. *So far, so good.*

"How did it go?" I ask, as she slides into the passenger seat.

Meret's hair covers her face as she ducks away from me. "Fine."

"How are the other kids?"

She shrugs. "They're okay. I sat with three girls who'll be in the same high school as me this fall."

"That's great." I wonder if the girl she walked out with is one of them. "Any interesting teachers?"

Meret glances away, and I realize that her chin is trembling.

"Hey," I say, touching her arm. "What's going on?"

The tears start. "Nothing. It's stupid. Everyone's nice. Everyone's *really* nice." She wipes her cheeks. "Everything was good, you know? Like, I thought I looked decent. And no one was saying anything terrible about me. But it turns out they didn't have to. I sat at lunch with people, but I didn't actually eat, because none of them did. Someone was talking about a kid who has alopecia and how terrible it would be to look like that, and I laughed. I *laughed* because I was so glad it wasn't me they were ragging on. Even though they're awful, I'd rather be like them than like me."

"Meret—"

"Then I had gym. Today we just got a tour of the locker room from Ms. Thibodeau—the tennis coach. She showed us the showers and the lockers and then she looked over at me and said there's a changing room, too, with a curtain, if you don't want everyone looking. I thought she was saying I need to be hidden. But—"

I am barely aware of getting out of the parked car, but I do. I jog behind the school to the tennis courts, where a woman in a track suit is carrying a wire basket filled with bright yellow balls. "Excuse me," I say, boiling. "Are you Ms. Thibodeau?"

She turns, smiling. "Yes, hi."

"I'm Meret Edelstein's mother."

"Meret," she repeats, as if she is shuffling a deck in her mind. I can see when she remembers my daughter.

"She told me what you said to her today during gym class."

The coach looks puzzled. "That she should try out for tennis?"

"Mom." Behind me, I hear Meret's mortified voice. "She *did* ask me to join the tennis team. I didn't get a chance to finish."

The coach puts down the bucket of balls. "I started playing in ninth grade," she explains. She takes out her phone and scrolls through photos until she holds one up to me. There is a younger, chubbier version of the woman with a bad haircut, a racket balanced in one hand. "I wasn't fast or strong but I was really good at video-games. That's the same kind of hand-eye coordination you get when you work in a science lab, like Meret has." She looks at Meret. "I hope you're still thinking about it."

"Yeah, maybe," Meret says. She grasps my arm and yanks, hard. "We, um, have to go."

I stare at the coach, then thank her for looking out for my child. We walk back to the front of the school. Just before we reach the car, Meret wraps her arms around me—in full view of other students.

"I'm sorry. I thought—"

"I know what you thought," Meret says, smiling a little. "It was lit."

We get into the car and I turn over the ignition. "So she wasn't saying that about the changing room to be mean."

"No. She's pretty awesome, actually. She's the first person who ever thought I'd be good at something with my body instead of my brain. Everyone else thinks I'm lazy because I'm fat."

"You *have* fat. You aren't fat. You have fingernails, too, but you aren't fingernails."

Meret looks at me from the corner of her eye. "I think that's the first time you've ever admitted that I'm . . ." She corrects herself. "That I *have* fat."

Talking about this, instead of dancing around it, feels right. "There isn't only one type of body. Anyone who makes you feel that way is only trying to make themselves feel better by finding someone to pick on."

"Yeah, but when you stand up, people listen. When I stand up, people notice my size. I'm literally the elephant in the room." She shrugs. "It's so weird. They can't *not* see me. But also, I'm invisible. I can walk down a hallway and see everyone looking away."

"I'm sorry," I tell her.

She looks surprised. "For ambushing Coach Thibodeau?"

"Well, maybe," I admit. "But mostly for not letting you talk about this with me. I figured if I did, it was like I was admitting that I agreed with you about how you look." I glance up. "And for the record I do not."

"Noted," Meret says.

"It doesn't matter how perfect I think you are, if you don't." I hesitate. "Are you going to start playing tennis?"

"Do you think I'd lose weight?"

"I couldn't care less," I say. "And that shouldn't be the reason why you do it. Our bodies are just what hold us together, you know. They're not who we really are. Everyone leaves them behind, eventually."

"Yeah, but I'd rather die skinny," Meret replies.

I roll my eyes. "Trust me. People who are thin aren't happier."

"Well, *you'd* know," Meret says. "When I was little, I used to think I was switched at birth."

"When *I* was little," I tell her, "people used to ask my mother if she ever fed me. I cut the tags out of my jean jacket so no one would know I was a 00. Literally, less than nothing."

"I don't think I was even a oo when I was born."

"You were." I smile at her, and pull away from the curb. "I was there."

BRIAN SENDS ME a text just before 5:00 P.M. I hear the ping on my phone, wondering what's going to make him late for dinner this time; forcing myself to not assume the worst.

*Thinking of you, so I thought I'd tell you.*

When he comes home, he brings me flowers: peonies and roses.

The smell takes me back to the perfume on his clothes, to Gita. But he looks so proud of himself, as if he's slayed dragons and reached through thickets to bring this to me.

Even though I've eaten, I sit at the table while he does. I put the bouquet in a vase. I tell him it's beautiful.

THAT NIGHT, WHEN Brian goes into the bathroom to brush his teeth, I roll to his side of the bed to turn out the light and accidentally upset the book he is reading.

With a groan, I lever myself down so that I can grab the spine. It's some god-awful tome about the mathematics of uncertainty. But when I pick it up, a piece of paper tucked inside it flutters to the floor.

It is a printout from a women's magazine. In the photo, a woman leans back in the circle of a man's arms, laughing. Then I notice the headline: *19 Ways to Tell Your S.O. You Care!*

My heart squeezes as I try to imagine Brian searching for an article like this. I glance down at the bullet points: *1. Don't talk, listen! 2. Say thank you. 3. A few blooms brighten anyone's day. 4. Text when you're thinking of them. 5. Hold hands . . .*

Next to the first four items are methodical little check marks.

With a smile, I slip the article back into the book and set it on his dresser. I reach for my phone and text him.

I can hear the ding in the bathroom; a moment later, he comes out in a towel, holding up the screen.

*Hi.*

"Hi," he says.

"I missed you," I tell him.

"I was twenty feet away."

I grab the edge of the towel and pull. "Too far," I say.

MY BROTHER GETS a day off maybe once a month, so when he asks to meet me for lunch, I immediately say yes. I pack chicken salad sandwiches and meet him in the Public Garden—his only requirement was that we eat somewhere outside. We sit underneath the arms of a gnarled tree, watching the ducks at the water's edge. "Are ducks the ones that mate for life?" Kieran asks.

"Pretty sure that's geese," I tell him.

He nods at a mallard. "You go, buddy."

"Speaking of which. Are you dating anyone?"

Kieran rolls his eyes. "You *could* just ease into it."

"Then I wouldn't be your big sister."

"I spend a lot of time with my right hand—" he says.

"Ew." I grimace.

"—doing surgery," he finishes, grinning.

"I'm scarred. You could have put that a different way."

"Then I wouldn't be your little brother."

"What happened to Adam?" This was his last boyfriend, a nurse.

"He decided to date someone less stressed out about his job. An air traffic controller." When I laugh, he shakes his head. "Hand to God."

"Right hand?"

Kieran throws a potato chip at me. "Moving on. How's Meret doing?"

"She's thinking about playing tennis and she's loving science."

"So much better than the way I remember fifteen."

"Which was?"

"Trying to explain to all my teachers why my sister was the one coming to back-to-school night. And actively avoiding gushing about the Jonas Brothers." He looks at me. "You did a good job, you know. Taking care of a little closeted orphan."

"Thanks," I say.

He crosses his legs and begins to tear at the grass. "I know I complain a lot, and I'm sleep-deprived, but I love what I do, Dawn. And I get to do what I love because *you* gave up what you loved, for me."

"I love my work," I argue.

"Okay, fair," he says. "But it wasn't your original plan."

I shrug. "Plans change."

"If Mom hadn't died, I don't know if I would have gone to medical school," Kieran muses.

This is news to me. "Really?"

"I felt so . . . powerless when it happened. I didn't want another kid to go through what I did, and I remember thinking that I could become an oncologist. But I got sidetracked by brain tumors."

"They *are* seductive," I agree.

"Well, they're also safer," Kieran says. "I never look at the patient and think of her."

We are quiet for a few moments. Kieran finishes his sandwich and tosses the crust to the ducks. "You know what's weird? I've been alive without her longer than I was alive with her, and I still miss her."

"Yeah."

"Like—I'll clip my fingernails and collect them—"

"—in case mice take them and steal your soul," I finish, laughing.

"What *is* that superstitious Irish bullshit, anyway?"

"Remember the Christmas she gave you a Swiss Army knife and insisted you pay her back with a penny, because if you didn't, you'd get into a fight?"

"Or that if you sat in the corner at the table, you'd never get married?" Kieran pauses. "Come to think of it, my seat *was* in the corner."

"She'd be so proud of you," I tell him.

"You, too."

I wonder why we always want to have conversations with the people we love when we've run out of time. The Egyptians wrote letters to the dead—they'd paint the message on a bowl and leave offerings in it and place it in the tomb. Even if the deceased hadn't known how to read, it was assumed that in the Netherworld, he or she was literate. A wife might write her husband if her daughter was sick, and she was worried that the girl had been attacked by an aggressive *ba* spirit. The dead husband could take that spirit to court in the afterlife.

What would I write my mother now, if she could read it?

*Why didn't you tell me earlier that you were sick?*

*Why did you leave me?*

*How am I supposed to be a mother when I can't turn to you for advice?*

*How am I supposed to understand marriage, when you never married my father?*

Out of the blue I remember a Saturday we spent the night at the aquarium. It was a special thing for kids, like a slumber party in a museum, called Sleep with the Fishes. My mom worked it because she got time and a half, and once, she brought us with her. We packed sleeping bags and snacks; toys for Kieran, homework for me. I was fifteen, and while my mother worked, I was expected to watch my three-year-old brother.

My mother was doing a tide pool lesson with a rowdy group of fourth graders. "The water in the ocean never stops moving," she told them. "Who knows what makes it move? I'll give you a hint . . . look out the window."

I had glanced out at the moon. Gravitational pull seemed romantic to me. Imagine being light-years apart, and unable to keep your metaphorical hands off each other.

I'm not sure how long I listened to her before I realized that Kieran was missing.

A lot of people have stories about losing younger siblings, but most of those stories do not take place in a building that literally has sharks in it, and ladders that lead into those tanks, and brothers who like to climb. I didn't want to panic my mother, so I slipped away, whispering Kieran's name in the psychedelic jellyfish exhibit and searching for him near the octopus tank. The last place I looked was the giant tank in the middle of the aquarium. I could see the orbiting shells of sea turtles, but I didn't see Kieran.

Panicked, I started running down the walkway that spiraled

around the tank, looking for a bright sneaker caught in coral and praying harder that I wouldn't see one.

I finally found Kieran sitting on a rock in the penguin enclosure. I was not sure how he got there without falling into the water surrounding it. "Jesus, Kieran," I said, and I literally jumped over the railing into the calf-high pool and grabbed him.

"Do you remember the time you got lost in the aquarium?" I ask him now.

"Yes. Penguins look so fancy, but it turns out they smell like fish and shit."

"I was having a heart attack, and you were just . . . sitting there."

"I was waiting for you," Kieran says. "I knew you'd come for me. You always did."

I consider this. I went to college when Kieran was six. In my mind, he stayed a baby, because I wasn't around when he was growing up. I was studying and taking finals and getting stoned for the first time and applying to grad school. Boston was a memory. I likely wouldn't have gotten close to Kieran at all if my mother hadn't been sick.

"Things have a way of working out the way they're supposed to," I reply.


I'M PUTTING ON my nighttime moisturizer when Brian turns to me from his own sink. "I was reading this article today about unsolved problems in quantum physics," he says. "It was talking about the concept of the past, and whether there's a single past, and if that means the present is physically distinct from the future—"

"Brian," I interrupt. "You lost me after the first sentence."

"Oh," he says, his face falling. "I just wanted to hear your opinion."

"Why me? I can name ten people at Harvard who could actually hold up their side of that conversation."

"But you're the one I'm married to."

Suddenly, it all clicks into place. I rub the remaining lotion into my hands. "Ah," I say. "Is this number seventeen on the list? Or eighteen?"

He blushes. I don't know if I've *ever* seen him blush. "You know about the list?"

"Yeah." I move closer to him and lean against the vanity. "I don't need a husband who brings me flowers or chocolate. I need one who watches the news with me and complains about how many ads there are. I need the guy who thinks the second verse in 'We Wish You a Merry Christmas' is *Oh bring us some friggin' pudding.*"

"*Figgy* isn't an adjective," he insists.

I smile a little. "The only person I ever wanted you to be is you . . . not who *Cosmo* thinks you should be."

I love that he wants to try. I love that he doesn't know how, any more than I know how to solve an unsolved problem in quantum physics. I love that he is actively thinking of me.

But none of this keeps my mind from drifting to someone else.

THAT NIGHT I dream of Egypt for the first time in years.

I remember a moment from my first season in Egypt, when I hated Wyatt Armstrong. I was sitting under a tent attempting to pick the grit out of my cheese sandwich as Wyatt and two undergrads discussed mythology and sex. "Greek myths are the weirdest," said one student. "Zeus gets it on as a swan."

"Pan stalked a nymph who turned into a reed to get away from him, and he made a flute out of her so he could blow her," said another student.

"Typical," I muttered, as Wyatt said, "Genius."

"I've got this all beat," he said. "Our story starts with Seth and Osiris, who are basically Sonny and Michael Corleone. You've got Seth, the hothead, always at odds with Osiris, who's all about staying calm and cool while he destroys his enemies as the King of Egypt. Plus, Osiris is married to his sister Isis, because divine royals are down with incest, especially when a relative is smoking hot."

He was telling the story of the tribunal of Horus, albeit the soap opera version. I rolled my eyes and looked up at the roof of the tent, which was snapping in the wind.

"Seth is crazy jealous of his brother, so he murders Osiris and hacks his body into forty-two pieces. Isis and her sister Nephthys hunt for the bits and they find everything but his dick. Anubis, the jackal god, mummifies Osiris. After that, Isis turns into a bird and sits on her dead husband's corpse and fucks him, getting pregnant with Horus."

"Wait," one undergrad said. "Without a dick?"

"Oh, they find that eventually," Wyatt said. "So Horus grows up and has an epic battle with Uncle Seth. Mind you, Seth is chaotic and probably shouldn't have chopped up his brother, but he also kills Apep, the serpent of evil, so he's more Loki than Thanos. Horus wins and becomes the divine template of the king on earth, while Daddy gets to be king of the Netherworld. All because his mother fucked a dead guy."

"That's messed up, man," one student said. "It's like Hamlet."

Wyatt grinned. "Ladies and gentlemen, I rest my case."

I stood, giving up on eating lunch. "Apologies," he said, not looking at all apologetic. "I think we've put Olive off her feed."

I took a bite, just to be contrary, and nearly broke my tooth on some grit.

"You do know it's called a *sand*wich," he said.

I left the tent and walked into the *wadi* to pee. I was just buttoning my pants again when I heard Wyatt's voice behind me. "Don't stop on my account, Olive," he said.

"What are you doing here?"

"The same thing as you, I imagine."

I stalked past him, wondering if someone's penis could get a sunburn, wondering why it was so easy for Wyatt to annoy me. At lunch he'd been showing off, but nothing worse than I'd heard before, and the other students found him entertaining. "Why does everything have to be a joke to you?"

He stilled, his hands at his belt. "Maybe it's not, Olive. Maybe that's just what I want people to see."

"I really don't think you have to work harder to get attention."

"You've probably heard that my grandfather has a wing at the Met named after him, and that I come from four generations of Yalies?"

What an egotistical asshole. "So what?"

"What you *haven't* heard is that my father effectively wiped out the family fortune in a single generation and he hates my guts because one of his sons died and it wasn't me. And that I graduated with a double-starred first from Cambridge because I worked my bloody arse off, not because I was given a free pass. But it's easier for people to assume I'm just another entitled idiot." He blinked. "Why am I even telling you this," he muttered.

"You should tell everyone. They'd like you more."

Wyatt was quiet for a moment. "You know, the Ancient Egyptians believed that words were so powerful that if you spoke them, things might happen you didn't want to happen. It's why when you read the texts about Osiris being murdered, they only allude to it. And it's probably why we keep secret what we wish for on our birthday candles, and why we never tell our wildest dreams out loud. It's too bloody terrifying to think how our lives might change, if you just put it all out there." I heard the buckle of his belt jingle. "I'd recommend you take your leave, unless you're kinkier than I thought."

As I walked out of the *wadi* I realized that although I had been working in close proximity with him for the past three years, I had only just met Wyatt Armstrong.

I DON'T SLEEP well, and finally give up the battle an hour before sunrise. I sit at the kitchen table, drinking coffee and picking at a stain on a place mat. I know why I dreamed what I did. All this discussion of the unfinished past with Win—no matter how hard I keep trying to focus on Brian, the memory of Wyatt keeps surfacing.

Brian pads into the kitchen in his pajama bottoms and a T-shirt, bleary, looking just as exhausted as I feel. He stands in front of me, rocking on his heels. "Hi." He sees the look on my face. "Did I do something wrong?"

I hate that this is his first assumption; that I've driven him to that. But it's not him; it's us. I force myself to look into his eyes. "Do you ever feel . . . broken?"

Brian stares at me for a long, quiet moment, the way I've seen him focus on a puzzle in his lab when he doesn't know why an experiment isn't coming out the way it is supposed to. Then he pulls me into his arms. "I know you by heart. I can put you back together."

He has made the assumption that I am talking about myself, not our marriage. Because our relationship has always been rock-steady. It's why he didn't think twice about going to Gita's apartment; it's why he was so shocked by how upset that made me. I've always trusted him with my heart; why would that stop now?

*You are so lucky,* I tell myself. *You have this wonderful man. Stop obsessing over what might have gone wrong and focus on what could go right.* I lean into him. "Brian? Even if I forget to say it . . . I love you."

His hand strokes up and down my spine. "I know," he says.

*I know.*

Suddenly I am in a rainstorm in Cairo, watching the world swim in front of my eyes. I start shaking.

Feeling me tremble, Brian holds my shoulders in his hands. "Are you okay?"

"Yes," I tell him. I tell myself. "Yes, yes, fine."


WIN IS ASLEEP when I arrive, and Felix is working, so I clean up the kitchen and check her medical supplies. Then I go to the desk in the hallway and take the ribboned key out. I enter the locked room with all its canvases.

I know exactly where the painting of Win is, the one that Thane created. I pull it free from its hiding spot behind three other canvases and I look at the secret in her eyes. She's almost daring the viewer to become complicit with her.

Or maybe I'm just reading into it.

I look at the gentle slope of her breast, the divot of her belly button, her hand between her thighs. I have helped Win dress and undress. I have bathed her. Her body, to me, is a responsibility, and I watch it for signs it is failing her. But this—this is an altar built to Win, to worship what he saw.

I put the canvas back, close and lock the door, and return the key to the desk. By the time I get down the hall to check on Win, she is awake and sitting up in her bed.

"I wrote something down for you," she says. "It's in my vanity."

I mentally note that she is not wearing makeup. She has dark circles under her eyes; Felix has told me she isn't sleeping well, but she is sleeping more. I cross the room to the little white mirrored table with her jewelry box on it. In a drawer, lying amidst a jumble of eye shadow and lipsticks and face creams, is a list.

THINGS I DO NOT WANT
1. Lilies
2. Religion
3. Pallbearers
4. Mosquitoes
5. Black
6. An open casket

THINGS I DO WANT
1. Red velvet cake
2. Fireworks
3. Sidecars

I pull up a chair beside her. "I'm assuming this is about your funeral," I say. "Mosquitoes?"

"I don't want people wishing it was over because they're getting eaten alive." Win grins. "Or maybe I should say getting bitten to death."

"What shouldn't be black?"

"The clothes. Tell people to come dressed in bright colors."

"I can do that," I tell her. "And by sidecars I assume you mean the drink, not the motorcycle attachment?"

"Do I *look* like a Hells Angel?" She pushes herself up higher on her pillows. "Oh, that's something else. I don't want one of those photos of me on an easel that looks like it was airbrushed."

"We can pick a photo that you like," I suggest.

"Maybe later," Win says. "I remember thinking at my wedding that it was the only time, other than my funeral, that all the people I cared about would be together in one room." She turns to me. "What do you think happens? After?"

"I have no idea," I say. "But then again, in utero, we probably can't imagine any other existence. And once we get here, we don't remember *that*."

"Do you believe in ghosts?" Win asks.

"I believe in the figments of someone's grief," I tell her. "I had a client whose wife died, and she still set her a place at the dinner table every day." I hesitate. "I think people assume death is all or nothing. Someone is here, or they're not. But that's not what it's like, is it? The echo of you is still here—in your children or grandchildren; in the art you made while living; in the memories other people have of you."

"Well, I think ghosts stick around because there's something they didn't finish," Win says. "Which is why you'd better help me write that letter to Thane. If you don't, I'm going to haunt the fuck out of you."

I picture that painting in the locked room.

"I'll help you find him," I tell Win.


EVERYTHING I KNOW about tears I learned from Meret, who had to do a science presentation on them once. She had four giant photographs on easels, X-ray crystallography of onion tears, tears of change, laughing tears, tears of grief. Close up, they look completely different from each other, because they are. Emotional tears, for example, have protein-based hormones in them, including a neurotransmitter called leucine-enkephalin, which is a natural painkiller. Onion tears are less sticky, and disappear more quickly from a person's cheeks.

Although all tears have salt, water, and lysozyme—the main chemical in tears—how the crystals form differs, due to other ingredients. So onion tears look as dense as brocade. Tears of change resemble the fervent swarm of bees in a hive. Laughing tears are reminiscent of the inside of a lava lamp, with smarter angles. And tears of grief call to mind the earth, as seen from above.

BRIAN IS GIVING me a lecture. Well, technically, he's practicing in front of me. I am supposed to be paying attention, but I am also on my computer, trying to find Thane Bernard, the man Win left behind.

"In the 1990s, physicists started running high-tech experiments to figure out how neutrons broke down into protons. That in itself wasn't so special—it's the core concept behind radioactivity. But weird things happened."

He pauses, so I smile and give him a thumbs-up.

"Neutrons that were created in particle beams—"

"What's that?"

"It's a particle physics thing, a nuclear reactor that shoots out billions of—"

"Never mind."

"Anyway, neutrons created in particle beams lasted approximately fourteen minutes and forty-eight seconds before breaking down into protons."

There are over a million Google results for "Thane Bernard."

"But neutrons that are put into a lab bottle break down a little faster. Fourteen minutes and *thirty-eight* seconds," Brian says.

Add "France" to that search and the results drop to five hundred and thirty-seven thousand.

Bernard is the second most common surname in France.

"I know what you're asking yourself."

Was Thane even French, or was he only visiting, like Win?

"What's the big deal with ten seconds?" Brian continues. "Well, there should be zero difference. That's the big deal. All neutrons are identical and their behavior shouldn't change depending on where they are."

Thane Bernard is not on Facebook or Twitter or Instagram or Snapchat. I can't use a missing person's website because he's not technically missing. There are zero T. Bernards in the French white pages, but in today's world of cellphones that means nothing. There is a Thane Bernard in academia, but he is on staff at USC and his field is ballet.

"There are two explanations," Brian says. "Either neutrons are breaking down into something other than protons—although there's no proof of this—or they somehow cross over into a mirror world and become mirror neutrons for ten seconds before flipping back. If that's the case, maybe another world—even a multiverse—exists."

I start typing Thane's name into an international search engine for finding people. There is a fifty-dollar fee. I type in my credit card number.

"Before you go thinking that your physics professor needs a straitjacket, I offer this: we know—we have known since the 1970s—that dark matter in the universe outweighs visible matter by a ratio of six to one. But no one has ever been able to find it. There's a world, literally, in which dark matter is hidden away. If that's the case, the mirror world those neutrons are disappearing to briefly is huge. Huger than our own."

Suddenly Brian's phone dings. He looks down at it and frowns. "I think our credit card just got stolen," he says. "I got a fraud alert from something called LocateTheLost.com."

I fold down the clamshell hinge of my laptop. "Actually, that was me."

"Who are you looking for?"

"I'm looking on *behalf* of someone who's looking for someone. It's one of my clients."

"Your client is missing?"

"No. She wants to write a letter to someone she lost touch with years ago."

"Like a secret love child?" For all of Brian's braininess, he has a melodramatic streak. It's why he insists on seeing Marvel Universe movies the day they come out, and why he conveniently manages to be in the room every time I'm watching *The Bachelor*.

"No," I tell him. "It's a man she used to love. She also wants me to deliver it to him."

"Wait, what?" he says. "Is this Win? The one with ovarian cancer?"

I nod.

"You can't do that," he says.

In all the years I have been a death doula, I can count on one hand the number of times Brian has questioned my judgment. The biggest argument we had sprang from a client who wanted me to look into assisted suicide for her. I just didn't feel right about it, and referred her to another death doula who does. Brian, however, was angry that I hadn't tried to talk her out of it. She had a son who was a sophomore in high school, and Brian felt that it was irresponsible to not try to stop her.

"She's the one who's married to the driving instructor?" Brian clarifies, and I realize that all the time I've thought he was tuning out, he has actually been listening carefully.

"Felix. Yes."

"And he's okay with this?"

"He doesn't know," I admit. "He won't find out."

"Do you really believe that? What if the missing guy writes back?"

"There won't be a return address."

Brian shakes his head. "It's still better to know than to be blindsided. What if, when Felix is putting away Win's clothes and her books and whatever after she's gone, he finds a note from this guy, or a ticket to a show he's never seen, or a photograph of his wife looking happier than she ever looked with him?"

I think about the canvas in the locked room and say nothing.

"The guy is already dying by degrees. You're going to kill him twice."

"That's not fair. Felix isn't my client, Win is." I gesture to his notes. "How do you know that in another universe, she isn't living happily with this other man?"

"How do you know that she *is*?"

"I don't really understand why, out of the blue, you've suddenly decided you're an expert in my field," I say coolly.

"Because you're being a hypocrite."

At that, I think of my dream of Wyatt, and my face is so hot I turn away.

"You're helping a woman on her deathbed keep a secret. No, actually, it's worse than that. You're the match that could burn down that whole marriage even after she's gone," Brian says. "But you were angry at me for not telling you about every moment I spent with Gita where nothing happened."

"I would have been angry even if you *did* tell me," I explode. "The only difference is that if you'd told me, I would have known right away that there was apparently something so wrong between us that you had to go looking for it somewhere else!"

My voice rings in the silence between us. One thing I've always told caregivers and clients is that last words are lasting words.

I've always wondered what's preferable: knowing the worst, or not knowing. Is it better to get a terminal diagnosis and count the days till you die, but have the time to say goodbye to everyone and everything you love? Or is it better to die immediately—an accident, a stroke, an aneurysm—and not have to wait for the inevitable? I think the answer is: neither. Both outcomes are terrible ones.

"There are things I've never asked you about . . . before we met," Brian says haltingly, and suddenly the reason for his indignation is laid bare. "I figured, after all this time, you'd have told me everything."

*There are things you wouldn't want to know,* I think. But I look him in the eye. "I have," I say, because what's one more lie.


FOR THE PAST few days, I've relayed to Win that I've been searching for Thane Bernard. She has had more energy lately, which happens sometimes before the end.

She knows that I haven't made any significant headway, but I think that the mere fact someone is looking for Thane makes her feel as if the world is righting itself. "Maybe we should write that letter," I tell her, multiple times, but Win shushes me.

"We have to do something else first," she insists, and then she asks me to run an errand.

I come home from the art supply store with everything on Win's list. She is too weak to stretch a canvas herself, so she directs me with military precision. The way you know if you're stretching a canvas right, Win tells me, is if there's tension.

I seal and prime the canvas, and we let it dry, and then Win asks me to go to the locked room and retrieve her paints. She keeps them in a plastic tackle box. Some tubes are so crusted over that I have to wipe their necks with warm water to get the caps unscrewed. I prop up Win with pillows on a window seat where the light is good. I watch her squeeze thumbnail-size bits of color onto a glass palette: white, cadmium red, cadmium yellow, ultramarine. From the primary colors, she blends purple and green and orange. She shimmies an entire scale from red to blue, filling the middle with purple shadows. She gives rise to rainbows.

I check out the window to make sure that Felix's car is still gone. "Do you know Thane's birthday?" I ask. "That would help me."

"Why?"

"Because when you use online search engines to find missing people, it's the first thing they ask."

"He isn't missing."

"Well, that's the other problem. *And* he's overseas. Almost every database I've found is American. Plus, I don't speak French, so I have to use Google Translate for everything."

"I know he's a Leo, that's all. But we didn't talk about our ages."

Why would they, when he was her professor? When it only highlighted the differences between them?

"I know he was nearly forty," Win says. "Which at the time, felt ancient."

It would, to a twenty-year-old. I remember Win telling me that his wife had been pregnant. I wonder how old she was.

"Tell me again where you've looked," she asks, as she touches her brush to the canvas.

"Facebook. Twitter. Instagram," I say. "Genealogy websites. The white pages. The prison system in France."

"What?"

"Well, I didn't find him there, if that makes you feel better. He doesn't show up in court records, either."

I haven't told her this, but I plan to check death records next. I don't think it's occurred to Win that Thane might have left this world without telling *her*.

"What are you going to paint?"

"Death. What else?" She glances at me. "Don't peek."

Instead, I catalog her. Her wrists are so fragile that the skin stretches tight over the bones; her complexion is ashy, her fingernails jaundiced. But her eyes are brighter than they've been in a week, darting from her palette to the painting and back again. There's something almost mystical about her looking at a blank canvas and seeing something that nobody else can, yet. I suppose it's not that different from peering over the edge of this world into the next.

Suddenly we hear the front door open, and Felix's voice calling for Win. "In here," she says, and his face peeks into the dining room.

His eyes are drawn immediately to his wife. "Look at you! I can't remember the last time I saw you painting." He kisses the top of her head. She tilts her face toward him, a cat stretching toward the sun. "Do you know how many Loew-Cornell brushes I've put in her Christmas stocking that she's never used?" he says to me. "You're a miracle worker."

Win meets my gaze, our secret held between us. "Isn't she, though?"

Felix cannot stop touching Win. His hand lights on her arm, her neck, between the wings of her shoulder blades. He has no idea that Win's animation is due to the fact that she is tying the last bow of her life with a note to someone she loved more than him.

"Could I ask you a favor, honey?" Win says. "I have a crazy craving for buttermilk biscuits. But we don't have any buttermilk."

Felix blinks, stunned. We both know how long it's been since Win finished a meal, much less *asked* for a specific one. "Coming right up," he says. "I'll even bake them from scratch." Over Win's head, he nods toward the hallway, a silent request for a private moment with me. I follow him out of the dining room.

"I know it's not likely, but doesn't she seem like she's rallying? I mean, people prove doctors wrong all the time—"

"Felix," I warn him. "Don't go down that path. Win's terminal. What you're seeing is something that happens a lot, just before death. There's like a power burst or something. I don't know how long it will last. But it won't be permanent." I hesitate. "I'm sorry."

"Right. Okay." He rubs the back of his neck. "I guess I'd better get the buttermilk fast, then."

By the time I return to the dining room, I'm angry at Win. For putting me into this position; for putting Felix second, when he so clearly idolizes her. For making me think that Brian is right— I shouldn't be aiding and abetting this betrayal. "Do you see how much that man adores you?"

Win nods. "I always have."

"Don't you feel like you're cheating on him?"

She doesn't even falter. "There are times I wonder if my whole marriage has been me cheating on Thane. If *that* was the life I was supposed to have." Win looks at me over the lip of the canvas. "I belonged with him long before I belonged with Felix. I'm not saying that I couldn't love two men. Just that if I'd stayed with Thane, there wouldn't have been a space in me to fill with Felix."

I sink down into a chair opposite from the back of her easel. She has turned my thinking on end. Felix was the one she ended up with . . . but he wasn't where she started.

"I can't stop thinking about it," Win continues. "Who I might have been, if I'd fought for Thane. An artist, maybe even a good one. A mother, definitely. But would I have moved to France? Would my son have lived? Would I have cancer? What if that one decision set off a whole chain of other forks in the path?"

I think of Brian's multiverses. "Even if Thane gets your letter . . . you're never going to know the answers."

"That doesn't mean I can't wonder," Win says.

"It also doesn't mean that this life wasn't the best one. The one you were *supposed* to have."

"Do you believe that?" she asks, putting down her brush. "That I deserve cancer?"

"That's not what I'm saying—"

"I don't think I do," Win continues. "I don't think *anyone* does. I think life is a roll of a die. I got a one, I could have gotten a six. It is what it is. But it isn't destiny. It isn't determined by three old witches snipping a thread at the minute you're born. Not cancer, not my profession, not even who I love. The real question is whether I'd still be sitting here, dying, if I'd made different choices." She looks at me. "Do you think that no matter what, everything you've done in the past, every decision you've made, would still have led you to this room, this discussion, this moment?"

"Yes," I say. "Probably."

Win laughs. "Those are two different answers. Besides, I can prove I'm right."

"How?"

"Close your eyes. Now picture the person you thought you'd wind up with."

I can see him as if he's standing in front of me. Drinking from a water bottle, his head tipped back, his throat working. His smile, when he catches me staring.

"You can ask that of anyone, and they always have someone in mind. *Always*. And here's the thing, Dawn—it's rarely the person they're going home to that night."

I imagine our legs tangled in the cooling sand, his hand a star on the small of my back.

Win raises her brows. "I knew it. Who is he?"

"Someone I knew in grad school," I say softly.

"You aren't in touch?"

"No."

"But you still think about him." A statement, not a question.

"Not very often," I tell Win. "Not until you told me about Thane."

She smiles. "Well, well, well. Methinks the doula doth protest too much."

"I'm happily married," I remind her.

"So am I." She starts to paint again. "So . . . why did it end?"

"I don't remember."

"Yeah, right," Win says. "You could probably tell me in excruciating detail the last conversation you two had." She dips her brush into the blue, and then into the red, and makes a small purple heart on her palette. *A medal for courage.*

"Why did you wait so long to find Thane, if you never stopped loving him?"

"Because I also never stopped loving Felix," Win says simply. "And women don't get to have midlife crises where they run off to find themselves."

I consider this—how many husbands have walked out in pursuit of some elusive happiness. Men leave their wives and children behind every day, and no one is shocked. It's as if that Y chromosome they hold entitles them to self-discovery, to reinvention.

*Was that how Brian felt?* I wonder. *With Gita?* It makes me feel unsteady. Brian has always been home base, my anchor, the knight who rescued me. To think of him faltering is to imagine the earth veering from orbit, the seasons reversing. What if he, like me, made the assumption that we were forever—but couldn't help his thoughts from straying to someone else. If love is, as Win said, just chance, then the only way to feel secure is to never pick up the die again after that first roll.

*Brian was my second roll.*

Felix comes back with buttermilk, and soon the house is filled with the scent of baking. He brings us a plate, biscuits still steaming, honey on the side. Win eats two, and after Felix goes to wash the dishes, she picks up the thread of the conversation. "It's okay, you know."

"What is?"

"To admit that you think about it. Where you might be now, and with whom. What *if.* It's not being unfaithful. It's not even saying that you wouldn't make the same choice, if you had to do it over again. It's just . . ."

I meet her gaze. "Part of life," I finish.

"Part of life," Win repeats.

She taps her fingertip against the center of the canvas. "Acrylics dry fast," she says, satisfied, and turns the painting toward me.

Her portrait of death lives in shadows. It's midnight blue and dusky violet and violent black, but if you stare at it hard enough, you can make out two faint profiles, a breath apart, unable to complete that kiss for eternity.

"Now," she explains, "we take it off the stretcher bars." She reaches for a tool in her fishing box, a staple remover, and starts to pluck out the fastenings that hold the canvas stretched tight. One end begins to curl like an eyelash.

"You're going to ruin the painting!"

"What painting?" Win replies calmly. By now the canvas is a coil of color, a scroll of pigment. She turns it over. "All I see is a piece of stationery for a letter I need to write."

ONLINE, I FIND all sorts of Thane Bernards who are not the right one. There's the man who runs a crab-fishing boat in Alaska. The public works director in Johannesburg. The hedge fund employee who is selling his house on the Margaret River in Australia. There are three Thane Bernards who have gotten married in the past year who are too young to be Win's Thane, and four that have died, but who are too old to be him.

I find one promising lead—a man of the right age who teaches figure drawing at a university in Belgium, and I pull a photo of him up on my phone. Win, in bed, actually sits up a little as I am doing this. She straightens her robe and dabs a little bit of Blistex on her chapped lips before she takes the screen from me, as if he might be able to see her.

It breaks my heart.

"Wait," she says. "What do you know about him?"

I know that he has been employed for ten years at this university.

I know that he belongs to a rowing club and has competed as part of a master's division four with coxswain. I know that he wrote a letter to the editor of his local paper about a town ordinance that would affect bike lanes.

I also know this isn't what Win wants to know.

"He's still married," I say softly.

Her hand tightens on the edge of the quilt, and then relaxes. She reaches for the phone. I watch her peer at the photo, touching the screen to enlarge the details of his face.

Win closes her eyes. "It's not him." Her voice is raw, her relief palpable. "It's not him."

AFTER DINNER THAT night, I tell Brian I have some paperwork to finish and I go into my office. On my laptop, I receive a notification from another search engine. This one has found the name Thane Bernard in, of all places, a 2009 *Rolling Stone* magazine. David Bowie had done an interview from his London home, discussing his collection of art by old masters like Rubens, Balthus, and Tintoretto as well as more modern art by Henry Moore and Jean-Michel Basquiat. He also mentioned a recent acquisition by artist Nathaniel Bernard. The painting, sold for $10,500, was called *Prometheus,* and styled like the famous Rubens, but instead of chains wrapped around the subject's wrists there were ethernet cables and telephone cords and power lines. The mythical eagle was not picking out the victim's liver, but instead a beakful of British pound notes. Part of the joy of art, Bowie said, was finding artists no one else had discovered yet—*like Thane.*

The reason I haven't been able to find Professor Thane Bernard is because he isn't teaching art. He is *creating* it, and signing the pieces with his full first name.

I keep searching, using this new information, and find sales from auctions in France, Belgium, Italy. An announcement of a show at a Gagosian gallery. An appearance at Art Basel. Although there is an e-trail of his career, there is almost no personal information about him. He doesn't have a Wikipedia page. I can't find a photograph.

But then, in Google Images: a picture from a charity auction in London to raise money for a homeless shelter. There are five men in black tie. *From l. to r.: A. Rothschild, T. Haven-Shields, H. Ludstone, R. Champney, N. Bernard.*

N. Bernard.

When I blow up the image, it's grainy. His head is bald. His eyes are dark as night, the pupils and the irises almost indistinguishable.

I print a copy of this photograph so that I can bring it to Win tomorrow.

Then I reply to the original email from the site that found the original reference. For another fifty dollars, do I want them to find a last known address?

Yes. Yes, I do.

I click out of my mail app. I've done what Win asked; I should close my laptop and go to my husband, who is in bed, watching Stephen Colbert. But instead I find myself opening Facebook. My fingers find the search bar of their own accord, and type in Wyatt's name.

I'm not sure if I'm relieved or upset when there are no results.

That should be it. I should feel like I've dodged a bullet. But then I think of Win's voice: *Picture the person you thought you'd wind up with.*

It isn't cheating, if I loved him first. It isn't cheating, if I never act on the information. It isn't cheating, if Brian was the first to look away.

There are so many ways to lie to myself.

If my relationship with Brian has any chance of stabilizing, and we can't go backward, maybe I need to even the distance between us. As Brian said: nothing happened. But for a heartbeat, he wondered what it might be like to be with someone else. And so will I.

Unlike Thane Bernard, Wyatt Armstrong has a robust Internet presence. He finished his dissertation in 2005 and published a book that analyzed the text and grammar of the Book of Two Ways. He became the head of Yale's Egyptology program after the death of Professor Dumphries—I skim the eulogy he wrote in our alumni magazine. I read about his search for the missing tomb of Djehu-tynakht, and his discovery of it five years ago. To date, he hasn't published his findings.

Then I click on the link for images.

It feels like a punch to the gut. Wyatt is still lean and long, folded like a jackknife as he looks over his shoulder in the cramped chute of a tomb toward a camera. His face is familiar and unfamiliar at once. His searing blue eyes—the ones that look *into* you rather than *at* you—are tempered by a wariness, and there are lines at the corners now. I am reminded of everything that has come between us: people, distance, time.

As if this was done *to* us.

As if I didn't do it to myself.

"Oh." I hear a soft voice behind me, and I turn to see the wound of Brian's face.

For a sinking, terrible moment, I wait for the ground to swallow me whole, and when it doesn't I follow Brian back into our bedroom and close the door. My mind is spinning so fast for an explanation that the words are already tumbling out of my mouth. "I was looking up Win's old boyfriend—"

"And you found yours instead?" Brian interrupts.

The pain in his expression is so acute that I stumble. "You . . . you know who Wyatt is?"

"I'm not stupid."

I sink onto the bed. "I don't understand."

"That makes two of us," Brian murmurs.

He sits down beside me. I glance at his dark hair, the raw knuckles of his hands, the slope of his shoulders, and wonder when I last really, truly, looked at Brian; when I saw *him,* instead of just seeing who I needed him to be.

"Are you going to leave me?" Brian asks.

"No," I say immediately, but it's just a reflex, like when the doctor taps your knee with a hammer and you can't do anything but watch it jump.

"Why were you looking him up, then?"

"Because finding Win's ex made me wonder what Wyatt is doing now." I try Win's question on him. "Isn't there someone in your life you thought you'd wind up with?"

"No," he says. "But by some miracle, I did anyway."

"I am a thousand percent sure Wyatt doesn't even know I'm alive."

"Why would you say that? He could be in a pyramid or God knows what looking you up, too."

"I didn't realize you even knew his name."

He hesitates. "He sent you letters that I found in your mother's bin of junk mail. I should have given them to you. But by then, I loved you. And you seemed to love me." He looks up. "I'm a physicist, Dawn. I know what makes things move. You came here for your mother—but no one rockets that hard and that fast unless there's a force driving them away."

I would do anything to erase the anguish threaded through his voice. "I wanted *you*. I chose *you*."

"Back then," he says. "And now?"

I bite back my response: *You decided you didn't want me first.* But this is not a game of one-upsmanship. This is not an eye for an eye. This is two people, peeling back veneer, to discover that the wall they expected to find underneath is disintegrating.

"Don't you think we have a happy marriage?"

He considers this. "Can you have a happy marriage if your spouse doesn't think so?"

I wonder if he is talking about me, or himself. "I obviously had a life before I met you," I tell Brian. "I wasn't trying to hide it."

"I never asked you to. But my wife told me recently that not talking about something can be just as bad as flaunting it."

My cheeks burn. "After fifteen years, do you really think I don't love you?"

Brian is silent for a long moment. I can see pieces moving in his mind. "After fifteen years, love isn't just a feeling," he says. "It's a choice."

. . .

AFTER A SLEEPLESS night, I take the coward's way out, and drive to Win's before Brian even wakes. When Felix opens the front door, he looks just as exhausted as I am.

"Rough night?" I ask.

"She couldn't get comfortable. No matter what I tried."

"Let me see what I can do," I offer.

Win is tossing and turning on the rented hospital bed when I enter, her legs kicking at the light cotton blanket. Her eyes open when she hears me.

"I'm still here," she says.

"I noticed."

"Dawn." Her voice is small, boxed, neatly folded. "I didn't think it would be this hard."

In the weeks I've been with Win, she has been plucky, angry, and pragmatic, by turns. But I've never seen her defeated, until now. "What's hard?"

Her fingers clutch at the bedding. "Letting go. All those times you read an obituary, or a neighbor tells you someone you know has died. It's so bizarre to think that I'm that person now. That I'll be the next one."

"I know, Win," I say simply.

"This world is such a mess. Who would have guessed I'd want so badly to stick around?"

"I would. Because, like me, you don't give up easily." I pull the piece of paper from my pocket and smooth it out.

Win picks up the printed photo. She brings it closer to her face, close enough to kiss. But instead she stares at Thane Bernard as if the world has just changed from black and white to color.

She rests against her pillow, the paper still clutched in her hand. She closes her eyes, and a single tear tracks down her cheek. "Dawn," she says, "I'm going to write that letter now."

# LAND / EGYPT

. . .

On paper, Anya Dailey is the perfect partner for Wyatt. She is technically *Lady* Anya, a distant cousin to the queen or something like that, who was present at Prince William's wedding and whose baby gift for Princess Charlotte was the first item of clothing in which she was officially photographed. She went to boarding school and then King's College. She is on the boards of a dozen charities. Her father owns half of the land that London is built on.

She met Wyatt at the British Museum, where she was planning a fundraiser; Wyatt was giving a talk. She heard his voice as she walked by the auditorium, and as she put it, he was honey. She was the fly.

She had grown up hearing about Egyptology, because her grandfather had been friendly with the late Lord Carnarvon, and when she was a little girl he'd taken her to visit Highclere Castle, before it became a set for Downton Abbey. In the bowels of the building was a treasure trove of artifacts from Lord Carnarvon's various concessions—the objects that hadn't been sold to the Met. Her grandfather had been an Egyptomaniac; when he'd passed away, she'd thought: *What better way to honor his memory than to invest in a current excavation?* She had entered the relationship as Wyatt's business partner. One thing led to another.

I learn all this within five minutes of meeting her.

I am bouncing along in the Land Rover, sitting in the back behind Anya and Wyatt because he has ordered Alberto and me to accompany them to the dig site. Anya wants to see the discovery her money has funded.

I am shooting daggers at the back of Wyatt's head as he drives. I know why he wants Alberto there—so that they can get some press photo coverage of the benefactor and the archaeologist. But I cannot figure out why he wants me there, except to suffer.

Now that we've taken the most valuable treasures out of the tomb, there is only a *gaffir* at the site, dozing on a piece of cardboard at the entrance. "Sleeping on the job?" Anya murmurs, as Wyatt helps her out of the Land Rover. The *gaffir* scrambles to his feet. I wonder if she even knows what portion of her funding goes to this man—a pittance, really, that wouldn't be considered a livable wage in a first-world country. *"Mudir,"* he says, nodding to Wyatt, opening the locked gate to the tomb so that we can get inside.

Because we have all been focused on the coffins back at the Dig House magazine, the generator that provides light in the tomb is off. It is stifling and dark in the main chamber, so I shine a floodlight on the painted walls. Wyatt translates some of the hieroglyphs when Anya points to a spot that interests her. When he starts talking about a scene of fishing and fowling, her eyes start to glaze over. Suddenly she jumps, crashing into his chest. "Spider," she says.

Alberto and I look at each other behind her back, our first meeting of the minds.

When Wyatt begins to describe the excavation of the coffins, Anya peers down the tomb shaft. The rope ladder is still staked at the top, unraveling its way down. "Come, I'll show you," Wyatt says.

"Oh, I couldn't—"

"You want your Indiana Jones moment, don't you?" he asks, grinning. He puts his hand on her waist. "I'll be right behind you."

He asks Alberto to monitor the stakes where the ladder is secured, and then turns to me. "Dawn, you'll go down first with the torch," he instructs. "And to prove to Anya that it'll hold."

I read that statement so many ways: I am the sacrificial lamb. I am to do what I'm told. I'm heavier than rail-thin Anya, so if the ladder can bear *my* weight it will certainly bear hers. I jam on my headlamp and set my foot on the first rung and suddenly realize whose boots I am wearing.

Jesus fucking Christ.

I scramble down the ladder into the hot throat of the tomb and turn on the lamp, shining it up so that Anya can delicately pick her way down the shaft. I am convinced she digs her heel into the rock wall intentionally, so that I will suffer a rain of debris. But I stand my ground, watching her come closer.

By the time Wyatt has crawled down, I've backed myself into the tomb chamber. There's not much to see here, now that it has all been excavated. Wyatt begins to describe to Anya what it looked like when he first pulled away the limestone blocks that covered the entrance. For a moment, I forget where we are, and let Wyatt's story settle over me. I fill in the details that he leaves out: the moment when I was pressed up against him, peering over his shoulder. The way he swung me around in the tomb chapel when he realized that there was a Book of Two Ways inside the coffin. I tuck these details away, savoring them.

"Here," Wyatt says to Anya. "Give me your phone."

Since Alberto is still above us, extra assurance that the ladder won't mysteriously unwind itself from its posts and leave us buried underground, Wyatt offers to play photographer. He waits for Anya to pose and smile, and then takes a few photos. She grabs the phone from him and scrolls through. "Do it over. The light's not right."

She looks directly at me as she says it.

Wyatt turns to me and clears his throat. I shine my headlamp directly in her eyes. "Oh," I say, unapologetically. "Sorry."

He eventually takes a photo of which she approves. "Now one of us both," she insists. She hands me the phone.

Wyatt stands next to Anya, near the shelf where the canopic jars had originally been set. His arm is around her. At the last minute, just as I take the picture, she turns and presses her lips to his cheek.

I give back her phone, hoping I've accidentally lopped off their heads in the photo.

"So how many tombs are in this necropolis?" Anya asks.

"There were thirty-nine," Wyatt says. "This is the fortieth."

"Do they all look the same?"

"Pretty much. Some have more than one burial chamber, for a wife and husband."

"How cozy." Anya touches the wall of the burial chamber. "I

wonder how many slaves it took to build a necropolis. At least as many as built the pyramids, I'm sure."

"Shockingly, it was the exact same number of slaves," I say. "Zero." I fold my arms. "I'm sure your grandfather told you this, but the pyramids were built by workers who were paid a wage, or who were paying off their taxes. There is absolutely no evidence of foreign captives working on the pyramids. Also, the pyramids were feats of engineering and detail, like how the corners line up to point to the Benben stone that was the focus of solar worship in Heliopolis. For that level of skill, you wanted an expert. I mean, isn't that why you picked Wyatt?"

"Dawn——" he murmurs, a warning.

"Oh. Sorry. I mean *Dr. Armstrong.*" I turn to Wyatt. "Hold your own damn flashlight." I thrust my headlamp into his hands and climb up the rope ladder, running out of the tomb before anyone can watch me fall apart.


I RACE SO fast into the *wadi* that the wind screams in my ears, and I cannot hear Wyatt calling my name until he catches up to me. He is stronger and faster than I am; I can't outdistance him—and even if I could, where would I go? So when he grasps my arm, I stop. "Why didn't you tell me?" I ask.

"I thought you knew." He lets go, falling back a step. "You knew her name."

"I thought *she* was a *he.*"

"Why does it matter?" Wyatt counters. "You're *married.*"

"I know that," I snap.

"Then you also know I don't owe you an explanation about what I've been doing for the past fifteen bloody years," he yells.

I want to hit him. I want to embrace him. "But you let me think that——" I swallow the rest of my sentence, kicking the sand at my feet.

Wyatt's fingers curl under my chin, lifting my face so that he can see my expression. "Think what?" he says, so gently it breaks me.

"Think that I meant something to you."

"You did," Wyatt replies. "You *do*, Olive."

His mouth crashes down on mine, and even as I grab his arms hard enough to hurt, I am pulling him closer. His hands spear into my hair, knocking off my hat, loosening my braid. The wind whirls in a frenzy, like we have manifested the weather.

When we draw away from each other, breathless and charged, Wyatt touches his forehead against mine. "You vanished," he says, raw. "When you didn't write me back, I tried to find you. But it was like you had dropped off the face of the earth."

Dawn McDowell had. She became Mrs. Brian Edelstein.

"Do you know why I was so determined to find Djehutynakht's tomb?"

"Yes," I say, and he laughs.

"Okay, fair point. But also because I thought if the discovery was big enough, you'd hear about it."

"And do what?"

"I don't know." He meets my gaze. "Did you tell him about me?"

I shake my head.

"Why not?"

I do not know how to put this into words. Possibly because I love Brian enough to protect him. If you don't tell a man that you came to him with a missing piece, he will never know to look for it.

But there is another reason: because if I kept Wyatt to myself, he was mine and mine alone. To tell Brian about him would be to give him up.

I touch his cheek with my palm, feeling the stubble of his jaw. He didn't have time to shave this morning, before Anya arrived. I know he's thinking about that, too, because he says, "I'll tell her everything, if you want me to."

"You'll lose your funding," I reply.

"I'll find more."

I feel my eyes sting. "I can't let you do that."

*Because,* it remains unsaid, *I still belong to someone else.*

Wyatt takes my hand from his cheek and kisses the palm. "We were destined for each other," he says ruefully. "Two people who live in the past."

I throw my arms around him for just one more moment. He smells like cedar, like summer. He always has. The button of his shirt presses against my temple and I push a little harder, wishing it would leave a mark.

We head back to the necropolis. I wonder what he will tell Anya; if she will be smart enough not to ask why he ran after me.

At first, as we walk, we hold hands. But as we leave the privacy of the *wadi,* we let go.

Alberto and Anya are waiting for us outside Djehutynakht's tomb. Wyatt immediately bounds up the stone steps and says, "Seen enough?"

"And then some," she replies.

We both freeze, but Wyatt recovers faster than I do. He leans down and whispers something that makes her laugh and turn in to his arms. The sun catches the diamond in her engagement ring, making light dance on the limestone pillars behind them.

Over Anya's shoulder, his eyes are locked on me.


ANYA ASKS FOR dinner to be served in Wyatt's bedroom, which is all I need to lose my appetite. I work in the magazine, carefully copying images onto my iPad, until I cannot see clearly. Then I go to my own room, but it is so stifling that I feel caged.

I find myself wandering to a closet that has a padlock on it, in which Wyatt keeps a crate of very good, very expensive French brandy. Harbi and his family do not drink; the lock is for the rest of the team. I decide that Wyatt owes me this, at the very least.

I haven't picked a lock since I was a grad student and we were opening this same closet to steal some of Dumphries's liquor, but it comes back quickly. I use two paper clips, making one a tension bar and the other a pick. The cylinder turns, the lock pops open. There is a case of Tesseron cognac, and on top of it, a padded box that contains a crystal bottle of Louis XIII de Rémy Martin. Taped on it is a note from Richard Levin, former president of Yale, congratulating Wyatt on his appointment as the director of graduate Near Eastern Languages and Civilizations.

I take *that* bottle.

The Dig House is quiet, too quiet. I find myself straining to hear a woman's laughter, or Wyatt's voice. I imagine him lying in bed with Anya and wonder if he changed the sheets. I wonder if he is thinking of me and then wonder why I am allowed to even ask that question when I spent years lying in bed with Brian.

I don't want to go back to my room, so I wander into the communal work space, where laptops and iPads are plugged in and charging.

I sit down in Alberto's chair, open the cognac, and drink straight from the bottle.

Alberto's computer screen saver is the Sphinx. It's probably a photo he took: human head and lion body, tail on the right side, the Dream Stele between its paws. I've read that Dream Stele—every Egyptology student has. It states that Thutmose IV, the father of Amenhotep III and grandfather of Akhenaton, was riding his chariot around the Giza necropolis and he fell asleep in the shadow of the head of the buried Sphinx. The Sphinx came to him in a dream, and said that if Thutmose IV removed the sand that covered him, he'd become king. And he did.

I don't know how long I sit swilling cognac before Alberto comes in, but he is fuzzy around the edges.

"What are you doing here?" he asks.

"I would think," I say, lifting the bottle, "that's obvious."

"You're sitting at my desk."

"This is true." I don't make any attempt to move.

He sighs and pulls up another rolling chair. He reaches for a coffee mug and holds it out; I pour some cognac in it. We clink, ceramic to crystal. "I have a Sphinx riddle for you," I say.

"Man."

"What?"

"That's the answer," Alberto says.

"But I haven't even asked it yet . . ."

He shrugs. "*What walks on four legs in the morning, two legs in the afternoon, and three legs in the evening? Spoiler alert:* Oedipus figured it out."

"No, I have a different one," I tell him. "Why is the tail of a Sphinx always on the right side?"

Alberto laughs. "You actually *do* have a Sphinx riddle."

"Because it matches the hieroglyph," I answer, and then my throat closes tight. "Wyatt taught me that."

"Fuck," Alberto says. "You're not going to cry, are you?"

"What difference does it make? You already hate me."

"I don't hate you."

I take a long drink. "Really. Since the first day I got here, you've been standoffish."

"Of course I was." He rolls his eyes. "You showed up here and it was like steak on a hot plate."

"Thanks?"

"The minute I saw the way he looked at you, I realized our funding was screwed. He knew better. We have been working for five years on this tomb. To jeopardize that, especially during the season when we were going to actually finally excavate . . ." He doesn't finish; he doesn't have to.

"Does he love her?" I ask.

Alberto looks at me for a long moment, and then holds out his mug. I pour another splash of cognac into it. "I don't know. I think he loves the *thought* of her."

I consider what Wyatt told me earlier, about wanting to make this discovery so that wherever I was in the world, I would see it. I think about Anya's long legs and her creamy skin and concede that if Wyatt sacrificed himself on the altar of Egyptology, it couldn't have been all that much of a hardship.

"Did you come here to find him?" Alberto asks.

I can feel the heat of his eyes on my face, waiting. His own livelihood may hang on my response. And it's a good question—one I would never have truly let myself weigh if I wasn't three-quarters of the way through a bottle of excellent brandy.

"I came here to find *me*," I say softly. "I just don't know if I like what I discovered."

What has my endgame been? To see Wyatt, yes. But then what? Was I planning to speak my truth and then walk away, as if my words wouldn't cause a ripple in the pond of his life? "I have to go home," I realize. "To my daughter, and my husband."

Alberto doesn't even flinch; I realize Wyatt has shared the fact that I'm married. "So you came here to hurt Wyatt?"

"No," I say immediately. "Why would you think that?"

"Because why else would you remind him he loves you, and then leave him. Again."

I haven't thought of it that way, but it is exactly what I will be doing. "I thought you were mad at him, not me," I mutter.

"I think I'll be mad at you both, now."

We sit in silence for a few minutes, drinking. Then Alberto glances up. "You know that the Greeks used to believe that people were made up of two heads and two bodies. But Zeus was afraid of how powerful that could be, so he split people in two. That way, instead of causing trouble for him, they spent the rest of their lives trying to find their other half."

"A soul mate," I say.

"Do you believe that there's only one for each of us, and that we have to sift through seven billion people to find it?"

"No. I think that you can love more than one person in a lifetime. There's the one who teaches you what love is, even if it doesn't last." *Wyatt*. "And then there's the one who makes you a better human than you were, even as you do the same for him." *Brian*.

"And then there's the last one," Alberto adds. "The one that you never get enough time with. But who sees you through to the end."

Given the caretakers I have seen at deathbeds, it's a valid description. Your last soul mate might be your spouse, or it might be your child. It could be a best friend, or maybe even a death doula. It's who is holding your hand when you finally have to let go.

He sets his empty mug down. "I don't know you. I don't know what you've been doing all this time. But I've seen how you finish his sentences, and how he knows what you're about to say before you say it: like you're twins with a secret language. I see the way you look at each other—not like you want to get under each other's clothes, but like you want to get under each other's skin. I think it's really pretty simple, Dawn: who do you want with you, when your time runs out?"

Alberto stands up. "I'm going to bed. Don't fuck with my computer." At the doorway, he turns. "I think he was a dick for not telling you about her," he says. "Just for the record."


MY MOTHER USED to say that if there was bad energy in the house, you could put a glass of water on top of the fridge to absorb it, and when you poured it down the sink the next day, your troubles would be gone, too. Hedging my bets, I stumble into Harbi's kitchen and fill a plastic cup with water, set it on top of the dingy old fridge. I pour a second cup to take back to my room.

I stop in the magazine first. It's dark, so I turn on a single work lamp, which blinks down at the exterior coffin on its trusses. I can so easily imagine Wyatt bent over it, his shirt shifting across his shoulders as he leans down to better see the text at the bottom. The shaft of light illuminates the *peret kheru* painted on the coffin, the invocation offering. There's such a beautiful simplicity in believing that by speaking a wish, you can make it happen.

"Dawn," I whisper. "Wyatt."

But this isn't Ancient Egypt, and I am alone and drunk.

I pad down the hall, holding my breath at the silence. The last thing I want is to hear them together. I let myself into my bedroom and sit down on the bed and see it—a limestone flake on my pillow, with a hieroglyphic message scrawled in Sharpie:

*Neheh djet. Forever and ever.*

# WATER / BOSTON

. . .

*I don't really know how to start this.* Hello *seems too formal, and* Remember me? *seems ridiculous. Besides, I know you remember me, because I remember you. That was never going to be in question. The bigger challenge was whether we'd ever be able to forget.*

*I imagine that it's a shock to get this letter. I mean, it's been years. Maybe I'm being presumptuous to think you would welcome hearing from me. Maybe you've done a better job than I ever did at taking the past and plastering over it. Now that I've made the decision to have this conversation, one-sided as it is, I am struggling to figure out what I want to say.*

*I guess I will start here: I haven't thought of you every day. But I haven't* never *thought of you, either. When I do, it isn't the kind of recollection that feels wispy or comforting. It is visceral, the clean cut of a sword. One moment you are not in my mind and the next, you are so sharp and intense that all my attention is focused there.*

*So you see, even after all these years, you take my breath away.*

THIS IS HOW a body dies: it's very intelligent, so it conserves the heart and the lungs and the brain. It starts to dump the things that aren't important. The first thing to go is peripheral perfusion, the blood to your hands and feet. If you press on the nail beds, color doesn't rush back in. Then the kidneys shut down. Bowel sounds disappear. Blood pressure drops. The heart rate increases. Body temperature lowers. Breathing becomes labored. And then you fall unconscious.

Win is actively dying now. As she requested, I will be with her more and more. Some days, we do not have a single conversation; others, she is lucid. When she can, we write her letter. Because she is too weak to hold a pen, I print her words in careful small letters on the back of her painting. In the middle of a sentence, she sometimes stops and drifts away for moments, hours.

Before my mother died, even when she was unresponsive, I found myself touching her, like I was the one tethering her to existence. I would hold her hand. I would rub her arm. I would curl up next to her. I was doing it because I knew that once she died, once the funeral home came and carted her off, I was never going to be able to touch her again.

I am spending so much time away from home with Win that by the time I get back at night, the household is asleep. I always tiptoe into Meret's room and kiss her forehead as she sleeps. Then I slough off my clothes in the bathroom and crawl into bed beside Brian.

We have maintained a fragile peace, in spite of our argument about Wyatt. I don't know if this is because we have so few hours together right now that we are making the best of it, or because we are afraid to reopen a wound. Even though he sleeps through it, I curl my body around him or wind my arm with his or tangle our fingers together. There's nothing sexual about it, just a desperation, like when my mother was dying.

I wonder if I touch Brian because I know my time with him, too, is coming to an end.

*Do you remember the day we tried to find the perfect blue? Some of the details are fuzzy, but I know it was raining. We were in the good studio, the one with better light where the radiator didn't belch like an old man. I couldn't mix my paints to match what was in my mind, and I was trying to explain it to you, but I failed in English and in French. I was sniping at you and you were snarling at me, and finally, you grabbed my wrist and pulled me out of the studio, out of the building, to the metro. First we went to the Louvre, and you dragged me through hallways from one painting to another: from* Lady in Blue *by Corot with its steely cadet silk highlighted against the orange fan tip to Colin Nouailher's* Melchizedek and Abraham, *vibrant and cobalt, to the Salle Henri II with Georges Braque's* The Birds *on the ceiling, rich midnight that bled into royal purples.* Like that? *you asked at each stop, but I shook my head. So you took me to the Musée d'Orsay, where we bathed in the teal of Monet's* Water Lilies, *and drifted in Van Gogh's* Starry Night over the Rhône. *Finally, we stood in front of* The Church at Auvers, *beneath the cool azure blanket of its sky.* Closer, *I told you,* but not quite.

*We sat on the banks of the Seine and looked in its depths. We lay on our backs and pushed the clouds away with our imaginations until we could see nothing but blue, blue that hurt, blue that became the black of the universe.* What are you looking for? *you asked, and I said,* I'll know when I see it.

*We tried to find my blue in the pottery sold by a Turkish man in a street market; in a handful of bursting berries. We stopped in front of a Chinese restaurant with a tank full of live fish and stared at their rainbow scales. We brushed our fingertips over the heads of pansies in window displays, and counted the navy knapsacks of schoolchildren in uniforms.*

*We went back to the studio, finally, and you mixed paint: aqua and cerulean, indigo, sapphire. You took your brush and stroked them in stripes on the back of my hand, up the inside of my arm. We watched the twilight, all the blues of night being born, and you turned me into art.*

*It was when you moved in me, when you cried out my name, that I found the color I'd been searching for. That blistering blue of your eyes. I've been looking for it ever since.*

YOU CAN'T HAVE death without birth. The Ancient Egyptians believed that before creation, there was only unity—no death, no birth, no light, no darkness, no earth, no sky. Just an undifferentiated oneness, into which something had to be carved.

Atum was the androgynous creator god. His name literally means *All*. The Coffin Texts say that Atum created the first male/female pair. He masturbated into existence Shu—the luminous space between sky and earth, and spat out Tefnut—the divine moisture. In Middle Egyptian, the word *hand* is feminine, so the male Atum has a feminine element of himself that he uses to fashion the world.

It's because of this belief that Egyptian religion uses the concept of syncretism. Two deities who appear as separate gods in temples can be taken back a generation, before they split. Amun-Re is the hidden Amun and his visible form, Re, together. You start with a unified whole, and then as time passes, you differentiate and organize and divide. Creation, by definition, is separation. Moving forward means being split apart.

This is what I think about, when I can't fall asleep at night. When I stare at Brian across the table and try to remember who I married.

*Time is a construct. Our brains take eighty milliseconds to process information, did you know that? Anyone who tells you to live in the here and now is a liar. By the time you pin the present down, it's already the past.*

*If you had asked me back then where we would be ten years later, I would have laughed and asked why, when we had today? I would not have admitted to you, to anyone, that every now and then when I lifted my head from your shoulder and peered into the future, I could imagine you, and me, but not us.*

*I guess that's the part no one ever tells you. You can love someone so much your teeth ache, so much that it feels like he is carrying your heart in his own rib cage, but none of it matters if you can't find a practical way to be together. It's like learning that you would be immortal if you could breathe nitrogen, but knowing you are bound to the oxygen of Earth.*

*I was the meteor that crashed into your life when you were already living it. I didn't have any more control over my landing than you did when you froze, looking up at the inevitable sky. You had a past and a plan and responsibilities. You had someone who already loved you. We were gasoline poured onto fire. With you I burned twice as high and hot.*

*This is why you and I could never have stayed together. We would have consumed each other until there was nothing left.*

*When I met the man I would eventually marry, I almost blinked and overlooked him. He was quiet and thoughtful and steady and sure, all the things you weren't.* This is boring, *I thought at first.* Where are the bursts of color? Why doesn't he talk over me when I'm talking because we have so much to say? *When you're used to flying, it's hard to walk with your feet on the ground. But the strangest thing happened. Moving so deliberately, I noticed things I never had before: the way he never backed out of a parking spot unless my seatbelt was fastened; the way he asked before he kissed me, as if what I had to give was not his to take; how, when I got appendicitis, he was more worried about me than I was about myself. How he would order food that he knew I wanted, instead of his favorite meal. How he charged my phone daily, when I forgot to plug it in. How, when he held my hand, I didn't just feel things. I felt everything. He wasn't staid and slow. He was steady. When I stopped careening between the highs and lows of emotion, I didn't feel bored. I felt safe.*

*For a while I was angry at you, because I had almost missed this—someone I didn't just want to be with, but someone I wanted to be more like. You were the bright shiny thing at the corner of my consciousness. I made myself look away.*

KIERAN IS SO busy as a neurosurgery resident that weeks at a time go by without my seeing him, and yet, I know him so thoroughly that the minute we meet up at Saks in Copley Square, I see something is wrong. I also know he can't talk about it without getting more agitated. "I don't understand why you need a suit," I say casually, as we wander through the store, fingering cashmere blazers as soft as a dream and shirts so fine they slip through my hand.

"Because I can't present my research at a conference in scrubs," Kieran says. He glances at a price tag and goes pale. "That's more than I make in a month."

"I thought neurosurgeons were rolling in dough."

"Residents aren't."

He's fidgeting, the way he used to when he was younger and nervous—when he had to take his SATs or when he finally came out to me. So I do what I used to do—I grab his hand and squeeze once, like a pulse. I wait for him to squeeze back. We keep this little heart-beat between us.

If I ever needed proof that I had made the right decision to stay in Boston after my mother's death, instead of going back to Egypt, all I had to do was think of Kieran. He excelled as a student, he went to Harvard undergrad and then Harvard Medical School; he was a resident at Mass General; and now, he'd been invited to present his research—aneurysmal therapy using retrievable Guglielmi detachable coils—at age twenty-eight. I know what a big deal this is for him. But I want to just smooth back his hair, like I used to when he had a fever, and tell him he can breathe.

"Hey," I say now, softly, "you're going to be great."

He looks at me with my mother's eyes. He nods and swallows, but his fingers are still clenched in mine.

"You could wear a burlap sack," I tell him. "No one is going to even notice what your tie looks like, once you open your mouth."

"That's easy for you to say," Kieran mutters. "You're not the one being judged. I know my shit, but I don't know if I can explain it to a whole auditorium full of people."

"You teach med students all the time."

"In groups of five. Not five hundred."

"Imagine them in their underwear," I suggest.

"The med students?" he says. "The ones I know don't wear any, because they have no time to do laundry."

He is joking, but his pulse is still racing. It's my job to read a human body, to see how close it is to crisis.

"Are you going to tell me what's really wrong?"

He stops wandering through the racks. "What if this is it? I've been number one in my class. Twice. I got the match I wanted. Everything's gone according to plan. Doesn't it seem like it's time for me to take a stupendous fall?" He drops his head. "It's a big deal to be asked to present research this early in my career. Maybe I shouldn't have said yes."

"Kieran, you've gotten where you are because you work hard at it. Take a deep breath," I suggest, and I inhale deeply, to model the behavior.

And nearly jump out of my skin, because I smell Wyatt.

Sugar and sunlight and something expensive. I yank my hand out of Kieran's and turn around like I'm being hunted.

"Dawn?" Kieran asks, but his voice sounds like it's coming from miles away.

I'm tangled in white sheets, in his arms. I am pulling his shirt around me like a robe. I breathe him in all around me.

The Ancient Egyptians believed that when a god came in its true form, there was an irresistible aroma. In the creation scene of the female king Hatshepsut at Deir el-Bahari, Hatshepsut's mother conceives when Amun comes to her. Even though Amun is taking the form of her husband, she knows he is really a god, because of his scent.

I feel Kieran's hands on my shoulders, shaking me back to reality. "Dawn? Are you okay?"

I want to be strong for him, the way I have been for years now. But to my shock, my eyes fill with tears. "No. I don't think so."

He drags me deeper into the men's department. He finds the fitting room, tugs me inside, and closes the door behind us. "What the hell is going on?"

I am shaking so hard that I cannot stop. Once I open my mouth, the words pour forth like an inundation. I tell him about Gita and Brian and the fight we had the night of Meret's birthday. I tell him everything, beginning with the moment I left home and ending with Brian behind me, staring over my shoulder at Wyatt's face on a screen.

I tell him I've made a mistake.

"You mean looking up Wyatt," he clarifies, and I shake my head.

"How many times have I heard Brian talk about alternative universes?" I pick at a thread on the bottom of a coat hanging behind me. "It's like I've opened Pandora's box . . . inside my mind. I can't unsee it."

"Unsee what?"

"What my life might have been."

My neck prickles with shame. What mother, what wife admits

this? The only solace I have is that Kieran can't possibly hate me any more than I hate myself right now.

But he doesn't tell me I'm a monster. He curls his hand around mine. He squeezes. He waits for me to squeeze back. When I don't, he tries again, and then I respond, and suddenly, there's a beat between us. Thready, erratic . . . but present.

I look into his face, seeing the boy he was when he cried himself to sleep after our mother died, the teenager who delivered the valedictory address, the man who'd just suffered his first heartbreak. "You," I say, "are going to be a great doctor."

Kieran lifts his hand and I think he's going to stroke my hair or my cheek, the child caring for the adult. Instead, he reaches behind me to the coat that is hanging on the dressing room wall. He flicks his finger to turn the price tag, and smiles wryly. "Fuck this," he says. "Let's go to T.J.Maxx."

*I thought about you whenever I painted. When I went to a museum. I wondered how you told the story of us, how different it was from the way I framed our story. To you, I was there one minute and then I was gone. You probably think that I stopped loving you. You didn't realize that the reason I left was because I loved you too much.*

*I didn't want to be a cliché and I didn't want you to be one either. But mostly, I didn't want to be the one left behind, and the only way to ensure that is to be the one who leaves. I kept thinking about your wife, about how she would feel if in the end you were mine. It was too easy to put myself in her shoes. I couldn't let myself be the reason you made a woman feel that way, so whether I stayed or not, I lost.*

*I lied to you, before. I told you that I could see you in the future and me in the future but not the two of us. This is not true. I did see us together, the very best of us, for fifteen years—in the face of our son.*

*This is the part where you are allowed to hate me—because not only did I keep him from you, but I also kept you from him, and now it is too late to fix. His name was Arlo and he had your blue eyes and height and my crooked front tooth. He loved Dixie ice cream cups, but only the chocolate half; he hated peas. He couldn't draw a straight line, so much for genetic artistic ability. He was not easy—but that only meant that when he decided to love you, it mattered more. I think maybe that he was born with fire instead of blood.*

*I guess you could say he got that from both of us.*

*Was. Got. Past tense. You noticed, I'm sure. The reason I know that you and I in tandem were not sustainable is because of Arlo. Whatever it was that raged in him could be soothed, but only for snatches of time. First, a toy. A piece of candy. A hug. But as he got older, the only thing that could lift him from himself were drugs.*

*He died three years ago.*

*I used to imagine him, walking the streets of Boston, and you, walking wherever you are, somehow being able to feel each other through the thickness of this planet. Like an echo in your footsteps, or a tremble in your pulse.*

*I used to imagine this because I can't bear to think that you never knew he existed. And it's all my fault.*


ONCE UPON A time, there is nothing but darkness. You stumble around blindly, so close to the edge that you are sure you'll tumble over it, and if you are going to be honest, you must admit you are so low already you don't necessarily think that would be a bad thing. Then one day, you meet someone. He finds you kneeling right at the precipice and instead of telling you to get back up, he kneels next to you. He tries to see what you are seeing. He doesn't ask anything of you, or beg you to snap out of it, or remind you that there are people who need you. He just waits until you turn and squint and think to yourself: *Oh, yes, I remember. This is what* light *looks like.*

You don't know how it happens, but you become friends. You find yourself looking in the parking lot to see if his car is there. You see something on TV or read it in a book and think, *I must remember to tell him.* You learn how he takes his coffee and what his favorite color is—not by asking, but by observation. Then you realize that your day speeds up when you see him. The hair stands up on the backs of your forearms when his shoulder bumps yours in the elevator. His presence is so filling, the absence of him aches.

You begin to reconfigure the puzzle of your life to fit him into it. You don't want to spend time without him, if you can help it. You introduce him to family. You suffer their elbow jabs and their raised eyebrows because later, it gives you two something to laugh about. You wish you could introduce him to the family members that aren't here anymore. They would have loved him. You see him around children and think, *One day*.

When he asks you to get married you let out a breath that you never realized you were holding. On your wedding day, your face hurts because you are smiling so hard. Your life isn't simple, but does that really matter if you have someone like him to help shoulder the burden? Money, jobs, promotions, failures, they are only speed bumps on a track that will go on forever.

You have a child. You do not believe he could love anyone the way he loves you, until you see him with her. She is not just a treasure, meant to be kept safe at all costs. She is the proof that the two of you belong together.

Not that you need proof.

You keep that baby alive like it's your only job.

One night when she is sick, you are so tired from taking care of her that you go to sleep in the office, on the couch. You think you will never be able to fall asleep without him beside you. You are wrong.

In fact, you sleep pretty well.

It happens again when he gets a cold; when you come home late from work; when you argue. It stops being a guest room and becomes a sanctuary. Your daughter asks if you are going to get divorced. *No,* you tell her. *We love each other.*

You move back into the same bed that night. You say *I love you,* but it's no longer like throwing open the windows of your heart. You say it the way you'd say *It's Tuesday* or *I'm a brunette:* matter-of-fact, a truth, a statement. Not an exaltation. Not a miracle. You wonder when the core of love changed from passion to compassion.

You never surprise him, anymore, by slipping into the shower when he's in it. He shuts off the light on his night table while you are still reading in bed, and turns onto his side. You remember how he used to stand with you in crowds, his hand at your waist, protective and possessive. Now he holds your daughter's hand, rather than yours.

The things that used to endear him to you now drive you crazy. How he clears his throat all the time. How he doesn't replace the empty roll of toilet paper. How he sings off-key to the radio. But that's the stupid stuff, you tell yourself. You have real love, not Hollywood love. You have a child. That's what's important.

Yet there are days that you fight with him just because it lets you feel *something*.

You begin to wonder if you still love him. You wonder if you ever did. The opposite of love, you think, isn't hate. It's complacency.

One day you find yourself in the darkness again, stumbling around, at the edge of a cliff. He's there, too. But you think maybe he isn't light, was *never* light at all. He was just sucking up what was left of *your* light, to illuminate his own shadows.

You've changed. You don't want to jump into that void. You don't have to, because the source of your pain is standing right beside you.

When you fall in love, it's because you find someone who fills all your empty spaces.

When you fall out of love, it's because you realize that you're both broken.

*Why now? Why write, after twenty years? Why turn up like an unquiet ghost, chains in my hands, disturbing whatever peace you have convinced yourself you have?*

*Because I'm running out of time.*

*It is the one thing we never had, and I'm sorry to say it's only gotten worse.*

*I'm sick, my love. I'm sick, and as my body decays around me, all I have left is my mind. I have had many long hours in this bed to mull over it, and even if we were never meant to stay together, we were meant to be together. Even if we had to lose each other, we were meant to find each other. I would not have had my marriage or almost sixteen years with my son if not for you. I don't think it could have gone any other way, and I don't think it should have gone any other way. You are the catalyst, if not the product of the chemical equation. You belonged with her, and I belonged with him, but for a tiny flicker, we belonged to each other. I just couldn't leave this world without telling you that you were the one, for me. The one I couldn't shake and didn't want to.*

*By the time you are reading this, I'll most likely be gone. But because you are reading this, I know that as long as you're here, so am I.*

THE SICKER A person gets, the more equipment there is. Win's bedside is cluttered with pill bottles, cups with straws, wipes to soothe her skin when she's feeling hot. There is a stack of Chux—the absorbent pads we slip under the sheets as incontinence becomes an issue. The cane she used when I met her became a walker, and now a wheelchair. The commode in the bathroom is now a commode beside the bed.

Win has her head turned toward the window. Felix has hung a bird feeder there, and juncos and squirrels and the occasional blue jay twitch nervously on its lip. "Is that a red leaf?" she asks.

I lean closer so that I can look where she is looking. It's summer, green as far as the eye can see.

"I don't think so. It's too early for the leaves to turn."

She sighs, rolling onto her back. "I was hoping I'd make it to fall."

"Is that your favorite season?"

"No, I hate it. Pumpkin spice is the work of Satan." Win folds her hands across her stomach. "You know, people who are dying always talk about the things they'll miss. A spring day. Orange Popsicles. Seeing your grandkids grow up. No one talks about the other stuff that you won't: shoveling your driveway or doing your taxes or getting arthritis . . . or pumpkin spice. But here's the kicker: I'm actually going to miss those, too." Win glances at me. "It feels like there ought to be a word for that feeling. Something long and German, like *schadenfreude*. Or maybe your Ancient Egyptians had one."

There is a Middle Kingdom text called The Dispute Between a Man and His *Ba*, in which a man argues with his soul, saying he wants to commit suicide. The soul counters by saying that we don't really know what happens after death, so why take that risk? The text doesn't judge the man for wanting to kill himself—it's not about going to hell, or sin, or even a warning. It's about missing out on the enjoyment of life on earth.

Win stretches out her hand, and I take it. Her bones are light and insubstantial. She is an hourglass, and there is so little sand remaining. "I have one regret, you know. That I didn't get to meet you under better circumstances."

I feel a telltale prickle of tears in my eyes. "Win, it has been a joy getting to know you."

"I think we would have been friends," she says.

"I think we *are* friends."

She nods. "That's why I want you to leave."

I look at her quizzically.

"To deliver my letter."

I shake my head. "I promised you I would get it to Thane, but right now, you're my priority."

"And I'm asking you to go now, to do this. I know it won't change anything. But I think it's going to be easier for me to . . . leave . . . knowing that he's thinking of me." Win's sentence ends in a whisper. "I trust you, Dawn."

"But—"

"You told me you'd make sure that whatever I wanted at the end, or needed, I'd have. I need this. I want this."

"Win," I say clearly, carefully, "you may very well die while I'm off finding Thane."

"I'll have Felix, here."

I nod, unable to speak for a moment. "I'll make sure that my friend Abigail comes. She's a hospice social worker."

"That would be good," Win says. "For Felix, too."

I believe that there are five things we need to say to people we love before they die, and I give this advice to caregivers: *I forgive you. Please forgive me. Thank you. I love you. Goodbye.* I tell them that they can interpret those prompts any way they like, and nothing will have been left unsaid.

I forgive Win for making me do this.

I hope she will forgive me for not being here, if she dies when I'm away.

I thank her for showing me a piece of myself I'd forgotten.

"I love you," I tell her, pressing a kiss to her forehead.

When I meet her gaze, she is crying, too. "Goodbye," I say.

She reaches up, which takes considerable effort, and holds on to my hand with both of her own, as if she, too, is having trouble letting go.

From a desk drawer, I take the rolled canvas, with its art on one side and my cramped handwriting on the other. Tied with a piece of string, it looks like the papyrus scroll of the Book of Going Forth by Day.

"Dawn?" Win's voice reaches me as I am about to cross the threshold of the room. "I hope you find him."

"Thane? I will. I promise."

"Not mine," she says. "Yours."


WHEN BRIAN COMES home from work, I am packing, and I have purchased a ticket to Heathrow. He sees me folding a change of clothes and underwear into a knapsack and goes still in the doorway. I realize he thinks I am leaving him.

Again.

"I'm going to London," I explain. "For Win."

He sits on the edge of the bed. "Did she die, then?"

"No. But I don't think it will be long now. She asked me to deliver her letter now, instead of waiting."

Brian nods, pulling at a thread in our comforter.

"I know you don't want me to go," I reply. "But I made a promise."

"A promise," Brian repeats. "You made one to me, too, a long time ago."

"What's that supposed to mean?"

Brian looks at me. "I found you looking at your old boyfriend online, but I didn't run. You keep saying that I'm the problem, that it's because of what I did or almost did, but I'm here. I'm sticking. I'm fighting for our marriage. You're the one who keeps putting distance between us." His voice breaks. "Jesus. Being with you is all I ever wanted. And being with me, for you, is torture."

"That's not true. I love you." I hesitate. "I can see us, twenty years from now, with wrinkles and white hair and grandchildren, all of it. I just don't know how we get from here . . . to there."

He holds my palm between his hands, turning it over like he could divine my future. "I do. I'll do whatever it takes to make you feel safe again. I'll quit my job and move to a different university. I'll go to counseling. We could take a vacation. Egypt—you could show me Egypt! Let's go to Meret's tennis matches together and be the loudest, most embarrassing parents. Let's try to remember how to be *us* again."

I want to. I want to so badly that I ache. But I can't figure out how to be *us* if I don't know who *I* am.

"It's like déjà vu. The thing I'm most afraid of happening keeps actually happening," Brian says. "Every time you walk out that door, I think it's the time you're not coming back."

I don't know what to say. The last time I ran away, I didn't think I was coming back, either.

Brian draws a shallow breath. "Do you think I don't know that you settled?"

"I didn't settle," I tell him. "I wound up exactly where I was supposed to wind up."

"Then don't go."

Logic. Brian has always been able to wield it. He makes it seem so simple: stay here, and fight for the marriage. But I have to deliver Win's letter.

"I'm not saying you shouldn't deliver it," Brian adds, reading my thoughts. "I'm saying you shouldn't deliver it *right now*."

"Sometimes the past matters more than the present," I answer, and he lets go of my hand.

We are saved from ourselves by Meret, who bounces into the bedroom, brandishing an envelope. "It's back. It's finally back!"

Brian and I both instantly morph into normal, untroubled parents. "Genomia?" Brian guesses.

"What's Genomia?"

Meret sits down between us. "The DNA test Dad got me for my birthday."

I vaguely remember her thanking Brian for the belated gift—but I hadn't actually ever asked what the present was.

"It's supposed to tell you if you have tendencies for, like, celiac disease or high cholesterol or Alzheimer's . . . or obesity," Meret says. "I just thought it would be cool to see why I'm the way I am."

A girl who looks nothing like her parents, who is trying to find her place in the world. I meet Brian's gaze over her head.

"Well?" he says. "Time for the big reveal?"

She tears open the envelope. "The first page is just ancestry," Meret says. "But I already know I'm Irish and . . ."

"Ninety-eight percent?" Brian looks at the pie chart on the paper. "That's weird. Your grandma and grandpa were Ashkenazi Jews from Poland. What's the margin of error for the test?"

Always the scientist.

Meret smirks. "Is now the time to tell me I'm adopted?"

I stare at the pie chart and suddenly I can't move. My blood, the same blood that runs in Meret's veins, is sluggish. That nearly complete circle graph. British and Irish, ninety-eight percent.

*The marquess is my father. I'm merely an earl.*

*All the way back to William the Conqueror, I'm afraid.*

*English,* Wyatt had said. *Through and through.*

# LAND / EGYPT

. . .

THERE'S AN EGYPTIAN myth in which Isis, hungry to get power from Re to give her own son, brings down the sun god by creating a poisonous snake out of his own spit. Re can't fight it, because it's part of him. That is how it feels when, the next day, I am working in the magazine and Wyatt comes in.

I already know that Anya is leaving. I heard the Land Rover pulling away; I assumed that Wyatt was in it with her, driving her back to Cairo to make her flight.

"I'm surprised to see you," I say.

He leans against one of the storage shelves. "Alberto had to go to Cairo to get some computer cable, so he offered to play chauffeur."

"He deserves a raise," I say, turning my attention to a line of hieratic I've read four times.

Wyatt comes closer, climbing up the scaffolding so that he is standing opposite me, the cavern of the coffin between us. "You're angry."

"You said it yourself: I don't have the right to be angry." I look away from him. "I got your note. Or was that a parting gift?"

I want to ask him what he said to Anya. And at the same time, I don't want to know. Either way, I can't see where we go from here.

"Dammit, Olive. I really want to talk to you."

"Then talk."

"Not here." Wyatt climbs down from the scaffolding and stands at the base of the coffin, his hand extended, like a knight rescuing a maiden from a tower. "Let's go for a drive."

. . .

IN 2003, ON the day that we found the rock dipinto, everyone else living in the Dig House had taken the day off. We were alone because they'd gone to visit Tell el-Amarna, the city where Akhenaton ruled with his queen, Nefertiti. It is only eight miles from us, thirty minutes, and it's remarkable that I have never actually been there, because Akhenaton is one of the most fascinating kings in ancient Egypt. A New Kingdom pharaoh from the 18th Dynasty, he is known for two things: for being the father of Tutankhamun, and for changing religion during the course of his reign.

There's no question that deities—plural—were important to ancient Egyptians. Many Egyptian gods seemed to clot into threes or multiples of threes—from Atum, Shu, and Tefnut to Amun, Re, and Ptah; from Osiris, Isis, and Horus to the Ennead—the nine main deities worshipped at Heliopolis. Temples in Egypt were stages for processions. The Egyptians would have come out to watch, and after the gods had sucked up all the spiritual sustenance from the offerings, the literal food was given to the masses. Feast days then were like Christmas now.

But when Akhenaton became king, he was the Grinch. He shut down the temples and the festivals. Instead of celebrating many gods, the Egyptians now had to celebrate one—the Aton, or sun disk—but Akhenaton wasn't a monotheist. Instead, he inserted himself into theology, rounding out a new trilogy with himself and his royal wife, Nefertiti. Every day in Amarna, his shining golden city, there were festivals celebrating himself, his wife, and his daughters. He was accompanied by a military escort at all times. It is the only era in Egyptian history where there are representations of people bowing all the time to their king.

He didn't just cancel Christmas, though. He also canceled the afterlife. Although he was a New Kingdom pharaoh, his tomb—unlike the tombs in the Valley of the Kings—depicts no funerary rituals involving deities like Re and Osiris, because that would negate the concept of Akhenaton as a creator god. By definition, none of those other deities could exist yet.

Wyatt and I are quiet on our way to Amarna. We stop first at the boundary stele, and then we continue to the necropolis.

Wyatt has been here often. The guard knows him by sight and hands him the key so that we can explore on our own. As we descend into the Royal Tomb, I breathe in the sweet, smoky smell of bat guano. Immediately, I am drawn to the images on the walls, which are so different from the art at Deir el-Bersha or *anywhere* else in Ancient Egypt.

Nefertiti and Akhenaton are hard to tell apart, because the figures do not look male and female. They are carved with elongated heads and round tummies, like the androgynous creator deities of Ancient Egypt. Their daughters are depicted, too, with the same alienesque heads and bellies, as if they, too, are eternally frozen at the moment of creation. In ritual temple scenes and private tombs, Akhenaton only portrayed his daughters, because a creator god could have as many female manifestations as he wanted, but the minute there was another male, the primordial clock was marching forward.

Suddenly I understand why Wyatt has brought me here. Akhenaton tried to turn back time.

"I didn't say anything to Anya," Wyatt confesses, "because I realized I had to speak to you, first."

Slowly, I face him. Wyatt stands in front of a sunrise scene depicting the royal family. His bright hair is exactly at the level of the sun disk, and for some reason, this makes me want to cry.

"Stay with me, Olive. Publish this tomb with me. It's not too late to start over."

It is so enticing to imagine that my life might have been different. That it still could be. But even as Wyatt reaches for my hand, I know what I have to tell him.

Like Akhenaton, we can pretend. We can squirrel ourselves away in Deir el-Bersha, just the two of us. We can spin an epic story of how we were always meant to be. But also like Akhenaton, we will never really be able to go backward.

I pull away, escaping into another chamber of the tomb as I press the heels of my hands to my eyes. I can't do this. I can't walk away from him twice.

I hear him come into the chamber behind me. I am in the room where Meketaton, the second daughter of Akhenaton, was buried.

She died near the thirteenth or fourteenth year of her father's reign. In the scene carved into the plaster on the walls, she is lying dead on a bier, as Akhenaton and Nefertiti hold each other and weep over her body. It is the most breathtaking portrait of grief.

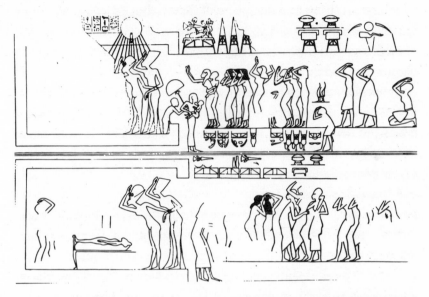

A second scene shows Akhenaton and Nefertiti again tearing out their hair in the act of mourning—*nwn*—in front of Meketaton's standing mummy or statue. In this image, a baby is being led away by a nurse.

When I was studying Egyptology, there was a lot of discussion about that baby, and who it might be. Some scholars said this proved Meketaton died in childbirth—and that the father was her own father, Akhenaton. But Meketaton died at age eleven, which was likely too young to be pregnant, even then. Some said the baby was Tutankhamun (then called Tutankhaton), although there was a question about a nearby determinative hieroglyph, which may show a seated female rather than a seated male. Others believed it was Meketaton herself, reborn under the healing rays of the Aton—the only way to show an afterlife, since there was no reference to Osiris or Re during Akhenaton's rule.

Although, academically, that baby is most likely Tutankhaton, I prefer the last analysis. Depending on your point of view, Akhenaton might be seen as a king, a narcissist, a visionary—but he was *definitely* a grieving father. In his heart, he would have wanted his daughter resurrected. To me, this is the only interpretation that hints at hope.

When you have a child, you will do anything for her. You may not do it well, but you will kill yourself trying. You will trip over obstacles as you clear them out of her path. You will give her the choices you didn't have.

I move closer to the image of Meketaton's parents, bent with sorrow. This is the remarkable part of history. As different as my life is now from that of an Egyptian pharaoh, I know what it feels like to wake up in a world where I have a daughter, and the next day, to face a future where I may not.

It's why I can't stay here.

The most difficult job I have ever had as a death doula was also the shortest. I was hired by a couple who knew that they were having a baby that would be born without a brain. You would think this was a fresh level of hell—having to carry to term a fetus that wasn't going to survive. But in this case, you'd be wrong. The mom used to love her OB visits, because hearing that heartbeat was the time she got to spend with her daughter. She said that when she had to get up at 2:00 A.M. to pee, she pretended those were her daughter's ornery teenage years—she was just living through them now.

I told this couple that I didn't want their birth plan—I wanted their *life* plan. If the baby survived five minutes, what was most important? Who would be in the delivery room? If the baby survived five hours, who could visit? If the baby survived five days, would they want to bring her home?

They said they wanted to celebrate every major holiday, in the time they had. They wanted her first year, in a matter of moments. So I hired a photographer. We took pictures of the baby in a Santa onesie, and with a Baby New Year sash, and with a little paper Valentine's heart. We knew when her grandparents could hold her, what music they wanted playing, when their priest should come in to administer last rites. The baby's name was Felicity. She lived for thirty-seven minutes.

I have told this story to many people who ask me how I can possibly work with those who are dying. There is beauty and grace at the end, I tell them, even for babies like Felicity. She never experienced war, heartbreak, or pain. She never struggled to make ends meet. She didn't get bullied in school or find out she had been passed over for a promotion or get left at the altar. She knew nothing in her short life but love.

I don't know why, when it comes to death, we say we *lost* someone. They're not missing or misplaced. They're whisked away from the tightest embrace.

In a world where some parents don't get the choice to keep their children close, I can't leave mine just so I can have a second chance with Wyatt.

I turn around, knowing that he is waiting. "You know what's the hardest part of watching someone die? The people who are left behind."

"That's why you should stay, Olive," Wyatt interrupts. "I love you."

"I know." All these years, and here I am repeating myself. Tears stream down my face. "But you're not the only one *I* love. Even if I could leave him . . . I couldn't leave her."

"Your daughter."

"Yes. Meret." I take a deep breath. "After Meretseger."

Wyatt is one of the few people I don't have to explain this to. The cobra-headed goddess of the peak, she was associated with the mountain above the Valley of Kings. The name means *She Who Loves Silence,* and she was worshipped by the workers from Deir el-Medina who built the royal tombs. She would blind or strike down those who stole or committed a crime, but she could also be merciful.

It had been hard to find an Ancient Egyptian deity who had, at her heart, forgiveness. "People screw up," I tell Wyatt. "We make mistakes and bad decisions and piss off the people we care about, and if we're lucky, a goddess like Meretseger takes pity on us." I meet his gaze, and finally say what I came all this way to say. "That's why I named our daughter after her."

# WATER / BOSTON

. . .

FIFTEEN YEARS AGO, when I had left Egypt during the *neshni*, when the roads had flooded and Wyatt drove me to the airport in Cairo, I felt sick. Once or twice I even thought I'd have to ask him to pull over. Now, looking back, I know it wasn't anxiety.

Wyatt and I had used condoms with the exception of that first night, so what were the odds?

The same odds, I supposed, as those of finding a painted rock inscription in the middle of a desert.

The same odds as those of falling in love with the person you thought you hated.

The same odds as those of finding a soul mate.

I think of the Coffin Texts, Spell 148: *Lightning flashes; the gods become afraid. Isis awakens being pregnant.*

A spark in the sky, another *neshni*, another child. It was that simple, and that unexpected.

I am sitting in the bathroom on the closed toilet seat, trying to keep myself from flying apart, when Brian finally comes in. He is not the man who begged me to stay just an hour ago. He is hard, his eyes flat and empty. "Meret's asleep," he says. "I managed to find her three studies on the Internet that showed flawed DNA test results due to foreign bodies in the sample."

I try to nod, but I can't even do that. I think that if I move an inch, I'm going to shatter. Brian leans against the vanity, the marble surface that has my face lotion and his shaving cream on it, side by side, as if it were that easy. "Why didn't you tell me?" he asks finally.

"I didn't know."

It is the truth, although now, I wonder if I was just trying to convince myself on some subconscious level. By the time I found out I was pregnant, I'd already lost my mother. I'd had what I thought was a period. I've always been irregular, and time had warped in hospice, so my last moments with Wyatt seemed months earlier, rather than weeks. Now, though, I remember how Meret was born two weeks before her due date, as the nurse reassured me she looked just as robust as any full-term baby. I remember holding her, staring at the curve of her ear, and thinking of the shape of Wyatt's. But then, there was Brian, rocking Meret when she had colic. There was Brian, tossing her in the air until she squealed with delight. There was Brian, teaching her how to jump in from the side of a pool. Eventually, I stopped looking for my past in my future.

Maybe I'd been blind. Or maybe I'd just *wanted* to be.

"I didn't know," I repeat, tears sliding down my face. "I didn't know."

Brian's jaw is so tight that it distorts his face. I barely recognize him. "You'll forgive me if I don't actually believe you," he says. "Can I ask you just one question? Did you pick me as an easy target?"

"No. I fell in love with you."

He shakes his head. "Guys like me, we live in our grandparents' basements and collect comic books and eat leftovers for breakfast. We might meet girls who are smart and funny and pretty, girls who don't have to coach themselves on conversation topics before they walk into a room, girls who see us as more than science nerds—but we never take them home. And we never, ever get lucky enough to marry them." He looks at me, so cold I shiver. "I should have known."

"Brian, I swear to you. I didn't know Meret wasn't yours."

"She's mine, goddammit," he snarls. "In every way that counts."

I nod, swallowing. "Yes. Of course." I wipe my eyes with the back of my hand. "So now what do we do?"

"We?" Brian says. "I don't even know who you are."

He walks out of the bathroom. I follow him, but at Meret's door he gives me a look over his shoulder that stops me. I watch him slip inside to spend the night watching over her.

She's in the best hands, I realize. Far better than mine.

Brian may not know who I am, but I do. I'm a coward.

Which is why I take the overnight bag I was packing before my world fell apart, and slip out of the house.

A FEW WEEKS ago when I left, I hadn't been the one at fault. After Brian had missed Meret's birthday dinner, when he came home swollen with an apology about Gita, I got in my car and started driving.

He'd texted. *Please, Dawn, I'm sorry.*

*Let's talk.*

*I made a mistake.*

*I'm getting worried.*

I had watched the messages rise on the GPS screen, ignoring each one.

Until one came in from Meret, who had been in her room as her father and I argued. She knew nothing about Gita; she—I thought at the time—did not realize that I'd even left the house.

*Come say good night?*

So less than an hour after I walked out of my house I walked back into it, and Brian apologized. He approached the way you would a feral animal, or someone whose world has gone to pieces around her. He said he thought I was gone forever. I went up to Meret's room, tucked her in, and pretended I'd never left.

But I had.

All these weeks, I have not told Brian where I was driving to, when I was interrupted by Meret.

The airport.

All these weeks, I have not told Brian why I left. He assumes it is because after he told me about Gita, I was shocked.

I was. But not at Brian.

When he confessed, when he waited for my fury or my absolution or something in between . . . I didn't feel angry. I didn't feel hurt.

I didn't feel much of anything.

And that scared the hell out of me—more than infidelity; more than realizing that I might have mistaken comfort for love. So I did what I've always done, when nothing makes sense: I ran. Had Meret not texted, had the universe not intervened—I would have gotten on a plane.

Three weeks ago, I thought I was running away from Brian.

But maybe, without even knowing it, I'd been running *to* someone else.

WHEN I ARRIVE in England, I have lost the entire day. I boarded the flight in the early morning, and by the time I land in London, the sun is just setting, and there is a stream of traffic on the road, people heading home from their workday. The zoom of headlights becomes a glowing snake, like when Meret would wave a sparkler around in the dark, and I tracked her by the firefly trail she left behind.

*Meret.*

The bus drops me off in the center of Richmond. I have Thane Bernard's address, thanks to the Internet search company, but I've realized too late that I do not have international service on my cellphone. So I stop at a pub, where a group of men and women who look like office mates are drinking pints and playing a trivia game on the television behind the bar. There, I order an ale and a meat pie, and I ask for directions.

I feel like I have jumped timelines. Like this version of Dawn is one who might be friends with the raucous crowd next to me, trying to remember the names of the characters on *Three's Company*. Like I might have moved here after grad school and taught at Cambridge. Except that this other me wouldn't be sitting on a pub stool feeling a hole where her moral core used to be.

"Another, luv?" the bartender asks, nodding at my empty glass.

I could sit here all night and delay the inevitable. But I have a flight back to Boston tomorrow morning, when I have to learn how to be brave, how to face the mess I've made.

I walk along the bank of the Thames and through a beautiful park where joggers rush past me, lost in their own music. I stop and pet a dog wearing a bandanna with the British flag on it. At last I find myself in front of the townhouse of Thane Bernard.

It is red brick, with an intricate black Victorian gate. I crane my neck, trying to see all the way up to the third story. It is narrow, rooms built in layers rather than sprawled. Several of the windows spill soft yellow light, like cat's eyes.

"Win," I whisper, "this is for you."

A letter can be a beginning, or so I try to convince myself. In Egypt there are multiple origin myths, and in the Memphite one, Ptah speaks creation, and the hieroglyphs become the world.

I take the scroll from my backpack and open the gate, walking up to the small stoop. There is no mailbox, just a little slit in the door. Before I can slide the scroll through the slot, a movement catches my eye. In the wide double window to the right of the door a woman is carrying a roast chicken on a platter. She sets it on the dining room table.

This, then, would be Win's other timeline. She might be here, cooking dinner. Calling everyone down for the meal. Healthy. Alive.

The woman is pretty. Taller than Win but less willowy; she has strong shoulders and sound hips and curves. As I watch, a teenage boy skids in, grabs a chicken leg off the plate, and starts eating it. I see her scold him, but he just grins and sits down at the table. A girl follows him, a few years younger, typing on her phone as she slumps down at her seat.

"Can I help you?"

I whirl around to find myself staring at Thane Bernard. He is lanky and lean, wearing the bright spandex of an avid cyclist. He carries a helmet in one hand, and smooths the other over his sweating, bald head. He has a slight accent, the *h* in *help* rising like a helium balloon. I try to take a mental snapshot, so that I can tell Win, and then I remember that she may no longer be alive.

For the first time I wonder if it is fair for Win to make dissatisfaction contagious. I had been thinking so much about allowing her to come full circle that I didn't realize I might be breaking the smooth track of someone else's life.

"I . . . I think I have the wrong address," I sputter, and I push past him back through the gate. I walk without turning around, my heart racing.

Four blocks away, I stop rushing. I sit on the curb and draw deep drafts of air into my lungs. The stars squint, shaming me.

I can't do it.

I can't break up two families in less than twenty-four hours.

I walk past the Victorian gate again, hidden in the folds of the darkness. Thane Bernard and his family are deep in a conversation I cannot hear, amidst the ruins of a picked-over chicken and a scraped plate of mashed potatoes.

*This* story, anyway, is not mine to finish.

I DON'T BOTHER to get a hotel. I take a bus back to Heathrow and stand in front of the giant boards of the British Airways international departures area, trying to figure out where to check in for Boston. I inch forward with my passport in hand, until I am the next in line. The woman in front of me is wearing the sort of sleek white suit I always wish I traveled in, instead of a T-shirt and cargo pants. "Where are you heading today, madam?" the desk agent asks, in her plummy British accent.

"Cairo," she answers.

The agent scans her passport, types into the computer terminal, checks her two matching pieces of luggage. Then she hands the woman a pass. "That flight's boarding in thirty minutes."

The woman moves into the throng headed through security.

"Next?" the gate agent calls, and I step forward. I hand her my passport, and she enters my name on her keyboard. "Ms. Edelstein. You're going to Boston?"

My fingers tighten on the strap of my backpack. "Is it possible to change my ticket?"

• • •

My mother, who lived and died by superstitions, used to make us say together before we went on a trip: *We're not going anywhere.* It was meant to trick the Devil. I can't say I believe in that kind of thing, but then again, I didn't say it before I left home, and look at where that got me.

Walking outside of the airport in Cairo in August feels like stepping onto the surface of the sun. Even late at night, the heat is a knife on your skin and comes in pressing waves. I can already feel a line of sweat running down my spine; I didn't come prepared for this. I find myself in the middle of other people's transitions: a rumpled, dazed group of tourists being herded into their minivan; a teen dragging duct-taped luggage from the back of an open cart to the curb; a woman securing her head scarf as it blows in the breeze.

Suddenly I am surrounded by men. "Taxi?" they bark. "You need taxi?"

There's no hiding the fact that I'm a Westerner; it's clear from my red hair to my cargo pants and sneakers. I nod, making eye contact with one of them, a driver with a thick mustache and a long-sleeved striped shirt. The other taxi drivers fall back, seagulls in search of another crumb.

"You have suitcase?"

I shake my head. Everything I have is in the small bag I carry over my shoulder.

"American?" the man replies, and I nod. A wide, white grin splits his face. "Welcome to Alaska!"


Planes and trains and taxis. It takes me a few hours to get to Middle Egypt. As the driver turns south, bringing me back to Deir el-Bersha, I glance out the window again, struck by the beauty of the sky yawning over the desert. It's blue and pink and orange, the stripes of a day that's only beginning. A star winks at me for a moment before it's swallowed by the sun.

Sothis. Sirius. The star that heralds the inundation festival at the beginning of *Akhet,* the season of lush crops and rebirth. In ancient times, it would have happened in July. But after so many years of the earth shifting slowly on its axis, the star now rises one morning in early August.

Today, in fact. And it would have looked exactly the same thousands of years ago when the Nile flooded and Ancient Egyptians gathered and celebrated, and one left behind a dipinto painted onto a protected rock face that, thousands of years later, was found by two graduate students.

I stare at the spot where the star has already vanished, a freckle in the rosy cheek of the horizon.

Just like the Ancient Egyptians, I see it as a sign.

# CAIRO TO BOSTON

. . .

My CALENDAR IS full of dead people.

When my phone alarm chimes, I fish it out from the pocket of my cargo pants. I've forgotten, with the time change, to turn off the reminder. I'm still groggy with sleep, but I open the date and read the names: *Iris Vale. Eun Ae Kim. Alan Rosenfeldt. Marlon Jensen.*

I close my eyes, and do what I do every day at this moment: I remember them.

At one point, they were my clients. Now, they're my stories to keep.

I wonder if Win is gone by now. I wonder where I will type her name into my calendar.

Everyone in my row is asleep. I slip my phone back into my pocket and carefully crawl over the woman to my right without disturbing her—air traveler's yoga—to make my way to the bathroom in the rear of the plane. There I blow my nose and look in the mirror. I grab a handful of tissues and open the door, intent on heading back to my seat, but the little galley area is packed with flight attendants. "Ma'am," one of them says, "could you please take your seat?"

I climb back over the dozing woman and buckle my seatbelt. A hand slips over mine, threading our fingers together. I lean against Wyatt's shoulder, breathing in the scent of him, touching him just because I can. In spite of all that has happened in the past six weeks—from the days spent trying to repair the sieve of my marriage, to Win's letter and the trip I made to London; from my last-minute decision to go to Egypt, to reuniting with Wyatt and unearthing the coffin—getting to this point feels both monumental and inevitable.

Wyatt blinks awake and smiles slowly. "Where'd you go?" he asks, his voice still rough with sleep, just as the overhead lights blaze and the cabin comes alive.


I HAD THE second hardest conversation of my life in a tomb in Amarna. After I told Wyatt that Meret was his daughter, he just stared at me, as if he had clearly heard the words wrong. And yet, what had I expected? Learning this after fifteen years? When his first assumption—like Brian's—was that I had hid this from him?

They had, I realized, this one thing in common.

I filled the stunned silence. I told him about my mother's stay in hospice. About feeling so overwhelmed and how Brian suddenly appeared. I told him that I slept with Brian because I couldn't remember what joy felt like, because for one night I needed to be the one taken care of, instead of the caretaker. I told him about the pregnancy. I told him how, a year later, we got married.

I also told him about Gita, and the night of Meret's birthday, when Brian didn't come home to celebrate with us. I told him how I had driven away and thought I was leaving for good, but didn't. I told him about Win and her lost love and how I searched for Thane Bernard and found Wyatt. I told him about the moment Meret came into my bedroom with a DNA test; how all the tumblers clicked into place.

I told him how, at the last minute, I changed my return flight to come to Cairo instead to Boston—because he deserved to know about Meret, now that I did.

When I finished, my shirt was sticking to my back with sweat. There was no air in that tomb. I felt frozen inside, an insect in amber. Finally, Wyatt raised his head. His expression was careful, guarded. "You found out you were pregnant, and it never crossed your mind that it could be mine?"

I didn't know how to explain to Wyatt the weeks that my mother was dying, the strange elasticity where hours bled into days and nothing felt linear. I didn't know how to explain how I'd felt torn apart from leaving him, and embarrassed because I'd used Brian to stitch myself back together. That I'd been drowning in a future that was uncertain, and grabbed on to someone solid and strong. That when I got pregnant, I truly thought it was Brian's baby, Fate pointing a giant neon arrow in one direction.

So I said nothing.

A muscle jumped in Wyatt's jaw. "Was I that easy to forget?" he asked. "Or were *you* just selfish as hell?" He brushed past me then, his footsteps echoing as he moved through other chambers of the tomb.

Leaving me. Which, frankly, I deserved.

I sank down beneath the scene of parental grief and cried. Nefertiti and Akhenaton had lost one beloved daughter; I had lost nearly everyone I cared about. I couldn't even blame Wyatt. Through his eyes, this was stupidity at best and betrayal at worst. Either I had set him out of my mind so quickly fifteen years ago that it seemed our relationship meant nothing; or I had made the calculated decision to hide his own daughter from him. I imagined him walking out of the tomb and giving the keys back to the *gaffir*. Maybe thousands of years from now, tourists would come to see my dessicated body: *Here lies the woman who destroyed her own life.*

An hour passed before I heard someone walking back toward the chamber. Wyatt sat down beside me, his shoulders against the rock wall. "When you left home the first time," he asked, "where were you headed?"

Of all the questions he could have posed, this was the one I had not been expecting. "I don't know. I didn't have a plan." I swallowed hard. "But I think I've been running in place for a long time, because I knew if I stopped, I'd wind up wherever you are."

In this tomb, where time stood still, I waited seconds, weeks, a lifetime, until I felt Wyatt's hand cover mine where it rested on the dirt. "I lost what I loved once, and I don't plan to do that again," he said quietly. "I'd like to meet my daughter."

. . .

"LADIES AND GENTLEMEN," a voice announces, "we have just been informed by the captain that we're going to have a planned emergency. Please listen to the flight attendants and follow their directions."

Wyatt had insisted on getting the first flight out of Cairo, in spite of the fact that he was in the breakthrough stage of an excavation (*He's been dead for four thousand years, Olive, he's not going anywhere . . .* ); although I thought he should sleep on his decision. I believed my anxiety had stemmed from the confrontation that would face us in Boston, which would not be easy, even if it was right. But maybe there had been a sixth sense warning me away from this flight.

Shock rolls through the cabin—but no screams, no loud cries. "We're crashing," the woman on the aisle whispers. "Oh my God, we're crashing."

*Fasten your seatbelts. When you hear the word* brace, *assume the brace position. After the plane comes to a complete stop you'll hear* Release your seatbelts. *Get out. Leave everything behind.*

I have heard that when you are about to die, your life flashes before your eyes.

But I do not picture Brian or Meret. I do not envision my mother or Kieran.

Instead, I think of Wyatt, only of Wyatt.

I imagine Wyatt in the middle of the Egyptian desert, the sun beating down on his hat, his neck ringed with dirt from the constant wind, his teeth a flash of lightning. A man who hasn't been part of my life for fifteen years. A place I left behind.

A dissertation I never finished.

A future we'd never get.

I try to imagine Wyatt and Meret and me, a family. I think about how many people we have wounded, just by falling in love fifteen years ago. I think about the feather of Ma'at, and whether I will pass to the afterlife, given all I've done.

I fumble for my phone, thinking to turn it on, to send a message—an apology?—even though I know there is no signal, but I can't seem to open the button on my pants pocket. Wyatt's hand catches mine and squeezes.

I look down at our fists, squeezed so tight a secret couldn't slip between our palms. "Dawn," Wyatt says, his voice breaking through my panic. "Listen to me. This is not how we die. We're Orpheus and Eurydice. We're Romeo and Juliet. Catherine and Heathcliff. Our story doesn't end before it can even start."

I wonder if he realizes that none of his examples have happy endings.

Wyatt's nails dig into my skin. "I love you, Olive. Always have. Always will."

I want *always* to be more than the next three minutes.

*Brace,* the flight attendants yell. *Brace!*

The plane plunges vertically. Bags fly out of the overhead compartments and the oxygen masks drop on their strings like macabre marionettes. Someone screams, and my head whips around. "Look at me," Wyatt commands, his words lost in the roar of the plane breaking apart. My world narrows down to those fierce blue eyes, which have criticized me, challenged me, surprised me, seduced me, loved me.

As we fall out of the sky, I wonder who will remember me.


I HAVE SUNK into the lake of fire, between the two routes of the Book of Two Ways. It roars around me, smoke billowing, coating the inside of my mouth and underneath my eyelids, making tears burn down my face. Flames grab at my clothes, my shoulders, my hair. I am shouting but no one can hear me.

Knowledge. I need knowledge. That's what will get me through the gates, past the demons. They are everywhere—a monster with half its body torn off. A mangled seat with a man strapped to it, shrieking as the fire consumes his fastened seatbelt. A girl with flame where her braids used to be. Their eyes are as wild as mine, and I try to get past, as I scream for Wyatt.

There are two ways out—land and water. I know this viscerally, as if it's been stamped into my heart. But I am not going without him.

*Wyatt,* I yell.

The smoke becomes a beast, clouds rolling into the blackened form of a person, coming for me. I stagger backward. *Wyatt! Wyatt!*

A flight attendant steps out of the smoke like she's shedding a second skin. She grabs my arm. *You need to come with me.* I can read her lips, but there's no sound.

I don't need to come anywhere. I wrench away from her and dodge through a hoop of fire and fuselage. As I am running I trip and fall flat onto the soft mattress of a man wearing a white shirt; a man, facedown, with yellow hair. *Wyatt.*

It takes all my strength to turn him over and I am coughing and my lungs are ribbons and his eyes, his sightless eyes, are staring up at the black sky.

But this man is wearing glasses, and has a mustache. This man is not Wyatt.

I start crying so hard that I can't get to my feet. A fine mist covers my face and my hair. The water route. I turn toward it and mark the distant glint of fire hoses, magical hydras fighting the breath of dragons.

But it also makes the smoke thicker and viscous until I am breathing soup, and I can't find my way through. The land route is nothing but an inferno. I'm trapped.

The smoke parts like wood split by an ax and another monster stalks toward me. This one has blood covering its face.

This one is shouting my name.

I get to my feet and he pulls me against him, holds the back of my head with his hands, kisses me like he could gift me the oxygen from his own lungs.

That's when I can see it: a way out. A next life.

# AFTER

...

WHEN I OPEN my eyes, everything is white, so white and bright that I wince. There are objects, unmoving, unfocused, surrounded by halos.

The first thing I notice is the pain.

My head is too heavy to move and it has its own pulse. My throat is a ribbon of desert. It takes a Herculean effort to open my eyes.

I can't be dead if there's pain, can I? But none of us knows what the afterlife holds. Maybe it's nothing *but* pain.

Immediately, as if a blanket has muffled all that light, it isn't quite so blinding. I let my vision adjust, realizing that a curtain has been yanked across a window. The objects become a chair, a sink, the foot of a hospital bed. Then I hear Brian's voice. "Better?" he asks.

His hand, warm, enfolds mine. His face rises in my field of vision like a blood moon, familiar, but unexpected.

He smiles down at me, and there are tears in his eyes, and I realize he is having the same trouble finding language that I am.

"You were hurt," he says finally. "You had to have surgery to relieve the pressure on your brain."

Gingerly I raise my free hand, feeling the edges of a bandage wrapped around my entire head. I try to stay calm, but inside, I am terrified. My brother has told me about some of the neurosurgery cases he's seen: Workmen who fall off ladders and never wake up. Award-winning professors who have seizures and cannot remember how to dress themselves. The brain, Kieran says, is a fascinating and frivolous organ. You never know what it's going to do.

The hammering makes sense now. I try to remember what happened, where I am, where I was.

Wyatt.

Egypt.

The plane crash.

I turn my head to the side and see stars, it hurts that much. I roll my eyes from side to side, searching. But there is only Brian, as if he is true north and I am a compass that needs adjustment.

Did I imagine it all?

Was Egypt and the tomb some fever dream? Was my reunion with Wyatt just a synapse firing beneath the probe of a surgeon?

At that thought, my own eyes swim. I close them, and a tear tracks down my cheek.

"It's okay," Brian soothes, gripping my hand more tightly. "It's going to be okay now. I've got you."

*I've got you.*

My lips press together around the one word that bubbles to the surface. "Meret," I whisper.

"She's home. With Kieran. She's fine." Brian hesitates. "When I got the call . . . I thought I should see you first."

To make sure that I was not hooked up to wires or cut into segments or burned beyond recognition. *What happened to me?*

I try to remember, but my mind is full of vivid textures: the sting of sand, the corona of the sun, the shimmer of the desert. Pictures that do not match the hospital room, with its blue chair and plastic water pitcher and wide, blind mounted television.

The only thing I can recall, other than Egypt, is Meret's DNA test. I close my eyes. "Sorry," I exhale. "So . . . sorry."

Brian shakes his head. "It doesn't matter right now. Let's just get you well enough to go home."

*Home* is such a loaded word. Is it still mine, if the last thing I remember is leaving it?

It hurts to move my head, but it also hurts to think. Maybe that's what happened. Maybe, when I drove away from Brian and Meret, I never got to where I was headed.

That tugs a string of pearls: Thane, England, Win.

Lose.

Can you miss something you never truly had?

Or *someone*?

That thought hurts even more than my skull.

Brian traces his thumb over the back of my hand lightly and exquisitely, like he is touching a butterfly that might take wing at any moment. "I should get a nurse. Tell someone that you're awake." A sob catches in his throat, and he bends over, kissing our joined fingers. "I thought you were gone for good," he says, his voice breaking.

He said that to me once before, too.

I lift my free hand and slowly touch it to the back of Brian's head. His hair is soft as down. I run my nails over his scalp, let my palm settle against his cheek. My eyes drift shut, entrusting myself to him, like I always have.

There is a commotion in the hallway, a muffled argument. Then the door bursts open, and one voice rises above the others: "I don't care if I'm not related to her. You can't bloody keep me out of there."

Wyatt pushes his way into the room. He stands, wild-eyed, assessing the bandage around my head and the machines I'm hooked up to and my husband, who has gotten to his feet and is still holding on to my hand.

And me. Awake. Alert.

A smile breaks over his face, and it feels like a sunrise inside me. *You're real, and you're here,* I think, and I know that is exactly what is going through his mind, too.

"Thank God," he breathes. He takes a step forward. "You're all right? You're truly all right? Say something," he demands.

"Wyatt," I reply. "This is Brian."


MY MOTHER USED to say that bad luck came in threes, and as usual, she was right.

The results of the DNA test.

The plane crash from Cairo to Boston.

And my heart. There is no way for me to come out of this without it breaking.

I explain to Brian that I flew from London to Cairo; that I found Wyatt; that I told him about Meret; that we were coming back to her on the plane that crashed. I thought I was fine, because I had walked away from the wreckage. I hadn't even been checked out by a doctor yet, because Wyatt was the one with a cut on his scalp that wouldn't stop bleeding. I was asking an airline representative about flights to Boston when the whole room spun. After that, I didn't remember anything.

I watch the two men take each other's measure. Neither of them speaks. Then Wyatt holds out his hand to Brian.

Brian stares down at it. "Are you fucking *kidding*?" he says.

My unlikely savior turns out to be a neurosurgery resident, who comes in to check on me and is delighted to find me conscious. Brian and Wyatt retreat to separate corners of the room while the doctor examines me, shining a light in my eyes and asking me questions and pressing down on my toes to test my central nervous system. He explains that I had an emergency craniotomy, after a CT scan showed an epidural hematoma. Surgeons relieved the pressure by removing the blood between the brain and bone in the epidural space. They drilled a burr hole into my skull, elevated a skull flap, evacuated the clot, refastened the skull with tiny titanium plates, and sutured the scalp. I had youth on my side, and the good fortune to collapse at a Level I trauma center, which meant that I'd had immediate care—all of which boded well for a positive outcome. I'd be monitored for two to three days here in North Carolina, but could do follow-up care at a hospital closer to home.

That word again.

By the time he is finished, I am sitting up, the headache is ebbing, and my voice is stronger.

"All in all," the resident says, "you have a lot to be thankful for."

He leaves us in happy oblivion, to write notes on my chart at a nurses' desk somewhere.

I glance at Brian, and then at Wyatt. I swallow. "Wyatt," I ask. "Can you give us a minute?"

The stricken look on his face nearly breaks me. "I'm not going anywhere," he says stubbornly. "Just outside the door." He narrows his eyes at Brian, as if he does not trust him not to hurt me.

When, clearly, it's been the other way around.

The door snicks shut behind Wyatt. "Brian," I begin.

He sits down on the edge of the bed. "Dawn, you have a head injury. This conversation . . . it doesn't have to happen now." He pulls out his phone. "But I know someone who'd really like to talk to you."

He hits a few buttons and before I can protest Meret's beautiful face blooms on the little screen. "Mom!" she screams. Her smile is a galaxy.

"Hey, baby."

"Are you okay? What happened to your head? Do you still have hair?"

I fight a grin. "I'm *going* to be okay," I tell her, and I realize that I will fight anyone and anything to keep this promise to her. "They drilled a hole in me. And I have no idea if I have hair."

"For real?"

"I could look like a bowling ball under all this gauze," I say. "Do you think you could stand to be seen in public with me?"

"When are you coming home?"

I flick a glance toward Brian. "In a few days. When the doctors let me."

The image on the phone tips and whirls and suddenly Kieran's face swims into view. "Hey," he says, peering at me through Meret's computer screen. "Brian said it was an epidural hematoma with mass effect. Sexy."

"This is why you're single," I say, and he laughs.

"You *are* okay," Kieran replies. Then he sobers. "Look. I don't have enough family for you to be disposable."

I feel my throat swell. For so long, it was just the two of us. "I know."

I hear Meret's voice scrambling with his as she tries to wrestle her computer back. I have so much to tell her, but now isn't the time.

Not when Brian is standing here; not when I don't know what the next five minutes will bring, much less the future.

For a few moments, I just stare at her on the screen, drink in the sight of her again. Her face transforms with the ghosts of emotions: fear, anger, relief. She seems to be weighing her words, and I wonder what conversation Brian had with her before I woke up; what conversations Brian had with her when I was in Egypt. I remember her email to me, asking if it was her fault that I'd left.

I wanted Wyatt to build a relationship with his daughter, but maybe he's not the only one who needs to do that.

"Mom?" she says quietly, finally. "I missed you."

"I missed you more."

In the dark her eyes are stars. "Don't die, okay?" Meret whispers.

"It's a deal," I answer.

She hangs up, and I hand Brian back his phone. He slips it into his pocket. I have tears in my eyes, and when I wipe them with the back of my hand, Brian brings me a tissue. "I didn't realize . . ." I begin, and the words evaporate like snow under sun.

Brian looks down at his feet. "I guess it's harder to think about what's not in front of you," he says quietly, and then shakes himself, as if he's trying to recalibrate.

"Does she know the truth?" I ask.

He hesitates. "You need to rest—"

"Brian."

"Yes," he says. "She figured most of it out herself. I mean, you went to *Egypt*. That would seem pretty random, unless . . ." His voice trails off. "You shouldn't be thinking about this right now."

"Brian," I say, "we can't pretend it away."

"You almost died," he says, his voice so soft I can barely hear it.

"But I didn't."

"It changes everything."

I wait for him to meet my gaze. "Does it?"

Just because I am lying in a hospital bed and he feels sorry for me doesn't mean all the emotions he felt yesterday aren't still roiling beneath that plastered equanimity.

He clears his throat. "Did you sleep with him?"

Of all the things I expected him to say, this wasn't it.

*"Did you?"*

I swallow. "Yes."

The pain in Brian's eyes makes me feel like I'm going to be sick. *I* did this to him; *me*. His silence hurts more than any of his yelling. He sinks into the chair beside the hospital bed, his elbows on his knees. "Did you fall in love with him?"

The kindest blow is the cleanest one. "I never fell out of it," I whisper.

Brian nods, studiously avoiding my gaze. "You know, when you're at a physics conference, physicists are always posing theoretical situations. Like, say you're a passenger on a plane whose engines fail and you're about to crash and die, should you take solace in the fact that there are other versions of you out there somewhere, that will live on? Or the inverse: should you feel worse knowing that there's a version of you whose life is a disaster—a you that flunked out of school or became a criminal or got bitterly dumped and divorced. These are honestly the things quantum physicists talk about." Finally, he looks at me. "They're supposed to be hypothetical."

"I didn't mean for this to happen," I falter, and at that, Brian smiles a little.

"Well," he says. "You're preaching to the choir there."

In an ideal world, the plane wouldn't have crashed. I wouldn't be lying in a hospital bed with a hole in my skull. I would have had time to introduce Wyatt to Brian, and to Meret.

In an ideal world, I wouldn't have *had* to.

"I'm going home to Meret," Brian says, and my jaw drops.

"What?"

He nods, scooting closer to the bed. He reaches for my hand. "There was no way I wasn't flying here to make sure you were all right," Brian says. "And I'll confirm with the doctors. But the prognosis is good. Meret needs one of us. And I assume he'll bring you to Boston when you're discharged."

"Yes, but—"

"Dawn. You want to be with him."

He says this so evenly that I hold my breath, certain that there is a *but*.

He stands up, his green eyes crinkled at the corners, even if the smile does not reach them. "All I've ever hoped for is to give you what you want."

Brian leans down and so gently, so tenderly kisses my forehead, framing my face in his hands. "You were coming back to me, when the plane crashed," he says. "You just don't know it yet."

He slips out of the room without looking back.

WYATT REFUSES TO leave my room and charms the nurses with his accent and his dimples so that he can camp out overnight, even though he isn't supposed to. He contacts Yale and talks at length to the dean of the faculty. The neurosurgeon comes by twice to tell me I'm doing better than expected. I nap, and when I wake, I feel like myself. We do a crossword puzzle and watch a few episodes of *Law & Order: SVU*. Wyatt eats the Jell-O from my tray. He tells me what I don't remember: how there were thirty-six survivors. How we were brought to this hospital; how I became woozy watching him get stitched up and slipped out of the room to get some air; how he heard the commotion and ran out to find me on the floor, surrounded by medical personnel. "Couldn't you have been less competitive?" he asks drily. "I was the one with the bleeding head wound, but you *had* to win the plane crash."

He is joking, because it is easier than facing the truth: had I been sitting in a different seat, had I struck the ground in a different way, I would not be here. Our story, which has just begun again, would be over. Somewhere, in a parallel timeline, there is another me at my own funeral.

That makes me think about Win. Is she still alive? If I'd died, would she have been waiting for me?

This, even more than the bandage around my head, makes me

realize how close I have come to death. I start to shiver and can't stop. Wyatt crawls into bed beside me. "Hey," he says, holding me close. "Hey, Olive. It's all right."

"It's not all right." I can barely breathe; it is as if I've only just seen the odds of my survival and I am crushed beneath the weight of them.

"It's going to be," he announces, and I have never been more grateful for his arrogance.

"What if the doctor's wrong?" I whisper. "What if I close my eyes and don't wake up?"

Wyatt stares down at me, fierce. "You do not get to die. Period."

I smile a little at that. "You know, if it came down to it, I think you could strike a bargain with Osiris himself."

"If you're afraid to close your eyes, I'll keep you awake. If you don't believe the doctors, I'll find a hundred more to convince you." He grins ruefully. "Plus, you have to stay alive if only for my own safety. If you die on my watch, your husband will kill me."

"I didn't want you to meet him that way," I say.

"Hematoma aside, I don't imagine there was any scenario where that would have been less awkward." He hesitates. "I can't believe I'm saying this, but *I* wouldn't have left you."

I don't know how to explain that the reason Brian went home was about not how little he cares for me, but how *much*.

I wonder, had the roles been reversed, if Wyatt would have given me the space to make a choice.

He takes my hand and places it over his heart, which beats steady and strong.

"Do you think anyone ever makes love in a hospital bed?" he muses.

I muffle a laugh. "I think if you're in a hospital, you're supposed to be too sick for that."

"What do they know?" His hand slips around my waist, coming to rest. "It's like this spot was made for me," Wyatt says. "Like we were carved from the same block of limestone."

I think about the statue of Ramesses II at Luxor, hewed from the same stone as his wife, Nefertari, who is depicted at a fraction of his massive image and nestled between his legs.

"Except when they build a temple for us," Wyatt says, "your statue gets to be the same size as mine."

"How do you always know what I'm thinking?"

He glances down at me. "Because I've been trying to get in your head for fifteen years, maybe." He reaches for my hand, tangling our fingers together. "I used to have a fantasy that you wrote me and told me you weren't happy."

"*That* was your fantasy?"

"One of the tame ones. I'd dream it, and then realize it was a dream, and then throw myself even harder into my work."

"Did you write me back?" I ask. "In the dream?"

He nods. "I told you to fix it. But in general terms. To get on a plane and travel. To stay up all night. To kiss a stranger. But I really wanted to tell you to travel to me. Stay up all night with me. Kiss me."

So I do. I press my lips to the rough edge of his chin. "What happened to that fantasy?"

"It pales next to reality," Wyatt says.

But reality is a plane crash, and a head injury, and a Gordian knot of relationships that is no less tangled than it was when I left Boston.

There is a literary text in Ancient Egyptian that says the gods made magic so that people could ward off misfortune. And yet, although you might be able to diminish something bad, you still couldn't prevent it from happening.

I look at Wyatt's hand, scarred from working in the field. I look at mine, still wearing a wedding band. "Where do we go from here?"

I am well aware that although we boarded a plane together and although Wyatt wants to meet his daughter, we haven't really discussed our own future. We haven't talked about Anya. In a way, I don't mind. I'm afraid to hear what Wyatt wants.

I'm afraid to hear what *I* want.

"As far from this hospital as humanly possible. Hopefully sooner rather than later."

"I meant figuratively."

"Maybe this is presumptuous," Wyatt says, "but I hope you'll go wherever I go."

"You have a fiancée."

"You'll have to excuse me. I've been too busy surviving a plane crash to actually call that off." When I don't laugh, he brushes a kiss across my lips. "I know we both made commitments to other people. I think we meant to love those people for the rest of our lives. But things don't always work out the way we've planned. We know that better than anyone."

"I'm scared," I whisper.

"You've a hole in your head," he murmurs, kissing my bandaged temple. "You're badass."

"That's not the same," I say. "I have so much to lose."

"So do I . . . and I've never even met her."

"I want her to like you."

"How couldn't she?" He grins, his usual cocky self. But in his eyes I can see it: that flicker of fear, that discomfort of being thrust into a role he hasn't prepared for. For two people who are obsessed with history, we are doing a lousy job of confronting our own.

I think of Meret, of her face when she saw mine on her screen, of all the work I have to do to fix what I've broken. "I can't just move overseas."

"Then I'll commute."

"To *Egypt?*"

"To bloody Mars, if I have to." He smiles at me, and light fills all my darkness. "Don't you get it, Olive?" Wyatt says quietly. "That's the *easy* part."

He wraps his arm around me. Any minute now, the nurse is going to come in and yell at us. But until then, I'm not budging.

"The other fantasies," I ask. "The less tame ones . . . ?"

I feel Wyatt's grin against my neck. "I had a particularly racy one about painting spells from the Book of Going Forth by Day."

"That's a *terrible* fantasy."

"Your naked body was my papyrus."

I laugh. "Tell me more," I say.

. . .

ON THE SECOND day, I have another CT scan. There's no reaccumulation of the clot, and no intracranial air. All in all, the doctor says, it looks like I will make a complete recovery. I stay under observation for another day.

Miraculously, my phone survived the crash, with only a cracked screen—which means I've been able to talk with Meret. Brian told her I needed to stay in the hospital for a few days, and I have a friend taking care of me. That, I realize, is so generous Meret doesn't even question it. She is FaceTiming with me the first time I sit up on my own in bed, and when I take a walk around the floor, pointing out the patient lounge with the television stuck permanently on Boomerang en Español, and the nurse that looks like Alec Baldwin. She is with me when the doctor unwinds the bandage and I first scrutinize the neat little scar in the shape of a question mark, held fast by glue and staples. My hair has been shorn on one side only, which she says makes me look like Natalie Dormer in *Mockingjay,* and she googles it to show me. She wins her first singles match on the tennis team and phones me on the ride home because she is so excited.

Whenever Meret calls, Wyatt steps out of the room. I know it is to give me privacy, but also because he is terrified to have his first interaction with her be over a screen. Or maybe he is just terrified to have his first interaction with her, period.

I am always careful to smile and to be upbeat, even if my head hurts or I'm tired. Meret is always careful to talk about superficial things. When the conversation begins to get strained, we can both feel it, like when you move over a frozen pond and edge back from the spots where the ice is too thin.

Each time, before we hang up, Brian asks to speak to me.

He scrutinizes me, and tells me I'm looking better. I relay what the doctors have said. We run out of words, because I will not mention Wyatt to him, and he doesn't seem willing to volunteer information about how he's spending his days. It's familiar but just a little off, like when you are watching a movie on TV and the sound doesn't quite match the mouths of the actors. He isn't angry and he isn't sad; I can't quite put my finger on *what* he is. Studiously *even*, maybe. Waiting.

On the third day that I'm in the hospital, Meret doesn't mention Brian. "So," I say. "I guess I should talk to . . ."

I don't know what to say. *Your dad?*

"Oh," Meret interrupts. "He's not here."

"Okay," I say. It isn't surprising that he's at his lab, and yet, somehow, it is. Somehow, I expected him to be there, just because I was asking.

After we hang up, I stare at the phone in my lap, thinking of Brian's brilliant mind. I wonder if he learned this lesson from *me:* that something has to leave before you realize it is missing.

FOUR DAYS AFTER I nearly died in a plane crash I board an aircraft again.

Because there was no air in my follow-up CT scan, the doctors give me a cautious thumbs-up to fly, since it's a short flight and there are neurosurgeons in Boston who can take care of any complications. Wyatt buys a silk scarf from the gift shop for me to wrap around my head, although it doesn't really conceal the fact that half my head is shaved and the other half is not. I think I will never be able to make myself step onto that jet bridge, yet I turn out to be less anxiety-ridden than I expect. I find myself looking at the other passengers as they stow their carry-ons and buckle their seatbelts. *Do you know how lucky you are to be flying with me?* I want to say. *The worst has already happened; what are the odds it will ever happen again?*

When we land, though, I grip Wyatt's hand so hard that my nails leave marks in his skin.

How many times have I come through Logan Airport—back from a trip to Orlando with Meret, or a conference in London with Brian—yet this is the first time I've been here with Wyatt. It's the first time I've been anywhere with Wyatt, really, other than Yale or Egypt. Having him in the spatial dimension of the city I call home is jarring.

It makes the most sense for Wyatt to check in to a hotel. We decide to rent a car, because when I had emailed Brian from Cairo, I had told him where mine was parked at the airport, so that he could reclaim it.

At the Avis counter, a clerk with a Boston accent as thick as soup asks Wyatt if he wants a full-size, a compact, or a subcompact.

"You Americans with your size obsession," he says. "Compact is fine. I'm not compensating for anything."

The clerk doesn't even bat an eye. "If your wife is driving, I need her license, too."

It's an assumption, but it stops us cold. "I . . . I'm not driving," I stammer. I can't, not for a couple of weeks, but it's also easier than saying I'm not his wife. It makes me think of Wyatt bellowing his way into my hospital room, because he wasn't my next of kin. I'm nothing to him—not legally, not practically, not in the way the world recognizes. This hammers home for me, firmly, the gravity of where we are headed.

"Just me, mate," Wyatt tells the clerk. He hands off his credit card—miraculously, his wallet also stayed in his pocket during the crash—and wraps his arm around me. "Isn't Boston all about lobsters?"

"Um, yes?"

"I'd like to have one. They're not exactly prevalent in Egyptian cuisine."

I am flooded with gratitude for Wyatt, for making this feel normal, instead of unbearable. For pretending, even if it's only for the next half hour, that I am not about to pull the thread that completely unravels the life I've been wrapped in.

"I can make that happen," I say.


IT IS JUST after 7:00 P.M. when Wyatt drops me off at my house. We have decided that it's best I do this first part alone. For a moment, we sit with our hands knotted on the gearshift. "Whatever happens, Olive," he says, "I don't blame you. I know full well that I'm not exactly a welcome visitor for anyone in that house." His voice roughens. "And if she isn't ready to see me right away, well, I've waited fifteen years. I can wait some more."

I nod and open the passenger door, but he doesn't let go of my hand. "I can't help thinking that once you walk through that door, you won't come back out," Wyatt says softly. He leans forward and stamps a kiss on my lips like a brand. I get out of the car before I can change my mind and walk up the steps. I hesitate at the door, not sure if I should knock, or just walk in. Wyatt is still waiting at the curb, as if he knows I might turn and take refuge again in his car.

Taking a deep breath, I enter my house.

I hear water running in the sink and follow it to the kitchen. Brian stands with his back to me, rinsing dishes and putting them into the dishwasher. I have a sudden, searing flash of memory: the summer that the dishwasher broke and we didn't have enough money to pay for a new one, so we'd flip a coin each night to see who got kitchen duty. How, when I lost, he would still come into the kitchen and dry the dishes for me, so I didn't have to do it all alone.

"I'm back," I say.

Brian knew I was being discharged, but I hadn't told him when, exactly, I was arriving back in Boston. He might have assumed I'd want to travel by car, which would take another day. I watch his shoulders square, and then he turns off the faucet and pivots, wiping his hands on a dish towel and seeing me upright and healthy, except for the scar in the shape of a question mark. For one glorious, unexpected moment, joy washes over his face, like gilding on a statue. In one step, he is across the room and I am in his arms and he's crushing me against him. He leans back, running his hands down my arms as if he needs to convince himself that I am real. But then, the space between us solidifies, pushing back at each of our edges, until we are standing a foot apart and no longer touching.

"The doctors say it's going to take more than a plane crash to get rid of me," I say, trying for cheer, and realizing too late that the sentence falls flat.

"Good," Brian says. "That's good."

"I have to get my staples removed in a few days. Kieran can do it."

He nods. We stare at each other. The room is full of the conversation we are not having. He doesn't say, *Where is Wyatt?* I don't say, *What happens next?*

"Where's Meret?" I ask finally.

Brian's eyes flicker toward the staircase. "In her room."

Every muscle in me wants to avoid the conversation we have to have, to run to her instead.

"Where is he?" Brian asks.

I drag my gaze to his. "At a hotel," I say.

Brian's hands ball into fists at his sides; I watch him force his features smooth again.

"You can't keep doing this," I say.

"Doing what?"

"Treating me like I'm made of glass."

"I'm not treating you like anything."

"Exactly. Because I almost died. But I didn't." I take a step forward. "We have to talk, Brian, as if I wasn't in a plane crash."

"If you hadn't run away you *wouldn't* have been in a plane crash," Brian blurts out. He falls back, as if the force of his anger has shoved him.

His voice is hot and low, a match touching tinder. *You asked for this,* I remind myself. Before the entire house goes up in flames, I reach for his arm, intending to pull him into the backyard for privacy. But the moment I touch him, he jerks like he's been burned.

Which, I suppose, he has.

"Let's not do this where Meret can hear us."

"Oh," he says. "So *now* you're thinking about her?"

My pulse is so loud in my ears that I am sure he can hear it. "I didn't mean for this to happen. I am so sorry, Brian."

"For what?" he asks, his voice deceptively soft. "For lying to me? For leaving us after that bomb dropped? Making me pick up the pieces for Meret?" His eyes narrow. "For fucking him?"

I flinch. A memory circles the drain of my mind: me, asking Win if she felt she was cheating on Felix. Win's response: *There are times I wonder if my whole marriage has been me cheating on Thane.*

"You left your *child* behind," Brian accuses. "You abandoned her, when she'd just found out . . ." He shakes his head, unable to even mention the DNA test. "Do you know how much she's cried these past three weeks, thinking she lost a father *and* a mother? Do you have any idea how selfish that was?"

Later, when I replay this, I will realize it was that last adjective that broke a bridge of clay in me, a structure that had remained standing far longer than it ever should have. "Selfish," I repeat. "Selfish? Do you know how many people I've put in front of myself for the past fifteen years? My mother. My brother. My clients. Meret. You. Even Wyatt. Everyone else's welfare was more important than mine. I am *always* the last person I think about. So just for a minute— one *minute*—I did. I know I didn't do this the right way, if that even exists. I know I should have told you what I was thinking, where I was going. But I had to go, for my own peace of mind. I couldn't stay here and pretend everything was fine, like usual, and let this eat away at me, wondering *what if*. Eventually, there would have been nothing left of me."

When I finish, I am breathing fast, like I've run a marathon to reach this conversation.

Maybe I have.

I realize that this white-hot anger is the most undiluted emotion Brian and I have had between us in a long time. I think he realizes it, too. This time, when our eyes meet, the storm between us is gone. It's just him and me, like it used to be, standing in puddles of regret. "Why wasn't it enough?" he asks softly. "Why weren't *we* enough?"

"I wanted it to be enough. I went to Cairo because I needed to know if this was all in my imagination. You know. If I'd taken a memory and blown it out of proportion."

"If you felt disconnected, we could have fixed that. Instead you tried to latch on to something new."

*Something old,* I correct silently.

"I thought we were a team," Brian says. "We made it through the deaths of people we loved. We built careers. We were raising a *teen-ager*. I thought I leaned on you and you leaned on me and even if it was lopsided sometimes, it always evened out."

"I thought that, too," I confess.

"Then . . . why?"

I do not have an answer for him—why we are drawn to certain people, why some soothe our angles and edges better than others.

Brian closes his eyes. "I keep thinking: I did this to you."

I realize when he says this that I have not thought about Gita for a long, long time. I wonder if he turned to her, after he came home from the North Carolina hospital. If he cried in her arms.

If I still have the right to feel like I've been punched in the stomach when I think about that. If I *ever* did.

But then I realize that's not what he's talking about. "Every night when you were away, I'd lie awake and hope you were miserable. You lie to me for fifteen years . . . you screw me over and you screw over our kid . . . and there's no punishment?" He swallows. "I feel like I manifested that plane crash."

He's wrong. The crash wasn't retribution, but there *is* a price I have to pay. No matter how happy I am with Wyatt, that joy is poisoned. It comes at the cost of someone else's happiness.

Brian reaches out, his hand stopping just short of my shaved scalp. "I wanted you to be hurt. But not this like, Dawn," he says. "Never like this."

I am stunned that scientific, methodical Brian could believe, even in passing, that his dark private thoughts had anything to do with an airplane malfunction.

"There's another universe where I got angry, and you were gone forever. So . . . I don't know. Maybe it's superstitious, but I thought if I didn't yell anymore, you'd . . . stay."

I open my mouth, close it. "I'm sorry," I finally manage. Again.

Brian's eyes are dark and soft. They move from my own eyes to the curved scar on my scalp to my lips. "I know," he says. "I am, too."

Over his shoulder, through the window, I see a flash of light on the road. I imagine it is Wyatt, driving away.

. . .

WHEN I OPEN the door, Meret is sitting on her bed with her laptop open. She sits up, yanking out her earbuds, freezing in place. I move gingerly, the way I would approach a wild animal, and sit down on the edge of the bed.

She throws herself at me.

I wrap my arms around her and bury my face in her hair. The reality of leaving her—leaving *this*—feels like a blow to the head. I'm dizzy, sick with the thought that I may never have had the chance to see who she becomes. I know I am hugging her too fiercely, that she can barely breathe, but I can't seem to relax my arms. I think of how, when she was a baby, I would lean down and nuzzle her neck, blow a raspberry, make her laugh.

"You always smell like bubble bath," she whispers.

"I . . . I do?"

"Last week I was at camp and I came out of a classroom and smelled that same soap and I started looking all over the place because I was sure you were there." She pulls away from me. "You weren't."

I try to imagine her, hope rising like yeast, turning in circles and not being able to find me.

She looks at my head. "Does it hurt?"

"A little." I touch my scalp tentatively. "Very Frankenstein-chic, right?"

"It's not funny." Meret wipes a tear away with the back of her hand. "You could have died."

"Anyone can," I say gently. "Anytime."

"But you didn't even say goodbye," she blurts out, and I wonder how I haven't seen it until this moment: the streaks of self-loathing that paint the walls, the stripes of insecurity woven into the bedding where she nests.

I decide to tell her the truth. "If I did," I admit, "I wouldn't have had the courage to go."

"You mean *leave*," Meret corrects bitterly. "Leave *me*."

I hesitate. "I had to find someone."

"My biological father."

I take a deep breath. "That's why I was in Egypt. I know that your"—I falter, trying to find the right word—"your other father told you."

"He's my *only* father," Meret says, loyal. "I don't even know the other person's name."

"I could tell you about him," I gently offer. "Wyatt."

She is nearly vibrating with—with what? Fear? Rage? Finally, she glances up again. Permission.

So I bring Wyatt, metaphorically, into this house. I tell her the story of the boy I hated at first sight, with his golden hair and sky eyes and swagger. I tell her about how we both jockeyed to be the best in the department at Yale. I tell her about Wyatt's upbringing in England and his brother's death and his title. I tell her about the Dig House and how still the desert is before the sun rises and how we were fighting before we found the dipinto. I tell her that when he kissed me, I realized the reason I'd been pushing him away was because if he came close, I wouldn't be able to ever separate myself from him.

"I didn't know about you," I finish. "I didn't know I was pregnant when I left Egypt."

"You expect me to believe that?" Meret scowls. "All the talks about being safe and using protection. The minute I got my period I practically had to wear armor to make sure I didn't end up like—well, like *you*."

"I guess I deserve that."

"So you dumped him and rebounded with Dad?"

I wince. "I guess I deserve that, too. But it wasn't a rebound. My life had fallen apart, and Br— your dad helped me put it back together. How *couldn't* I have fallen for him?" I take a deep breath. "I'm not expecting you to forgive me. I'm not expecting you to even understand. But what I had with Wyatt—I buried it deep on purpose, because I needed to move forward, not backward. I wanted a life with your dad. I wanted our family. When I looked back at Egypt, all I had were questions, because I didn't have the luxury of being a scholar anymore. I had to be a sister and a mother. When I looked forward, where your dad was waiting, I saw answers." I clear my throat. "But the feelings I had for Wyatt, somehow, they got dislodged. And took root. And grew. I could cut them down, Meret. But if I did, I'd always be looking at the spot where they bloomed."

In a very small, cramped voice, Meret asks, "What about me?"

"What about you." A smile heats the words. "He wants to meet you."

Her head snaps up. "Now? *Here?*" I watch as it all crystallizes for her. "He's the one who was with you at the hospital."

"He brought me back to you," I correct. "He's at a hotel. It's up to you, whether or not you want to meet him."

She pulls at her clothes, billowing her shirt away from her curves, the way I've seen her do a thousand times when she's nervous.

"You don't have to like him. You don't have to make him part of your life."

She looks at me curiously, as if she's just seeing a piece of me she never noticed before—a crooked finger with a story behind it of how it was broken; a tattoo that was previously hidden under layers of clothes. "So what happens to us? To me and you and Dad?"

"I don't know."

Her eyes flash. "God, can't you ever stop *lying?*"

"I'm not lying."

"Oh, okay. So he's here to say *Hi, daughter, nice to meet you,* and then he's going to leave and go back to Egypt and you're going to stay here and we all pretend nothing's changed?"

I don't know how to respond, because there's no good answer.

"Yeah," Meret mutters. "I thought so."

There's a moment when, as an adult, you realize that the child you are speaking to is no longer a child. With Kieran, it happened when I had to tell him that our mother was dead. I remember looking into his eyes and seeing a shift in him, a realization that the solid foundation he'd been leaning against had turned to dust and he was falling. For Meret, it's now. When she was a little girl, I'd told her all the fairy tales about love: how it could wake you from death, how it could triumph over evil, how it could make the poor rich. But today, I am drawing back the curtain, revealing not just pretty stories but facts: that love can also kill you; that for you to triumph, other people have to be hurt; that the wealth love brings comes at a staggering cost. "I don't know what will happen with your dad. We have a lot to work out. But I'm also not going to tell you that I don't want to be with Wyatt. I love him in a way that I never thought I'd love someone."

Truth vibrates when it's drawn across the bow of pain; Meret hears that note, and listens intently. "Some people never get to feel that way, much less find someone else they love . . . and I did love your dad. I do. But the greatest love I've ever known is *you*." I reach for her hand, and she doesn't pull away. "I lost Wyatt once, and I survived. I may lose your dad, and I will survive. But you?" In her face, I see my eyes, Wyatt's jaw, strength from us both. "I wouldn't survive losing you."

With a sob, Meret throws herself against me again. I hold her close and stroke her hair, the way I used to when she was tiny and monsters took up residence in her room. They may not have been real, but her fear was, and that was all that mattered. "What if he doesn't like me?" she asks, and I realize she has made a decision.

I frame her face in my palms. "Baby," I say. "How couldn't he?"


I TEXT WYATT. But it doesn't feel fair to ask him into the house, not with Brian there. So instead, Wyatt parks at the curb and waits on the front porch, sitting on a little wooden swing we bought five years ago that we thought we would use more than we ever did. When I open the door, Meret a step behind me, he stands.

And lights up like a candle.

"Hello," Wyatt says.

She shifts from one foot to the other. "Hi."

"Would you, um. Would you care to sit down?"

She doesn't move, so I put my hand on the small of her back and give her a little push. They sit down together on the swing, boxers in opposite corners, sizing each other up.

"Well," I start. "I'll just give you two a minute—"

"No," Meret interrupts, just as Wyatt says, "Please, stay."

So I lean against the sturdy bones of the house, trying to blend into the shingles.

Wyatt clasps his hands between his knees. Meret folds her arms. "I hear you're a scientist."

"You don't have to patronize me," she replies.

"I wasn't. I just . . ." He rubs the back of his neck. It is the first time I have ever seen Wyatt in a situation where he isn't effortlessly comfortable. "Your mother told me a little bit about the camp you went to this summer."

"I can catch you up on the rest. I've always wanted a Bernese mountain dog, I know every word of *Hamilton* by heart, and I'm terrified to eat fish with bones in it. I can't cook but I can make nutrient agar. Oh," she says, too sweetly. "And I'm a Taurus."

He bursts out laughing. "Well. I can certainly see the resemblance."

"There's a DNA test for that, if you want proof."

To Wyatt's credit, he doesn't look to me for help. "I don't need to see the results." He keeps his gaze solely on Meret, who isn't giving an inch. "Look, you should know that . . . I'm glad. I don't know how, but I'd like to try to be your father."

I flinch, because I know that's exactly what Meret did not want to hear.

"Thanks, but I have one of those," she says. "You're just genetic material."

"Dashing and preternaturally brilliant genetic material, I hope," he jokes.

"I wouldn't know," Meret replies. "We don't seem to have a lot in common."

"But that's where you're wrong." He looks up and grins. "We both love your mother."

Meret's lips are pressed tightly together.

"And," Wyatt adds, "I, too, know all the words to *Hamilton*."

Meret's eyes widen. "You do?"

"No. But I can stumble admirably through the first song." He sobers. "I know you didn't ask for any of this. I know it must feel like the carpet's been ripped out from beneath you. Something else I believe we have in common. I also know it would be demeaning to you for me to assume that I could enter your life and be treated as anyone more important to you than a stranger on the street. I have no misconceptions that you think of me as a friend. But I'd like to hope that you'd give me the chance to become one."

He fumbles in his pocket for his phone. "Oh, and there's this," he says.

He scrolls to a photo that has the chromatic richness of old Kodak prints. In it is a boy, with Wyatt's telltale golden hair and wry smile, sitting beside a Bernese mountain dog on the steps of a stone building.

He means to show her a childhood pet, but both Meret and I are staring at the image of a young Wyatt—a boy who was chubby, husky, with round cheeks and the hint of a double chin.

"I don't know if a passion for dog breeds is genetic, but—"

"You don't look like that now," Meret says, taking the phone from his hand.

He glances at the photo. "No." Wyatt shrugs. "I suppose not. I was always big for my age, or at least that's what they called it back then, to be polite. When it became clear that I couldn't play rugby for shite I had to find a way to hide from the coach. He never went to the library on the school campus—I'm pretty sure he never read a book in his life. But I did. About pyramids and mummies and pharaonic dynasties."

I stare at him. For all that I always imagined Wyatt to be perfect, there was a time when he felt he wasn't.

I watch Meret touch her finger to the picture, enlarging it, as if she has to see it better to believe it. She sucks in her breath, and I can see all the answers falling into place: finally. *This* is where I came from.

"People change," Wyatt says quietly. He looks at me, still speaking to Meret. "You may not think so right now, but sometimes it's good to remember who you used to be."

I feel my eyes sting. With one photograph, Wyatt has not only given Meret a sense of history, he's also absolved me.

Meret hands him back his phone. "I loved that dog," Wyatt muses. "I wanted to name him Narmer, after the first king to unify Egypt. But he was my brother's pet, technically. So his name was Bailey." His mouth twists. "How pedestrian."

"Do you ever listen to podcasts?" Meret asks. An olive branch.

"No."

"There's one called *The Weirdest Thing I Learned This Week*. It's awesome. There's an episode about how hair goes white overnight and deer that eat humans and death by molasses. One time they talked about monks who turn themselves into mummies," she says. "I could send you a link."

Wyatt nods gravely. "I would very much like that."

A smile transforms Meret's face. "I just started playing tennis. The coach says I'm a natural."

"I'll bet you are. I was the highest ranked singles player at boarding school when I was your age."

"Really?"

"Yes." He hesitates. "I haven't played in a while. Maybe you could show me a few tricks, one day."

"Maybe," she says. "One day."

I watch them for a little while, trading conversation as if it is a checkers game, one red piece taking one black one and vice versa, until each holds the full measure of the other's color. An hour passes, and then another. I wonder what Brian is doing. If he is sitting somewhere in his own house, wondering how a stranger might be stealing his daughter's allegiance.

As if I have conjured him, the door opens, and Brian steps outside. Wyatt immediately stands. I realize that where I am sitting, with my back against the porch wall, I am equidistant between them.

Brian stares at him, his jaw locked. Wyatt doesn't blink under his regard.

It's like a pissing contest. Even Meret can't stop looking from one man to the other.

"It's getting late," Brian says to Meret. "You'll never wake up in the morning."

She rises from the swing. "I hope we can pick up where we left off," Wyatt says. I can see her struggling to figure out what to do: shake his hand? Hug him? Neither?

He steps off the porch, off Brian's property, saving her from making the decision. "Well," Wyatt says awkwardly. "Good night."

I take a step toward Wyatt, but Meret grabs my wrist before I can join him. "You're not leaving again, are you?"

Brian and I have not talked about it: where I will stay, *if* I will stay. But Meret's face is so guileless, so fragile. I have just come back to her; how could I leave again?

"No," I say, as if I never intended anything but this. "Of course not."

At this, Brian turns and walks into the house. Meret waves to Wyatt, and follows. "Come say good night," she tells me.

Wyatt stands underneath the field of stars. "I'm sorry," I whisper. "I . . ."

"I know. I get it." He takes the rental car keys from his pocket and flips them in the air. "Meret needs you tonight more than I do," Wyatt reasons. "I'm willing to share."

"You're terrible at sharing."

"Okay, that's true," Wyatt admits. "I'm willing to share this *once*. But I'll be camped out at the curb at first light."

He starts down the driveway, but turns around.

"She's remarkable," Wyatt murmurs, a grin playing over his mouth.

"I told you so."

"You've been dying to say that to me, haven't you?" He laughs.

I watch the taillights of the rental car disappear down our road, and then turn to the house where I've lived for fifteen years. I know every loose plank in the floor and where there is water damage to the ceiling and which rooms have the newest coats of paint, but tonight, it seems unfamiliar. A mausoleum, a crypt.

I find Brian making up the bed in my office. "You . . . you don't have to do that," I say.

He turns around, his cheeks reddening. "I figured you'd want to . . . I didn't think . . ."

Now *my* face is burning. "I mean, yes. But. I can do it. You can . . . you can just leave everything."

He sets the quilt and pillows down on top of the sheet he's already tucked around the sofa cushions. He's a foot away from me, and I suddenly remember being on the honeymoon we took with an infant Meret and my brother, to Miami. Kieran had spied a red-spotted newt that darted underneath a hedge before he could get a good look. Brian had spent a half hour laying a minute trail of crumbs and sugar, waiting for the little lizard to inch into the sunlight again.

The difference between him and Wyatt, I realize, is that Wyatt will dig till he finds something. Brian will wait until it comes to him.

"I'm going to say good night to Meret," I tell him.

"I'll leave my door open so I can hear you," Brian replies, just before I cross the threshold. "If you need anything in the middle of the night, just call."

Wyatt and a nursing staff have been monitoring me at night; this will be my first stretch alone. Brian realized that, even if I didn't.

I know, without him saying it, that he will wake up like he used to when Meret was little and wheezing with the croup. That he will tiptoe down the hallway, and listen for my even breathing.


IN MERET'S BEDROOM, I lie down on top of the covers beside her, the way I did when she was tiny. Moments before she tumbles into sleep, her voice curls like smoke over her shoulder. "It's just like it used to be," she murmurs.

But it isn't.

When I slip away, the door of the master bedroom is ajar and the lights are off. I go into my office and lie down on the couch. I stare at the ceiling, but I toss and turn, unable to grab sleep every time it darts within reach.

Finally I give up and reach for my phone and FaceTime Wyatt. He looks like he's been in a deep sleep when his features swim into view. "Dawn? Is everything all right?"

Too late, I realize that when the phone rings this late, it is usually bad news.

"I'm fine," I say immediately. "How did you know it was me?"

"Who else knows I'm in America?"

I crawl into bed and tuck him into the space beside me.

"So," Wyatt murmurs. "Are you checking up on me? Making sure I didn't bring any other nascent Egyptologists back to my room?"

"I just missed you."

"I wish you were here," he says, his voice soft.

"I wish I were, too."

"Why do you look like you're on the verge of tears?"

Because, I realize, getting what you want isn't instant gratification. It's a slow pulling apart, a realignment of bones and sinew. There are aches involved. There is bruising.

"I don't know," I say. "I can't sleep."

"You can't sleep without *me*," he corrects, so cocky that it makes me smile.

Suddenly I feel guilty, dragging him into my insomnia. "You were tired, and I woke you up. I'm a terrible girlfriend."

"Girlfriend," he muses. "Is that what you are?"

Given that he still technically has a fiancée and I still have a husband, I don't know what else I *could* be. I feel like I am in seventh grade again, whispering to my crush. I feel my heart hammering, while I try to figure out how to respond. "Co-parent?"

"So clinical."

"I'm open to suggestions."

"*Are* you." Wyatt's voice licks the inside of my ear. "How about *my other half,* then. *My heart. My love.*"

I fall back against the pillows, filled with stars. "Those work," I manage.

"Good. Now, may I go back to sleep if I promise to dream about you?"

"I suppose," I say, grinning. "Good night."

"Olive," he sighs. "You have to hang up."

"You first."

"Count of three?"

"One," I say.

"Two," he whispers.

I disconnect the call. I feel so buoyant I am barely touching the mattress. I close my eyes, but after a few more minutes, I give up and pad downstairs to the kitchen.

Suddenly I'm grounded again. Brian sits in a small pool of light cast by the hood of the stove. In front of him is a bottle of whiskey. He turns when I stop a few feet away from him, looking at me as if my appearance is inevitable. There are dark circles under his eyes, and his hair is spiky with sleep, or lack thereof. He stands up, immediately alert. "Are you all right? Does something hurt?"

*Everything,* I think. *Just not the way you imagine.*

"I'm fine. I just wanted some water."

As I run the faucet and fill a glass, I hear Brian sink back down at the kitchen table. I turn around and stare at him. "You don't drink," I say.

He lifts his glass and drains it. "There's a lot of stuff I never did before that I'm doing now."

It is so strange to be here in our kitchen, to see him in the flannel robe I bought him two Christmases ago, to know what it is to be held by him and how our bodies fit together and to think I will likely never do that again. I will never kiss him, I will never taste the salt on his skin, I will never pull his hips to mine.

We've sat here dozens of times before in the middle of the night—celebrating a promotion of Brian's, talking about a client of mine, worrying about a fever Meret has, crunching numbers for a monthly budget. This is familiar ground, and also completely unfamiliar.

How do you undo intimacy? How do you go back to being acquaintances, when the other person knows every inch and groove of you, every irrational fear, every trigger?

He turns, his eyes tracking me. "There's one thing I can't figure out. Why were you so mad at me for what happened with Gita?"

Her name, inconceivably, still shivers through me. "I don't know. Maybe because a part of me felt like I'd given up Wyatt years ago, and it wasn't fair that you'd get to think about someone else." I hesitate. "Maybe because you stopped short of . . . cheating. And I don't know if I could have."

At my confession, a shocked laugh bursts out of Brian. "Wow," he breathes. "Okay."

We sit in the silence for so long that it presses against my eardrums. "I know it's not worth much, but I'll always love you."

"Just not enough," he murmurs, and I flinch. When he looks up at me, though, it is with kindness. "You should sleep. *One* of us should, anyway."

I nod, setting my glass in the sink.

"I know it's stupid, but the house feels different with you here. More . . . right."

When I turn around again, his hands are curled around his whiskey glass. "It's not stupid," I say quietly, and I leave him sitting in the near dark.


I AM SWIMMING in flames. Ash sits on my tongue, my eyelashes, my skin. I roll to my side and see a dragon made of smoke, fire belching from its jaws. I turn the other way, and stare into sightless eyes.

I stagger to my feet, trying to find my voice, but it's muffled by the cries of others. I am walking on cobblestones made of the dead. I need to find him. I need to find him.

The soles of my feet are bare and pressed to glowing coals. I look down, squinting through a blizzard of cinders, and see a faint line. One blue. And beside it, one black.

I start moving.

Demons scream to me. One in the shape of a child without a face. One is a woman broken over a metal spike, her arms and legs still wheeling. I keep my eyes on my feet, shuffling one foot in front of the other, each ankle rocking on two syllables: *Wyatt. Wyatt.*

In front of me is an inferno. Behind me is an angry ocean. I am supposed to know the answer to something but I cannot remember it.

A monster rears up in my face, bloody and clutching me.

But this one is shouting to me. *Dawn! Dawn.*

I choke on his name.

"Dawn!"

My eyes open on a gasp. I am sweaty and trembling in Brian's arms. "You were having a nightmare," he says. His hand skates down my spine. He seems to realize that he is sitting on the edge of the sofa and that I am wearing a T-shirt and underwear, and he lets go of me as if I really am on fire.

I can still feel the shape of his hands on my skin. "You're okay," he whispers, and I believe him.

WHAT SURPRISES ME is how slow the break is. Not a clean cut, not a guillotine, but tugging and pulling and dislocation. So much has to happen before that final separation. I realize that, partly, this is because neither Brian nor Wyatt will force my hand. I can envision my future, but it's superimposed on my past. When I am with Wyatt, it feels like seeing the world for the first time, in colors so rich they don't have names. When I am with Meret and Brian, it feels like sifting through every treasured tapestry of memory. Who could ever choose one at the expense of the other?

The day after I get home, Kieran bullies me into going to the hospital for a CT scan to be read by his supervising doctor, the best neurosurgeon in Boston. Although I haven't had any pain or complications, I know he will not trust my health until he sees me with his own eyes.

Wyatt takes me to the appointment and goes to the cafeteria to get us coffee while I'm in the waiting room. I am skimming an old magazine when my brother comes through the door, still wearing his scrubs from surgery.

He catches me up in a tight embrace. "Goddammit, Dawn," he murmurs. "You don't get to leave me like everyone else did."

"Doing my best not to," I say. I close my eyes, clutching him. I have been with my brother in Boston for fifteen years. I have been so busy thinking about Meret in this messy equation I have completely forgotten that if I go to Egypt with Wyatt, I'll be leaving Kieran, too.

He draws me back at arm's length and examines my scar critically. "Nice work," he concedes. "Who's the surgeon from North Carolina? When do the staples need to be removed?"

Suddenly, Wyatt is at my side, holding two coffee cups. He smiles widely, trying to figure out how to extend a hand for a shake while still holding the lattes.

"You must be Kieran. I'm Wyatt Armstrong. I've heard so much about you." He passes me my coffee. "Here, Olive."

"He doesn't know your name?" Kieran murmurs. "Did he have a head injury, too?"

"He knows my name. It's a long story."

Stunned, Kieran shakes Wyatt's hand. "I didn't realize he came back with you . . ."

"He came to meet Meret. He's her biological father."

Kieran's eyes widen. "Did not see that one coming."

"That makes two of us," I murmur.

The nurse behind the desk looks up. "Ms. McDowell?"

"Back to the maiden name?" Kieran muses.

While I change into a hospital gown and robe, Kieran waits outside the little dressing room. "So let me get this straight," he says. "You brought your boyfriend home to your husband?"

"Shut up, Kieran." I step out of the dressing room and let him lead me to the imaging suite. "I had a plan. And then I wound up having brain surgery."

"If I had a dime for every time I heard that excuse . . ." He talks to the radiology assistants, who help me climb onto the table and lie down. I am covered with a sheet. Kieran steps into the glass booth, his arms crossed, watching me as I slide into the metal tube.

"Okay, Dawn. This won't take long." I hear his voice over a speaker. It's even and calming, but I know him well enough to hear the thread of anxiety. He is just as afraid of what he might see as I am. "Hold still. Don't move."

As if I am not already paralyzed.

I close my eyes and hope that whatever Kieran is seeing on that computer screen is normal, and clear, and perfect. *Please let it be all right*, I pray.

*I've only just found him again.*

After a few minutes, I am wheeled back out. Kieran pushes a button and speaks to me through the glass. "I never thought I'd say this, but your brain is perfect."

I let out a long breath of relief. Now if I only could figure out my heart.

"On the other hand," Kieran continues, "your hair looks like a freak show."

I sit up, clutching the sheet to my chest. "Dr. McDowell," I say. "Fuck you."

THE NEXT DAY, when Brian is at work, Wyatt comes over. He uses my laptop to write a draft of an article while I read a novel; we take a slow walk around the reservoir. We pick up Meret at camp. In the late afternoon, Wyatt and Meret play Monopoly until he insists he's going to die of boredom and begs me for a deck of cards so he can teach her Spite and Malice. "Okay, the goal of the game is to clear your personal deck," Wyatt says. "You've got five cards in your hand. You have to play your aces and twos. Jokers are wild, but can't be an ace, two, seven, or king . . ." He laughs. "Get ready to throw shit."

Meret's eyes light up when he swears. "Dammit. I'm probably not supposed to curse," he says, and he smiles twice as wide.

We are careful not to touch each other when Meret is nearby. Or maybe I am careful, and Wyatt respects my space. It lets me hover at the edges of their conversation, pretending to do things like clean the kitchen counter or answer email.

I am sitting in an armchair, chipping away at the mountain of unanswered messages in my inbox, when they finish their game and Wyatt shuffles in preparation for another.

"That was beginner's luck," he says sourly.

"You're a sore loser."

"That's what you think. You're going down, *sukar*."

"*Sukar?*"

He looks surprised to have said it himself. "It's Arabic. For sugar." His cheeks redden. "Like a . . . nickname."

Over the edge of my laptop I watch the blur of cards in his hands—a waterfall, a fan, rising against gravity.

"Are you going to go back to Egypt?" Meret asks, and the cards fly all over the place.

He glances at me sidelong as he begins to gather them together. "I plan to, eventually."

I don't realize I'm holding my breath until I hear Meret's response: "Can I come?"

Wyatt grins. "I'd like that."

"I want to see the Great Pyramid."

"No, you don't," he insists. "It's cramped and touristy. I'll take you to see tombs that haven't seen the light of day in thousands of years—"

"But the Great Pyramid is the one where they found that new inner burial chamber by using muons."

"Using *what?*" I ask.

They both turn to me. "Muons," Meret repeats. "They're subatomic particles. Kind of like electrons, but with more mass. They hit Earth all the time and they can go through stone and solid matter, but then they peter out. Physicists used them in the Great Pyramid to see places where they were zipping through empty space."

"A Japanese and French team carried out the tomography in Giza. But," Wyatt argues, "it didn't really tell us anything. Rather than being a new burial chamber, it's likely to be an architectural feature, taking the weight off the Grand Gallery of the pyramid."

Meret shrugs. "Still, you have to admit it's a really cool tool, using natural radiation for mapping."

"And bloody expensive," he counters.

I watch them argue amiably. Wyatt's eyes are dancing as he matches his daughter's verbal parries.

I let myself imagine it. Maybe we three will go to Giza, and shuffle into the cramped tunnel of the Great Pyramid, breathing in sweat and stale air until we stand in the center of the Grand Gallery, surrounded by history.

Glancing down at my screen, I open an email from Abigail Trembley. The subject line is *WIN*.

Before I left for England to find Thane, I had called my social worker friend. Although Win had absolved me of my duties, I didn't feel right leaving her and Felix without someone to watch over them. Then I had emailed Abigail from Egypt, but I hadn't heard back.

I click on the message, waiting for it to load, expecting the worst.

Wyatt is dealing a new hand. Out of the blue, Meret asks, "What should I call you?"

*Don't say* Dad, I think silently. *She isn't ready for that.*

"Mighty is the Ma'at of Re, Chosen of Re?" Wyatt suggests, giving the translation of Ramesses II's Egyptian name.

Meret's lips twitch. "I was thinking *Wyatt*."

"That works, too," he says.

The body of the email loads.

*Dear Dawn,*

*When I last spoke with Brian, you were still out of town. In case you are checking your mail, you should know that Win is still with us. Fading, unresponsive, but here.*

*I think she's waiting for you.*

*Let me know when you're back.*

X

*Abigail*

I look at the date of the message: this was sent two hours ago.

I stand up so abruptly that both Meret and Wyatt turn in unison. "Everything all right?" he murmurs, getting to his feet.

"I need to go see someone. A client."

"Now?" Wyatt looks down at Meret. "Don't cheat," he says, and he pulls me into the hallway. "Someone who's dying?"

"Yes," I reply, impatient. "That's what happens to my clients. I need to sit vigil."

"Olive, is that really a good idea? You're barely out of surgery—"

"I'm not dying," I say simply. "She is."

He nods. "All right. Get what you need and I'll take you."

It never occurred to me that he would think to come. But there are things I have to say to Win, confidences that can only stay between us.

"I need you to stay here," I say gently. "To babysit till Brian gets home."

Wyatt rubs the back of his neck. "It's not babysitting when it's your kid," he replies.


THE UBER DRIVER drops me off at Win's house and I find the key that they used to leave for me under a flowerpot to let myself in. "Hello?" I call out. "Felix?"

The rooms are dark, musty. But the kitchen is clean and the dishes are all rinsed on a rack. It's clear that Abigail has been taking care of them, as the inevitable hurtles closer.

"Dawn?"

Felix has gotten so thin that his clothes hang from his shoulders and hips. His hair is matted down on his scalp, and I would guess that he hasn't had a shower in a couple of days. His eyes are red, with weariness and tears.

I fold him into my embrace, feeling him shudder against me. "It's going to be all right," I murmur. "I'm here to support you both."

He draws back, as if he hasn't trusted his own eyesight. His gaze locks on my scar and the shaved swath of my head. "What . . . what happened to you?"

"It's a very long story and it's not important right now," I tell him. "You are. *Win* is. I'd love to see her, if that's all right."

Abigail is sitting beside Win when we enter her room, reading aloud from a novel. Her eyebrows fly up to her hairline as she looks at me, at my angry red wound, but she is a professional. Instead of making this about me, she says, "Win, Dawn's come to see you."

She puts the book aside and stands up, relinquishing her chair to me. A host of unspoken communication passes between us— gratitude, curiosity, and acknowledgment. I reach for Win's hand, which is a canvas of skin stretched over bone. Her eyes are dark hollows, her cheekbones are blades. We are the same age, but she looks double her years. Her breathing is erratic and soupy. "Cheyne-Stokes?" I murmur.

Abigail nods. "All morning. She's been unresponsive about twelve hours now." She squeezes my shoulder. "I'm glad you made it."

Because there isn't much more time.

She turns a soft smile on Felix. "Why don't you freshen up, and I'll make some fresh coffee while Win and Dawn visit?"

He nods, grateful to be told what to do. Following directions is so much easier than staring the unknown in the face.

I settle in beside Win. Her son's blanket has been spread over her. The door closes behind Abigail.

"I told you I'd be here when it happened," I say softly, when I am really thinking: *Thank you for waiting for me.*

Her skin is cold and dry. Her breath saws from her lungs in gusty, uneven wheezes. "I found him for you," I whisper. "He's so handsome, Win. He had just come back from biking and his cheeks were red."

Beneath her closed lids, her eyes shift. "I have something to confess. I didn't give him your note. I know I promised. But you see, he has a daughter, and a son, and a wife. When I saw that, I thought, *That's not what Win wanted*. And then I thought a little more, and wondered if maybe it *was*. I think that what you really hoped I'd get for you was knowledge, which you could take with you, when you go. The understanding that he's all right. That he was as happy in his life as you have been." I smile sadly. "I mean, who gets such an embarrassment of riches? One love that sends you into orbit . . . and then another that guides you home?"

I let go with one of my hands to wipe away a tear. "If you want to hate me for not carrying out your wish, I understand," I tell her. "But I hope you don't. Because even though I was the one who was supposed to be giving you the tools to make the most out of the life you had left, you turned out to be the better teacher. What I did . . . what I found . . . Oh, Win. There's really no such thing as a right or wrong choice. We don't make decisions. Our decisions make *us*."

I bite my lip. "You asked me once what it was like, when we die, and I said I didn't know. But now, I do. I almost died in a plane crash. I've been trying so hard to remember it, to feel every minute of it again, so I could tell people in the future what to expect. I felt like I had to go somewhere, but it was so hard to stick to the path. It's like when you finally reach the top of a mountain you're hiking, but look down and realize how small you are by comparison. Your heart is in your throat, because it's beautiful and terrible all at once, and if anyone asked you to describe it, you wouldn't be able to find the right words, because how can you be so alone and insignificant and also so full and complete at the same time?" I shake my head. "I know this isn't what you were hoping for. You want to know if there's a white light, or a hundred dogs, or an angel who comes to get you. I don't know any of that. But I do know that all the answers were there, to questions I would never even think to ask."

Win's chest stops moving. I stare down at her, waiting. I search for the broken thread of her pulse.

"But I came back," I tell her. "Maybe I wasn't ready to hear those answers."

I feel it then, the slightest squeeze of my hand.

One more shallow breath. A long pause.

"Felix?" I call out. "I think you should come now."

I lean down and press my cheek to hers. "It's okay to let go, Win," I whisper.

The door flies open and Felix stands there, wide-eyed and frightened. "Is she . . . ?"

"Not yet," I tell him. "But now would be a good time to say whatever you need to say to her."

Felix sinks onto the edge of the bed. He leans down, whispering something into her ear that I cannot hear. Her breath rushes out, a soft susurration stirring his hair, and then she is gone.

He folds himself into her, an origami of grief.

I step outside the room to give them a final moment of privacy. I take my phone from my pocket and add Win's name to my list of ghosts.

· · ·

ABIGAIL TAKES ONE look at me and my scar and tells me she will take care of contacting the funeral home but she'd really like it if I didn't keel over myself, so I should go home. She calls me an Uber and even though the ride is only fifteen minutes, I fall asleep. Sadness sits with me, another passenger.

I text Wyatt to tell him Win has died, and then I text Brian, but neither of them responds.

When I enter my house, I witness something I never expected to see. Brian and Meret and Wyatt are all sitting around the kitchen table, eating pizza. Wyatt and Brian have bottles of beer, and Wyatt is telling a story about how, as a graduate student, he licked something fossilized to figure out if it was bone or rock, and had a coughing fit and inhaled it. "I'm likely walking around with a piece of a pharaoh in me," he says, and then he looks up when I walk through the doorway.

Immediately he gets to his feet, reacting to something written across my features. He takes two steps forward, and there's only one more before he can reach me and let me fall apart in his arms— but then he stops abruptly and jams his hands in his pockets, remembering where he is. "Your client . . . ?"

"Died," I say, and for the first time the word is not a statement or a fact but something as delicate as an egg that I have to deliver over rough terrain.

"I'm so sorry, Olive." The endearment slips out. Brian's eyes narrow when he hears it.

Brian rises, too, and takes a plate from the cupboard. On his way back to the table, he squeezes my shoulder. "Sit down. I'll get you a slice."

Even Meret is sympathetic. She brings me a paper napkin and hugs me. She is the glue, I realize, that connects this oddly shaped group of people before me.

I push my grief behind a curtain, the ugly sweater I will take out and try on later, before closeting it for the next time. I force a smile. "I hope you got sausage."

"God, Mom," Meret says. "You realize pigs have been taught to play videogames and are smarter than chimpanzees?"

And just like that, everything should be back to normal. As normal as it can be to have Wyatt and Brian sitting on either side of me at a table. To be methodically eating pizza even though a wide swath of my hair has been shaved away. And the most important point: I am here. Win is not.

I hope that Abigail takes care of Felix. I hope he can make it through this first night in an empty house, which is always the worst.

If my clients are afraid of dying, then my clients' caregivers fear being alone. There is something bleak and barren about a world that is missing the person who knows you best.

As Brian relays an explanation of an experiment in his lab, I stare at him. He would win, if that were a contest. He knows the tiny details that make up a life: where I hide the gingersnaps, so no one else will eat them and leave me with an empty box. Which drawers hold my socks, my bras, my sweaters. How to pick the cilantro off my food, because it tastes like soap. Where my back always hurts the most, when he offers to rub it. How to undo the clasp of the necklace I can never manage myself.

But Wyatt, he knows who I *could* be. An academic. An author. An archaeologist.

A colleague whose ideas he seeks out, whose vision he trusts.

A woman who comes apart so easily in his bed that I have to sink my teeth into him, sometimes, just to stay grounded.

The mother of his child.

The person he sees first in the morning, and last at night.

When I remember to pay attention to the conversation again, Meret is talking about her next tennis match. "I'm not great, but—"

"You're not great *yet*," Wyatt corrects.

She rolls her eyes. "There are kids who've been playing since they were three."

Brian lifts his beer. "Then the fact that you've improved so fast in so little time is even *more* impressive."

Maybe this is what Meret has needed all along. An extra parent to build her up, when she is certain the world is tearing her down.

"I may not be entirely objective," Brian says, "but she's smart, you know? She doesn't just have a hundred-mile-per-hour serve—"

"I *don't* have a hundred-mile-per-hour serve—"

"—so she makes up for that with strategy."

Meret turns to me. "He hasn't missed a meet. He even changed his summer session's final exam time so he could come to the last one."

Brian smiles at her. "She's really something to see."

"I bet she is," Wyatt says.

There is an uncomfortable silence as we process why Brian is the only one who's seen Meret play tennis.

Brian begins to fold his napkin into quarters, then eighths. "I meant to tell you, Meret. I think my perfect track record's about to get shot down. I can't make the match on Thursday. I tried, but there's a tenure review meeting." He clears his throat. "Maybe your mom and . . . and Wyatt could go."

It is one of the purest, humblest gifts I have ever received.

When I was a social worker doing my clinical rotations, I was called to a hospital room where all hell had broken loose. A girl who barely looked old enough to be in high school was still in stirrups, having just delivered a premature baby. Beside her was a shell-shocked boy with peach fuzz on his upper lip. The delivery suite was crammed with medical professionals who were performing a full code on their impossibly tiny daughter. I was paged because the teen mother was hysterical, and no one else had time to deal with her. I immediately grasped her shoulders, trying to get her to look at me, and when she wouldn't I followed her stare to her baby.

The skin of the newborn was blue and as thin as tissue. With every compression of CPR, it tore, and a new wound started to bleed. The air was ringing with the girl's shrieks and the terse fugue of lifesaving, but it was clear that the effort was futile. The doctor glanced at me over his shoulder, still pressing down on the tiny rib cage, his hands covered in blood. "*Do* something," he ordered.

I let go of the girl. Instead, I touched the boy's shoulder. "You have to be the dad," I said firmly. "They are looking to you to make a decision."

His face crumpled. "I thought . . . I thought we'd have more time."

"Everyone thinks they'll have more time. But a father has to give away his daughter, and you're doing that today."

The boy looked up, his eyes dead. "Stop," he said. "Just stop."

Now, Wyatt smiles at Meret. "I would love to come to your match. Tell me your camp colors, so I can paint my face and wear Mardi Gras beads and be obnoxiously loud in my cheering."

She laughs, and I think: *He is so good at this; at gaining a child.*

But my eyes drift to Brian, who is so gracious at losing one.

AFTER DINNER WHEN Wyatt goes back to his hotel, I walk him to the car. We lean against it and Wyatt pulls me close, stroking the uneven sheet of my hair. He is solid and strong and vital, the best argument against death anyone could give. "I wanted to do this when you came in," he murmurs. "You looked so . . . crushed."

I tighten my arms around him. "I wanted you to do this when I came in," I reply. "But I know why you didn't." He is painted against the night sky, wearing a crown of stars. "I almost died my-self, when I saw you at the table with Brian."

"I must admit, I wasn't expecting that invitation." Wyatt hesi-tates. "He's . . . he's a good man, Olive. If I couldn't be with you, I'm glad he was."

I know how much it cost Wyatt, with all his casual confidence, to admit this.

"But not *that* glad," he adds, and he kisses me.

I don't know how or why it always feels like the first time, when this happens. I press even more close to him, craving him, desper-ate. It shouldn't surprise me anymore, but it does: after I fill my senses with Wyatt, I am only hungrier.

He rests his forehead against mine. "Easy, Olive," he murmurs. "You don't have to try to crawl under my skin. You're already there."

"I miss sleeping next to you," I say.

"I miss waking up to you. This is a bit like some gothic fairy tale, isn't it, where you're mine during the day, but he gets you after sun-down." He brightens. "Let's take a nap tomorrow and break the curse."

If only it were that simple. If only it weren't a curse of my own making.

I watch him get into his car and drive off. Instead of going inside, I sit on the porch swing. I think about Win, and about Meret, and then—as if I have conjured him—Brian steps outside.

He doesn't say a word, just sits down next to me. I can hear the whistle of crickets, and the peepers calling from a pond in the woods. "It's late for them," Brian muses. "Almost fall."

I wonder if our conversation will be boxed into things like weather and flora and fauna, because it's safer that way, until there's virtually nothing we can talk about at all.

I force myself to look him in the eye. "Thank you for doing that."

He knows I am talking about stepping aside, so that Wyatt can go to Meret's match. One of Brian's shoulders lifts and falls. "Well. I can't undo it." Meaning: Wyatt. "So."

He leans forward, clasping his hands together between his knees. "About Win."

"Yeah."

"Was it peaceful?"

"I suppose. Her husband was there when it happened." I glance at Brian. "I didn't deliver her letter, just so you know."

He looks at me, surprised. We sit in the pool of porch light and watch as one prematurely red leaf lifts in the wind and detaches from a tree, beginning a death spiral.

"Dawn," he says, "I'm sorry."

I smile a little. "I think we've both exceeded our lifetime quota of those two words."

He continues as if I haven't spoken. "I feel like that," he says, gesturing to the leaf, which looks like a splash of blood on the grass. "There are so many winds pushing me around, but they're all *feelings*." He says this as if it is a curse word. "For a scientist, that's like kryptonite."

I sit very still, giving him the space to finish. "I was mad at you," he admits. "When you left, I was so angry. I couldn't wait to tell you off. But then, I almost didn't get the chance, and that changes everything. It was like I was seeing from a completely different vantage point, from a view I hadn't considered. We have fifteen years of a foundation. Maybe the hurricane has knocked down the house, but the bones, they're still there." Very slowly, so that I have time to draw away if I want, Brian threads his fingers through mine. "We can build on it again, and this time, it'll be twice as strong because we know where the flaws were, and how to fix them." His eyes hold me captive. "You can't discount what we had, Dawn. I know you can't."

Once, when Meret was in elementary school, she came home and burst into tears because she had told a friend about a secret crush she had on a boy, and by the end of recess, everyone knew. *I will* never *trust anyone again,* she sobbed. My first instinct was to tell her *Yes, you should only trust me, forever and ever.* But instead, I asked Meret how she decided if someone was trustworthy. She thought about this for a few moments, counting down her small list of friends. One girl had shared half her Kit Kat. Another slid to the side of her seat at the lunch table when there wasn't any more room, so Meret could sit with her. Such tiny acts, and so critical. You trust someone who makes space for you in his or her life . . . so much so that if you leave, they will feel the absence. You give someone your vulnerable, un-shelled heart wrapped in a question: *What will you do with it?*

"It's hard not to see this as Fate—you surviving a plane crash, so you can be with him," Brian muses. "But if Fate is the notion that you're destined for a given outcome, based on who you are and what you were meant to do, then a quantum physicist has to say that's bullshit, by definition. On the other hand, if Fate means the lack of free will—the idea that you have no control over which timeline you wind up in—then you're just a pawn experiencing whatever the multiverse throws at you." He glances up. "In which case the chances of you winding up with him, or you winding up with me, are completely random."

"You're saying this isn't my fault?"

He smiles ruefully. "Well. In a quantum sense. That doesn't make it hurt any less."

When Brian leans forward and kisses me, I let him. In that quiet, simple touch of his lips to mine are fifteen years of knowing how he folds his T-shirts, and buying satsumas the one time of year they show up in the grocery store because they are his favorite, and feeling him press a packet of M&M's that he's smuggled from home into my hand at the movies. It's his shoulder against mine while we watch Meret's back rise and fall in her crib, and the smell of his skin and the way my snow tires magically appear on my car every year without me thinking about it.

His hands frame my face for another moment. "Tell me that means nothing to you," Brian says, "and I'll let you go."

But I can't.

He leaves me alone on the porch, where I sit for an hour, or maybe a lifetime.

WHEN WIN'S OBITUARY is printed in the newspaper, I read it twice. It is a pale imitation of the friend I knew, but words are like that. They never quite capture what you need them to, the way a panoramic photo of a mountain range somehow misses the vibrance and the grandeur.

I take out the pair of scissors we keep in the kitchen drawer with all the other bits and pieces that don't fit, and cleanly snip the column of text.

I put this into an envelope and write down a name and an address in Richmond upon Thames. I do not write down my own return address. I add stamps and slip this into the mailbox.

I find Brian reading the paper with a big hole in the middle. Somehow, this feels fitting. As if everyone will have to imagine the singular story that once fit into that space.

WHEN YOU LOSE someone you love, there is a tear in the fabric of the universe. It's the scar you feel for, the flaw you can't stop seeing. It's the tender place that won't bear weight. It's a void.

But the universe tends toward Ma'at, toward order, so even though there's a rip, it gets camouflaged. The edges overlap, and after time, you might even forget that this is the spot where something went missing, the spot where—if you push—you'll fall through. And then there's a scent or a thought or a heartbeat and suddenly it's clear as day: the light behind that ragged tear, so blinding that you cannot imagine how you ever mistakenly believed it had woven itself back together.

On the fourth day after I arrive home, I attend Win's funeral. There is red velvet cake and sidecars crafted with excellent cognac. It is held at night, because there are fireworks. People wear a rainbow of colors, and take turns telling stories about her. Wyatt comes with me to the funeral, holding tight to my hand and passing me a handkerchief when I tear up.

Win will haunt me, even if it's not in the way she thinks. When you lose someone, you see them everywhere in a hundred different ways. I will think of her when I go to an art museum, or a dog park. On a blank canvas. When I eat a buttermilk biscuit.

The sky is bruised. Purple in the center, blue at the edges, an unaccountably pretty record of damage. I watch the injury spread, staining the whole sky. Win's friends and relatives sit on blankets, waiting for the fireworks. Wyatt and I lie down to watch them. I tuck myself beneath his shoulder and pretend that those shooting stars never fall; that they become a whole new constellation with Win at its center.

Gradually, everyone disperses. I give Felix a strong hug and tell him I will check in on him in a few days. But instead of leaving, I shake out the blanket again, and sit down.

Wyatt settles beside me. "Making a wish?"

I reach for his hand. "Looking for the Big Dipper."

I scout out the star in the middle of its handle. Along with a second star in the Little Dipper, it revolves around due north. Because they never set, these undying stars were a perfect metaphor for the afterlife of an Ancient Egyptian soul. Just as the deceased wanted to be integrated into the solar cycle with Re, he also wanted to join the circumpolar stars.

"Those Who Do Not Know Destruction," Wyatt murmurs, using the Ancient Egyptian term for those stars. "That's what we are."

"I want to believe that."

"I want the fifteen years I didn't have with you," he says.

"Only fifteen? Then what?"

"Then I'll renegotiate." I turn to find him looking at me, sober. "How long?"

I know what he is asking. How long will we be here, in this limbo?

"It's only been a few days," I hedge. "I just need . . . I need to catch my breath."

He rubs his thumb over the back of my hand. "I know. But I lost fifteen years. And then I almost lost forever. I spent so much time thinking that you'd disappeared off the face of the earth that I can't let you walk away again, and if that makes me a bastard, so be it. You and I, we're still young. There are plenty of Egyptologists who don't strike the motherlode until they're ancient and doddering. There's a lot we missed out on, Olive. But there's so *much* ahead of us."

It is easier to dream about the future with him than it is to untangle the messy knot of the present. Maybe that is what's so appealing: the simplicity. The effortlessness.

"I don't want to leave Meret," I say.

"Then don't."

"I can't take her away from Brian."

"Then I'll move. I'll defect to Harvard."

I shake my head. "You were not meant to sit in a classroom, Wyatt. And Harvard doesn't own the concession in Bersha."

He sits back. "You're having doubts." He speaks slowly, as if he has never heard those words in his life.

"Not about you," I say quickly, because he needs to hear it, and so do I. "About . . . the logistics of home."

Wyatt kisses me so gently it already feels like a memory. "Home isn't a where, Olive. It's a who."

There's an ancient text, the story of Sinuhe, who flees his native country. When he leaves Egypt, he says, *My heart is not in my body.* To the Ancient Egyptians, for whom the heart was the site of intellect and emotion and faith, it was the same as saying: *I have lost my mind.*

Whatever happens, whatever I gain, it is going to be tempered by loss.

*My heart is not in my body,* I think.


THAT NIGHT I dream in blue.

I imagine Win and Thane, traipsing through Paris to find the perfect pigment.

I see Meret the moment she entered the world, her skin porcelain until oxygen pinked through her like a sunrise.

I picture how Brian's hands shook when he reached across the blue tablecloth and asked me to marry him, as if he still wasn't sure after a year that I would come home every night to him.

And I remember Wyatt's eyes, after the plane crash, when the hospital walls spun and I fell to the floor and couldn't speak or move. He had leaned over me, filling my field of vision. Although there was only buzzing in my ears, I could read his lips:

*Olive.*

*Olive.*

*I love.*

"You," I had gasped, my last word when I thought I was dying.


ONE WEEK AFTER I am back in Boston, Kieran comes over to remove my staples. Wyatt is at his hotel, taking a phone call with Mostafa, the antiquities director. Brian is at work. Meret finds me alone in the bathroom after my brother leaves, staring at my scar in the mirror. A misshapen braid of the remaining half of my hair snakes over my shoulder.

Herodotus wrote that around 499 B.C.E., Histiaeus—the deposed King of Miletus—wanted help revolting against the Persians. He tattooed a note on an enslaved man's head and sent him to a sympathizer months later, with the instruction to shave the man's hair and read the message.

Even after there is hair on this side of my head again, I will know there's a story hiding beneath it.

"It'll grow out," Meret says, looking at the shadowed stubble of the buzzed section of my head.

"Yeah," I reply. "Eventually."

Meret grabs my hand and pulls me out of the bathroom. She tugs me down the stairs and snags my purse off the counter before leading me outside.

"What are we doing?" I ask.

"Trust me."

In Brookline, we are only a few blocks from Coolidge Corner. Meret leads me down the main block, into a salon where I get my highlights done twice a year. My normal hairdresser, Siobhan, turns as the door jingles, takes one look at me and the scar on my head, and her jaw drops.

"Hi," Meret announces. "I know we don't have an appointment but my mom recently nearly died and it would be really cool if you could squeeze her in just this once."

Every client in the salon is staring at me. The woman in Siobhan's chair, whose wet hair is wrapped in a towel, stands up. "You can have my spot," she says.

I sink down into the seat, Meret hovering beside me. Siobhan clearly doesn't know if she should ask me why I have half a shaved head, why I have a scar. "Brain surgery," I explain.

"My God," Siobhan breathes. "What happened?"

"I was in a plane crash." I lean back and close my eyes. "I just . . . Make me look more normal?"

Her eyes widen. She picks up the scissors and assesses me critically. "We're going short," she announces.

A moment later, the rope of my braid falls to the floor.

She spins the chair so that I am not looking in the mirror as she works. She uses a clipper to buzz the fine hairs at the back of my neck and to blend where my scalp has been shaved with the parts that haven't. Twenty minutes later, she pivots the chair so that I can see.

If you approached me from the right, you might mistake me for an Ancient Egyptian. My hair ends just above my jawline, hanging in a sleek bob. But if you approach me from the left, I am buzzed, punk, cyborg. I am history and I am the future, all at once, depending on where you look.

"What do you think?" Siobhan asks, holding her breath.

I burst into tears.

It is not that I look ridiculous, because I don't. Somehow, as a haircut, it works. It's that I am split into halves and I don't know how to put myself back together.

Before Siobhan can react or soothe me, Meret grabs the electric razor from the table and swoops it over the side of her head, clearing a path that matches the one I was given in surgery. "Do me next," she says, plunking down in the empty chair beside Siobhan's. When the hairdresser doesn't move, she challenges her with a look. "You're not going to let me walk out of here like *this*, are you?"

While Siobhan cuts Meret's hair into a bob on the right, and buzzes the left side of her scalp, I watch, speechless. Meret's hand snakes out from beneath the plastic cape they've settled over her to catch the curls that slip to the floor. "It's only hair, Mom," she says softly, meeting my eyes in the mirror. "I know it doesn't matter what you look like on the outside. But just in case, it's nice to know you match someone, isn't it?"


WE TAKE THE long way home, my brave daughter and I. We walk around the reservoir, like we did before I left for Egypt. There are leaves floating on its surface like small, jeweled boats.

I feel lighter without the bulk of my hair, like the wind exists just to touch me. Meret and I fall into step with each other. I realize that she is taller than I am now. Not by much, maybe a quarter of an inch, but it's unsettling. I think of her, fierce as a Valkyrie in that salon.

"I love you," I say.

She glances at me. "Okay, boomer."

I laugh. "I just thought I should say it out loud."

We take a few more steps in silence.

"I like him," Meret says finally. "I didn't think I would."

I stop walking and take a deep breath. "Love is messy," I tell her.

"Sometimes you hurt the people you love. And sometimes you love the people who hurt you."

This is how I want her to remember me: as someone who told her the truth, even when it was a razor. As someone who learned the hard way, so she would not have to.

I can see Wyatt in her features, and Brian in her mannerisms. I blink, and Meret is no longer just my daughter. She's someone who is on the edge of becoming a woman, who one day will be subject to the same gravitational pulls on her heart.

"So," Meret asks. "What are you going to do?"

Maybe this is all love is: twin routes of pain and pleasure. Maybe the miracle isn't where we wind up, but that we get there at all.

I open my mouth, and I answer.

# AUTHOR'S NOTE

. . .

AFTER MY SON Kyle Ferriera van Leer declared his major in Egyptology at Yale in 2010, he mentioned the Book of Two Ways in passing. Without knowing a thing about it, I said, "That's a great title for a novel." It was only after he began to explain what it actually *was* that I realized what I needed to write about—the construct of time, and love, and life, and death. I scheduled a trip to Egypt to learn more—and that turned out to be the year of the Arab Spring. My trip was canceled, and I moved on to other books and other stories that needed telling.

But I didn't forget about this one. In 2016, Kyle got married, and invited his former thesis advisor, Dr. Colleen Darnell. I told her how much I wanted to write this novel, but couldn't do it without traveling there. "I'll take you," she said, and a year later, I found myself in Egypt, the grateful recipient of a private tutorial from one of the foremost Egyptologists in America, traveling in the footsteps my characters would eventually take.

For the sake of fiction, certain liberties have been taken:

The coffins of Djehutyakht and his wife, Djehutynakht, in the Boston Museum of Fine Arts are described as they were installed after a landmark 2009 exhibit alongside a catalog: Rita E. Freed, Lawrence M. Berman, Denise M. Doxey, and Nicholas S. Picardo, *The Secrets of Tomb 10A: Egypt 2000 B.C.* (Boston: MFA Publications, 2009). For the timing of this novel, I predated the display to 2003. However . . . the FBI really did crack the case of the severed head's identity, in 2018: https://www.nytimes.com/2018/04/02/science/mummy-head-fbi-dna.html.

Yale does not actually have the concession at Deir el-Bersha—it belongs to the Leuven mission. They are indeed copying the tomb of Djehutyhotep II and carrying out important epigraphic and archaeological work within the necropolis. For more about the work the Leuven mission is doing, go to http://www.dayralbarsha.com. Many of Dawn's theories are based on the work of Harco Willems, the real-life director of that mission, particularly *Chests of Life: A Study of the Typology and Conceptual Development of Middle Kingdom Standard Class Coffins* (Leiden: Ex Oriente Lux, 1988) and *The Coffin of Heqata: A Case Study of Egyptian Funerary Culture of the Early Middle Kingdom (Cairo JdE 36418)* (Leuven: Peeters, 1996).

After I turned in this book to my publisher, Harco Willems published a study of a burial shaft that his team reopened in 2012 in Deir el-Bersha, in which they found the remains of a sarcophagus of a woman named Ankh, with two cedar panels that had the Book of Two Ways drawn on them. Based on its inscriptions, this is now the oldest known version of the Book of Two Ways, roughly forty years older than any previously discovered.

Djehutynakht, son of Teti, was a real nomarch in Ancient Egypt, as proven by actual hieratic ink graffiti. To date, his tomb has not been found—although it is possible that it could be discovered at some point in the future. Djehutynakht was an antiquarian committed to making his ancestors' names live forever, so I'd like to think this novel is belated wish fulfillment, for him.

The layout of the Book of Two Ways in the fictional coffin of Djehutynakht is borrowed from the actual Book of Two Ways in the coffin of Sepi, after Adriaan de Buck.

I am beholden to many people for bits and pieces of this novel: Nicole Cliffe, for her Twitter feed about superstitions.

NBC News for Brian's mirror universe lectures (https://www.nbcnews.com/mach/science/scientists-are-searching-mirror-universe-it-could-be-sitting-right-ncna1023206).

Ava and Stan Konwiser, for information about oppositional defi-ant disorder and holding therapy.

Dr. Claire Philips, for the science of tears: https://twitter.com/DocClaireP/status/1163511118901448707?s=20

For donating their names as part of charitable contributions: Maureen Beauregard and Abigail Beauregard Trembley, for sup-porting Families in Transition New Hampshire; and Lauri Nebel Cullen and Joe Cullen, for supporting Trumbull Hall Troupe.

Eleni Lawrence, for teaching me about the grading system at Cambridge; and Carolyn Mays, for correcting everything else I got wrong about being British.

Mania Salinger, my bonus grandmother, who shared her real-life story about Dorie and Pionki work camp during World War II and asked me to include it.

For assistance with crashing a fictional plane: Chris Bohjalian, Heather Poole, Chris Manno, Ashley Nelson.

For endless information (and rewrites) about neurosurgery: Dr. Elizabeth Coon, Lisa Genova, Dr. Eric Stiner, Dr. Nevan Baldwin, Betty Martin, Dr. Christopher Sturm, Dr. Kamal Kalia, and Julia Fox Garrison.

For six-mile uphill walks where we thrashed out plot details, Joan Collison and Barb Kline-Schoder. Joan was the source of Brian's Mars and Murries story. Barb made me realize that Dawn would be involved in hospice work, and kindly shared her own experience with me.

For my family: Kyle Ferreira van Leer, who translated Middle Egyptian for me ad nauseam and who fell in love with this subject long before I did; Kevin Ferreira van Leer, for being an early reader; Jake van Leer, who shared everything from the Marvel Universe to the rules of Spite and Malice; Melanie Borinstein, for giving me a crash course on modern art; Francisco Ramos, for answering end-less questions about head injuries; and Samantha van Leer Ramos, for helping me figure out the complicated structure of the book.

For Jeremie Harris, who managed to teach me quantum mechan-ics so I could teach it to you.

For the wonderful people I met who work in end-of-life care:

Todd Starnes-Williams, Alua Arthur, Amy Morales, Rebekah Duplechin, Marcela Navarro, Cara Geary, Samantha Colomer, Lynn Spachuk, and Loren Goldberg. The world is a better place because you're in it.

For my beta readers—all of whom read multiple drafts of this beast: Elyssa Samsel, Jane Picoult, Laura Gross, Katie Desmond, Gillian McDunn. Brigid Kemmerer gets a special shout-out, because I think she cares about these characters even more than I do, and without her, this book would have taken twice as long to write.

For the small army that is my publishing team—I am so grateful for all you have done for me, and continue to do. You are the gold standard: Gina Centrello, Kara Welsh, Kim Hovey, Deb Aroff, Rachel Kind, Denise Cronin, Scott Shannon, Matthew Schwartz, Theresa Zoro, Paolo Pepe, Erin Kane, Madison Dettlinger, Emily Isayeff, Jordan Pace, and everyone else at Ballantine who is part of Team Jodi.

Susan Corcoran gets a special thank-you. She may be my publicist, but she might as well be life support, because I seriously don't think I can exist without her at this point.

Jennifer Hershey is the best editor I've ever worked with, and this novel is a testament to her brilliance. This story had a *very* different ending—one that was quite hard for me to let go of. But Jen, *you were right*. I respect you so much; you make me a better writer every time I set out to tell a story.

My biggest kudos are reserved, however, for those who didn't just introduce me to Egyptology but immersed me in it. It's not every author who can have Dr. John Darnell *create* a fake dipinto for her, in addition to providing all the translations and concepts that have come from his published work. I had the pleasure of meeting Alberto Urcia when I was in Egypt, and he taught me how technology intersects with Egyptology (and became the namesake of the fictional Alberto). But the MVP of this research is, far and away, Dr. Colleen Darnell. Not only can she take the highly academic and present it in a way that a novice like me might understand, but she can crawl into a tomb and translate hieroglyphics on the spot (while spectacularly dressed in vintage gear). Colleen's passion for this subject is infectious—whether she is pointing out a specific sign in an ancient necropolis or answering my hundredth email for clarification. The level of detail in this novel exists because of her attention to minutiae, her superb teaching skills, and her generosity of time and spirit. Without her, Wyatt and Dawn would not exist; I'm honored to call her a mentor *and* a friend.

And finally—because this is a love story—thanks to Tim van Leer, whom I would find in *any* timeline.

JODI PICOULT, *December 2019*

# BIBLIOGRAPHY

. . .

EGYPTOLOGY

Baines, John, and Jaromir Malek. *Cultural Atlas of Ancient Egypt*. London: Andromeda Oxford, 1980.

Darnell, John Coleman. "Hathor Returns to Medamûd." *Studien zur Altägyptischen Kultur* 22 (1995): 4794. *JSTOR* 25152711.

———. "A Midsummer Night's Succubus—The Herdsman's Encounters in P. Berlin 3024: The Pleasures of Fishing and Fowling, the Songs of the Drinking Place, and the Ancient Egyptian Love Poetry." In *Opening the Tablet Box: Near Eastern Studies in Honor of Benjamin R. Foster*. Edited by Sarah C. Melville and Alice Slotsky, 99–140. CHANE 42. Leiden: Brill, 2010.

———. "The Rituals of Love in Ancient Egypt: Festival Songs of the Eighteenth Dynasty and the Ramesside Love Poetry." *Die Welt des Orients* 46 (2016): 22–61.

Darnell, John Coleman, and Colleen Manassa Darnell. *The Ancient Egyptian Netherworld Books*. Atlanta: SBL Press, 2018.

———. *Tutankhamun's Armies*. New Jersey: Wiley & Sons, 2007.

De Meyer, Marleen. "Restoring the Tombs of His Ancestors? Djehutinakht, Son of Teti, at Deir al-Barsha and Sheikh Said." In M. Fitzenreiter, ed. *Genealogie: Realität und Fiktion von Identität*, 125–36. London, 2005.

Dodson, Aidan, and Salima Ikram. *The Mummy in Ancient Egypt*. London: Thames and Hudson, 1998.

———. *The Tomb in Ancient Egypt*. London: Thames and Hudson, 1998.

Faulkner, R. O. *The Ancient Egyptian Book of the Dead.* rev. ed. London: British Museum Press, 1985.

Gardiner, Alan. *Egyptian Grammar.* 3d ed. Oxford: Griffith Institute, 1988.

Grajetzki, Wolfram. *The Middle Kingdom of Ancient Egypt.* London: Duckworth & Co., 2006.

Griffith, F. L., and Percy E. Newberry. *El Bersheh II.* London: Egypt Exploration Fund, 1895. For color images of Djehutyhotep II's tomb, http://www.griffith.ox.ac.uk/archive/GI-watercolours /Deir-el-Bersha/GI_wd_Deir_el_Bersha.html.

Haggard, H. Rider. *She.* Oxford: Oxford University Press, 2008.

Hornung, Erik. *The Ancient Egyptian Books of the Afterlife.* Translated by David Lorton. Ithaca: Cornell University Press, 1999.

————. *Conceptions of God in Ancient Egypt.* Translated by John Baines. Ithaca: Cornell University Press, 1982.

Kemp, Barry. *Ancient Egypt: Anatomy of a Civilization.* Abingdon: Routledge, 2006.

Lesko, Leonard H. *The Ancient Egyptian Book of Two Ways.* Berkeley: University of California Press, 1972.

Parkinson, R. B. *Voices from Ancient Egypt.* London: British Museum Press, 1991.

————, trans. *The Tale of Sinuhe and Other Ancient Egyptian Poems 1940–1640 BC.* Oxford: Oxford University Press, 1997.

Robinson, Peter. " 'As for them who know them, they shall find their paths': Speculations on Ritual Landscapes in the 'Book of Two Ways.' " In D. O'Connor and S. Quirke, eds., *Mysterious Lands,* 139–59. London: UCL Press, 2003.

Shaw, Ian. *The Oxford History of Ancient Egypt.* Oxford: Oxford University Press, 2000.

Sherbiny, Wael. *Through Hermopolitan Lenses: Studies on the So-called Book of Two Ways in Ancient Egypt.* Leiden: Brill, 2017.

Taylor, John H. *Death and the Afterlife in Ancient Egypt.* Chicago: University of Chicago Press, 2001.

Van de Mieroop, Marc. *A History of Ancient Egypt.* West Sussex, UK: Wiley-Blackwell, 2011.

Wilkinson, Richard H. *The Complete Gods and Goddesses of Ancient Egypt*. Cairo: American University in Cairo Press, 2003.


DEATH AND DYING

Buckman, Robert. *"I Don't Know What to Say . . ."* Toronto: Key Porter Books, 1988.

Callanan, Maggie, and Patricia Kelley. *Final Gifts*. New York: Bantam Books, 1997.

Dunn, Hank. *Hard Choices for Loving People*. Naples, FL: Quality of Life Publishing, 2016.

# ABOUT THE TYPE

. . .

This book was set in Fournier, a typeface named for Pierre-Simon Fournier (1712–68), the youngest son of a French printing family. He started out engraving woodblocks and large capitals, then moved on to fonts of type. In 1736 he began his own foundry and made several important contributions in the field of type design; he is said to have cut 147 alphabets of his own creation. Fournier is probably best remembered as the designer of St. Augustine Ordinaire, a face that served as the model for the Monotype Corporation's Fournier, which was released in 1925.